Armistice Day

Septimus Brass thriller 1, Volume 1

John Fullerton

Published by Partisan, 2024.

ARMISTICE DAY

First edition. June 28, 2024.

ISBN: 979-8224732760

Written by John Fullerton.

Acclaim for John Fullerton's books

Spy Game

'This is an informed thriller, authentic and vividly written, set in a now almost forgotten conflict that helped to shape our modern world.'

– *Adam LeBor, Financial Times*

'A first-rate tale, with all the authority of first-hand experience.'

– *Luke Jennings, author of the Killing Eve series.*

Spy Dragon

'Fullerton knows the ground, knows the game, and his novel has the authentic reek of personal experience.'

– *Martin Walker, author of the Bruno of Chief Police series, France.*

'It's a joy to read a series of novels that can inform as well as entertain...'

– *Michael Garin, United States.*

'A gripping story of which one can honestly say Le Carré would be proud.'

– *Karen Wood, United Kingdom*

Spy Trap

'A fitting finale to this exciting trilogy that kept me enthralled to the end...A brilliant read & I did not want to put it down. Highly recommended & if I could give it more stars I would.'

- *Deb's Books*

'A very good read. Indeed his best writing yet.

Authentic, rewarding, relevant, fascinating, entertaining, well written novel that left me looking forward to the next one.'

-*Sinclair Molloy*

Emperor

'John Fullerton surely ranks high among the gods of thriller writers.

His "Emperor" is taut, polished and as throat-gripping as you're likely to find in this world.'

– *Alan Bradley, New York Times bestselling author.*

'Chillingly realistic, stunningly well informed...a rattling good read.'

– *Martin Walker, author of the Bruno of Chief Police series, France.*

'This is bloody good – especially the fast pace and mastery of detail.'

– *Shyam Bhatia, author & war reporter*

John is clearly a talented, accomplished and inventive writer – with a knowledgeable grip on the dark machinations of global politics.'

-Toby Jones, editorial director, Headline

'I was on the edge of my seat for most of the ride.'

– Tom Vater, author & journalist

'A vivid portrait of a tyrant that oozes authenticity.'

– Andrew MacLeod, novelist

'I thought this was a thought-provoking, timely novel, from a talented writer..he is a huge talent.'

– Finn Cotton, senior commissioning editor, Transworld

'Hauntingly prescient.'

– Jeremy Clift, writer & publisher

'Emperor is gripping, well researched and realistic...The characters, their actions and motivations are very believable and make the book hard to put down.'

– Jaidev Jamwal, military analyst & journalist

The Monkey House

'Absolutely first-rate...shocking enough to steal the breath and bruise the heart...Too good to miss.' - Literary Review

'The most convincing thriller I've read in years.'

- Andy McNab

'Highly accomplished...This is writing of the first rank...'

- Irish Times

'Powerful and authentic'

- Mail on Sunday

'Fullerton captures the grit and cut of the imploding city beautifully'

- Observer

'With a clarity that its sharp and painful, Fullerton's first novel captures the emotions of small people trapped in a mad war: terror and privation, compassion and Balkan gallows humour.'

- Daily Telegraph

A Hostile Place

'Wake up thriller writers, a talent has arrived.'

- Bernard Cornwall

'Harsh, cold-eyed thriller...Fullerton puts the politics on hold and tells the story with heart, guts and go. A brilliant performance, with a fierce uncosy intelligence setting off the fireworks'

- Literary Review

'Fullerton's sour, clever postcolonial tale, permeated with double-crosses, puts the west in a very bad light...His bounty-hunter tale moves swiftly, with a sharp eye for rugged landscape...impressive.'

- The Guardian

The Reticent Executioner

'Anthony Burgess always preferred the word cacatopia to dystopia, and it certainly describes the setting for this excellent thriller. The Party, "generously funded by two aged American billionaires with links to nationalist-religious zealots in a Near East pariah state" has gained power in England, and the country has descended into Big Brother tyranny with added ethnic cleansing and guillotines. Enter our anti-hero, a seedy detective who has his own ideas for fighting back. Very pacy, relevant, and keeps you guessing. More please.'

- Ned (GoodReads review)

'As for revenge, what leads someone to destroy another individual is rancour or the need for redress, enduring hatred or overwhelming grief; as for punishment, it's more a chilling warning to others, the desire to set an example, to teach others a lesson, to make it perfectly clear that such actions will have consequences and will not be permitted.'

- Javier Marias, *Tomas Levinson*, translated from the Spanish by Margaret Jul Costa, Penguin, 2024.

Chapter 1

<big>11</big> *:01:32 November 11*
The prime minister doesn't hear the shot that kills him.

Neither the crack of the bullet flying towards him at one thousand metres a second nor the muffled bang of the weapon itself.

The round enters an inch above his bushy left eyebrow, blows away the back of his skull and removes much of his brain.

The 15-gram, steel-jacketed projectile is deflected a smidgen to the left as it exits. It smashes the jaw of the defence minister standing behind the prime minister and a step to one side, ripping away half his face.

A second round, fired immediately after the first, strikes the prime minister again, this time in the throat. His feet leave his lace-ups on the ground, and he flies backwards from the impact of the first, letting go of the wreath of poppies he's been holding. He's dead before the wreath hits the pavement; it then rolls and wobbles away, falling over into the street.

The shooter fires a third time, striking the leader of the opposition between the eyes, slicing off the top of her head. The shooter squeezes off a fourth and final shot. This round is also intended for the Labour Party chief, crashing through her chest cavity, exploding her heart, severing her spine and killing the home secretary behind her.

Four shots in under eight seconds.

Time: 11:01:40

Two targets double-tapped.

Three senior politicians dead.

One critically wounded.

Range 488 yards or 446 metres.

Wind: north-easterly, 10-12 knots.

Nine degrees Celsius.

There's no more shooting and no return fire.

No one seems to hear the detonations. The first visible sign something has gone wrong is a flurry of movement around the victims as they collapse, and as their immediate neighbours — also members of the cohort of stern-faced politicians draped in black winter overcoats decorated with

1

plastic-free Flanders poppies — flinch, rear back like black roses opening, duck down and throw themselves to the ground. Those few who aren't frozen in terror manage to scamper or crawl for cover. Only then does the screaming start. Several of those closest to the targets are hysterical; they're liberally spattered with blood, brain, and bone fragments.

The attack has been carefully timed, right at the end of the two minutes' silence.

The troops from the three armed services are standing to attention when the shots are fired. So too the 1,500 additional police officers deployed along the route in case of riot. They face the onlookers penned behind metal barriers. The military massed bands are silent. The veterans of Britain's small wars, in berets and blazers, many of them frail and some in wheelchairs, tremble in the cold as they await the march-past but are otherwise still. The horses of the Household Cavalry are on their best behaviour; some shake their well-groomed heads, making their polished harness jingle, one enormous bay snorts, a restless roan paws the ground with a clatter of her iron-clad hooves. The armed forces standards on the Cenotaph hang damp, limp and move listlessly in gusts of wind.

The shooter seems to have waited for these moments when everyone is sure to be still, right up to the moment before the king in admiral's uniform will take a first step forward to lay his wreath at the foot of the monument.

His Gracious Britannic Majesty King Charles lll, Duke of Cornwall, Duke of Rothesay, Earl of Carrick and Baron of Renfrew, who, for all this feudal flummery as hereditary head of state, is not a target. Unhurt, he's visibly shaken as he's bundled away.

Millions see it live on television. It is, after all, Armistice Day, commemorating the British and Commonwealth dead, military and civilian, of two world wars. The assassinations occur in the very heart of the British state. Many millions more will watch the replay on news bulletins around the world over the next twenty-four hours. For many, it's simply entertainment.

Chapter 2

E *arlier*
Merrick devotes three months to selecting and preparing the kill zone and would wholeheartedly agree with the adage that time spent on reconnaissance is never wasted.

One visit a week to the building at 55A Whitehall to prepare the firing position. Twelve visits in all.

Getting in has proved easier than expected, first as an office worker in a natty two-piece suit, wearing specs and carrying a civil service briefcase, a little later as a housepainter in paint-stained white overalls and a cap, with dust sheets under one arm and a small aluminium ladder under the other. And, right down to the last recce four days before the mission itself, as a plumber wearing a wig and carrying a battered toolbox.

Stashing the gear has proved easier than expected, too. Merrick isn't stopped or interrogated, not once. It's almost disappointing. He'd enjoy talking himself out of trouble.

The weapon, bipod, sound suppressor, the ammunition, scope, rangefinder, two burner phones, dry rations, tea bags, electric kettle, wet wipes, face towel, the tactical patrol bag, protective clothing and sleeping bag are all in place.

Merrick patrols the site every day at different times, and if it's dry, and the sun appears, Merrick will dawdle, hang out on a park bench and occasionally feed the ducks in St James's Park, an opportunity for a little static countersurveillance. If it's pissing down, Merrick watches the streets from the comfort of one of three coffee shops.

It's odd how people react to a stranger. When Merrick is kitted out in uniform and takes a turn around local streets, people nod and even smile — especially those wearing the same or a similar uniform. Brothers-and-sisters-in-arms, or something of the kind. Mutual recognition as members of the same tribe charged with protecting the state and enforcing its laws. If they bothered to stop to inspect the badge around Merrick's neck, they'd see it's genuine. Stolen, yes, but they wouldn't know that.

Important civilians — important in their own estimation — such as the civil servants and politicians who infest the killing zone, take no notice of someone so humdrum, so lowly. They don't make eye contact. Nor do their drivers and bodyguards.

Which is all to the good.

He isn't afraid. Most people would be, or at least nervous. Not Merrick. Since birth — indeed, while still in the womb — the possibility of violent death has never been far off. While living — if it could be called living — under the regime, all beings were in danger of summary execution by young soldiers trained to think of the likes of Merrick as evil, as less than human and to be exterminated. Merrick's mother was threatened on the way to hospital to give birth. 'So,' a soldier at a checkpoint had said, pointing his loaded rifle at the expectant woman's bump, 'you're bringing yet another terrorist into this world!'

That immortal line is the family leitmotif.

Merrick is ordinary and revels in ordinariness. It's a form of protection, not unlike camouflage. Merrick appears to most people to be much less than Merrick is, just as Merrick speaks much less than Merrick knows.

Too ordinary to matter is the objective. Too ordinary to kill. Not worth the effort or the price of a bullet. A member of the proletariat, like the cleaners, the post and local council workers, ambulance drivers, parcel delivery van drivers and Deliveroo cyclists in high viz vests carrying pizzas or chicken katsu and sticky rice to six-figure salary clients at their high-rise office desks. This is the working class in the twenty-first century under late capitalism: people on infamous 'zero-hours' contracts. The lowest of the low, blending into the background, an invisible category whose existence says, 'Carry on, don't mind us, please; we don't matter 'cos we're nobody!' They're shift workers, mostly drawn from minorities, often immigrants and many of them undocumented refugees, a hidden, subterranean sub-species labouring unsocial hours, huddled on Underground trains or dozing at the back of London's double-decker red buses during the hours of darkness. They don't speak good English. They're likely not even white. They're the small boat people. No self-respecting trade union would have them.

They keep London afloat on a pittance.

Merrick likes to think he's one of them, these nobodies huddling in corners, eyes closed, trying to sleep. He hopes he is seen that way.

The first task has been to plot all comings and goings and monitor changes over the twelve weeks. The elderly caretaker who lives in a basement flat, the cleaners, the office workers on the first and second floors. It's a listed building. Stucco for the ground floor, red brick above, four windows wide, three floors plus an attic with a tall, black-fronted door and two steps down onto the wide Whitehall pavement. Merrick has installed four miniature digital cameras high in the recesses of the hall and corridors, which can be monitored from afar, even from his bed.

The state owns the place. The name of the department has changed with dizzying frequency. In the space of less than ten years, it has gone from being named variously as the Department of Energy and Climate Change to the Department for Business, Energy and Industrial Strategy, then it was split into several entities, its latest bureaucratic incarnation being the Department for Energy Security and Net Zero (DESNZ). The reorganisations are so frequent that the building managers seem to have given up keeping the nameplate above the door up to date. It's left blank, ready for the next change. The front door lock is old-fashioned and presents no difficulty. The third floor and attic are deserted. The only visitors to these upper floors are the cleaner and the caretaker, and they're predictable. All the latter does is take the rickety old lift — Merrick thinks it could be an antique, ideal for a 1940s film set — up to the third, steps out, points his torch this way and that along the corridor and descends again with a metallic clatter. He doesn't try the individual office doors. Big mistake, for which Merrick is grateful. The caretaker never bothers to visit the empty attic, deep in dust, rat droppings and pigeon feathers.

Other people's errors are Merrick's opportunities.

For the civil servants who staff the place, working from home is still preferred (hardly surprising, in Merrick's view), with the result that only a handful turn up on weekdays, and sometimes none at all.

One of the cleaners — a woman named Suellen (or is it Sue-Ellen?), originally from the Ivory Coast — pushes a mop up and down the corridor floor and staircase, dipping it now and then in cleaning fluid carried in a yellow contraption on wheels, and chatting loudly all the while with her fellow cleaners on different floors. She's a cheery soul. She has a rich contralto that carries far and punctuates her melodious humming with an infectious laugh. She bursts and shimmers with life. Nothing seems to ever get her down; bless her.

Does she get the so-called living wage, which no one could live on in reality, not even a dog, and especially not in London? Merrick doubts it. She probably has three jobs to feed the kids and pay the bills.

Making impressions of Suellen's office keys, while she's on a break and gabbing with her workmates out on the fire escape, is easy-peasy.

Outside office hours, the building is silent, save for London pigeons strutting, cooing, copulating and crapping on filthy windowsills.

The killing zone will be missed by Merrick once it's all over — it's become familiar, a temporary lodging. It covers the conservation area extending west to the edge of St James's Park and all the way to the river along the eastern edge, with Whitehall running north-south down the centre. Merrick could navigate this wedge of real estate blindfold after wearing out shoe leather for so many weeks. The Admiralty. The Banqueting Hall. The Clive Steps and Horseguards' Parade, the old Scotland Yard.

It's so much fun, running the gauntlet, especially when laced with a dose of high risk.

Around a million people flow like a tide back and forth through it five days a week. Roughly a third of that number are employed in security duties of one sort or another, official and commercial.

Three days before the police searches and lockdown begin, Merrick is in position.

Ready.

The lazy bastards are complacent. They don't check the roof spaces, and even if they did, they wouldn't find anything amiss. Merrick has made sure of it.

Chapter 3

Kandahar Province, Afghanistan, 15:30 local, November 11
Septimus Brass talks to the dead man next to him. He does so quietly, hardly moving his lips so no one will notice.

'Sorry about this,' he whispers. 'This won't take long, and they'll have you back just the way you were. That's a promise, okay?'

As the sun climbs, Septimus sweats a torrent inside his white plastic overalls. In desperation, he manages the Houdini-like feat of unzipping, then peeling down, the upper section of the protective suit to around his waist, revealing a drenched white t-shirt. He keeps his white baseball cap on and his face down as if bowed in prayer. Salty perspiration rolls down his face, stings his eyes and drips off the tip of his nose. It doesn't help that he's on his knees in a shallow grave, and to accomplish the tricky manoeuvre, he's had to down tools — these comprising a small, blue, plastic-backed brush and an equally small, blue, plastic bucket not unlike the kind he supposes toddlers play with at the seaside.

Septimus is forbidden to touch the remains beside him in the grave — bones and disintegrating clothing — on pain of being shot, or at the very least beaten, by one of the armed men watching the forensic research team's painstaking progress. All Septimus may do as the team's most junior member, and as someone who is not a co-religionist of the victim, is look for evidence in the immediate surroundings consisting of materials other than the human remains themselves, the remains being that of a young, adult male. These might include weapons, cartridge cases, bullets or fragments of bullets, edged weapons, blades or anything else that might have constituted a weapon, as well as buttons, fragments of clothing. Any artefact that might help identify the deceased and his killer or killers is in his bailiwick, so to speak. Excluded from his excavation would be hair, teeth, fragments of bone or other human tissue, which would have to be extracted, examined, bagged and labelled by someone else.

It helps that he's not the only white-clad blob sweating on the plain. He doesn't stand out; there are several others on their knees, bent over, suffering in the heat. Others stand or stride around with an apparent sense of purpose, some with clipboards displaying authority and providing immunity from beating and shooting, or so they must hope. The truth of the matter is that it isn't the rising heat of an Afghan sun that makes Septimus sweat from what feels like every pore of his pale northern skin, but fear and guilt. Guilt that he's an imposter and a liar. Fear that he might be found out. And fear, as he knows only too well, is a chemical compound. A man may stink of fear.

Especially if that same fearful character is sweating from apocrine glands in the hands, feet, armpits and genital area. Septimus knows he is. He wipes his hands on his protective suit. Not that it helps. His fingers are still slippery when he snatches up the toy bucket and spade to resume his work, disturbing glossy black flies that buzz and crawl.

The telltale, sweetish stench of death is slight. That surprised Septimus at first. The desiccated remains of the twenty-two-year-old give off little odour now. The lad died more than a decade previously, and the dry air — so dry it seems to Septimus to crackle with electricity — ensures that outwardly the body is well preserved, while Septimus imagines that the dry, loose sand of his resting place must have absorbed what fluids he would have secreted at the time of death.

There is hope of relief. It's hot enough now to drive the two gunmen out of the sun and into the shade cast by a mud wall some eighty paces distant, where they light up their cigarettes and seem to lose interest in the diggers. They prop their AK-74s against the wall and fiddle with their turbans. The imam brought in by the Taliban to supervise the entire process has already moved inside with Abdul, and both men are no doubt enjoying sweet green tea, dried fruit and nuts in the cool interior.

Septimus hopes everyone will break for lunch very soon.

His eyes are on the doorway through which the imam and Abdul vanished. Abdul works for the Afghan Red Crescent, the local counterpart of the International Committee of the Red Cross. He's also a malik, or elder. He wields much influence, has innumerable contacts and not inconsiderable charm. He's respected by all parties. It's Abdul who keeps the whole show on the road, and that means keeping the Taliban appeased and at arm's length to allow the team to work. Abdul manages to enter areas others can't. When required to do so, he collects cadavers in his beat-up Toyota taxi and returns them to their families, or in the case of members of so-called Western aid agencies, to the refrigerated mortuaries overseen by the ICRC.

If Septimus's secret were to leak out, it could all go pear-shaped, and not even Abdul Ishaqzai could save the day. He probably wouldn't even try. Septimus is someone of no importance to the excavation, but his real identity, if revealed, could lead to a great deal of trouble for everyone.

The graves are not what Septimus had expected. He wasn't sure what to expect, but not the rows of almost identical hummocks of sand covered with stones - the latter no doubt used to keep the sand from being blown or, in the rare rainstorms, washed away. The stones would also help protect the dead from the predations of packs of feral dogs. The cemetery is huge, in what amounts to a flat field of pink and beige dust. It's colourful, too, thanks to the prayer flags fastened to long poles protruding from each burial mound. The poles bend, and the tattered fragments flutter like frayed battle pendants in the fitful desert breeze. The team is interested in just eleven graves among the scores that are visible. These eleven are all to one side, and, while they look pretty much indistinguishable from the others, they have been pointed out by villagers as the resting places of the eleven people killed violently — martyred — in two incidents just hours or days apart.

Lunch is called. The announcement takes the unusual form of a loud squawk from a two-foot-long plastic horn known as a vuvuzela, the controversially loud apparatus of South African football fans. This is thanks to Robert, a cheerful Kenyan graduate of the African School of Humanitarian Forensic Action. They won't resume work until 4 p.m. when the heat should start to lessen.

'Alright, Septimus?'

He turns, surprised. 'Fine, thanks.'

The deep, cheerful voice, as well as the sight of the big man striding towards him while pulling off latex gloves and unzipping his white suit, is reassuring. Everyone calls him The Boss. He exudes confidence, a toughness of spirit and an intellect people trust.

The distinguished Dr Starr Richards heads the team's specialists. Septimus knows he has two doctorates to his name — forensic anthropology and archaeology — and is board-certified by the Royal Anthropological Institute. He's the chief forensic scientist on the mission and at the peak of his career, and he lets everyone know it. He's also party to Septimus's guilty little secret.

'So, how are you getting along with our pal Mirwais Yusufzai, otherwise known as KA08/23?'

He's referring to the remains Septimus has been crouching next to for much of the past hour — a collection of bones wreathed in rotting cotton shalwar kameez and held together by a few remaining sinews. The jaw is still attached to the skull. Septimus has tried not to look too closely at Mirwais, who appears to be grinning up at him — a knowing grin, sightless, of course, with a third eye created by a neat bullet entry hole above the right eye socket. The impact appears to have cracked the skull across the top and has sheered the back of it clear off.

'Splendidly,' says Septimus. 'I think we've established something of a rapport, he and I, despite his insistence on speaking only Pashto.'

'Ah. You must work on that. The Pashto, I mean. Find anything?'

'Sorry. No.'

'Never mind, old chap. Let's clean ourselves up and have a bite to eat, yes?'

They splash their faces and upper bodies, then scrub their hands at a long zinc trough fed by an enormous bladder storage tank. Other teams descend on the open-sided canvas tent, where potable water and a lunch of cold cuts and salad await on trestle tables. There's coffee too, and the smell makes Septimus salivate. The new arrivals have come over from the village where the eleven people buried in the cemetery are alleged to have been killed, ten of them inside their homes, the eleventh in an alley behind his family's house. Accompanied by the local imam and watched by relatives, technicians have noted bullet holes, measured angles of fire, recorded distances and photographed everything as they've proceeded from one crime scene to the next. Alleged crime scene, rather.

Of the eight, seven were shot, and one was stabbed, either with a large knife or bayonet. The latter seems the most likely.

'Want to talk to them — the technical guys? Did you have a word with Hamilton, our ballistics specialist?'

'Already did, thanks,' says Septimus, chewing on a chicken and rocket wrap.

'The families?'

'Those too. First thing. They're still angry, even though it was years ago.'

'Of course they bloody are.' Richards nods in apparent approval and wipes his fingers on a paper napkin, his blue eyes still on Septimus.

"Tell me something, if you would, Dr Richards.' Septimus looks around quickly and lowers his voice. 'You're not allowed by the religious authorities to remove the remains or any part of them, right?'

'Correct. Our Moslem colleagues will restore the graves this afternoon, a process supervised by the two imams.'

'OK, good, but what about DNA? If you can't remove anything organic —'

Dr Richards leans forward. 'It's called stealth. Invaluable in this line of work. As you've no doubt found out yourself. Now, answer me this. Have you had enough? Want a rest? I ask because I'm visiting two sites in Helmand Province tomorrow if you're interested. Three, if we have time.'

'I don't need a rest, thanks.'

Dr Richards will not spell out how they collect the DNA or even confirm that it has been harvested. Septimus, playing the innocent, is taken aback to discover his mentor is using sleight of hand — deceit — to get what he needs. Quite a subversive fellow, our Dr Richards.

'Sure?'

'Sure.'

'Splendid. Then we'll pick you up at zero-four-hundred tomorrow. On the dot. Good?'

A moment's hesitation.

'Very good. Thank you.'

'You've got all the data so far, Septimus. You're up to date. You don't have to visit all the locations in person. Give yourself a break, why don't you? I'll send you daily updates for as long as we're here.'

'I think I need to see as many as I can.'

'Fine. Your dedication is commendable. But don't keep us waiting in the morning is all I ask.'

Septimus isn't satisfied, so he tries from another angle.

'How can anyone tell who the shooters were?'

'We ask the relatives. They provide the initial identification.'

'Would they know the difference between a British special ops soldier and an American? Or a Dane? Or a Czech?'

'Almost certainly not.'

'So — '

'So we don't take saliva samples from the relatives if that's what you're wondering. Sticking a cotton bud into a living Afghan's mouth or nostril wouldn't be a good idea. Far too intrusive and upsetting, with unpredictable consequences. But there are alternatives.'

That must mean hair. Match the DNA of the victims to that of their closest surviving relatives.

But Septimus can't press the issue further. Two team members have come up, carrying plastic trays and wanting to join Richards. Septimus recognises one of them as a senior Canadian forensic science technician and the other as none other than Dr Fabiani from Milan, a man with a professional reputation as formidable as that of Dr Richards, if not more so. They're rivals, then, though they seem to remain on good terms. They're working together, after all. Dr Fabiani is renowned for his work in exhuming, examining and identifying the remains of hundreds of Bosnian Moslem civilians gunned down by Serb nationalists at Srebrenica and Gorazde in the early 90s. He subsequently went on to court controversy and no little antipathy by publicly identifying beyond all reasonable doubt the killer of a female Palestinian journalist as an Israeli military sniper in the Occupied West Bank. A deliberate, targeted killing. For this commendable public service, Dr Fabiani has been wrongly labelled an antisemite.

Septimus doesn't hesitate — he pushes his own tray along the table and follows it, shifting along the bench to make ample room for the two men. He knows his place. It's not subservience or modesty on his part; the last thing he wants is to be drawn into a technical conversation or to be asked about himself. The falseness of his claim to be a junior colleague of theirs wouldn't bear a minute's scrutiny by professionals.

His satellite phone beeps. He takes it out of his pocket, sees the caller's ID, gets up from the table, takes a few steps away and presses 'receive.'

Septimus listens in silence to an encrypted message. He doesn't react at all when he learns of the shooting in central London.

'Okay,' he says at the end. 'All right. I'll be there asap.'

He'll have to give Helmand Province a miss. In any case, he has all he needs. His draft report is done. Just a tweak or two, and it'll be submitted well before the start of the formal inquiry, an inquiry into allegedly unlawful deaths of Afghan civilians at the hands of British special forces.

Septimus looks out of the tent at the site of the investigation: white tape, yellow pegs, dust whirling in a stiffening breeze, graves open to the sky. He sees where KA08/23 lies. He pockets the satphone, puts the rest of the chicken wrap in his mouth and, chewing and swallowing, picks up his tray. London might be in crisis, but he'll not deny himself the small pleasure of a coffee before leaving.

Goodbye, Mirwais Yusufzai, whoever you were.

Chapter 4

West London, 13:16 GMT, November 11

Bridie Connor wasn't watching television.

There would be colleagues who would say it was remiss of her had they known. She seldom did watch because she loathed what the BBC had become and refused to pay the licence fee despite letters in heavy black type threatening to send inspectors around to her home, to impose fines or to launch criminal proceedings.

She was only vaguely aware it was Armistice Day because of the contentious peace marches she knew would be taking place later in cities across Britain. To her, they were only contentious because they were expected to draw a million marchers and because the extreme culture warrior (and, in Bridie's view, dangerously unhinged) anti-woke home secretary had made it so by kicking up a fuss, calling the protests 'hate marches.'

Bridie had to wonder if the home secretary had any idea what 'armistice' meant.

Instead of ogling daytime telly, she was outside in her wellies, an ancient waxed jacket and gardening gloves, working up some warmth this chilly morning by slashing away at the old summer growth like an explorer hacking through jungle, trying to create order out of chaos — blackberry, wild strawberry, clumps of rogue grass, nettles, thistles and a dozen other sharp, pointy things she couldn't name had run amok over the unusually hot, dry summer. She heard the phone ring in the house — the special green phone in what she called her library. It rang rarely. Even so, she didn't rush to answer it once she recognised it for what it was, though a small voice told her in a disapproving tone she was supposed to jump to it, night or day, and never to ignore it.

It's your job, you nincompoop.

The tinny voice of professional conscience told Bridie something else she knew: the Office didn't call her reserved landline unless the situation was FUBAR — fucked up beyond all recognition. But then, wasn't everything FUBAR nowadays, from floods and dying seas to raging wildfires, failing childcare to education, potable water to sewage, carbon emissions to energy, transport to health, trade to investment, air pollution to NHS waiting lists? The Barbarians weren't at the gates. They were inside and in charge while filling their own pockets with loot from the public purse.

She was a lifelong pessimist; Bridie thought the country was like her back garden — a decaying ruin of willful, malevolent and possibly criminal neglect, and she had long come to terms with the realisation that she could fiddle with both but fix neither. It was all going to hell.

It rang again when she reached the door to the conservatory, but she couldn't get her boots off in time. She swore long and loud and didn't care if the neighbours heard her profane rant. She was damned if she was going to go inside with her boots on and scatter dirt everywhere because there was no one to clear it up except Bridie herself, and she hated housework. Ditto her partner, Alec, who had his own life and refused to consider such mundane tasks part of his marital contract, especially at weekends.

By the time it rang a third time, Bridie was ready and waiting at her desk with a large mug of steaming Yorkshire Gold in hand. Inscribed in black on the white mug — a birthday gift from Alec — was the following: 'My work is top secret. Even I don't know what I'm doing.'

'Ma'am? We're sending a car.'

How kind. 'Okay, what's happened?'

'Seen the news, by any chance?'

'I'm turning on my radio now.' That wasn't true, but who would ever know?

'All will be explained once you get here.'

'Give me a headline or two.'

The caller did better. He provided a succinct summary. 'PM's dead. Shot. National emergency declared, all points of entry and exit being shut down as we speak. National unity government being formed. Security forces on alert. Airspace closed; flights grounded. Deputy PM taking over. Parliament summoned.'

Bridie is momentarily stunned.

She pulls herself together.

Not that arse Carstairs, for Chrissakes!

'And you are?'

'Weekend duty officer for my sins. Ma'am. Cuttle.'

'Cuttle?'

'Bernard Cuttle. Ma'am.'

Bridie was grappling with the implications of what she'd just heard. 'And how does this affect us, Mr Cuttle?'

'All hands on deck. Ma'am. Director-general's orders. He's on his way from Scotland by road. That's all I know.'

'You're too modest, Bernard. That's right, isn't it — Bernard? How are things at the Office?'

'Honestly?'

'Speak your mind.'

'Total madhouse. Ma'am. As you might expect. Scores of headless chickens running around squawking in ever-decreasing circles. The good news is that it must be even worse over at Five, if that's possible.'

'I think I get the picture, thank you.'

'Of course. Ma'am.'

'And stop calling me Ma'am. You can call me Ms Connor or Bridie. Bridget, if you really must.'

'Yes. Ma'am. Sorry.'

Bridie remembered Bernard Cuttle for one reason: he invariably added a respectful 'sir' or 'ma'am' when addressing senior officers of the Service, but only after a pregnant pause. Well, good for him. Scepticism towards authority was healthy, even when Bridie happened momentarily to be that authority.

'I'll see you soon then, Bernard.'

'That you will. Ma'am. I mean, Ms Connor. Traffic permitting.'

She was going to end the call when he spoke again. 'Oh, this is just in. A flash from the Press Association. I'll read it if I may.'

'Go on, if you must.'

'Police shoot dead suspected gunman at Dover — Kent Police spokesperson.'

'Thank you,' Bridie said for lack of anything better.

'Bloody idiots and their itchy trigger fingers,' Bernie spluttered. 'Now we'll never fucking know who did it.'

Chapter 5

Central London, 14:22 GMT, November 11

The phone rang on Bridie's desk the moment she walked into her office in the Ziggurat, with Bernard Cuttle in her wake.

She picked up, hit 'encrypt speech' and signalled to Bernie that he should stay.

'Yes?'

'Bridget? Bridget Connor? Henri Picard.'

They switched to French.

'Good to hear from you, Henri, as ever. How's the weather in Paris?'

'Cold and wet — just like London, I suspect. I wanted you to know we're here to help in any way we can. Just let me know. We can do it formally or informally. Your shout.'

'Thank you so much.'

'Is this line secure your end?'

'It is, Henri.'

Picard was Bridie's opposite number at the DGSE, France's external intelligence service, the equivalent of SIS, but larger and primarily responsible for strategic intel and counterintelligence outside the French mainland.

'Thanks to Brexit, as you're well aware, the wheels of bureaucracy grind awful slow. So, I want to bend the rules and make you aware that eight days ago, a right-wing fanatic with a military background travelled from Marseille to the United Kingdom as a tourist. Scheduled flight to Luton. Single ticket, one-way.

'Name of Karscher, Erich. Born in Brandenburg, Germany, not far from Berlin. Former warrant officer in our Foreign Legion under the name Jean Martin, which is how he became a naturalised citizen after five years' service. A qualified army marksman. Active service in Mali and Syria. Not a bad record. Since then, politically active on the far right in both France and Germany as well as Hungary. A hardcore racist. Worships Putin. Arrested three times in demonstrations but no convictions, hence no record. He must have a good lawyer, no? Too good, I'd say. Age thirty-six. Source of income not established. Thought you should know. Official notification is on its way. It will reach you— eventually.'

Bridie tapped the details into her computer.

'Henri, thank you. I really appreciate this.'

Picard spoke in English. 'It's your Christmas present from me. Stay in touch, Bridie. Hello to Alec. *Joyeux noel*.'

Meantime, word went round that 'C' had arrived at the Ziggurat — the grandiose Secret Intelligence Service headquarters at 85 Albert Embankment in Lambeth — from Scotland. A Puma helicopter from the RAF's S&D Flight, a unit of a dozen pilots attached to special forces and the intelligence services, had ferried him most of the way.

If SIS staff had hoped for a firm hand on the tiller in time of crisis, they were to be disappointed. 'C' declined to see anyone. He made his way alone from the Ziggurat's helicopter pad to his office on the top floor, still in his tweeds, brogues and in a foul temper, or so it was said, presumably because of the police checkpoints, vehicle searches and intrusive questions — and the delays all this had caused on the A1 — until the S&D Flight came to the rescue and plucked him off the hard shoulder.

Sequestered in his office, with its plush caramel carpet, wood-panelled walls, and a copy of his favourite picture above his desk, an enormous Landseer oil of a twelve-pointer stag being clobbered by Prince Albert while Queen Victoria looks on (a picture everyone else in the Office loathed, including Bridie), 'C' made it clear he didn't want to see anyone until he'd found out for himself what had happened and what was being done about it. He needed to catch up. The red light above the door of the DG's office was switched on, and it stayed that way. It meant he was busy with his several secure phones and the SIS computer messaging system. Or maybe he wasn't. There were to be no interruptions, but from the muffled sounds leaking from his office, he was flicking through television news channels. It was all about the same thing. Bursts of Cantonese, Mandarin, Korean, Portuguese, Russian, Spanish and Swedish could be heard by anyone paying attention in the outer office. That 'anyone' was his long-suffering and long-serving personal assistant, Madge, who was almost old enough to be his mother (which was why she was called Mother behind her back) and who'd nannied three 'C's in succession, and who'd been told in blunt terms to keep out.

Eventually, the light went off, and Controllers were summoned to the DG's lair one at a time and swiftly dismissed, followed by the Director Requirements and Director Production, whose interviews with 'C' were equally short.

In a huff, Mother had cleared her desk, locked its drawers, picked up her handbag, stormed out, and after an unconscionably long wait, caught her usual number 36 bus, standing room only, though it took her almost two hours from Vauxhall to her home in Paddington instead of the usual forty minutes.

• • • •

'C' SUMMONED BRIDIE to his office suite just after 4 pm when most people compelled to work on a Saturday were clearing their desks and sneaking out, hoping to find trains or buses to get them home, just as the DG's PA had done. The lights along the Thames embankments were already aglow in the gathering murk of winter.

It was just Bridie's bad luck to be called upstairs now, after the seven Controllers had already fled, and the light was fading.

Sir Thomas Avery was on his feet with his back to the door by a drinks table in a corner behind his immense Georgian desk of walnut, fruitwood, and oak. He turned and smiled as she entered. Charm personified.

'Thanks for coming, Bridie. I've been deserted in my hour of need by Madge, so we're alone. Shut the door, if you would.'

The huge and dying stag, its nemesis Prince Albert and the doting Empress Victoria stared down on them from a vertiginous Highland glen. Haughty looks all round.

'Scotch?'

'Bit early for me, Sir Thomas.'

'Oh, balls, Bridie. Sun's well over the yardarm. Sit.'

'C' brought over two cut glasses containing what looked to Bridie like triples. No ice.

'Dash of water?'

'It's fine the way it is, thank you.' She knew that was the answer he wanted. She despised herself for trying so hard to please, especially someone who'd been on the same Intelligence Officers' New Entry Course (IOENEC) as herself but who'd overtaken her at warp speed.

'I would hope so. Good to see you, Bridie.'

This was to be a friendly chat. Just how friendly remained to be seen.

'C' left his desk and plonked himself down in a leather club armchair opposite his visitor. Bridie knew what was in their glasses: the DG's favourite tipple at this time of year was twelve-year-old Bowmore single malt. In summer, it would have been enormous pink gins. Again, without water. The DG hated water except for shaving and showering.

'Slàinte Mhath!' 'C' lifted his glass.

'Slàinte Mhath,' replied Bridie and took a sip, feeling the liquid fire burn her tongue and roll down her throat.

The hit was instantaneous, blood rising to her cheeks and tears to her eyes.

'It's been a rotten day,' said 'C'.

You poor baby, was Bridie's unspoken thought. If it wasn't for some deranged assassin, her boss could still have been out where he was happiest, on some freezing peat bog or moor on the edge of the Cairngorms slaughtering legions of poor wee defenceless grouse, hobnobbing with millionaires and gentry — and all of it to reinforce his macho sense of self-worth at immense cost to the natural environment. There was nothing natural about a grouse moor, not even the grouse, bred to be killed.

'C' had one striking peculiarity: he spoke, dressed and behaved like an old fogey at least twice his age. He liked tweed, the MCC tie and double-breasted, three-piece suits. Bridie thought he wanted to appear old for the gravitas that only age could bestow. Despite his best efforts to age, Sir Thomas resembled an undergraduate, still innocent, fresh-faced, red-haired and horribly fit. He booked a game on the Ziggurat's squash courts at least twice a week. He seemed to Bridie to be a rather serious and bookish schoolboy, which was closer to the truth than the huntin' fishin' Old Etonian image he liked to project. He had been a scholarship boy from a Leeds grammar school all the way to Oxford and a double first. Bridie felt old every time she saw 'C', which thankfully wasn't that often. She thought some women were probably attracted to him because they felt he needed mothering. She was not among them.

He had his fucking 'K' already, and Bridie didn't.

'What are you up to?'

'We're looking for any foreign links. I've invited Five and GCHQ to join a working group to investigate just that.'

'C' nodded and sipped his whisky. 'I've just come off the phone with Five. Special Branch report that the man shot at Dover carried no identification. When he was stopped by police, he was said to have reached for his back pocket, and he was warned a second time. He ignored the warning and appeared to brandish something black and solid that looked like a pistol. They warned him a third time, but he ignored them yet again. So they shot him. That's their version, and I've no reason to doubt it.'

So why mention it if there isn't any doubt?

Bridie hadn't forgotten the case of Jean Charles da Silva, the innocent Brazilian killed by Met police at Stockwell Underground Station on July 22, 2005. He'd been mistakenly identified as a fugitive involved in the previous day's failed bomb attacks. Only two weeks earlier, on July 7, terrorist bombs had killed fifty-two people in the capital. Bridie remembered it because she'd been a sixteen-year-old at school in west London at the time, and the bombings and shooting had terrified her.

'C' drank again.

'Turns out it wasn't a gun, but a phone. A burner. Only one number on it, which Special Branch passed to Five, which has traced the number to Nice. A private address. We await DNA, prints, blood group, etcetera. There's your first foreign link. No doubt there'll be many leads of this nature before we're done.'

We?

'Who shot the suspect?'

'One of the CTSFOs. Does it matter?'

Bridie knew what they were — Counter Terrorist Specialist Firearms Officers. Clumsy, aggressive brutes in her view, dead from the neck up and politically well to the right of Genghis Khan. She'd find out in the fullness of time which one had taken the poor sod down. Maybe whoever it was had a personal agenda. It was unlikely but not impossible, knowing the Met.

'I'd better let Picard know.'

'C' drained his glass.

'The French military are bound to have records on their wayward legionnaire — fingerprints, dental records, DNA. We could try to match that with the fellow we shot today.'

'Good point,' Bridie said. She decided not to confess to having already kick-started the process. 'I'll get onto it.' The chief had to take credit occasionally for bright ideas he never had.

'C' asked, 'Do you have anyone in your bailiwick who might sniff out the lie of the land in Nice? Don't think we should ask your DGSE friend to do it for us.'

'I think we might,' Bridie said.

Why not give it to Paris Station? But she didn't suggest it.

'Excellent,' Sir Thomas said, beaming. 'Keep me posted. Just so you know, I've put RWW on full alert.'

The Revolutionary Warfare Wing was a Special Air Service (SAS) Regiment detachment based at Hereford and part of the SIS 'Increment' — experienced special forces with intelligence training and specialising in the arcane skills of sabotage and improvised explosive devices, as well as covert insertion and exfiltration by sea or air.

Bridie waited. There had to be more to this tête-à-tête, and there was.

'C' put his glass down and cleared his throat, putting a fist to his mouth.

Here it comes.

'What I'm about to say is not only official but a direct order from the Cabinet Office — and me.'

Shit, here we go.

'You will, with immediate effect, lead a multi-agency task force to identify and hunt down the killer or killers responsible for today's attack. This wasn't simply the assassination of a couple of unpopular politicians but an assault on the UK itself, as I'm sure you understand. You have all the emergency powers you need at your disposal. You're to start immediately. You'll report in every day to the home secretary and me, though not necessarily in person. You will copy your daily reports to the heads of all the agencies involved...'

Oh, Christ. What did I do to deserve this hell?

'C' continued to speak. Funding. Location. Secure communications. Transport. Investigative staff and administrative support.

'Questions?'

'None, sir. Not now, anyhow.'

'Good. That's what I wanted to hear. I know I can rely on you, Bridie, which is why the Service put your name forward to manage it. It's a credit to you and SIS that you've been chosen.'

She would have liked to ask 'why me' but knew she wouldn't get an honest answer. Like it or not, her days in the field were over. She was DCI, after all. Director of Counterintelligence, though what counterintelligence had to do with a police murder inquiry she had no idea.

'C' leaned forward and passed her a note with a printed list of the eight names of her leading investigators. She didn't get to choose, and neither did they. She'd never heard of the first name.

Septimus Brass.

Bridie polished off the single malt and stood up with care, holding the arm of the chair as she felt the liquor anaesthetise her frontal lobe. Wow! Not at all an unpleasant sensation, just not appropriate on duty and in the presence of 'C'. She needed to eat something, and soon.

Sir Thomas put out a hand for Bridie's glass. 'The other half? I'm going to. Join me, might as well.'

'No, that was great, Chief, thank you, but I'll keel over if I have another.'

'May I offer some advice, Bridie? It's more of a reminder, actually. If you don't awfully mind.'

'Please.'

'As always, Five is the lead agency when it comes to counterintelligence, as you know better than anyone. We must be seen to defer to them on all CI matters, at least on home ground. Officially, your department exists to detect any penetration of our Service and its fifty-four Stations abroad, a big enough burden for anyone as it is. Trust me: you need to delegate as much as possible, or you won't be able to cope with the task force as well as your day job as D/CI. You can't do it all, so use others to take up the strain. Delegate, Bridie, okay? I must remind you once more that we keep Five informed at all times, and we do not go tearing off on our own bat without sharing. Clear?'

'Goes without saying, sir.'

A little obeisance went a long way with 'C'.

'I know you, Bridie. We trained together, you and I, and I watched your progress. Once you scent blood, there's no stopping you. You're our top bloodhound.'

A back-handed compliment?

'C' continued his homily. 'Take this as friendly advice from a colleague. What happened this morning was horrible. Despicable. We're all shocked, of course. But we must crack on and play a team game. You will have to show your collegial side because everyone will be taking a very close interest.'

Here endeth the lesson.

'Off to the Garrick now, sir?'

'Very funny, Bridie.' He wasn't smiling.

All the usual clichés applied. Bridie knew 'C' didn't like rocking boats, which was why he'd been plucked out of the field for the top job three years earlier. A weekend sailor on calm waters. A safe pair of hands, it was said, a team player, it was said, a Whitehall insider, oh, yes, very much so, someone who knew how to play the game and was adored by the stiffs on the Joint Intelligence Committee, with a glittering, uninterrupted ascent in record time from station chief in Berlin and Moscow to the sixth floor, leapfrogging even the seven 'dwarves' — the controllers. So talented. So professional. Such a wunderkind that his rivals and detractors who'd dared whisper their envious misgivings to one another in their cups at the Travellers, White's and Boodles had nicknamed him, somewhat unkindly — and to Bridie's secret delight — as The Greased Piglet.

Or, as the Germans might say, *gefettetes Ferkel.*

And no, of course he wasn't a member of the Garrick Club. He was far too smart to be caught up in a row over the white, male, stuffed-shirt membership of that august institution.

Bridie's brow furrowed as she stepped into the lift. She wasn't looking forward to heading up the new Task Group. It seemed to her to be an invitation to almost certain disaster, and who wanted to be associated with failure? There were no solid leads. They had no idea at all who was behind the shooting or what the motive was.

And who the blazes was Septimus Brass?

Chapter 6

Central London, 11:06, November 11

Merrick slipped out of the building, pulled the front door shut behind him and turned to face Whitehall.

No need to run. Better to stay put on the top step for a minute or so, counting the seconds, feet apart, arms akimbo, bag at his feet, aware that the CCTV would pick up the image. This wasn't someone fleeing a crime scene, scared and trying to hide. This was a police sergeant very much in control of himself and his situation.

Calm. Collected. Professional.

Who was it who said, 'Some men improve the world just by leaving it'?

Wasn't it Oscar Wilde?

Merrick walked down the steps through the gate in the black iron railings to the pavement, stopped again, turned and stared up at the building he'd left as if seeking signs of the assassin in the upper windows. Just then, a phalanx of riot police jogged past in helmets and body armour, turned at the steps, burst into the building next door and raced up the stairs. They carried a battering ram, and two of them lugged a bulletproof shield. Merrick noted that at least two officers were armed with Heckler & Koch G36 5.56mm assault rifles along with Glock 17 pistols strapped to their thighs.

Christ. That was fast.

They've come for me. Well, here I am, lads, and you're at the wrong address — that's No. 54.

They ignored Merrick.

Chaos helped. The soft, peaked police cap, the Met police navy blue tactical firearms coverall and sergeant's stripes on the epaulettes did the rest. Merrick carried nothing but a patrol bag and wore blue latex gloves on both hands.

A standard patrol belt completed the look, along with standard Met attachments.

Keys and cash in a thigh pocket.

He held his patrol bag in his left hand.

That was it.

Merrick set off with a purposeful stride and a facial expression that said, 'Don't fuck with me.' Someone on official business, even if heading away from the crime scene. He felt strong, his muscles and sinews in good working order, his spirit adamantine.

Through and around the crowds of bemused tourists, cops, ambulance drivers and paramedics, troops, television crews, metal barriers, yellow police tape, the scuffles and pushing, Merrick kept moving, ears ringing with shouts of command, the plangent chorus of ambulance and police sirens, the racket of helicopters hovering just above the trees of St James's Park, above Buckingham Palace and over the Thames.

A uniformed police inspector shouted something from across the street and tried to get Merrick's attention by waving an arm. He was ignored; Merrick appeared to have seen and heard nothing but marched on, arms swinging. Merrick was hot now, sweating under the polyester and cotton coveralls, not from stress but the layer of protective clothing underneath the coveralls.

K9s on the street, German Shepherds and Malinois, their handlers awaiting orders to begin their search.

CCTV everywhere, as usual.

Nowhere to hide but in plain sight.

Merrick spotted three police vans with facial recognition cameras mounted on the roof.

But what did they see, any of them? A copper — one of 1,500 deployed in the vicinity — striding with confidence yet without haste into Westminster Underground. The 'officer' held up a warrant card, moved through a turnstile, took the elevator down to the platforms, facial features obscured by the cap. The first train east-bound wasn't crowded; it was probably the last before public transport shut down. Then again, maybe folk were too scared to venture out after the shooting. Merrick boarded the train, but just as the doors were about to close, he stepped out again onto the platform and retreated up the elevator to the street. Staff were urging people to leave. The shut-down had begun.

It was gloomy outside. Pewter sky, streets the colour of lead. Storm on the way, most likely. Merrick headed through the glow of sodium street lights and walked to Marks & Spencer opposite Green Park Underground, made for the food hall, picked out a sandwich and a bottle of juice, paid for these plus an M&S bag with cash at a self-service till, then set out for the clothing section, selecting from the racks a deep-red hoodie, a pair of standard fit indigo jeans and a grey baseball cap. All on offer, fifty-percent off. Paid again in cash. Merrick ignored the junior sales assistant's curious looks and smile. She seemed to hesitate as if wanting to say something, but Merrick turned away.

Why would a uniformed police officer buy civvie clothing, especially a copper wearing blue latex gloves?

There could be a dozen reasons, the big discount being one of them.

Now for the toilets. Merrick followed the signs. Up to the second floor by elevator, watching for surveillance going up and coming down. Nothing. Wonderful thing about M&S was the age profile of ninety-nine percent of customers — they all seemed to be well over sixty. Youngsters — anyone under fifty — would stand out. Once inside a cubicle, the purchases were set to one side. Merrick took off the uniform cap, then the waterproof patrol boots, unzipped the coverall, stepped out of it and pushed all the police paraphernalia into the M&S bag, followed by the protective clothing worn under the police clobber. Merrick ripped the sales tags off the new gear, tugged on the jeans, put the boots back on and dragged on the hoodie. Last of all, the grey cap — the peak pulled low.

Sandwich, juice and receipts went into the bag on top of everything else. All done.

In a couple of minutes, Merrick was out on the pavement again and heading for his next bolthole.

Chapter 7

South London, 16:18, November 11

London's transport links had been brought to a standstill in the immediate aftermath of the murders, but road traffic started to crawl again in fits and starts by 3 p.m.

Mobile networks were also down for hours, then restored by mid-afternoon. Much of Whitehall and Westminster began to be reoccupied by a trickle of glum staff summoned for emergency weekend duty. Doors opened; lights went on in offices shuttered for the weekend.

Members of the public — many wearing Remembrance poppies in their lapels — stood on street corners, gazing at their phones, feeling no doubt helpless and hopeless, incredulous, anxious and annoyed. Tourists seemed to have evaporated, at least in central London. Uniformed cops popped up all over. Many were armed, strolling around in pairs, clutching Heckler & Koch automatic weapons. It was like a Bank Holiday with guns, Bridie thought.

According to her radio, paras from the Army's 16th Air Assault Brigade — an emergency formation always on standby — along with members of the Royal Marines' 40 Commando had been deployed to patrol seaports, ferry terminals, airports and railway stations. Their armoured fighting vehicles, bristling with cannon, machine guns and radio antennae, stood at intersections, strange armoured behemoths in camouflage. A menacing demonstration of strength by the British state. Were they expecting a coup, perhaps? Mobile checkpoints manned by soldiers and police were thrown up along major roads, seemingly at random, the M25 ring road especially.

Helicopters buzzed back and forth like enraged hornets. The sound reminded Bridie of a dozen electric hairdryers on full throttle. Others hovered or moved in slow circles, no doubt their surveillance gear watching, listening, recording heaven only knew what.

Bridie passed on Picard's tip to the Security Service, or MI5 as it was known, as well as to GCHQ.

Her transistor was on all the time, preset to Radio Three. All scheduled programmes had been interrupted by running news and commentary. Bridie would have much preferred Bach's soothing 'Cello Suite No 1' to the nasal tones of the newsreader and his solemn reports.

Messages dropped into her in-basket from Five and the Donut, as GCHQ was called because of the shape of its Cheltenham headquarters: it turned out that the German-born French national Erich Karscher aka Jean Martin wasn't on anyone's radar. Bridie sent off a brief query to Germany's BND, the *Bundesnachrichtendienst* or foreign intelligence service. She wasn't holding her breath; it might be a week or even longer before she heard anything back, if she heard anything back at all — thanks to the xenophobe architects of Brexit and the formalities of German intelligence liaison.

By lunchtime, according to the news, Special Branch had begun raids on the homes of right-wing extremists of the English Defence League and their affiliates, along with the addresses of several anarchists and communists. They'd started working through their 'watch list' of Moslems they considered as suspected militants, not just in London but at addresses in Birmingham, Bradford, Brighton, Glasgow and Leicester.

They went for the Greens, too, reminding Bridie that dear Alec was a paid-up Green Party member and supporter of the Campaign Against the Arms Trade or CAAT.

By 2 p.m., seventy-five people had been detained under the Terrorism Act.

A new home secretary was appointed. Bridie had never heard of him, an obscure backbencher with an odd name.

In Glasgow, the appearance of armed police outside one tenement block in the city's south prompted a rapid response from neighbours, and the police were forced to withdraw as several hundred locals closed in on them, using fireworks, bricks and Irn Bru cans as projectiles. The residents helpfully removed the tyres of two police vans.

The flow of messages on Bridie's screen did not let up.

GCHQ's Cheltenham headquarters were placed on alert. The director called in all available staff (a difficult task until digital communications were restored), cancelled all leave and used its immense computers to comb its database of UK telephone numbers and email addresses for signs of unusual activity they might have missed over the past week. The Onion would never admit it, but Bridie knew Cheltenham held data — unlawfully, in all likelihood — on the entire adult population of the United Kingdom.

Overseas listening stations, belonging to the 'Five Eyes' intel alliance from the U.S. funded Ayios Nikolaos (Saint Nicholas) Station on the island of Cyprus to Australia's Pine Gap near Alice Springs, were asked by GCHQ to check any unusual transmissions as a matter of urgency.

Bridie moved away from her desk and stood staring out of her window — the rare privilege of a corner office with a view of the Thames came with her rank as SIS Director of Counterintelligence, a joint affair with Five and GCHQ. Reporting to her was a range of eleven joint TCIs — Targeting and Counterintelligence Sections, divided by overseas regions, a spider web of anti-spy spies.

It had taken her twenty-three years at SIS to earn her window and corner office on the fifth floor, just below 'C' himself. It wasn't large, just a glorified glass box. No Landseers, thank heaven, only an out-of-date calendar Bridie kept on her wall for its stunning pictures of the Greek islands in summer.

She was reminded that she had one year to go before the big Five-O and six years left before she reached statutory retirement age in the Service.

She couldn't see much. The window glass was a special, multi-layered type of woven fibre to protect the interior against projectiles such as rocket-propelled grenades as well as laser and microwave attacks. It made everything dim and unfocused to the human eye. Was there a lesson in there, that after decades as a spook and counter-spook, she still couldn't see clearly? Bridie could just about make out the brown stain of the Thames snaking its way towards the sea, the outline of Tower Bridge and the priapic monstrosity called The Shard, but not much else.

There was no point in going back to her garden; even if Bridie left now, she knew that by the time she got home and put her boots back on, it would be too dark to see a damn thing.

A Metropolitan Police report — from the Anti-Terrorist Branch — came through, flagged urgent. She was on the long distribution list. Bridie turned back to her desk and clicked on it.

About bloody time.

According to the radio presenter, fingers were already being pointed at the Met and Special Branch amid a chorus of demands from politicians and journalists for an official statement or at least a press release. Why was the shooter (or shooters) up on a rooftop or window ledge? Hadn't the buildings on Whitehall been searched and sealed off? Weren't teams of police snipers and spotters deployed on Whitehall's balconies and roofs, or were they sleeping on the job? Bridie wondered who it was who'd tipped off the media about a rooftop sniper in the first place.

SECRET

NOFORN

EX MET POLICE COMMISSIONER

PRELIMINARY REPORT ON CENOTAPH MURDERS

1. AT 1101 TODAY, NOV 11, THE PRIME MINISTER, LEADER OF THE OPPOSITION AND HOME SECRETARY WERE SHOT DEAD AND THE DEFENCE SECRETARY SERIOUSLY INJURED BY AN AS YET UNIDENTIFIED INDIVIDUAL WHO FIRED FOUR ROUNDS OF .338 MAGNUM AMMUNITION FROM A SNIPER RIFLE DURING THE ARMISTICE DAY CEREMONY AT THE CENOTAPH ON WHITEHALL. (NOTE: THE RIFLE, CALIBRE AND TYPE OF AMMUNITION IS IN USE BY SPECIALIST UNITS OF UK LAW ENFORCEMENT & ARMED FORCES).

2. THE LONE SHOOTER WAS POSITIONED WITHIN THE LOWER SECTION OF THE ROOF OPPOSITE, AND FIRED FOUR ROUNDS AT A RANGE OF 446.6 METRES (488.5 YARDS) AT TWO TARGETS, NAMELY THE PM, AND THE OPPOSITION LEADER STANDING NEXT TO THE PM.

3. IT DOES NOT APPEAR THAT THE HOME SECRETARY WAS INTENDED AS A TARGET BUT WAS STRUCK BY A SECOND BULLET AIMED AT THE OPPOSITION LEADER. (NOTE: THE 'DOUBLE TAP' IS A STANDARD PROCEDURE FOR ENSURING A KILL).

4. THE WEAPON USED WAS EQUIPPED WITH A SILENCER. AS A RESULT NO CHARACTERISTIC

'CRACK' WAS HEARD BY BYSTANDERS. THE FOUR SHOTS WERE FIRED DURING THE TWO MINUTES' SILENCE WHEN BOTH TARGETS WERE CERTAIN TO BE STATIONARY.

5. THE SHOOTER WAS POSITIONED APPROX. 45 METRES OR 148 FEET VERTICALLY ABOVE THE STREET. (THE GRADE 1 LISTED BUILDING WHERE THE SHOTS ORIGINATED COMPRISES THREE STOREYS AND AN ATTIC OF STUCCO AND RED BRICK WITH PROJECTING GABLES, TOPPED WITH A GREY, TILED AND PITCHED ROOF).

6. FROM AN EXAMINATION OF THE LOCATION, FORENSIC & BALLISTICS OFFICERS' INITIAL FINDING IS THAT THE SHOOTER LIKELY GAINED ACCESS TO THE BUILDING AND ITS ROOF SOME TIME EARLIER, ALMOST CERTAINLY PRIOR TO SECURITY MEASURES IMPOSED FOR THE CENOTAPH EVENT, POSSIBLY AS LONG AS A WEEK PRIOR, AND THAT THE SHOOTER WAS CONCEALED IN THE ROOF SPACE FOR THAT PERIOD, HAVING REMOVED SEVERAL TILES TO PROVIDE A FIELD OF FIRE AND REPLACING THEM WITH A TEMPORARY COVERING OF PLYWOOD PAINTED TO RESEMBLE GREY TILES.

7. NO FINGERPRINTS, DNA OR OTHER USEFUL EVIDENCE HAVE SO FAR BEEN RECOVERED FROM THE SITE. THERE WERE INDICATIONS THE SHOOTER HAD OCCUPIED THE SPACE FOR SOME TIME BUT THIS HAS SO FAR PROVIDED NO LEADS. THE SHOOTER IS THOUGHT TO HAVE WORN SOME FORM OF PROTECTIVE CLOTHING AND GLOVES, POSSIBLY FROM COVID STOCKS. IT IS NOT KNOWN HOW THE SHOOTER DISPOSED OF PERSONAL WASTE.

8. A NATIONWIDE MULTI-AGENCY HUNT IS UNDERWAY FOR A DETERMINED AND SKILLED SHOOTER, POSSIBLY WITH A MILITARY OR LAW-ENFORCEMENT

BACKGROUND. HE OR SHE IS LIKELY TO BE YOUNG, PHYSICALLY FIT, WELL-TRAINED AND ORGANISED. IT IS NOT POSSIBLE TO SAY AT THIS STAGE WHETHER THE SUSPECT WE SEEK IS WORKING ALONE OR AS A MEMBER OF A TEAM. WITHOUT FURTHER INFORMATION, IT IS NOT POSSIBLE TO SPECULATE ON MOTIVE, IE. WHETHER THE SUSPECT IS A LONE FANATIC, A NON-STATE ACTOR OR AFFILIATED TO - DIRECTLY OR INDIRECTLY - A FOREIGN POWER.

9. CCTV FOOTAGE FROM WHITEHALL AND THE ADJACENT AREA IS BEING RECOVERED AND URGENTLY EXAMINED.

How did the killer escape? No mention of it anywhere in the police report.

• • • •

CUTTLE KNOCKED ON BRIDIE'S door, which was anyway half-open, peered around it and shuffled in.

'What is it, Bernie?'

'Nothing to do with today's events, boss, and sorry to disturb you, but I thought you might want to be the first to see this. It should be there now on your monitor....'

It was.

CX

TOP SECRET

NOFORN

D/CIS

EXLUCY TCO B. CUTTLE

SUBJECT: UK DEPUTY PM RICHARD CARSTAIRS AT ROME PARTY

1. THE UK'S DEPUTY PM (UKDPM) R.C.M. CARSTAIRS ATTENDED A PRIVATE PARTY IN ROME ON THE EVENING OF NOV 10 UNTIL THE MORNING OF

NOVEMBER 11 AS A GUEST OF RUSSIAN BILLIONAIRE AND SHIPYARD OWNER IGOR TARAS VISHINSKY AT A PRIVATE ADDRESS ON THE CAMPO DEI FIORI. THIS MAY HELP EXPLAIN THE DPM'S ABSENCE AT THE CENOTAPH WREATH-LAYING.

2. CONFIRMED GUEST LIST (SEE APPENDIX) HAS 370 NAMES OF A-LIST CELEBRITIES, INCL HOUSEHOLD NAMES IN ITALIAN FASHION, THE VISUAL ARTS, CINEMA, POLITICS, MEDIA AND BUSINESS. THE LEADERS AND DEPUTY LEADERS OF SEVERAL FAR RIGHT EUROPEAN PARTIES WERE PRESENT.

3. THESE INCLUDED: GERMANY'S ALTERNATIVE FOR GERMANY (AfD), SWEDEN DEMOCRATS (SD), FRANCE'S NATIONAL RALLY (RN), ITALY'S FRATELLI D'ITALIE (FdI), UNITED RUSSIA AND THE UK'S CONSERVATIVE AND UNIONIST PARTY (AKA TORIES) AS REPRESENTED BY UKDPM R.C.M. CARSTAIRS.

4. VISHINSKY IS KNOWN IN DIPLOMATIC CIRCLES AND ITALIAN MEDIA AS ONETIME CLOSE BUSINESS ASSOCIATE AND SUPPORTER OF RUSSIAN PRESIDENT V. PUTIN. THEY BOTH SERVED AS OFFICERS IN THE FORMER KGB AT KARLSHORST IN THE FORMER DDR (EAST GERMANY). VISHINSKY IS REPORTED TO BE AN ACTIVE INVESTOR IN MALI'S EXPANDING GOLD INDUSTRY AND IN OIL EXPLORATION. RUSSIA'S 'WAGNER' MERCENARIES ARE ACTIVE IN MALI.

5. UKDPM CARSTAIRS IS BELIEVED TO HAVE STAYED OVERNIGHT AT THE PARTY VENUE, A MANSION OWNED BY ITALIAN BILLIONAIRE INDUSTRIALIST, OIL MAGNATE & SHIPBUILDER LUCA PACIOLI, A SELF-PROCLAIMED SUPPORTER OF ITALY'S FdI. ITALIAN MEDIA CLAIM HE IS AN IMPORTANT PARTY DONOR.

• • • •

'YOU DO KNOW CARSTAIRS is now our Prime Minister, don't you? Or will be in a few hours?'

'Yes. Ms Connor. I heard.'

'This is interesting, Bernie. Thank you.'

Bridie read it again. It was nothing that couldn't have been drawn from the local Italian media, coupled with a little online research. Hardly worth compiling as CX — except for the fact that the subject of the report was about to become the latest resident of Number Ten.

'There's more,' said Bernie.

• • • •

CX

SECRET

NOFORN

APPENDIX: PARTIAL VERBATIM TRANSCRIPT

D/CIS

SOURCE: CODENAME LUCY, UKN

INTERVIEWER: TCO BERNARD CUTTLE

SUBJECT: SIGHTING OF UK DEPUTY PM CARSTAIRS AT LEONARDO DA VINCI–FIUMICINO AIRPORT 1130 HRS NOV 11.

BC: How did Carstairs seem to you?

LUCY: Like what? I dunno (shrugs).

BC What did he look like? How did he appear?

LUCY: A right mess, yeah. He looked like shit, to be honest.

BC: How so?

LUCY: He looked, I don't know, sick. Totally. Like he hadn't slept. Pale, you know. Eyes all red and puffy, yeah? Hair standing on end as if he'd crawled out of a bush backwards and seen a ghost. His suit, a navy blue suit, yeah, was all creased. Dirty. Shoes covered in dried mud. No tie. Collar and shirt buttons undone. He looked like a homeless drunk, if you must know. Like he lived on the street or had slept at the Lido, you know, the beach just outside Rome?

BC: I know the Lido. You took these five snaps?

LUCY: Yeah.

BC: With your mobile?

LUCY: That's right, yeah. And the vid.

BC: You don't have more than this?

LUCY: No, that's all there is.

BC: Okay, so what were you going to do with them?

LUCY: (Laughs) Dunno, do I. I thought maybe sell 'em, yeah, to the media. Like, you know, The Sun. Or The Mail. Crap papers both, but they pay better than you lot.

BC: I'm sure they do. Did you see anyone else recording this — um — gentleman's disorderly state?

LUCY: Nah. Doesn't mean they didn't though, right?

BC: But you didn't sell.

LUCY: Had second thoughts, didn't I? My duty to King and Country, yeah? (sniggers).

BC: What was he carrying?

LUCY: Carrying? Nothing.

BC: No luggage, no briefcase?

LUCY: Nah.

BC: Not even a book or a newspaper? What about a phone? Surely he used a cellphone while waiting?

(LUCY seen shaking head, doesn't reply)

BC: What did you think was the matter with him?

LUCY: How would I know? Hangover, maybe. From booze and coke, that's what I thought then. He had that Bolivian marching powder look, if you know what I mean.

BC: I don't, no. Then what happened?

LUCY: Nothin'. Airline people came to open the gate, and we all got up and formed lines, showed our boarding passes and passports. The usual thing, yeah, with people trying to push in, duck under the tape. I think he tottered off into business or first class. I didn't see him after that.'

BC: And his close protection team?

LUCY: What close protection? There wasn't any.

BC: No security? No bodyguard?

LUCY: Like I said. No one.

BC: Carstairs was alone?

LUCY: I just said. Yes.

BC: No female in tow? No secretary? No wife, no girlfriend? No one from the embassy to hold his hand, not even a third secretary commercial?

LUCY: Nope. Nada.

BC: Thank you.

LUCY: You can call me Bianca.

BC: Thank you, Bianca. Good job, and much appreciated. Great initiative on your part. We know where to reach you if we need you again, do we?

LUCY: Oh, yes. Sure. You know, or your colleagues do, right? I'm always, like, on call. That's the deal, yeah? It's why I'm on the payroll, you know. You've got my cell number and my email address and, like, I'm not going anywhere any time soon. Oh, and like, I'm looking forward to the bonus.

. . . .

BRIDIE DECIDED SHE wasn't going to pass this up the chain of command. No way. It would be professional suicide. She gave both reports from Bernie a two-star rating so they'd sink deep into the pile of mediocre sludge that formed the bulk of SIS product, in a category that could have been labelled 'interesting if true' and which wasn't therefore distributed to SIS customers. The CX slush pile. That way, no one else would pay the two reports any attention, and the matter wouldn't go further, not to the controllers, let alone 'C' and the Joint Intelligence Committee. She could always retrieve them from the mountain of low-level CX stuff if she needed them. But for now, they would stay buried.

The alternative was to withdraw the reports, but the procedure might in itself alert colleagues to their existence.

She said, 'That's it?'

'There's a little more, but it's inconsequential.'

'Seems she's quite a character,' said Bridie. 'A Londoner by the sound of her, this LUCY who calls herself Bianca. I'm guessing it's not her real name.'

'Correct. Lives not far from here, in fact, in Southwark; LUCY gets a modest wage from us because she's on permanent twenty-four-hour call as a core member of UKN. Her thing is countersurveillance and anti-surveillance both. She's good at it. She loves to play a role, so much so that it's hard to know when she's playing herself.'

'And her remark about a bonus?'

'Her idea of a joke.'

UKN members were trained at Fort Monckton, but they were categorised as agents, not intelligence officers. Bernie Cuttle was LUCY's temporary case officer (TCO) or handler. Code names only on CX, never real names. Sometimes, suitably qualified UKN agents worked abroad under natural cover. Some, like LUCY, were full-timers. For security reasons, no UKN staff could set foot in the Ziggurat.

Bridie asked, 'How come LUCY was watching the Deputy PM — soon to be the PM?'

Bernie seemed to stoop more than ever. 'Coincidence. M'am. Sorry. I mean, Ms Connor. She just happened to be at the airport and was booked on the same flight. She has an Italian boyfriend at SISMI and was returning after a weekend tryst in Rome.'

The acronym stood for the Italian secret service.

'Lucky girl,' said Bridie. 'How romantic.'

Bridie had a sudden thought.

Mali. Hadn't Henri said that the former French Foreign Legion noncom and extremist Jean Martin, aka Erich Karscher, had served with the Foreign Legion in Mali?

Chapter 8

London, 21:10, November 11

L Forensic technicians might have finished their work, or so they said, but the newly arrived investigators, Septimus Brass included, were nevertheless invited to don face masks, gloves and overshoes before their guided tour of the crime scene and shooter's location. Just a precaution. No one objected.

The eight came from all over, from as far afield as Belfast and Bristol, Cardiff, Edinburgh, and Sunderland. They'd arrived mostly by bus and train. Two had driven their own cars to London. The eight were reputed to be the best in the business. The five men and women from outside London were booked into Travelodge and Premier Inn hotels — clean if basic accommodation but conveniently located to be able to walk to Whitehall and back.

Four were detectives — sergeants up to inspector — from four different constabularies, including the Met. One was a Special Branch detective sergeant, another a counterintelligence officer from Five, and then there was Septimus himself, who — because he didn't fit into any of the standard categories — claimed affiliation with the National Crime Agency or NCA. The NCA dealt with organised crime, especially what it called terrorist funding and money laundering. Well, this was a national crime, and it was organised. So Septimus would argue if challenged.

In the dark, with masks, raincoats and umbrellas, they could barely make each other out, let alone see much else. Hunching their shoulders and pulling their collars up, the eight turned their faces from the sting of sleet. They ducked under crime scene police tape to stare at the spot where the victims died, the blood and gore mostly washed away. They then trooped across Whitehall in the shadow of the Cenotaph, with its rain-sodden wreaths, and into the building and up the stairs to visit the sniper's lair. No one wanted to risk being stuck in the antique lift. The smokers gave themselves away by coming last and gasping for breath long before they reached the top.

One of the senior Met technicians made a few introductory remarks, which Septimus understood to mean that nothing of any value had been found so far, and given all the comings and goings since the shooting, it seemed unlikely to Septimus that anything more significant would be discovered in the way of useful evidence.

White light was provided by a couple of rechargeable camping lanterns.

It made the visitors look deathly pale, almost ghostly, as they stood dripping in a semi-circle in the attic space around the pièce de résistance: the long rifle used to murder three senior British politicians and critically wounded a fourth. A devastating blow to Britain's political class in the heart of government.

The rifle sat on a table with the bipod attached.

Like tourists confronted by some inexplicable masterwork in a museum, perhaps a marvellous baroque Bernini marble statue or a crazily beautiful Basquiat, no one said a word. What could they say? They stared in silence at the remarkable instrument of destruction.

In horror or in awe? Impossible to tell.

Septimus hung back as their police minder and senior technician led the way out, taking the lanterns with them, and still he waited, listening to them tramping back downstairs, a few words and phrases from fragmented exchanges floating up, male and female.

Got to say...you know...it's kinda hard...really weird...don't see why it can't wait till morning, yeah...why not, like...don't think he could...you think?

When he heard the front door pulled shut, Septimus climbed up onto the table in the dark and inched forward on his knees. He picked up the rifle, stood slowly, then rested the bipod on the top rung of the aluminium ladder. The killer would have taken all four shots standing up, he decided. Septimus pulled the weapon into his shoulder, tilting his head to the right so his cheek was supported by the cheek rest.

It was steady enough and pretty comfortable.

Septimus put his right eye to the scope and, with the fingers of his right hand, opened the breach.

How very odd. There was a full magazine of five rounds attached to the rifle.

Safety on.

Was this how it was for you, fella? Did it feel good?

Septimus leaned into the target, left foot planted forward, knee bent, right leg straight. He aimed down, through the gap where the fake tiles would have been. Ambient light from the street outside exposed a rectangular slit, perhaps four inches deep and ten inches wide. The distance from the aperture to the muzzle of the rifle was about three feet or roughly a metre.

Enough distance, Septimus thought, to avoid being spotted by anyone outside with binoculars or a sharpshooter with a scope — perhaps from a position on a balcony or window opposite. No reflection from the lens and no movement or muzzle flash would have been visible.

The trajectory was at an acute angle to Whitehall and to the left of the Cenotaph itself, the austere, tapered stone monument just over thirty-five metres or 110 feet high and 103 years old.

You're a pro, aren't you? Only a champion shot could get off four rounds so quickly and accurately with a bolt-action rifle.

There was enough orange light outside for Septimus to make out the spot where the victims had stood on a pavement now shiny with rain. There were London plane trees on sections of this, the western side of Whitehall. In summer, taking the shot would have been impossible, but by now, the trees had lost most of their leaves. The twigs and branches would not have obscured the killer's view, Septimus decided, nor the paths of the four rounds. Seen through the scope, the victims would have seemed so close that the stitching and buttons of their clothing would have been seen by the shooter, even their expressions and the colour of their eyes as the shooter squeezed off the four rounds, leaving just one in reserve.

So, let me get this straight. You fired four of five rounds at two targets, then ejected the magazine with one round remaining and replaced it with a second clip with a full load of five bullets, none of which you fired.

Why?

• • • •

SEPTIMUS USED A SMALL pocket torch with an infrared filter to examine the rifle, checking it over inch by inch, especially the markings and working parts, from the breech and bolt to the safety catch, the trigger and trigger guard. He extracted the second magazine, ejected each of the five rounds in turn and examined the clip inside and out. The suppressor he unscrewed, weighed in his hand, and looked at it in the torchlight.

Getting down off the table, Septimus picked the four cartridge cases up off the floor where the shooter had left them after they were ejected. He used the torch to check and compare each one. He lined them up on the table.

He took the last round out of the first magazine and looked at that, too.

He looked under the table and inspected its under-surface. He ran a palm under it and found a switch and a wire.

Now, my friend, where did you brush your teeth, take a piss and a dump?
Not in the attic.

Septimus breathed in slow and steady. He knew he had a good sense of smell and taste, but there wasn't much here. Gun oil. The smell of a firearm after discharge, though very faint. Dust aplenty. Damp. No smell of shit, urine, food or drink. No whiff of tobacco, soap or toothpaste.

So where did you go?

It had to be the government offices occupying the first, second, and third floors. The doors off the corridor were unlocked, so the shooter had either picked them or borrowed and then copied the keys. The third-floor office was bare of furniture and seemed to be used exclusively for storage, with identical boxes piled up from floor to ceiling. Paperwork. It struck Septimus as odd that the mass of paper hadn't been disposed of or digitised. There was a small, filthy bathroom, its old white tiles covered in thick grey dust, and the toilet didn't look as if it had been flushed in months or even years.

Septimus went down to the second floor.

He tried all the doors. One was unlocked.

There was an alarm, but it had been deactivated.

How did that happen?

You're no fool, either.

Several desks, 90s computer monitors, loads of paper, in-trays and out-trays, files, a coffee machine. Cheerful calendars, a noticeboard, holiday postcards, plastic flowers, desk diaries, family photos, get well cards and a cheery teddy bear. Even a plastic Christmas tree and festive lights. This was more like it.

Gender-specific bathrooms and toilets, regularly cleaned by the look of them. Air freshener. Bins. Cleaning materials in a cupboard.

This is more your style.

Nothing like a busy government office for a touch of humanity, with civilised washrooms, eh?

Did you trip the light fantastic down here of a night for a civilised dump and a wee? A wash and brush, too, yes? All good for morale, and your DNA hopelessly lost or mixed with everyone else's. Perhaps you helped yourself to an espresso while you were about it. Well, why not relax after all your hard work? Using a torch with a low light or infrared like mine, mebbe, so as not to spook anyone who happened to glance up at the windows. Switching on the alarm and shutting the door again when you left.

But not the last time you were here because there *was no longer any need. Right?*

Chapter 9

*V*arious locations, 2003

Merrick would be the first to admit he hasn't done well at school. He doesn't do spectacularly badly, either; he's at best mediocre and hence all but invisible, floating just above the bottom of the class in all subjects except English and French, both of which he does passably well without having to exert himself. He turns out to be especially good at English essays on Milton and Shakespeare.

As for sports, he enjoys playing rugby but only manages to obtain a place as a reserve for the second XV. How pathetic! He hates cricket, which is a black mark against him. He does manage to get on the school shooting team, and that's about it. Just enough to qualify him as a member of humankind in the view of his schoolfellows and the teaching hierarchy. His final report — the last bit written by a headmaster who is clearly mystified by a pupil whose face and name he can't remember, states that Merrick 'is quite an able boy who has seldom given of his best.'

Which is true. He's learning to hide in full sight.

Nonetheless, the seventeen-year-old contrives to surprise by securing a place against all expectation at Glasgow University, where he scores an undistinguished second in English literature, and in those four years of lacklustre striving, loses his cherry, becomes a keen Celtic supporter (though never a Roman Catholic), and learns, not to his credit, how to drink far too much Tennent's lager without falling over or throwing up in Sauchiehall Street of a Saturday evening.

Thanks to a friend of a friend, he accepts an offer from a private bank in the City of London to sign on as a trainee manager. He knows nothing of banking and has no clue what a trainee would be required to do. The offer follows a brief 'interview,' lasting some ten minutes of amiable and drunken conversation at a drinks party, with someone who turned out to be the bank's public relations director and father of one of Merrick's contemporaries. None of this is achieved on merit but has everything to do with copious infusions of alcohol and a tenuous connection to the old school tie.

As it so happens, and contrary to the assumptions made by the people who run in what might have been called Merrick's social circle had he had one (he doesn't), the sad fact is that he has no private allowance or inheritance. It's a matter of some personal shame that he can't keep up with the crowd at the bank, or with his old schoolmates, and it soon becomes clear to him that thanks to inflation and the neoliberal policies of so-called austerity, he can barely afford the rent on his cupboard-sized bachelor pad in south London, let alone buy a round of drinks when it's his turn. As hard as he works to keep up, the world seems to be running off without him. Already Merrick lives modestly; he doesn't run a car in London, obviously, doesn't allow himself the luxury of credit cards; he doesn't gamble, doesn't dine out at La Gavroche, avoids West End and City bars, keeps away from pubs altogether, drinks wine from Aldi at under ten quid a bottle — alone — and buys most of his clothing second-hand in the better sort of charity shop. He doesn't hunt, shoot or fish. There are no trips to the Scottish Highlands to slaughter red deer on private estates. If anyone asks, he has his lie ready: he doesn't enjoy killing things. He tightens his belt still further; he buys and cooks the cheapest cuts of meat, such as sheep's hearts, turns down the odd invitation to spend a weekend in the country and stops taking friends' calls.

He leads what his acquaintances regard as a dull and solitary life. The more monastic it becomes, the faster his pool of so-called friends and their invitations evaporate until it isn't even a muddy puddle. He knows he isn't fun, and he isn't interesting. He doesn't blame them. Merrick is fast becoming not only alone but invisible out of necessity. Even so, something has to be done, and quickly, before he ends up sleeping under the arches.

The answer takes the improbable form of an ad for the Territorial Army in a free newspaper he picks up one day on a bus from Peckham to Marble Arch. It occurs to him it might be fun. More to the point, he can earn a couple of thousand quid extra each year, tax-free. Regular Army rates of pay, it says, for time served. And for what? Every other weekend and a fortnight's annual camp, and as commitments go, that doesn't seem excessive. He can handle that, no problem. It will get him out into the fresh air and absorb some of his excess energy — and hopefully put cash in his pocket. That couple of thousand will make all the difference between being homeless and keeping a roof over his head. It never occurs to him it might change his life.

Almost casually, Merrick chooses at random from a host of different formations featured in the glossy recruitment brochure the Army sent him. It was like sticking a pin in a map. It takes him less than twenty minutes. He could opt for the infantry, for the engineers, for artillery, for signals. The Light Infantry looks promising. He avoids those posh regiments that he reckons will require a private income. So no Guards regiments and, of course, no cavalry, not even the Royal Scots Dragoon Guards, known as the Royal Scots DG, which he rather fancies. Merrick likes the cut of the very ancient Honourable Artillery Company for its social cachet in the City, for example, but social cachet means mess bills he couldn't afford.

He picks the Regiment at random. He isn't sure why. It seems more interesting than most. He calls the number and is told in a brusque Mancunian accent to present himself at the Duke of York's barracks on the King's Road in Chelsea with trainers and tracksuit for a preliminary fitness test the following Saturday. He knows where it is. So he reports as ordered, and for all the wrong reasons.

The first test surprises him, if only because he passes it with ease: five miles around the track in under forty minutes. He hasn't passed many tests in his twenty-two years; he could no doubt count them all on the fingers of one hand. If he feels proud of himself, he feels less so when told he faces a series of fitness challenges every two weeks, challenges that will test his stamina. And if somehow, miraculously, he gets through all that without failing, he'll have to endure a two-week selection camp at the end.

What has Merrick got himself into?

At the second test, he runs eight miles in brand new army boots that cut into his flesh and give him blisters the size of party balloons, losing him three toenails and turning said toes purple. Around a quarter of those who turn up for the second run drop out. Merrick digs deeper; he will not allow himself to be 'binned' because his fucking feet hurt. He resents the patronising comments of some of his fellow recruits who clearly have claim to some form of previous military experience — shaved heads are much in evidence — and think themselves superior to the civilians in their midst. They look down at him, his untrimmed hair and his posh accent. Well, fuck 'em and the class war. Their sneers of contempt only make him more determined.

What matters to Merrick now begins at 1930 hours of a Friday evening. The volunteers are issued rations, and there's a kit inspection by instructors known as the Directing Staff (DS) to ensure there's no cheating — no importing civilian, private gear that would make their tasks easier, such as buying comfy hiking boots for a couple of hundred quid from a sports shop rather than using the standard Army issue that has turned his soft feet into a bloody pulp. They are already an ugly, suppurating mass of pus-filled blisters, especially around the Achilles tendon, on the heels and on the ball of each foot. Blisters that grow on top of earlier blisters. Layered blisters. No matter. He tells himself they look worse than they really are.

Once on board a four-ton Bedford truck two hours later, dozing between his comrades, Merrick finds himself driven out of London and down the M4 to Wales, debussing in the early hours somewhere in the Brecon Beacons where they are encouraged to use what equipment they'd been issued — a sleeping bag, waterproof bivvy bag, water bottle, compass and Bergen — to make a bivouac among the dripping firs and to snatch a little sleep on the sodden ground.

Reveille at 0600. Then breakfast — a stiff and bleary-eyed Merrick brews himself a mug of tea, eats canned bully beef and dehydrated porridge (he doesn't differentiate between them but mixes everything together), stows his gear away in the Bergen, and then listens to the DS issue the day's first objective, a grid reference several kilometres distant. Off they all go together in the rain, at the double, Merrick stumbling, swearing and bleary eyed. Oh, fuck, fuck, fuck.

The fittest and the best navigators emerge at the front with their compasses and waterproof Ordnance Survey maps in hand. On arrival at the checkpoint, they are given a new grid reference a further ten kilometres away, this time over more rugged terrain. Merrick can't believe it. Somehow, he manages. And then another. No one knows how long the route will be or how many hours the ordeal will last. Merrick is numb inside and out by this stage.

At least he's still in the game.

He finds it odd they don't shout at him. The DS is civil and speaks quietly. Commands are given in the form of polite questions. 'Would you like to get your kit together....' And he's struck by the kindness shown to those who give up or are sacked. 'No problem,' he hears the DS tell an exhausted volunteer who's twisted his ankle. 'Put your Bergen over there on the bank, and someone will pick it up. Get on the truck. You'll be back home in no time.'

The courtesy is almost sinister.

Merrick seldom arrives in the first dozen at the final checkpoint at around 1800. He's usually in half an hour or forty-five minutes after the frontrunners but several hours ahead of the laggards. There's still time to heat the remaining rations he's carried all day and to get some rest. He's woken again at 2100 — shaken roughly until he stirs — to be briefed by the DS on the night march, which is carried out in pairs because of the risks of moving in the dark across precipitous mountains.

Each weekend, the task is tougher, and the volunteers fewer.

Merrick takes it very personally. He will not throw in the towel. No way. Something stubborn and angry rises in him. They might well bin him at any stage, and for the slightest misdemeanor, but he won't give up without a struggle.

No bloody way.

By now, he's mastered the business of blisters, having learned an effective technique from a New Zealander and former Olympics medallist. This involves the use of a small bottle of Dettol, a needle, cotton thread, and a tiny pair of scissors.

The latest night march ends before first light. Merrick falls asleep immediately, only to be woken after what seems like a few minutes — it's two hours — for what the DS describes as 'beasting.' This full hour of physical exercise is, to an exhausted Merrick, beastly, if not downright sadistic. Another run follows, euphemistically called a 'warm-up,' with Merrick blundering about giddily like a drunk, narrowly missing trees and boulders. *You can't be serious!* But the DS is serious. This torture finishes at 0330 with sit-ups and press-ups. By this point, Merrick is almost out of his mind and certainly out of his body. He's hallucinating, convinced it's snowing, and he speaks aloud to someone he swears is his deceased aunt, Corinne, lover of the Tarot and a self-styled spiritual medium. It seems the DS didn't notice or care how utterly fucked he truly is.

The worst and final weekend arrives. It's known as the 'long drag.' It's held deliberately in unfamiliar territory — the Peak District in northern England. The objective: sixty-five kilometres or forty miles across strange country in under twenty hours, with full webbing, a 50 lb Bergen with all the gear and rations, and a heavy, self-loading 7.62mm FN rifle - without a sling just to make it that much more awkward to carry.

Bastards!

Of the 130 candidates who began the course, only seventeen have survived.

One of them is Merrick. No one could have been more surprised.

Or pleased.

• • • •

THERE IS STILL MUCH to be achieved before Merrick can be 'badged' with the distinctive regimental beret, motto and emblem of winged sword.

For the next six months, every second weekend is taken up with military skills training, from long-range recce patrols, camouflage, survival behind enemy lines, weapons training, fire-and-movement to unarmed combat and covert communications in the form of encrypted radios and high-speed morse.

There are not a few times when Merrick thinks the process is designed to make him fail or break him.

One rainy weekend, Merrick is accepted into the Regiment and badged by the CO, a colonel. It's a proud moment, yet also something of an anti-climax. There is no parade. It's a low-key affair. He knows what he's achieved is nothing compared to the selection tests for the Regulars.

To maintain and improve his fitness in the weeks that follow, Merrick runs around Battersea Park every morning and then runs to work, while in the evenings, he runs again around Hyde Park. Some weeks later, he achieves the necessary twelve jumps at RAF Brize Norton and so receives his parachute wings.

He's done it and yes, it does feel marvellous. Finally! He can call himself a reserve member of the Special Air Service Regiment. How fucking great is that?

There is a price to be paid, though. Climbing the corporate ladder in the world of finance is not for him. Something in Merrick has changed, though he isn't sure what. Or perhaps it was there all along, and he didn't know it. It isn't that he is physically lean, his hands and feet toughened, blisters and pain in the past. He's shifted emotional gears without knowing it. He is more stubborn, more bloody-minded, more capable of withstanding discomfort than he'd realised.

He is more himself. His true self.

Although he sees them every weekday, he discovers he has nothing to say to his City colleagues, nor they to him. They seem to him to resemble soft, overgrown, entitled male children, obsessed with booze, haute cuisine, ridiculously expensive cars and the tiresome women they try to impress at nightclubs such as The Ned or Eight. None of it appeals to him. At least he can just about pay the rent of his Tower Hamlets cupboard and occasionally eat something more appetising than sheep's hearts.

He no longer cares about his day job, and management senses his indifference. What can he do now? He has to get out before he's kicked out.

Merrick is becoming desperate. He tells himself he might as well try to make good use of his new skills. He's found that his primary skill is shooting. He's exceptionally good at it, or so he's told. As luck has it, he receives his first call to arms in the form of a brown envelope from the Ministry of Defence.

He is going to war.

Chapter 10

Cabinet Office Briefing Rooms, 70 Whitehall, London, 22:45 November 11

Newly appointed home secretary Jem Turan — just a few hours into the job following his predecessor's murder that same morning — chaired his first ministerial meeting in an underground conference room, effectively a bunker, at what the media called COBRA, not a hundred yards from the scene of the assassinations.

Turan was a big man. He had presence. Tall, stout, fifty-five years old with fashionable glasses, a brown, polished and completely bald head the shape of an egg and a salt-and-pepper goatee, he was known to be a successful, millionaire financier of Turkish origin on his father's side. Bridie recalled that there had been some 'silly fuss' in the tabloid press over his substantial parliamentary expenses, which had allegedly included charges for heating an Olympic-sized swimming pool, stabling for twelve horses as well as repairing a tennis court at his sixteen-bedroom Palladian mansion and five-acre grounds in Berkshire.

'Silly fuss' had been Turan's response to negative media reports.

Why shouldn't the taxpayer fund his few pleasures in life?

'I've come to listen and learn on behalf of the prime minister, not make speeches. So please, guys —' He beamed at those present before sitting down and shooting his French cuffs. He'd dressed up for this first official occasion as secretary of state, or so it seemed.

The scent of Creed aftershave spread around the cramped room.

The Metropolitan Police Commissioner Sir Max Susman, on Turan's right, casually dressed in jeans and a black, sleeveless puffer jacket, opened the innings.

Susman began with a slow ball in the form of lists.

Police had so far received over 220 calls from members of the public claiming to have seen the shooter, based on an image distributed to the media, a Photofit which the commissioner admitted was already out of date because it was based on the features of the unidentified, unarmed man shot dead by police at Dover that afternoon.

Most were 'crank' calls. They had all been eliminated but for two alleged sightings of a suspect boarding a train at King's Cross, heading north. CCTV at the station also had the image.

For the benefit of the home secretary and officials present, a fuzzy image was shown on a large screen.

Maybe it was the shooter, maybe not.

Transport police had boarded the train in question and were watching the train at all scheduled stops.

Consulting his notes, the commissioner continued.

The unidentified individual 'tragically' shot dead at Dover appeared to have no link to the murders, but his physical details were being compared with data provided just an hour previously by French authorities on a right-wing extremist and former military sniper thought to have flown to the UK from Marseille.

The visitor, who'd flown into Luton, was being actively sought.

A list of all known UK-based marksmen (and women) was being drawn up, with a total so far of 6,300 names. Restricting this to ex-military and police below the age of fifty, the figure had been reduced to 1,284. Those licensed to possess a bolt-action rifle and ammunition of .388 calibre — similar to that used that morning — stood so far at thirty-three.

House-to-house visits to the gun owners were underway. Everyone on the list would be contacted, in person or by phone.

Turan interrupted the police chief. 'How many people are in custody as a result of today's events?'

'In total, Minister, three hundred and twenty have so far been detained for questioning under the Terrorism Act, but the number will increase. These include extremist circles of the far left and far right, as well as suspected Islamic militants.'

'Of that figure, how many are foreign nationals?'

Susman glanced down at his iPad. 'Forty-eight.'

'Are we investigating any foreign links, aside from the French national you've mentioned?'

The Met commissioner glanced across the table at Helen Sweeney, head of MI5's Counter-Terrorism Directorate.

She was ready for the question. 'We are indeed, with the help of our sister service.'

'You're referring to SIS?'

'Yes, Minister.' Sweeney smiled at Bridie, who sat further down the table.

'Is GCHQ in the loop?'

'It is, yes.'

'Five Eyes?' The home secretary was referring to the 'club' of five so-called Western states that routinely shared secret signal intelligence — the United States, Australia, Canada, New Zealand, and the United Kingdom.

'Requests for urgent assistance have been sent out, yes,' said Tim Lombard, a GCHQ deputy director who sat across from Bridie. 'We've already had several positive acknowledgements and offers of help.'

Turan leaned forward and glared at those sitting at the table, making eye contact with each, one by one. 'How long, in your estimation, before we catch the evil bastard? Or bastards?'

The officials stared down at the polished table, the blank notepads, unused pens, untouched glasses and carafes of water. None replied. They looked like children being asked to own up to something they hadn't done.

Someone slipped into the room, glided soundlessly behind Turan, looked for whoever it was he wanted, stopped next to the commissioner, bent down like an obsequious waiter, whispered, and handed him a note.

The commissioner read it, slipped it into a jacket pocket and turned back to the table.

No one had yet answered Turan's question. There was no true answer.

Bridie would not mention an offer of assistance from her equivalent in the CIA's directorate of counterintelligence, one Wayne Bernstein, and she was sure that Sweeney wouldn't bring up the message of support Five had received from Quentin Mulcahy, director of the FBI, either. Quite what help the Americans might offer was left unsaid, especially under a newly elected U.S. president whose policies seemed contradictory, if not at odds with HMG in several disturbing ways.

'So let's be clear,' Turan rumbled in his deep baritone. 'For all the hundreds of millions of quid your organisations receive from the public purse each year, and the thousands of people you employ on this kind of work, you've got fuck all. You had no advance warning, and you have no clue what or who is behind it. Have I got that right? We're talking massive intelligence failure.'

Embarrassed silence — whether embarrassment at Turan's choice of Anglo-Saxon or the failure of the agencies represented at the meeting to have known about the attack in advance, or their failure to have nabbed a suspect wasn't clear.

Susman wouldn't let the charge of ineptitude pass unchallenged. 'That's not quite true, Minister.'

Turan fixed him with a frown, waiting.

'Then tell me what or who's behind this. Is this Russia's dirty work yet again? Is it China? Iran's Revolutionary Guards Corps? Some vengeful Middle Eastern terrorist dreaming of a martyr's paradise? Or a crazed Zionist fucker acting alone for Greater Israel? Someone seeking revenge for our colonial past, perhaps? One of those Green lunatics, militant Stop Oil climate protestors or animal rights activists? Well?'

Turan fixed Susman with a frown, waiting.

'We're following up several leads, Secretary of State.'

'I'm all ears, Commissioner.'

'For example, we have in our possession the weapon used in this morning's incident: a rifle manufactured by Accuracy International along with specialised 8.59mm or .338 Lapua Magnum ammunition, a type in service with UK armed forces and law enforcement. We've also recovered a Schmidt & Bender 5-25X56 PMll 25X magnification scope. This type of optics is in service here in the UK, along with an M110/SR25 KAC suppressor, which is also among those in current service.'

Turan's scowl deepened. 'You mean to tell me the shooter or shooters left these items behind for you to find?'

'That's right.'

'That was thoughtful of him or her. Why?'

'The killer took great care not to leave prints and DNA,' said Susman, 'and presumably the message was that he or she had no further use for them. Job done.'

'So it's a dead end,' Turan thundered.

He slapped the table with his big, fleshy right hand, shaking the thing and startling everyone in their blue–cloth–covered seats.

'Let me be clear,' he bellowed. 'This wasn't simply an assassination of three of our leading politicians in government and the official opposition, but a calculated, cold-blooded and cowardly attack on this country and its sovereignty. It would never have happened had you — and your respective departments — done your jobs properly in the first place.'

Silence. Not so much as a sneeze.

Overdoing it a bit, Bridie thought. At least Susman was too seasoned a copper to allow himself to appear at all browbeaten or put out by Turan's bullying. He'd so far survived four home secretaries, each one worse than his or her predecessor.

Bridie let her mind wander. She thought about stables, tennis courts and Olympic-sized pools, and how Turan had made his pile. She thought about the murdered prime minister and his unelected successor. The fourth unelected prime minister in a row. She thought about Alec waiting for her at home. She thought about bed and a good night's sleep. She thought about the bloody housekeeping she hadn't done and had no intention of doing.

Turan glared at everyone in turn.

No one would meet that ferocious look.

Turan planted his elbows on the table, gold cufflinks winking under the strip lights. He leaned forward, jaw jutting. His voice dropped to a stage whisper.

'I don't suppose it's occurred to any of you, has it, that the murderer might, just possibly, be one of our own? One of us?'

Chapter 11

South London, 18:58, November 11

Merrick ran the tip of his tongue along the jagged palisade of front teeth. He was voraciously hungry. He backed off under cover of the overhang of an ugly, nameless shopping centre, out of the rain and away from the orange glow of streetlights and put the bag down between his feet. He bent, unzipped one pocket, took out the sandwich, ripped off the plastic-and-cardboard wrapping and devoured the contents.

He could have eaten three of them and still not have been full.

He swallowed the juice, all the while watching people walk past. His eyes followed a police van, siren wailing, as it sped by, blue lights pulsing, heading towards Battersea.

He felt better, but after the food, which seemed almost tasteless (he wasn't sure what it was, probably chicken and bacon), he felt weary. He'd have to rest soon. His muscles ached, and he knew himself well enough to understand that fatigue made him impatient and short-tempered. That's how mistakes were made. He picked up the bag, swung it onto his left shoulder, took a few steps forward and with his right hand dropped the litter into a bin on the pavement, along with the protective clothing he'd squeezed up into a ball and kept in one of the hoodie's pockets until this moment.

Merrick knew he was no poet. He would have laughed at the suggestion, but the words kept coming.

I know you're not here,
My head tells me it makes no sense,
But there's some part of me that still feels you,
Hears, sees, knows you, still.
Your hand warm in mine,
Your slim, crooked fingers that turn up at the ends like Ottoman slippers,
Your tiny, plump and perfect feet.
I hear your laugh as bright as birdsong
It always makes me smile,
Welcome back! Where were you?
Never mind. I'm back now, you say.

I feel your warmth, breathe in your smell.
It's impossible, of course.
You can't be.
You're dead, Zala.
Aren't you?

He kept moving. He reckoned that criminals who'd just committed a bank heist, possibly a murder, would make a run for it, and as far from the crime scene as they could — out of guilt, disgust, fear. It was instinctive. They'd steal a car, head north on the M1 or try to catch a boat or plane abroad.

It would be a mistake. He'd learned from his military training, escape and evasion exercises in particular, to do the contrary, to stay put, go to ground at the start, to stay close to the enemy. He's learned that his pursuers and their dogs would expect him to run hard and fast, and they'd widen the search cordon by degrees, hour by hour, yard by yard. They'd try to work out how quickly the fugitive was likely to move, and the last place they'd look would be right under their own feet.

So that's what Merrick would do. He would not go anywhere.

A big cop shop sprawled at one end of the street. Lots of lights; police vehicles coming and going. At the other end, he could see the upper floor of the SIS headquarters all lit up. A bloody Christmas tree.

He headed for the eight huge bins lined up outside the back of Sainsbury's at Nine Elms, and after making sure there was no one about and no camera was pointed in his direction as far as he could tell, he lifted the lid and tossed the patrol belt into the first, where it joined an immense pile of putrefying food waste, and into the next one went the blue latex gloves. The skin of Merrick's hands was unnaturally white, soft and rumpled like parchment, as if they'd been submerged in water for days. Except for the two burners, he threw the police coveralls into the third, and the rest of the contents of the patrol bag into the fourth.

Maybe they'd find the gear, maybe they wouldn't. He reasoned that dump divers weren't the kind of responsible citizens likely to rush off to the police to boast of their lucky finds. More likely, they'd sell them on in a boot sale or exchange them with their friends for something else, such as hash, ecstasy or speed.

He moved around to the front and entered the store, where he knew the cameras would inevitably pick him up. After a few minutes, he found cheap black sneakers that should fit. He bought a pair for cash, along with a bottle of Jameson's whiskey.

That done, he sauntered down the South Lambeth Road some fifty yards like a man without a care in the world, paused, took one of the two burners out of the patrol bag and tapped in a number.

It was answered immediately. 'Ruthless, toothless Andy Bircher speaking. Who's this?'

'Andy. It's Peter. Peter Merrick.'

'I don't fucking believe it. Mate, is that really you?'

'Yeah, pal. It's me alright.'

'Christ, it's been ages. Are you okay?'

'I'm fine. But I've just arrived in London, and I need a place to crash. Just for a night or two. You were the first person —'

Andy interrupted. 'Sure. No probs. Come on over. We've plenty of room, and you're most welcome. Astrid's away. It'll just be the two of us. It'll be good to catch up.'

'And the kids?'

'With Astrid and her parents.'

'I'll be there in an hour.'

'Brilliant, mate. Christ, this is a pleasant surprise.'

'Are you sure?'

'Fucking hell — you want a printed invite from Buckingham Palace or what?'

'Andy, just one thing, if you don't mind.'

'Yeah?'

'Not a word. To anyone. I'm not here. We never spoke. I never made this call, and I never visited, okay?'

A moment's silence during which Andy digested this.

'No worries, pal. It'll be great to see you.'

Merrick destroyed the burner by dropping it in the gutter and stamping on it.

En route, he stopped and sat on a low garden wall opposite Vauxhall Park, took off the boots, put on the trainers and discarded the boots in another waste bin.

It rained again, hissing down.

• • • •

ANDY BIRCHER, TWENTY-two-year veteran and regimental sergeant major of the 3rd Battalion, The Royal Parachute Regiment, lived with his family in a three-storey terrace of London brick, built around the beginning of the twentieth century. It had suffered from subsidence at some point, as had many properties in south London. The only sign of it was a jagged crack in the brickwork above the front portico, which a visitor would only notice if looking for it. The front was paved over so Andy could park his Kawasaki Ninja H2R alongside his wife's Fiat 500, though the latter was absent when Merrick arrived on foot.

The inside was pretty much as Merrick remembered it. It still boasted the previous owner's yellow Colefax & Fowler wallpaper in the hall and corridor leading to the kitchen and, beyond that, to the conservatory. The wallpaper was starting to peel in places where it met the high ceiling. Andy had bought the house during London's last property crash. It had been repossessed by the bank and was going cheap. He had offered an even lower price, which the bank, keen to get it off the books, had accepted. He put down a deposit he'd saved over the previous decade of soldiering. On what was then Andy's army pay, the mortgage was a heavy burden. Since then, the value of the place had risen tenfold, and thanks to Andy's civilian career as a management consultant — whatever that might mean — he'd paid off the loan, not without his wife's considerable help. Merrick thought the place must have been worth a couple of million by now.

A bottle of Stolichnaya stood ready on the pine table in the conservatory along with two shot glasses and a plate of crackers, cheese and sausage.

'Only the best for my best pal,' said Andy.

'And something for you,' said Merrick, producing the whiskey from his bag.

'Ah, you beauty. Two nights, did you say? We'll polish off this lot in no time.'

They sat, toasted each other in silence, drank. The bottle went from one to the other. They drank the vodka neat. They agreed the Latvian-made Stolichnaya was the only vodka that tasted good enough to be drunk without a mixer. Merrick helped himself to the snacks. He could feel the drink take effect, softening the edges and blunting pain.

'Are you in any kind of trouble?'

'What makes you think that?'

Andy shrugged. 'Dunno. Just a feeling. And what you said.'

He was right, of course. They knew each other well. Andy had served two tours in the Regiment, and both times they'd fought together. Merrick thought there was nothing more intimate between male friends than being on active service together. It was a brotherhood, and it imposed a sense of both belonging and loyalty that surpassed all other relationships, even marriage. Women were for love, affection, sexual intimacy, making babies, building families. Men — well, if they were on the same side, it was comradeship. Nobody in the trenches fought for a king, a country, a flag or a god — not when the shit was flying. A soldier fought for the comrades on either side of him or her.

'All I ask is that you never saw me. I was never here. We never spoke. This, here, never happened. For your sake and mine. And if you don't mind, no questions.'

'Fine, mate. Whatever you say.' Andy smiled, but his eyes weren't smiling. They were watchful, and there was worry in them.

He'd seen the news; of course he had.

He suspected Merrick; of course he did. He had both the skill and the motive.

The only question was what he'd do about it. For Merrick, it was a calculated risk.

Andy started out as a boy soldier. He served in Northern Ireland in a hush-hush army surveillance unit, then the Gulf War, Bosnia and finally Afghanistan. He'd come far in life, built a new career and seemed to have adjusted well to being a husband and a dad. Not everyone made the transition successfully. Merrick had every reason to be envious.

They drank. The bottle was nearly empty.

'Are you short?' Andy asked. 'I've got plenty of cash lying around, and you're welcome to it. Take a grand at least, two or three if it helps.'

Merrick shook his head.

'Sure?'

'Sure. Thanks, though.'

'I'm truly fucking sorry about what happened. You know that, right?'

Merrick nodded several times. He couldn't speak of it. The words refused to form in his head. It was probably the vodka.

'It was a rotten business,' Andy said. 'I don't know how I'd cope if it happened to me. I really don't. Are you managing okay?'

What the hell could Merrick say? Not the truth, that was for sure.

'It gets a little easier with time,' Merrick mumbled. 'But it's always there. It never goes away.'

'Course it doesn't. I understand, mate. Truly.'

Andy frowned, his expression one of concern.

Merrick looked hard at Andy. 'Do you, pal?'

Andy tried to lighten the mood by switching subjects.

'Still living in that tiny flat of yours. Newham, isn't it?'

'Nah. Sold it for a ridiculous price. Tower Hamlets.'

It was a lie. Merrick asked himself why he'd lied to his best mate. It was instinctive. Andy was loyal to the Crown. An old-school patriot. He took loyalty seriously. If he was questioned about Merrick, if he was leaned on hard, he'd say what he knew, bit by bit. He'd feel conflicted, but ultimately he'd do his duty to King and Country, the bloody fool.

'They're all ridiculous prices in London,' Andy was saying. 'Russian criminals laundering billions through dodgy London estate agents, lawyers and banks. Pushes up all the prices. Saw a documentary about it on Netflix, yeah.'

Merrick had rented the cupboard at first, then bought it. He knew he should sell it now while he could. His savings were running low, and he needed a heap of cash to pay for his special project. The gear wasn't cheap, and the same went for two fake passports, both stolen and then 'adjusted' with his details. There wasn't any reason to lie to Andy about his studio flat other than instinct.

Andy was a decent sort, but Merrick told himself he wouldn't hesitate to kill his friend — his only true pal, in fact — if it turned out that Andy sounded off about any suspicions he might have had — must have — about what Merrick had been up to. Looking at Andy now, seated across the table, Merrick knew he couldn't take him on face-to-face on an equal footing. Andy might be short, but he was built like a tank and as hard as you'd expect of a paratrooper. Merrick thought he'd have to take him by surprise, when he was drunk and his guard was down, approaching him from behind and breaking his neck. It would be quick, almost painless, and relatively merciful.

For such a friend, Merrick could do no less.

What kind of evil monster have I become?

Andy grew up in a working-class district of Edinburgh, a place known for its high unemployment and crime. Andy had once explained to Merrick that there were two ways for a lad to get off the street: the life of the professional criminal or an Army career. His brother-in-law had chosen the former and had been sent down for eight years for grievous bodily harm. Andy chose the military path and started out as a boy soldier. He survived the bullying and abuse, and he had what it took to join the Parachute Regiment.

Andy owed Merrick. While serving with the UN in Kosovo, Andy was arrested and later court martialled over an incident in which Andy had taken it upon himself to stalk and kill a sniper without authorisation. He had stood to lose his rank, his pension and his reputation. He was charged with a number of offences, from being drunk and disorderly on duty, being in possession of a firearm while drunk, and for discharging said weapon without authorisation. But he got off, with more than a little help. Merrick had perjured himself on Andy's behalf. He'd submitted an affidavit vowing that Andy had never once been drunk to his knowledge, that he'd served his country with distinction and without blemish, and that he'd acted in self-defence. So keeping his tongue in check, whatever Andy might think privately about what Merrick had been up to, would be a favour returned. Or so Merrick hoped.

By the time Merrick crawled into bed in the spare room, it was after 1 a.m. He knew he'd be left to sleep as long as he liked. Andy would leave him be. He'd rest up for whatever was left of Sunday, and first thing on Monday, he'd set out.

His last thought was to wonder what Andy would do about his guest. He was possibly the only person Merrick knew who would understand his motive, even if he didn't approve. Andy was smart enough to work it out, but the last thing Merrick needed were veterans like Andy blabbering on the paras' grapevine — or worse, making a call to the cops and turning him in.

Because it wasn't over. Saturday's little drama at the Cenotaph — Merrick knew the word was Greek for empty memorial — was just the start.

Chapter 12

Task force headquarters, London, 08:00, November 12.

Sunday morning, and everyone who should have been present was, though their expressions suggested they were far from happy about it.

Tea and coffee steamed in big urns on a trestle table, dispensed by a friendly tea lady whose smile and Yorkshire accent brought some warmth into an otherwise frigid gathering of strangers who looked as if they'd have much preferred an extra hour in bed on this damp, grey Sunday morning. Better still, the entire day off.

It was Remembrance Sunday, after all.

The coppers huddled in one corner as if defending their exclusivity, exchanging information in low voices and getting to know one another. The lone oddities who didn't fit into this exclusive tribe, such as Septimus, stood about on their own, sipping weak tea, munching on a ginger biscuit and watching everyone else.

They did not have long to wait.

Bridie was on time. Septimus was quite taken by the boss at his first sight of her. She walked in quickly, businesslike in manner, shedding her winter overcoat on the move — and before it fell to the floor, it was grabbed by a tall, skinny and melancholy man Septimus assumed must be one of her staff who followed on her heels and who turned out later to be an intelligence officer named Bernard Cuttle.

Septimus saw that Connor was of medium height and slight build. A brunette with hair cut short in a smart bob, she wore a colourful blouse of blue and red lozenges under a black trouser suit. Her eyes were large and dark brown. She was a serious person, but the way the corners of her mouth turned down when she pursed her lips, especially on one side, hinted at a strong sense of ironic humour she sought to suppress while on duty. She reminded Septimus of one of his favourite film stars, the late and great French actress Jeanne Moreau, whom he'd first seen as a teenager in Francois Truffaut's film *Jules et Jim*. He put her age somewhere in her mid-40s. Quite young, he thought, for the senior role of Director, Counterintelligence, SIS.

He noted no visible jewellery save for a wristwatch. She wore a belt with a silver buckle and sensible boots with two-inch heels.

'Septimus? Septimus Brass?'

He realised with a start that she was calling his name, so he took a step forward from the back wall he'd been leaning against. 'That's me,' he said in surprise.

She nodded, those velvety eyes on him. He thought it was like being caught in the beam of a pair of searchlights, only much nicer. Septimus was being examined, and he felt his pulse quicken.

'Right. Listen up. Septimus Brass will be in charge of this investigation on a day-to-day basis. He will coordinate what we do, who does it and when. You will report to Septimus, who is on loan from the National Crime Agency. He will report to me every day on your progress. Just so you know, Septimus recently returned from Afghanistan, where he spent the best part of six months heading up an investigation into allegations of unlawful civilian deaths at the hands of UK special forces, and he was the author of a preliminary report on the subject submitted to the Supreme Court judge heading a new inquiry that has just begun its deliberations.'

Septimus appreciated the introduction, but it sounded like ancient history. Afghanistan seemed a long way off, another world. Septimus himself would not attend the inquiry, nor would he be required to give evidence. His last act should have been to sit in on interrogations of former and serving Special Air Service Regiment members by the specialists of the Joint Services Interrogation Wing and to offer advice on how lines of questioning might be developed. But the interrogators were so skillful that he was sure there would have been little he could have contributed.

Afghanistan was over. It was done. Time to move on.

'As for me, my name is Bridie Connor, and I hold an executive position in the Secret Intelligence Service, which some of you will know as MI6. Perhaps you've worked with us before, or our counterparts at the Security Service, which the media insist on calling MI5. My specialty is counterintelligence, but don't let it distract you from your work here.'

She started handing out sheets of paper.

To Septimus, Bridie said, 'I've set out today's plan and divided up our resources. You don't have to stick with this; it's only for starters, and you must make whatever adjustments you see as appropriate.'

She addressed the room again. 'Okay, everyone?'

He saw she'd divided up the officers into pairs. Each pair had a specific task to undertake, starting now.

His own 'partner' was the tall, sad fellow. Bernard Cuttle.

Her welcome remarks done, Bridie snatched her coat back from Cuttle and without another word, she marched out.

• • • •

THE INVESTIGATION HAD been set up in an SIS outstation, one of several in and around London. For some peculiar reason, it was owned by the Ministry of Defence but used by SIS for training, mostly lectures, supplementing the facilities available on the six-month-long IONEC run at Fort Monckton near Gosport on England's south coast.

The venue was a square, detached, three-story office block, probably post war (it bore no signs of the World War Two bomb damage commonplace along the Thames, especially on the south side) and had all those hallmarks of pseudo-classical design the Victorians and Edwardians loved. Located on Kennington Road just to the south of the Vauxhall railway tracks and bridge, its next-door neighbour was a pub known as one of London's biggest and most popular gay venues, the Vauxhall Tavern, and it backed onto what used to be known as the Vauxhall Pleasure Gardens, where there was a big cut-price wine merchant's. On the other side, two Portuguese guys ran a cafe, and next to that was a print shop owned by a cheerful man of Nigerian origin, whose articulate and friendly teenage children helped out from time to time.

The place did not stand out. Rather the opposite: it seemed to do its best to be invisible, and it worked well enough. There were no signs, no street number, no nameplate. The sash windows were protected by concertina burglar bars that could be opened and closed on the inside, anti-blast net curtains and plain white blinds that always seemed down, never up. There were external clusters of video cameras on all four corners and above the front door. Two uniformed doormen — Septimus thought they might have been retired police officers — were on duty at a reception desk on the ground floor with a row of video monitors to one side.

Not a building most people would look at twice, which was the intention, but it was within easy walking distance of the Ziggurat and another half mile to Five's headquarters in the former ICI building across the river. It was a minute's stroll from Vauxhall rail, Underground and bus stations.

It was late afternoon and almost dark before anything happened of any significance.

Out on the streets, pairs of uniformed officers were carrying out interviews with members of the public, stopping people on the street, entering shops, knocking on doors and filling in questionnaires. Bog standard procedure for major crimes. They also spoke to taxi and bus drivers at intersections when the lights turned red. They'd set up big yellow signs on the pavements asking for information and giving a confidential number to call. On some roads and bridges leading in and out of the area, vehicle checkpoints had been set up which were covered by armed officers.

Meantime, DI Gavin Purchase from Special Branch asked if Septimus would join him and a DS Caroline Bacri from the Met's Serious Crimes at their screens for a moment. 'Over here, boss, please,' said Bacri. They'd been looking at CCTV video feeds in the Whitehall area for the past four hours — for the second time — and it was giving them both headaches. Lombard was crunching on a couple of paracetamol tablets.

Now, they'd found something for their trouble.

'Take a look,' said DI Purchase. 'This is from a private security set-up. This is two minutes and forty seconds after the last shot fired. That's the building. You can see the front door open just wide enough for someone to step out. Here he comes. He stays on the step for a minute or so. Definitely a *him*, yeah.'

'Can you get in close?'

'Sure, but we lose some of the focus.'

'He's a cop,' said Septimus.

'Yup,' said Purchase. 'So it would seem. A Metropolitan Police sergeant, no less.'

Septimus grimaced and scratched his cheek. 'Looks pretty confident if he's the shooter. Most people would get away as quickly as possible via the back. Not this guy. He's just standing there, hands on his hips, admiring the view. It's hard to imagine —'

Purchase interrupted. 'Now, almost three minutes after the last shot, he's still there, watching a bunch of uniformed police jogging along the pavement, d'you see? They're armed. They approach and pass him. He doesn't seem at all bothered. Maybe he says something to them. They turn next left at No. 54. They smash the iron gates in, then attack the front doors and rush inside. Our police officer doesn't move.'

'Wrong fucking address,' said Septimus. 'Our sergeant seems to be smiling. Maybe he's telling him they're at the wrong address, but they've taken no notice.'

The assault team had been quick to respond, but then they'd been on standby anyway in case of public unrest during the ceremony, which far-right hoodlums had sworn to 'protect.'

It seemed a particularly stupid mistake to Septimus. The building the police had broken into was markedly different from the adjacent offices the killer had used: buff terracotta in Franco-Flemish Renaissance style, including the ornate ironwork the police had managed to bend and break during their forced entry. But then, he thought, no one's perfect.

'Now, our man picks up his bag and steps down to the pavement,' Purchase said. 'He looks back and up at the building he's just left as if trying to spot where the shooter was.'

The pavements on both sides of the street were unusually wide, Septimus noted, with dozens of black bollards protruding from them, which he knew to be steel obstacles to block any attempted truck bombing. The changes had been made by Westminster Council at a cost of around twenty-five million pounds as part of a security review. There were also temporary barriers set up on both sides: fifteen-foot-high, wood walls painted white and shielding the buildings behind the street — the immense fortress of the unreformed and unapologetic bumbling bureaucracy that was the Ministry of Defence to the east and, on the opposite side, to the west, Richmond House, the handsome, sprawling home of the Department of Health.

'He can't be the killer,' said Septimus.

Purchase agreed. 'Far too calm and collected, if you ask me.'

'Unless it's for our benefit,' said DS Bacri. 'A performance for the CCTV he knows is there. Like he's mocking us or trying to persuade us he's not our killer.'

Purchase and Septimus looked at Bacri. Septimus agreed it was possible. But the shooter must have had strong nerves to carry off such a deception.

DS Bacri's first name was Caroline, but everyone, regardless of rank, called her Caro. Her fellow officers seemed in awe of her. It was rumoured that she belonged to a minority of minorities: an ancient Jewish family from the Maghreb and, oddly enough, came from a wealthy family and was third-generation British. Minorities were disliked in today's Britain, and even more so in the several racist institutions of the state, including the Metropolitan Police. Septimus wondered what it was that had drawn Caro to a police career in the first place.

Purchase asked, 'See what he's carrying?'

Septimus leaned in and looked hard. 'A standard patrol bag. And most of the kit you'd expect on his duty belt. There's a CS spray in its holder, if I'm not mistaken, a body cam, standard police radio, notebook holder. Standard gear, but I don't see a baton.'

'Right,' said Purchase.

'Because of the police soft cap, we can't get a good look at his face,' said Bacri. 'I don't think our facial recognition apps would either.'

'Try,' said Septimus.

'Already in the works,' said Purchase.

'Now we lose him,' said Caro. 'He's in the crowd, see, dodging television crews, onlookers and emergency vehicles. He moves fast, yeah? He passes three dog handlers and their mutts.' Her cursor followed him on her screen. 'Last we see of him here, he ignores a senior police officer trying to get his attention. Or maybe he doesn't hear because of the noise.'

'That's it?' Septimus said.

'Almost.' Caro used her mouse to fast-forward.

'Just a glimpse. See? He's headed into Westminster Underground. There.' Time: 11:23

He could be miles away by now. The London Underground had 272 stations on eleven lines covering 400 square kilometres. A near impossible task.

As if he knew what Septimus was thinking, Purchase said, 'We expect London Transport Police feeds any moment.'

'Good work,' said Septimus. 'Think you might be right, Caro.' He was referring to her remark on the suspect standing in full view as if he wanted to be seen. 'Take twenty minutes, grab a bite to eat, then let's try to find out where he went. You two have the only real news in twenty-four hours.

I'll send you more people to help. It's a shitload of work. I'll ask London Transport to lend us a hand.'

Septimus thought it might well be the breakthrough they so badly needed, but he wasn't about to say so. He didn't want to raise false hopes.

They had to find the suspect first.

Chapter 13

Nice, France, 15:25 local time, November 12.

LUCY aka Calista was enjoying herself. The TGV was everything British trains were not. It was affordable, clean, comfortable, fast and on time. A miracle, no less! This second leg of Calista's journey wasn't nearly so crowded as the Eurostar. At least a third of the seats were empty. She buried herself in another twenty pages of a 1981 crime novel by Jean-Patrick Machette, *La position du tireur*, a noir tale of a cold-blooded gangster who leaves bodies all over the place, and then she thought about the story — which she read in the original French — while watching the countryside slide past.

She must have dozed off, rousing herself and struggling out of her seat to take a leak and buy a coffee. Just as she'd washed and dried her hands and opened the lavatory door and was about to emerge, Calista saw a woman who'd been at the Gare du Nord where the Eurostar train had ended its journey, and then again at the Gare de Lyon for the TGV to the south. Coincidence? She hadn't seen Calista, or at least Calista didn't think so. But one could never be sure. The woman was heading away, striding down the next carriage. Taken by surprise, Calista went into reverse, stepping back at once and shutting the door, just in case the stranger looked back. Calista was sure it was her. The jeans, the hair, the scarf. She counted up to thirty — slowly — before stepping out again into the corridor. The woman's Coco Chanel eau de parfum still hung in the air.

Calista's mission was, on the face of it, straightforward. She was to meet someone codenamed SPENDTHRIFT in a Nice cafe, at a certain time on a certain day, using standard identification signals. All she knew — all she was permitted to know, given her limited clearance — was that SPENDTHRIFT was an Englishman and convicted criminal who couldn't return to the UK unless willing to spend several more years in prison. He was a pederast. In other words, he was attracted to boys and had failed to restrain himself. He had a sadistic streak — he liked to pinch and beat as well as fondle his prey. A nasty piece of work, he'd served several years in a South African jail after working as a teacher at an exclusive private school in

Cape Town. Despite this, he'd then taught science for twelve years at Fettes College in Edinburgh, another private boarding school where it was said there were several of his kind teaching.

Charged with yet more sex offences, this time in a Scottish court, he'd been bailed. Instead of returning to face trial, he'd bolted.

The SIS station chief in Paris had thrown him a lifeline but regarded him as expendable, deciding to use him for risky or low-level tasks of a menial nature, paying him a subsistence allowance — just enough for rent and food. Perhaps, Calista thought, SPENDTHRIFT was used to being treated with contempt by now.

After all, he deserved it.

Calista was, for the purpose of this assignment, a head agent, and SPENDTHRIFT her agent. She was to debrief SPENDTHRIFT about the address where the mysterious call had been made. The call, that is, traced to the burner found on the unidentified man shot dead by police in Dover. She was to report the meeting with SPENDTHRIFT, write up any CX and pass it on, via a dead letter box, to HAMISH, a courier working out of the Paris Station who would have further instructions.

Then she was to go home.

Simple, right?

Calista changed at Marseille for a slower connection to Nice. She had forty minutes to wait, having just missed a train. Given the choice, she would have preferred France's second city, the rambunctious and fascinating Marseille, with its cosmopolitan population befitting a major Mediterranean seaport.

Much smaller, tranquil and bourgeois, or so she read in her guidebook, Nice was charming and pretty, and for many French people, it would be their first choice for retirement if they could afford it, so she couldn't complain. If it had been good enough for Graham Greene, Calista told herself, then it was good enough for her. The late Somerset Maugham, long a resident of Cap Ferrat, had said of the Riviera that it was a sunny place for shady people, which might well be true still, given the number of Russian oligarchs and their private armies of ex-Mossad thugs who'd set up shop along the coast.

It was Calista's first visit. Her glimpse from the train of the Bay of Angels on a hazy, muggy evening persuaded her that there were far worse places to practise tradecraft and agent handling. It was warm. The light was wonderful. It was unlike London in every way. On arrival, she took a cab to the three-star Hotel Monsigny, changing once en route. Ringing the changes, the Office called it. Her destination was popular with tourists, or so its website claimed, and it was located off the Avenue Malaussena.

Calista signed the register as Miss Shatz and handed over a passport in that name. She carried her own bag up to her second-floor room, unpacked, kicked off her shoes and threw herself down on the double bed. The room was pleasant, and it had a small balcony. She couldn't sleep; she had far too much to think about. She told herself she needed exercise, so she launched her route surveillance detection, something which her training had taught her could take a full day or night — if done properly.

And like any tourist, she was eager to explore.

Though it hardly seemed necessary just for a meeting with the expendable nonce SPENDTHRIFT.

. . . .

THE NEXT MORNING, AFTER a leisurely coffee, Calista walked to the Quartier du Port, taking her time, going again through the standard route surveillance detection, wandering off into side streets, hesitating in chi-chi shops, trying on hats, peering inside art galleries, taking off sunglasses and putting them back on, entering and leaving museums, doubling back, heading off in the wrong direction like any confused tourist, stopping to consult an inadequate tourist map. After all this, she was confident she was still black, in the clear. She was conscientious, but it was hardly a burden. It was such a beautiful day, with the temperature around eighteen degrees Celsius — twice that of dreary, damp, polluted and overpriced London.

She wore a summery print dress in red with a wide skirt and a wide black belt, a short black leather jacket and a pair of chunky Doc Martens boots. Her hair was cut very short. She called it her urchin trim. Calista circled around the Colline du Chateau and found what she was looking for just ahead: a small, family-owned cafe, le Café du Port, looking out onto the Quai Lunel. It had a few tables and chairs outside. Only one was occupied, by a solitary, middle-aged man in a short-sleeved white polo shirt not tucked in, a blue pullover slung around his shoulders, tan chinos, brown deck shoes and no socks. Tres chic. On the table next to his empty coffee cup was a copy of *Private Eye*. Both it and the pullover were recognition signals.

Making her way past to another table, Calista paused and turned. She spoke in English. 'Forgive the intrusion, but is that the latest, by any chance?'

The man looked up, removing his sunglasses and squinting up at the newcomer. 'Oh, no, I'm afraid not. It's at least a month old. Sorry. I blame Brexit.' He offered a fleeting and rather cold smile, showing perfect teeth.

'*Tant pis*,' Calista said.

Their credentials established, the man put his sunglasses back on. He was square-jawed, thin-lipped, blond, blue-eyed, sunburned. He looked tough. He'd have made a convincing SS type as an extra in a Hollywood movie, Calista thought.

'Why don't you join me? I don't meet many Brits these days. I've got out of the habit.' The accent was received English with just a trace of the underlying grittiness of an English-speaking South African. Unlike an Afrikaner accent, the English-speaking South African voice had a whine to it that grated. Calista pulled out a chair, turning it so she could watch the street and the quay by sitting sideways to the table.

A young woman in an apron bustled out and took her order with a smile. Calista asked for a croque monsieur and citron pressé.

SPENDTHRIFT ordered a café noisette.

The sun on Calista's face felt wonderful.

So it began. Still black, as far as Calista could make out.

Godfrey, as SPENDTHRIFT called himself, got right to it. He said the address she was interested in was in the old town and within easy walking distance. It was registered to an Argentinian national by the name of Costa. Like the coffee chain. SPENDTHRIFT had hung around for hours hoping to catch sight of the man the previous day, or so he claimed, but he hadn't appeared so far.

'My local police contact says Costa arrived in France several weeks ago, that he comes and goes, that his business is not known, that he rents the flat and pays a month in advance on the first of the month, that he lives alone, and that his French is adequate but not fluent. The French won't contact the

Argentine consulate until or unless this Costa breaks the law, which, so far, he hasn't done. Or so I'm told. Not so much as a parking ticket.'

It interested Calista that SPENDTHRIFT, a convicted pederast, would have a local police contact.

'Will you take me to see his place?'

SPENDTHRIFT shrugged. 'If you wish.'

He wasn't thrilled about it. Calista noticed that SPENDTHRIFT, or Godfrey, avoided looking at her and kept his face averted. A misogynist, or ashamed of what he was? He seemed more interested in the boats in the port, especially the luxury yachts.

Calista paid cash for them both and made sure she took the receipt. She left what she thought was a respectable tip for the friendly server. Not too much. She didn't want to give the young woman a reason to remember either of them.

• • • •

THEY WALKED TO THE address in the old town. They weren't followed. The pavements and cobbled streets were narrow in some sections, so Calista let SPENDTHRIFT lead and kept a distance of several paces. He didn't try to make small talk when she drew level.

'Been here before, Godfrey?'

SPENDTHRIFT didn't reply.

A flight of crumbling stone stairs ran up the side of an old but pretty building with fading yellow walls and a red-tiled roof. Very Mediterranean. Washing was drying on lines strung between the buildings that were squeezed and jumbled together. There were red and pink geraniums in pots on the ground floor, as well as on the windowsills of the first-floor flat despite the time of year. Calista gestured for SPENDTHRIFT to lead the way up to the second-floor flat under the eaves.

It had its own front door, painted green, the paint worn and chipped by age, neglect and scorching summer sun.

SPENDTHRIFT tapped lightly with his fingernails.

No response.

He tapped again, only louder, using the knuckles of his right hand. Two taps, a pause, then two more.

Nothing.

'Mr Costa?'

SPENDTHRIFT took hold of the round, metal doorknob and turned it.

Calista stood close behind SPENDTHRIFT and to one side. She saw for herself that the door wasn't locked.

To enter or not was the question.

'Go for it,' said Calista, even though she knew it was probably illegal.

SPENDTHRIFT pushed, and it swung open a few inches.

She knew that smell.

This wasn't bad drains. It wasn't shit. It wasn't a squirrel or rat. It wasn't a cat or dog.

It was far too strong.

SPENDTHRIFT aka Godfrey clamped a hand over his nose and mouth and stumbled back, turning away from the entrance in disgust. Calista thought he was about to throw up right there and then, so she jumped aside to avoid being splashed with vomit.

He pushed past, ran down the steps, all the way to the bottom, and she heard him spilling his guts noisily into the street.

A sensitive pederast, she thought.

Calista knew what it was. It wasn't her first time. It was an overpowering, sweetish stench that permeated everything, sticking to hair, clothing, skin. It wouldn't wash off easily, not even after several attempts with hot water and soap. It could linger for days, even weeks.

Chapter 14

Southern Afghanistan, 2003

Merrick is both excited and apprehensive.

All that effort over months of selection, and all the training he's received, are about to be put into practice, courtesy of 9/11 and al Qaeda. He's never been on active service, and never under fire, nor has he faced people who will no doubt do their utmost to kill him.

Merrick worries about those things every young man unproven in battle worries about. Will he cope, will he manage, will he be a credit to his comrades and the Regiment? Will he rise to the occasion? Will he demonstrate leadership? Will he excel at being a special forces soldier? Will he, at the very least, show himself to be dependable under fire?

Dawn finds Trooper Merrick scrambling up an immense pile of near-vertical rock that appears to pierce the sky. An eight-man, high-altitude, low-opening (HALO) squad has jumped at 20,000 feet to take and mark out an improvised landing strip for American C130s. These aircraft then bring in everyone else — around 140 troops in all from the Regiment — and their vehicles. They wrestle their DPV 110s or 'Pink Panthers' — stripped-down Land Rovers in distinctive pink camo — as far as they can uphill. The bone-shaking rides along gullies and ridges finally converge on the objective, an al Qaeda opium plant and training camp in the form of a network of caves, tunnels and bunkers dug into the mountain. Once on foot, Merrick and his mates use the available cover as best they can; they zig-zag up the slope, using toes, knees, elbows and hands, dodging from boulder to boulder.

Operation Trent comprises a regimental task force that fields a tactical headquarters and two squadrons of fifty men each. The huge mountain, a natural fortress named Koh-i-Malik, rises majestically from the semi-desert some twenty clicks north of the Durand Line that marks the porous frontier between Pakistan and Afghanistan, and 250 clicks southwest of Kandahar, the old royal capital. It's located at the southern end of Helmand, the largest of Afghanistan's provinces. At this stage, Kabul is still in the hands of the Taliban, and although both the British and American special forces have by now mounted several raids on the Taliban and their al Qaeda 'guests,' this is a more substantial affair.

It's winter and cold, especially at night and at altitude. It becomes colder as Merrick's fire team climbs. Rain alternates with hail and even the odd snowstorm. Not that Merrick minds; it helps him stay cool as he sweats his way up with a Bergen on his back, along with ammunition clips, grenades and his preferred weapon, an M-16 rifle.

Even as Merrick crawls, scrabbles, slithers and grapples with rock and vegetation, he cannot fail to be struck by the beauty of the place, the sheer scale of the terrain, the sense of isolation and the awesome silence.

Through his scope, he sees that the multinational enemy is well dug into terrain that's in the defenders' favour. Al Qaeda's fighters occupy several stone buildings and trenches, caves and a network of tunnels dug inside the mountain. While the British attackers receive air support from U.S. Navy jets, this is going to be of limited use once the soldiers close with the enemy.

The F-18s' smart bombs turn the enemy positions into a storm of fire. Smoke from the explosions wreaths the target area in a drifting white-and-grey mist. All Merrick can do is flatten himself on the shaking ground, keep his head down, and wait for the hurricane of rock-and-steel fragments to pass. It's like lying on the edge of a volcano, and within minutes it's clear that while al Qaeda forces might be bloodied and shaken by the hammering they've taken from the precision air strikes, they are far from beaten.

The clatter of AK-47 fire over to his left announces the surviving al Qaeda fighters' response, followed by the thump of their rocket-propelled grenades or RPGs. Small arms rounds start to hiss and snap around Merrick, with bullets splashing the dirt and ricocheting off rocks. Merrick gets to his feet. He doesn't know how, nor does he give it any thought. He and his squad stumble into a mad run, covered by fire from light machine guns and MILAN anti-tank missiles slamming into caves and bunkers.

He's taken half a dozen paces inside a tunnel entrance when he sees his first enemy closing in on him — a man running flat out, a mad dash, eyes wide, mouth gaping, screaming while firing his AK-47 in bursts from the hip. Not unlike a man with a rugby ball heading for the touchline. Merrick will keep every detail of that face in his mind for as long as he lives. He does what he's been trained to do and has practised countless times. It's instinctive, the way he's been taught. He doesn't have to think. Or feel. Merrick double taps him. The enemy is thrown back by the two rounds, twisting to one side as his legs go and he collapses. Several more figures emerge, charging towards the tunnel entrance. There's no time to consider his options or the nature of what he's doing. Merrick's actions are second nature. He isn't frightened. If he feels anything at all, it's elation. He double taps each target in his sights, moving from left to right, reloading, firing, shuffling his way forward deeper into the tunnel, firing again, moving from one form of cover to the next.

The crash of grenades, the flash of explosions, clouds of smoke and dust, Merrick keeps moving through it, coughing and spitting out dirt. He's aware of a bullet ripping through a comrade's water bottle like a slap, and he sees someone else, a senior NCO, shot through the calf — straight through, it seems.

A round strikes his own Bergen and knocks him off balance.

Merrick recovers, pushes on, rounds a corner, the gloved left hand of one of his comrades — Andy — right behind him on his right shoulder. They move as a pair, and just as he's thinking how extraordinary it is that the enemy has lighting and power lines rigged up in the tunnel, he's knocked flying by something big and solid. It's a colossal figure of a man who's cannoned into him. The collision knocks them both over, a confusion of legs and arms. It reminds Merrick of being trapped at the bottom of a rugby scrum in the mud at school. Whoever it is, the fucker's on top of Merrick, crushing him and trying to throttle him. The al Qaeda guy doesn't seem to have a weapon — maybe he's dropped it in the impact — and he uses his immense hands to probe Merrick's face, pushing his head back and trying to drive his fingers into Merrick's eyes and throat.

Merrick has lost control of his rifle, which is connected to the sling around his chest but is now also trapped under his enemy's body. They snarl and grunt as they fight, but the animal sounds are drowned out by gunfire. Merrick gets his right hand free, reaches down and fumbles for his Italian Fulcrum combat knife, grasps it, draws it from its sheath and plunges it into his opponent's side. Again. And again. He feels the steel grate on bone and then break through. He keeps it up. He keeps driving it into his adversary. The enemy's hands fall away.

Merrick pushes and kicks and rolls the inert body away and, rising, plunges the blade into his enemy's neck. He stabs again and again. He's rewarded for his efforts with a spurt of hot blood in his own face. It washes over his uniform, momentarily blinding him.

He's unaware that Andy has already shot the man twice.

Merrick is on his hands and knees. He has his rifle now. Someone grabs his webbing from behind and pulls him to his feet. It's Andy.

How long does this go on?

Merrick has no clue. Seconds, minutes, hours? All at once, the firing lessens then ceases. Merrick is drenched in his own sweat and his opponents' blood. He feels his exhilaration drain away, followed by an overwhelming sense of well-being. He squats down with his back to a rock and checks his weapon, clears the breech, reloads.

He tears the top off his water bottle and drinks. He realises he wears an idiotic grin on his face. He's still alive. Others aren't, but he is, and by God, it feels good. The complex human organism that is Merrick has survived unharmed. Every nerve, cell, muscle seems to quiver with joyful relief. Aside from the extraordinary effect of dopamine, he's still thirsty, and his water bottle is empty.

He's sitting next to Andy.

'Alright, pal?' Andy's grinning at him.

'I'm fucking great. You?'

'Never better,' Andy says. They both laugh as if it's all a tremendous joke.

Merrick's hands shake. Someone passes him a cigarette although he doesn't smoke. He's shaking so much he has trouble holding it, but he smokes it anyway. He notices how filthy he is, his hands covered in dirt and dried blood, the nails black. His combats are stiff with the enemy's blood. He spits out a mixture of grit and what tastes like blood, rust and salt.

He smells his own bitter body odour.

What strikes him most in the immediate aftermath when he thinks about his experience, is the courage and fighting spirit of the enemy. Those al Qaeda guys — apparently, they come from all over, from China to Iran — were quite something. They were not afraid to die. They'd not gone to ground or run away. They didn't fall to their knees, pleading for their lives. Not at all. They'd come out fighting. They'd worked as a team. In Merrick's way of

thinking, they were no more extremists and religious fanatics — the terms
the UK and U.S. authorities liked to use — than the eleven officers and
men of the 66th Foot who'd launched that final bayonet charge at the Battle
of Maiwand in 1880, a charge they'd known full well would cost them
their lives. To the Afghans, their victory at Maiwand over the British was as
important as Agincourt was to the English. And right here, they'd risen to
the occasion, knowing they wouldn't come out of it alive. Mentally, Merrick
salutes them. Brave fuckers.

Only later, back at the Kandahar base, does Merrick learn that the
Koh-i-Malik gun battle lasted five hours, that seventy-two al Qaeda fighters
died, and an unknown number were wounded. His own side has suffered just
four wounded, none of the injuries life threatening. Chinooks flew in and
extracted them. And only now does he overhear the chatter of senior officers;
Operation Trent — which depended entirely on the Americans for logistics
and fire support — resulted from the personal intervention of the prime
minister, Tony Blair, who'd wanted to show what British special forces could
do. Something he could boast about at Davos, the Bilderberg meeting or the
forthcoming G20 summit. For Merrick, this is a sorry anti-climax after the
high of his first close contact with the enemy, and a tacit admission that the
British vassal state has done something its American masters could have more
easily and cheaply achieved themselves with a few more airstrikes. London
had added a wrinkle to U.S. plans, forcing an extra burden on planning and
resources in order to prove the Britons' worth so that Mr Blair would have
something to boast about as Washington's leading *condottiere*.

It was about the bloody man's prestige, his fucking ego on the world
stage.

As Merrick gorges on three helpings of sausages, fried tomato, eggs and
tea, surprising even the Army cooks, he realises that politics has nothing to
do with his desire to fight. He has found something he can do fairly well,
that's all. That and the camaraderie.

Merrick belongs.

He shovels apple pie and custard down his throat and gets up yet again
to help himself to more coffee. He wants to go home to his south London
cupboard. Merrick tells himself he'll take a long, hot shower, put on some
clean and comfortable civvies, and his wish for profound forgetfulness will

be achieved by drinking far too much. And like so many young men who've faced violent death, his inebriation will lower any remaining inhibitions and will result in him getting laid, or so Merrick hopes.

He remembers that he's put his name down for a sniper training course the following month. It should be fun. Marksmanship is Merrick's thing.

After that, he'll come back and do this all over again.

Chapter 15

After a change of shift starting at 6 p.m., the work would go on all night. The original eight investigators stay just long enough to bring their successors up to speed, while the overnight team would now number fifteen people, having been reinforced by Transport Police.

GCHQ reported no spike in encrypted traffic, at home or abroad, something which might have been expected in anticipation of a terrorist attack.

The Met reported nothing unusual from the Automatic Number Plate Recognition (ANPR) system either.

The Interrogation Wing has harvested nothing useful in the screening of those detained under the Terrorism Act. People were being released in batches as new suspects were brought in.

Bridie, Bernie and Septimus got together in a spare office to draft a brief report on the day's efforts for the home secretary and heads of departments. Septimus wrote the first effort, Bridie adjusted it, and at the third attempt all three agreed on the text. It was then copied to the eight lead investigators. There were no objections. It was very short, which helped. Only a paragraph.

'You think it wise to tell Turan about our mystery man?' Septimus asked.

Bridie pursed her lips. 'I don't have any other option, Septimus. Sorry. I can't conceal it. More than my job is worth.'

'You know what he'll do, don't you?'

'What will he do?'

'I know the answer to this,' Bernie said. 'Turan's the new boy in the Cabinet. He wants to prove himself. Goes without saying he's ambitious — and eager to take the credit for anything he can get his hands on. After reading this, he'll want to issue a media release or, better still, hold a news conference. With himself in the spotlight, naturally.'

'Fuck that,' said Septimus. 'We don't want our suspect to know we're on his tail. We want him to relax, to think he's got away with it. Yes?'

'For what it's worth,' said Bridie. 'I'll oppose any attempt to feed this information to the media on national security grounds. I'll say we have to be certain this is our man, or we could end up with egg all over our collective face if it turns out he's innocent. We'd look stupid. Turan would look stupid. We need to nail down his identity and have him in custody before we go public.'

Everyone agreed.

Bridie wasn't sure her argument would work.

Bernie was right, of course. Not half an hour after they sent off the first daily report, Turan's shiny egg-shaped head popped up on their screens, insisting a release be sent to the media. People wanted to know what was happening, he said. What efforts were being made to bring the 'terrorist' or 'terrorists' to justice. They deserved to know, he added, as if he was a lifelong proponent of open government. He was under immense pressure.

Like hell he was a believer in open government. Bridie knew he'd already turned down a dozen Freedom of Information requests on his first day in office.

Bridie was at pains to be both courteous and rational when she spoke to him, but Turan wasn't buying it. Bridie had to accept his decision with regret; she would have no option but to report their difference of opinion to her boss, 'C'. She didn't need to spell out to Turan the realities of political life: 'C' answered to the foreign secretary, one of Turan's rivals, both in the ruling party and in Cabinet.

The episode was shaping up to be a confrontation when it was swept aside by breaking news. Turan's face and voice vanished from the monitor.

The secretary of defence Sir Kevin Tomlinson had that afternoon succumbed to his injuries sustained the previous morning at the Cenotaph. He had died as doctors tried to remove part of a bullet from his brain.

• • • •

THERE WAS NO POINT in hanging around the office after the daily report had been filed. Bridie went home, and she managed to obtain the all but impossible, an SIS driver and car from the Service pool; an electric Jaguar no less. When she opened her front door, she could smell Alec's cooking. She knew at once what it was — his favourite. Steak pie.

He came out of the kitchen wearing a striped apron. 'Well, this is a welcome surprise. My wife is home before midnight and just in time to eat. Miracles never cease.'

He put his arms around her and kissed her forehead. Bridie reciprocated by holding him close, though she felt she probably didn't smell that great. For his part, Alec smelled of cooked beef, spices and pie crust.

'Mind if I take a shower, first? I'll be quick, darling, I promise.' She saw he'd even laid the table and put out their best glassware and cutlery.

Aw, sweet man.

He was fortunate in that he worked regular hours most of the time, as a senior lecturer in nuclear physics at Imperial College. But the commercialisation of academia was spreading fast and led to much unhappiness among teaching staff, including Alec.

An hour later, they were almost done. Bridie was pushing bits of crust round her plate in pursuit of the last of the gravy. She'd polished off the veg. Alec reached for his wine glass.

'Tell me something, if you would, Bridie. You know I stay well clear of your work if I can, and I keep my nose out of it. But I know you're involved in dealing with the mayhem at the Cenotaph —'

Bridie interrupted. 'Alec, you're right, I am, but only in the managerial sense. I'm tied to a desk, so you don't have to worry. No more gallivanting around the globe in pursuit of the unspeakable. I leave all the fun to others.'

Neither of them had so far mentioned the politicians who'd been murdered. Neither had words of sympathy or regret. In that, they were probably representative of the majority. Even so, what had occurred was a shock, even if the victims were universally disliked — except possibly for a diehard cabal of the far right.

But Alec did talk about it now.

'Sure. I get it, and I'm relieved. But my question is this. Whoever did it had the temerity and the skill to breach some pretty intensive security at the Cenotaph, just to bump off a trio of the most unpopular and divisive politicians in the country. I mean, you wouldn't have voted for them, and I sure wouldn't have. The great British public thinks they stink. They're criminally corrupt, and everyone knows it. So why bother? I'm trying to say that if the perpetrators wanted to attack the British state for whatever reason, they'd target the king. Wouldn't they? Why bother with these third-rate, treasonous types?'

'You have a point, sweetheart. Is there any more of this red? It's delicious.'

'I'll open another bottle,' Alec said. 'I'd like some more, too.'

He returned from the kitchen, bottle in hand.

Bridie said, 'We should let it breathe, shouldn't we?'

'To hell with that.' He poured the wine into her glass, then his own.

'So, Bridie, what's your view?'

She'd hoped he wouldn't press the issue, that her mention of more wine would distract him long enough to forget that he'd even raised the topic.

'Well, if someone did assassinate the king, heaven forbid, it would achieve three things. One: it would unite a country that's falling apart. Two: it would restore faith in the monarchy — and you know the monarchy has never been less popular than it is now, except possibly for the reigns of Edward II or Charles I. Three: it would bring in a younger generation of royals. The next heir to the throne himself doesn't hold with all this Disneyland feudal ritual and cringey fancy dress, but more important, he's not going to smile and nod through the current slide to fascism. He'd resist it, I'm sure.'

'Crikey. That's a tall order.'

'It's only my opinion, mind.'

'So an assassin would kill the king to preserve the monarchy? And he or she would be a conservative traditionalist of the old school, probably a Tory voter over seventy and living in Guildford, Haslemere or Henley. Is that what you're telling me?'

Bridie sipped her wine and laughed. 'Something like that, but it sounds ageist.'

'I've got your favourite pud. Are you ready for it?'

'Alec, you know something?'

'What?'

'You're adorable.'

He laughed in turn. 'You know the old saying, don't you — that the way to a woman's heart is through her stomach?'

Bridie didn't get a chance to reply. Her green phone was ringing.

When she came back and sat down, she picked up her glass and drained it in a single swallow.

'Fuck,' she said with feeling. 'Fuck.'

'What's happened?'

'It's not what happened that bugs me. Well, it does, of course, but what gets my goat is that people think that because I'm of senior rank in the Service I have to be kept informed all the time of just about everything that happens. It's nonsense. I don't know why they bother, because if they gave it a moment's thought, which they don't, they'd realise I can't do anything about it. Jesus.'

'Why don't you tell them to stop?'

'Because if I did, and I missed something really important, they'd say it was because I ordered them not to alert me. I *can't* stop them.'

'What did happen?'

'Our new, unelected prime minister has asked the king to prorogue parliament. The king has agreed, naturally. The old bird never has had the gumption to resist. It's obvious why this has happened: Carstairs doesn't want Parliament to debate the State of Emergency he's just declared.'

'You're not serious.'

'Fraid so, love. Habeas Corpus suspended, no right to silence, public protests and marches banned. D Notice issued on the subject of the shootings. Now, was I imagining it, or did you say something about pudding?'

Chapter 16

*P*arish *of Normandy, Surrey, 11:15 November 13*

A tall, spare, silver-haired man stood in his modest conservatory, preparing for the first spring planting, sorting out his gardening paraphernalia, and emptying seedboxes and pots.

He'd stacked spade, fork, rake, long-handled brush and bamboo poles outside, along with smaller hand tools such as a trowel, leaning them up against the side of the aluminium and glass structure to make room so he could clean the place. His tools weren't new, but he'd kept them clean, and the steel shone in the sun.

Who wouldn't be outside today, given the chance?

After all that rain, the sky was eggshell blue, cloudless, and the low winter sun was just enough to shower the distant Hog's Back in gold. As the name suggested, the Hog's Back was a narrow ridge in Surrey's North Downs — well known among the southern English and mentioned at some point by Jane Austen.

Between that and the silver-haired gardener — who hummed to himself while he pottered about in his wellies, worn corduroys, tweed coat, yellow leather gardening gloves and flat cap — was a broad and level array of green fields that formed a market garden. Then came a line of what used to be farm cottages, each one on a third-acre plot, with almost identical mansard roofs, but 'gentrified' by London incomers and their new money.

This was Normandy parish near the border with Hampshire; it lay in the lea of the Hog's Back and was connected by bus and a train service from Wanborough Station to Guildford — where London commuters could change for Waterloo — in six minutes. The garrison town of Aldershot was some ten minutes by rail. The parish straddled the busy A323 or 'Aldershot Road.'

The gardener's home was a sprawling thatched cottage of mostly wood and plaster dating back to the early 1700s. It lay concealed in a strip of lush woodland between the A323 and the Army's firing ranges, an expanse popular among horse riders, runners and dog walkers, except for those occasions when the Army hoisted red flags to warn of imminent firing.

Despite increasing pressure from a growing population and expansion of residential housing, the woodland somehow survived as a quiet, rural oasis, full of birdsong, and populated by foxes, stoats, rabbits and occasionally, roe deer.

Something, perhaps a crackle of gravel underfoot, made the old man stop humming, turn his head towards the open door of the 'orangery' — his name for it — and straighten up.

A stranger stood there. He held the gardener's fork across his chest with both gloved hands. He wore black — a watch cap, a jacket of synthetic material, jeans and grey walking boots. He smiled at the older man, but there was no humour in it.

'Sir Humphrey?'

'Yes? Can I help you?'

The gardener's voice was firm, clipped, and not in the least nervous. It smacked of the officer class and institutional life: Wellington College, Sandhurst, the Coldstream Guards, and any number of camps, garrisons, parade grounds and military campaigns the world over. It was the voice of command, a voice self-consciously superior that was accustomed to being obeyed.

They were Sir Humphrey's very last words.

Chapter 17

Taskforce HQ, London, 15:53, November 13.

At the afternoon conference, several people were absent, being out and about and doing their investigating or resting after a twelve-hour night shift. Septimus mentioned to Bridie that over forty-eight hours had passed since the Armistice Day murders, yet there had been no claim of responsibility. Not a single one.

None of the usual suspects had wanted to take the credit. Not the so-called Houthis of Yemen, Islamic Jihad, Hamas, Hezbollah, nor the extreme Zionists of the Kach group, Otzma Yehudit and others.

No boast from al Qaeda or its several offshoots, no triumphal gloating from IS.

The Middle East's 'terrorists' and would-be 'terrorists' were silent. In any case, Septimus muttered, the term terrorist was itself reduced to a vague, derogatory term bandied about so much and so often by all sides that it meant very little.

No new militant group had surfaced to claim the deed, no ecoterrorists or white supremacists, for example. No neo-Nazis, no Stalinists, no nihilists, no Scots or Welsh nationalists, neither Republican nor hardline Loyalist splinter groups from Northern Ireland.

Septimus sounded almost disappointed. At least a claim, real or false, would be something to follow up.

Someone, perhaps DI Purchase, had put on the television. People gathered to watch the market news. London equities had dropped by twenty-four percent in the first hour of trading, the pound by thirty-four percent, and both were still declining by the close. Gold was at an all-time high. The trading boards were blanketed in red.

Bridie asked for it to be switched off. She told the meeting — only four people were present — that governments regarded as hostile to the UK and its interests had hastened to pass on messages through their diplomatic missions to the Foreign Office that very morning, some expressing sympathy, offering their condolences and all disclaiming responsibility for the killings. These had included Iran, Iraq, Israel, Syria, Russia, China and North Korea.

'What do you think, Septimus?' Bridie asked.

'Motive,' said Septimus. 'We need motive. If we have that, then we'll know who it was.'

'So?'

'I did look closely at the sniper rifle.'

Bridie asked, 'So did the ballistics people, didn't they?'

'Not close enough, it seems. Or maybe we were looking for different things.'

'Meaning?'

'It had been cleansed. No serial numbers. They'd been removed. Something else: I believe — but can't prove — that all the parts of that weapon came from other rifles of the same type, manufacture and calibre. The bolt and firing mechanism were from other rifles of the same make. So too the trigger mechanism and magazine. It had been assembled by parts from elsewhere.'

'But why?'

'I can only conclude that whoever it was had had this on his mind for a long time, and that he'd smuggled the parts into London — or maybe the UK — piece by piece. Probably over several months, if not years. He'd get hold of a component, perhaps steal it, and smuggle it into the country, or out of a military base or shooting club, or both, and do it again and again until he had what he wanted: a complete weapon system, along with the ammunition.'

Caro said, 'A member of the armed forces, right?'

'It's probable,' Septimus said, 'maybe not our armed forces, but almost certainly someone with a military background. What does seem certain is that he was in and out of that Whitehall building frequently, that he spent several nights there, and that he'd scoped the Whitehall area for months. We should widen our search of CCTV to the past fortnight, better still, the last month.'

DI Purchase groaned. He'd had enough of watching CCTV clips, and who could blame him?

Bernie Cuttle raised a hand. 'What makes you so sure, Septimus?'

'Did you see what he stood on when he took those four shots? No? It wasn't a trestle table, which is how the Met described it. It was an ergonomic

desk with a small, electrically powered control panel under the leading edge
— meaning its height could be raised or lowered, even tilted. Very solid piece
of kit. Made in Germany in 1996, according to an old label on the underside.
Ikea, it isn't. My guess is that it was left forgotten on the third floor, which no
one seemed to use, except for storing files. No doubt it was covered with box
files and gathering dust when the shooter discovered it. It broke down into
two sections: a very heavy iron base and the top, also heavy and pretty big.
It would require two, maybe three people to carry it all up the stairs to the
roof. I think our shooter did so alone, in the dead of night. Not impossible,
but it would have required considerable strength. And the time to dismantle
and reassemble it.'

Bernie again: 'Your point being?'

'That the shooter is a young male, fit and strong — and military, past
or present, with a patient, determined attitude. Sure of his own abilities. He
thought it all out and took his time. Persistent is the word I'd use.'

Caro had something to add: 'Imagine we were all, everyone sitting here
now at this table, skilled assassins of one sort or another. What would
prevent us? Family, for one. Or partners. And two: the job. We're all trying
to hold down our jobs and maintain our relationships outside work. Right?
Some of us even have kids. We wouldn't have the time, and we wouldn't be
able to afford it, either. Even if we wanted to do something like this. I think
you should add both single and unemployed to your profile, Septimus.'

'A professional, single hit man on benefits,' said Bernie.

• • • •

SEPTIMUS WAS A BELIEVER in going backwards. That meant looking
at the victims' pasts. The victims of a crime, any crime in his view, would
sometimes offer up crucial information about the perpetrators. It wasn't
much different from Bridie's counterintelligence brief: the key lay in details,
details in the past that had been forgotten, overlooked or concealed.

That afternoon, he kept to himself, stayed out of discussions and stuck to
his own desk. In the main room, meanwhile, television screens were showing
the politicians' funerals, flocks of people in black, the grieving families
weeping, the friends and political allies looking sad and solemn for the

cameras. He didn't want to watch or listen to any of it. Instead, he concentrated on gathering as much open-source information as he could, starting with the intended victims, namely the late prime minister Sir Edwin Lufkin and the late leader of the opposition and head of the Labour Party Dame Tasmin Quaife.

Septimus didn't want to read about it on his computer screen, so he printed stuff up, using coloured markers to highlight what he thought relevant, and setting it out in neat piles on his desk until he'd formed ramparts of files and paper stacks around himself.

The other victims, accidental or otherwise — the late home secretary and the late defence secretary — well, they weren't going anywhere. They could wait.

Septimus asked himself: what had the two intended victims done — or failed to do — during their political careers or personal lives to attract an enemy so angry, so filled with hatred, that he'd be willing to risk his own life and liberty to murder?

And the follow up question: of those deeds, which — if there were any — did they have in common, given that they were political rivals on opposite sides of the House of Commons, and subscribed to opposing views of the United Kingdom and its future?

Lufkin was what, superficially at least, Septimus might have expected. Eton. PPE at Oxford. Private equity firm that shorted the pound and made him a personal fortune reported to be in excess of 200 million. Inherited three million quid when he turned eighteen through an offshore trust set up by his father. 'Stunning' townhouse in north London (according to *House and Garden*), and a country pile in Oxfordshire that featured in the *Tatler* and where he held a safe seat. On the right of the right-wing Party. Political obsessions: pro-Brexit, so-called austerity (neoliberal economics), selling the NHS off to his pals in the private sector. Anti-immigration and an outspoken climate change denier, which upset some of his party colleagues. Signed off on twenty-seven new oil and gas exploration permits, including the licence for the enormous Rosebank field which he'd flogged to the Norwegians.

Lufkin had pushed hard for anti-protest and strike ban laws. He was a self-confessed Zionist 'and proud of it,' refusing to back a Gaza ceasefire and instructing his government's representative to abstain during the UN

Security Council vote. Eighty percent of the parliamentary Party were members of the 'Friends of Middle East Defence Force' lobby group. He'd enjoyed three 'free' trips to Israel, thanks to the FMEDF. Junior minister at the Foreign Office 2010-11, hawkish on China and Russia, promoted to immigration minister in 2012, but a year later, in 2013, was rewarded with the Foreign Office. Had sworn to stop what he called the invasion of small boat refugees and had notably failed in that endeavour. It was only a step from there to the Party appointing him to the (unelected) premiership.

'Delivering for the British people' was his slogan.

A likely target, then, for environmental, pro-Palestinian, socialist and Remainer activists.

He might be deeply unpleasant, morally bankrupt and hopelessly out of touch to many people, but murder?

Dame Tasmin Quaife was an enigma. Of modest origins, she grew up in a council flat, proving to be exceptionally bright. Her dad was a factory worker, her mum a primary school teacher. A scholarship student at Birmingham, and National Union of Students organiser, she appeared at the head of demonstrations and marches, notably 'Stop Oil' and 'Free Palestine' campaigns as well as the Campaign for Nuclear Disarmament. Active in local protest groups on issues relating to housing, rent control, refugees, asylum seekers, the homeless and domestic assault. A master's with distinction in human rights. Anti-Brexit and pro-European. The ideals of youth. Taking the path of the broad Left. So far, so good.

Then everything changed.

In the two-year run-up to the general election, Dame Quaife dropped or 'U-turned' on all twenty-four of her Party's manifesto pledges, even the much publicised — and popular — twenty-eight billion pound Green Deal, a plan to tackle and mitigate climate change and to invigorate a sluggish economy and employment.

News reports emerged of 'missing' emails in exchanges with senior U.S. administration officials during and after visits to Washington. Informing no one, she reportedly attended meetings of the Trilateral Commission, a mysterious body alleged to have CIA links — all of which she denied.

In the House of Commons, Dame Tasmin had voted against a ceasefire in Gaza. She was a leading light of the FMEDF lobby group and had twice been abroad at the group's expense. She'd purged her party of left-wingers, especially Jewish members opposed to Zionism. To be anti-Zionist was to be antisemitic, in her view. She insisted there was no prospect of rejoining the European Union, not even the customs union and free trade zone, despite a shift in public opinion in favour of closer European ties. 'Now is not the time' was her favourite and most often repeated phrase in response to reporters' questions about pretty much everything.

As darkness fell and everyone else in the office prepared to pack up and head for home, Septimus stumbled on a name that kept cropping up in relation to a Tufton Street think-tank: a billionaire named Ivor Brodzinski.

He was said — in very different reports spread over eighteen months in the *New Statesman*, *The Spectator* and *Private Eye* — to be a major donor to the election campaigns of both Quaife and Lufkin. *Red Pepper* said so, too, in an opinion piece picked up by *Tribune*. If the media reports were accurate, he'd slipped Quaife eleven million pounds over the previous six years, and Lufkin eight million over four years.

He appeared to have 'bought' both of them.

Who was Ivor Brodzinski?

· · · ·

BERNIE KNOCKED AND, without waiting, pushed open the door. 'I'm off,' he called out while pulling on a rumpled, fawn-coloured coat.

'So I see.'

'You have been busy,' Bernie said, waving a hand at the mass of paper and file covers. 'What is all this?'

'Revisiting the past,' Septimus muttered. He did not elaborate.

'Uh-huh. Good.' In his turn, Bernie wasn't interested in whatever it was Septimus was doing. He was being polite. 'I thought you might find this interesting.' Bernie took out his phone and offered it to Septimus, who was disinclined to accept it. Septimus wanted to be left alone to get on with his work without further interruption before his eyes failed.

'Go on, Septimus. Won't take a minute. Tell me what you think, please, then I'll leave you in peace. Promise.'

It was called *SurreyLive*, apparently live updates online from a newspaper called the *Surrey Advertiser*. He scrolled past riveting headlines such as 'M3 closure causes huge delays' and 'I thought I had tonsillitis but it turned out be cancer' and reached this:

'WAR HERO STABBED TO DEATH IN SURREY GARDEN.'

Septimus read on.

General Sir Humphrey Ocean, GCB, CBE, DSO was stabbed to death with his own garden fork in the Surrey village of Normandy on Monday, and police said they were treating the death of the war hero as suspicious.

No shit, Sherlock.

Sources close to the inquiry said Sir Humphrey, 66, had been stabbed through the heart in his conservatory and that he died instantly.

His body was discovered when a delivery driver tried to leave a parcel at the general's 17th-century home. There were no signs of a struggle, but the sources said police had ruled out suicide.

Since his retirement from the Army, Sir Humphrey worked as a consultant at the think tank State Strategy Institute, registered at Tufton Street in London. The institute is linked to several major UK arms firms. Its members include MPs from both major political parties, including the late Prime Minister Edwin Lufkin.

A widower, Sir Humphrey was born in Hong Kong and commissioned into the Coldstream Guards. He served in Northern Ireland, the Gulf War and with the UN in Bosnia. He held several top posts, including command of UK forces in Basra, Iraq, and of the Helmand Task Force in Afghanistan, as well as serving as Deputy Chief of the Defence Staff.

He is survived by a son and a daughter.

. . . .

'DIFFERENT MO,' SAID Septimus, handing the phone back. 'But thanks.'

What a glittering career! Septimus thought to himself how wonderful it was that an officer who shared at least some of the responsibility for the humiliating British defeats in Basra and Helmand could continue to be promoted and receive yet more decorations from the state and army he'd served so poorly.

'Of course, you're right,' said Bernie. 'Except that a local resident told police she saw what she described as a young man stride from Wanborough Station through the parish towards the general's house an hour before the murder was reported. It's around half a mile, maybe a bit more. He walked confidently and fast, and, as the witness put it, "moved like a soldier." He was also picked up on his way by a security camera outside the local butcher's on the Aldershot Road intersection. Surrey police then issued a Photofit. Here it is.'

Bernie held up his phone so Septimus could see it.

Septimus stared at it for several seconds without speaking. A male of military age, certainly, but no clear facial features. Could have been anyone.

At length, he sat back in his chair, sighed, and then said, 'Hard to tell, but I think you might have something there, Bernie.'

And wasn't the State Strategy Institute in Tufton Street the one funded by the mysterious Ivor Brodzinski?

Cuttle buttoned up his coat. 'Okay. So, shall we both go take a look? Body's in the Woking morgue. Given the man's reputation and the media interest, the pathologist will do the autopsy tomorrow.'

Chapter 18

Nice, France, 14:40 local time, November 13

Calista aka Bianca aka LUCY wasn't squeamish, and she wasn't about to allow the overwhelming stink of putrefaction to prevent her from having a look around.

She took a deep breath to fill her lungs, flung her right arm around her face so that her nose and mouth were buried in the crook of her elbow, and marched in, leaving SPENDTHRIFT to throw up his guts in the street.

A cat — a black furry blur — raced outside between Calista's legs, startling her. It took a couple of seconds for her eyes to become accustomed to the gloom, for the curtains had been drawn across the only living room window. The first thing she noticed was the loud buzzing. Thousands of bluebottles were already busy at work on the corpse of a man face down on the floor, no doubt laying their clusters of eggs, several dozen at a time.

It seemed to Calista that whoever he was, the victim had been dead for at least seventy-two hours. The stink suggested the rot of his internal organs was well advanced, emitting the foul gases that attracted the insects and had made SPENDTHRIFT nauseous. Calista forced herself to move closer, prodded one of the victim's hands with her foot. The hand was soft and shifted easily. Rigor mortis had come and gone, but the movement stirred up a cloud of flies so thick and loud that Calista was forced to turn away lest they fly into her face and hair.

She noted that the back of the victim's shirt was caked in blood that had turned into black treacle, and it seethed and shimmered with a metallic sheen as if he wore chain mail armour. The floor around the body was also black with blood.

Pale bluebottle maggots wriggled in the sludge.

Calista wanted to see the dead man's face, but when she tried to step around the body, she realised there wasn't much of it left to see. He looked as if he'd been shot in the face. To get closer, she would have to step in the blood and might slip. She would also leave footprints.

Not a good idea.

If he'd been shot from the front, why was he lying face down? Had the killer or killers turned him over to search him?

Calista took shallow breaths, trying to minimise the stench.

The flat was sparsely furnished, painted white and magnolia. What little furniture there was appeared to be of the Ikea type, inexpensive and simple. The place seemed to her to resemble a short-term holiday rental.

She padded down the corridor to the only bedroom.

Another body lay face up on the double bed. That of a man, fully clothed. Bluebottles undulated on his torso. If anything, it stank worse than the living area.

Shot in the chest by the look of him. A man in his forties, overweight, unshaven.

She'd seen him before, but when and where?

Calista needed air. She needed to breathe.

She fled, running for the front door and out onto the step outside, taking in a lungful of air the moment she was out. She realised she was dripping with sweat. Her hair was soaked, her arms and legs slippery with it.

SPENDTHRIFT had returned, along with a French municipal police officer, to the top of the steps. They stared at her, as surprised to see Calista in her current state as she was startled to see them.

'Two,' she said, holding up two fingers. 'There are two of them. Both shot dead.'

· · · ·

THE POLICE OFFICER asked for identification, and Calista said, truthfully, that she'd left her passport at her hotel's reception. He wrote down her name and asked for the name of the hotel but otherwise seemed satisfied. He gave her a card and asked her to attend the address on it the next morning for an interview about what had occurred. She should ask for an Inspector Couture. She must on no account leave Nice until then.

The flat and its neighbouring properties were soon surrounded by police, their patrol cars flashing blue lights, exclusion tape set up, and neighbours being questioned. A forensics team trudged up the steps into the property in white, hooded coveralls, masked, and with blue overshoe covers and gloves, carrying white cases. And the pathologist? Presumably, everyone was waiting for him or her.

Calista wasn't happy. She fidgeted, arms across her chest, turning this way and that, bothered by the possibility that the media would arrive any moment and that her face might be caught on camera, something she needed to avoid. Little by little, she moved away from the building, crossing the street, standing in the shade like any inquisitive onlooker outside the police tape, gawping at the crime scene.

In the general ruckus, she'd told SPENDTHRIFT — without being overheard, thanks to the crackle of police radios — that they didn't know each other, they'd met by chance, thanks to his copy of *Private Eye*, that they'd left the cafe together and on hearing a cat howling in distress, she'd followed the sound, climbed the steps and smelled human decay. SPENDTHRIFT — Godfrey, as he called himself — had found the door unlocked, and she'd gone inside as the cat fled.

End of story. It was true, as far as it went.

After a hot shower, much scrubbing to get rid of the stench and a change of clothing back at the hotel, Calista wrote up her report and strolled out again, down to the seafront and the Promenade des Anglais.

She was still black.

The splendid Hotel Negresco had a tiny front garden bordered by a hedge, and it faced the street and the sea. There was just enough room for a single table and two chairs where Calista sat down. A tall, lone palm towered overhead. Opposite, on the far side of the road, was a blue-and-white bench, one of several along the pavement, matching the blue balustrade above the seashore. The palm marked this as her destination and the site of her dead letter box.

She ordered an espresso and took her time drinking it. A couple of large American tourists in shades and identical Tilly sun hats — hardly required in November — waddled past Calista and into the hotel, dragging identical white, wheeled suitcases. No one approached the bench. No one sat down on it or stood at the balustrade close to it.

No cars, no scooters, no bikes slowed or stopped next to it.

Better still, no one showed any interest in Calista.

She paid for the coffee and, watching out for traffic, ran across the dual carriageway, sat on the bench and waited a minute. Inserting the thumb-drive into a cavity between the wooden bench and the iron frame took seconds. She sat there for a while, admiring the view, watching yachts and fishing boats.

In Calista's opinion, she had had nothing worth reporting, but report she must. Those were her orders. She'd met SPENDTHRIFT, who'd taken her to the flat associated with the phone number. The two dead men she discovered had so far not been identified by the French police. The whereabouts of the person named Costa weren't known. The flat did not seem to have been otherwise disturbed or ransacked. What else was there to say?

• • • •

THE FOLLOWING MORNING, Inspector Couture invited Calista to sit, took from her the fake passport in the name of Shatz, thumbed through it without discernible interest, and asked someone who appeared to be a civilian assistant to photograph it. While this was happening, Couture sat back in his office chair and looked at Calista across his desk without speaking. It was a look neither friendly nor hostile, but a frank and neutral inspection, if anything a little bored. Which was the best Calista told herself she could hope for in the circumstances.

'The man you were with —'

'Godfrey, you mean?'

'Is that his name?'

'That's what he calls himself.' Calista gave what she thought was her best imitation of a Gallic shrug.

'You know this Godfrey?'

'No. Not at all. We met yesterday for the first time.'

'Where?'

'A cafe at the port.'

'You planned to meet there?'

'No. It was by chance.'

'Tell me.'

'We happened to sit outside the cafe at separate tables, and I noticed he had an English magazine, which I like. I buy it sometimes. I asked him if it was the latest edition. He said it was months old. He then asked if we could talk, for he missed speaking English, or so he said.'

'What's his family name? Do you know?'

'No.'

Couture grunted. 'What do you know about him?'

'Nothing, other than that he told me he lives here and is retired.'

'That's it?'

Calista nodded.

'You don't know his family name?'

'No.'

'And what were you both doing at the flat?'

Calista told her story, keeping it as brief as possible.

'This Godfrey did not go inside the apartment with you?'

'No. He couldn't. He was sick outside. In the street. The smell —'

'Ah. I see.'

Couture handed back her passport.

'May I ask a question, Inspector?'

'Please.' He took off his glasses and rubbed his eyes.

'Who were those people, and why were they killed?'

'We have still to investigate, but so far, it looks like some settling of scores by rival gangs — over money, over drugs. Who knows? We have to wait for the DNA test results.' Now, it was Couture who performed a Gallic shrug, the genuine article this time.

'They were shot?'

'They were both shot, yes.'

'Thank you. It's really none of my business.'

Couture gave Calista another long look as if trying to weigh her words and decide how he should categorise her, into which pigeonhole of humanity he should place her. As a police officer, she thought, he must deal with all kinds, all the many variations from saintly to evil. He seemed neither hostile nor friendly but disinterested. They probably shared a rather negative view of humanity, Calista thought, namely that the majority were both greedy and stupid.

He rose to his feet, and she followed suit.

'You return to London today?'

'That's right, I do.'

'But Godfrey stays here. His family name is Mahoney. He's resident in France. Did you know?'

'I think he said something of the sort.'

'Did he tell you he cannot go back to the UK?'

'No, he didn't. Why?'

'Because he would go to jail for many years, I think.'

Calista glanced at the police officer but said nothing.

'I wish you a safe journey, Ms Shatz.'

'Thank you.'

He went with her to the door and opened it, but he held it halfway, forcing Calista to pause.

'Oh, by the way, Ms Shatz. I meant to ask — does the name Jean Martin mean anything to you?'

Calista blinked, pouted as if thinking hard, shook her head. 'No.'

'Otherwise known as Erich Karscher? Ring a bell, maybe?'

'No, I'm sorry. I've never heard of either name.'

'Fine. It's still to be confirmed, as I said, but it seems one of the men in the flat was a French citizen named Jean Martin. He also went by his original name of Erich Karscher. The one you found lying on his back in the bedroom, in fact. He visited your country very recently.'

'And the other one?'

'We don't yet know. But we will.'

Chapter 19

L ondon and Gosport, 2005
On graduating from Sussex University with a surprising First in Modern Languages, Bridie isn't certain what she wants to do. She does know she wants to travel. Beyond that, she's unsure. Yes, of course, she wants to earn a living so she can have her own place, even if it means sharing. Her parents aren't so well off they can buy her a flat all to herself. She keeps working part-time at a local Marks & Spencer food outlet while she ponders her future. She lives at home and does not as yet have a steady boyfriend. The last one she sacked at uni for cheating on her, and while she felt bruised by the betrayal, she didn't care for him that much and recovered quickly.

After the stress of the Finals, the chance to waste time is exhilarating at first, from endless browsing in bookshops, long walks, going to the cinema and pub with a couple of her old school friends, to drinking coffee and reading in her favourite coffee shop. These are the small pleasures of life she's missed while studying her butt off for her degree, and it's wonderful to reconnect with old pals.

But as weeks fly by, she feels bored, aimless, and guilty at her own indolence.

The phone call from Professor Roger Trent at Sussex is a surprise. He's never been her professor. She's known him only vaguely. Bridie went to a couple of his lectures, and they met socially. He's a history lecturer and department head, well-liked, and is said to have a brilliant future ahead of him. He congratulates her and asks her about her plans. She blurts out that she doesn't have any. She's thought about publishing...and then she remembers to congratulate him on his professorship.

'Have you considered the Foreign Office?'

'I can't say I have, no.'

'With your languages, I would have thought they'd snap you up. You want to travel, don't you?'

How does he know that? Perhaps, he's assumed all students want to, or perhaps she mentioned it when they met at a faculty party. She doesn't remember.

'I'm not very diplomatic, to be honest, professor. Kind of you to suggest it, but I don't think I'd be much good trying to explain, let alone support, a British foreign policy I find somewhat wanting.'

Understatement of the year.

'Of course, I understand, but I think they'd find a place for you in which you might well thrive.'

That's it.

The unsolicited call is forgotten by the time a brown envelope flutters onto the doormat, containing a single sheet of paper printed with the Foreign and Commonwealth Office letterhead, inviting Ms Bridget Connor to an interview at Carlton Gardens. There's an illegible scrawl of a signature and a telephone number to call.

She goes. Well, why the hell not? She's curious.

Bridie takes her passport with her as requested.

A young woman not much older than herself opens the door of the elegant Nash terrace a few minutes before the appointed hour. She introduces herself as Jenny and welcomes Bridie into a large, high-ceilinged room with four tall sash windows overlooking St James's Park. Jenny invites her to take a seat on an old leather sofa. Well-thumbed copies of *Country Life*, *The Spectator* and the previous day's *Financial Times* lie on a glass-topped coffee table.

Twenty minutes later, a Mr Jones bustles in, clutching what appears to be a file and apologising for having kept his visitor waiting. He is a small, middle-aged man with an enormous nose and a comb-over in a nondescript, off-the-peg navy suit and rumpled shirt with cuffs that almost cover his pale hands. His shoes look shabby and are in need of a polish.

Bridie hands over her passport. She's asked to read and, unless she has any objection, to sign a form, classified secret and which turns out to be the Official Secrets Act. She signs with a biro supplied by Mr Jones and is handed a folder containing thirty-six laminated pages, and she is asked once again to read them in his presence.

The folder explains what a government department called the Secret Intelligence Service is, and what it does. It sets out the selection process and describes what it calls enhanced positive vetting. It lays out the SIS career path, starting with a training course of six months' duration, then a succession of three-year postings, starting in London and alternating between home and abroad, and culminating with retirement at the relatively young age of fifty-five.

The pay isn't brilliant, Bridie notes, but it's pretty much what she thinks can be expected from the civil service, though perhaps a little better given the nature of the work. Anyway, fifty-five is a long way off, and she can worry about it later.

Mr Jones explains that the inadequate pension reflects the view that officers retiring at fifty-five are expected to turn to the private sector to find further work, at least until what is regarded as the normal retiring age of sixty-five. What, wonders Bridie, would that amount to? Security officer for British Aerospace or perhaps BP? How delightful. A marketing executive for Thales or sales manager at Raytheon? Missiles R Us — great! Assistant to the Assistant Security Adviser to the Sultan of Oman or the royal family of Bahrain? Jones has a few questions, which Bridie thinks she answers with confidence. That's that. Her passport is returned.

Bridie receives another letter a few days later, similar to the first, ordering rather than inviting her to a second interview, this time before a board of some kind. It means she has plenty of time to think about what she's doing. Does she really want to be a spy? She isn't sure what being a spy involves, though she's pretty sure that acts of deceit and dishonesty are almost certain to come into it, no doubt in the name of the national interest, whatever that might be, so it might be rather fun and just the sort of thing she could carry off without too much difficulty.

· · · ·

TRAINEES FOR THE LATEST IONEC course — No 97, starting in May, 2005 — are invited to present their passports at the entrance before being shepherded through the security gates up by fast lifts to the top floor of the new-ish SIS headquarters in London, where they gather in a conference room next to the director-general's office. This part of the building has deep carpeting — Bridie thinks it's the colour of dark honey — to match the wood-panelled walls. It has a hushed, sombre feel like a five-star hotel. She and the other eleven 'students' eye one another with not unfriendly curiosity as they crowd in and find chairs for themselves around a long, polished table roughly the shape of a coffin.

Bridie notes she's the only woman among the twelve student spies, and that she seems to attract more stares and glances than anyone else.

Not only are all the others male but also white and, by the look of them, probably middle class with possibly one exception — a hoodie-wearing nerd. *Fuck 'em.*

The two course instructors are serving SIS officers known as TD12 and TD11. TD12, the senior of the pair, introduces himself as Tom Gowers, large, florid, easygoing and sympathetic in manner, wearing a shirt that never stays tucked in and a colourful tie permanently askew. A good listener, is Bridie's impression, and a lot smarter than he appears. He likes a drink, does Tom. She can smell it on his breath despite the mints he chews. His 2ic, TD11, is Andrew Cornwall, short and compact, bearded and fit, a long-distance runner by the look of him. When there's talking to be done, he seems to be the one to do most of it.

The highlight of this welcoming session is an introductory talk by 'C'.

First, over weak, lukewarm tea and ginger biscuits, TD11 briefs them on the training, on the what and where and when and how. SIS has fifty-five overseas stations at this time, most staffed by one or two Intelligence Officers (IOs) and usually aided by an assistant. Stations in Washington, Brussels, Vienna, Paris, Berlin, Moscow, and Beijing have more staff, obviously, so too the Stations in those places with fossil fuel interests— Caracas, Lagos and Riyadh — to name just three, and these might have as many as a dozen IOs. TD11 says he has a few security matters to mention. Yes, live-in partners can and should be told the truth in general terms, but no one else. The trainees' cover for the duration, should they need it in the face of prying friends, neighbours, one-night stands, and anyone else, will be the FCO in Charles Street.

For now, and the foreseeable future, they are junior diplomats.

• • • •

AS FOR 'C', HE IS A surprise, at least to Bridie. He might well possess worldly gravitas, a weighty, idiosyncratic character with an intellect to match, someone with presence, but she initially mistakes the old man who shuffles in with dandruff on his shoulders and odd socks on his feet for a clerical assistant or misplaced doorman. He doesn't inspire confidence. He seems confused. He mumbles, looks down or away. He appears to have passed the retirement age by a decade or two. He's shy, Bridie realises. Not that Sir Stephen Saunders lacks experience in the field as an agent handler. Deputy chief of station in Vienna, chief of station in Delhi and then Controller Eastern Europe have marked his ascent.

He speaks in a gravelly voice to the newbies without notes but interrupts himself to clear his throat several times as if he's forgotten what he's about to say next.

'Welcome. Congratulations to you all at the start of your careers with our Service, and I wish you every success at the start of IONEC '97.

'We're a small service, tiny if you judge us solely by our numbers. We specialise in one aspect of intelligence that some of our rivals, allies and critics may regard as archaic, unfashionable, time-consuming, and in this digital age, extremely costly.

'I'm referring to HUMINT — human intelligence. We gather secret intelligence from people who have the access we need to help secure this country's safety and well-being, and to assist government in formulating policies to that end. It's one thing to estimate a potential adversary's capabilities, but another entirely to know their *intentions*. To do that, we need to *position* our people close to decision-makers. We work closely with our partners, the Security Service, and of course, GCHQ. You will get to know both in the course of your duties.

'SIS is global in its reach. To that end, our most important foreign partner is, of course, the Central Intelligence Agency, and this is likely to remain so for the foreseeable future. It's a partnership that has withstood immense changes, but despite ups and downs, it remains a steadfast alliance. We also work with our opposite numbers across Europe, in NATO and the European Union.

'Afghanistan and Iraq are among our current priorities. The terrorist threat has taken the number one spot previously occupied by the Cold War, and it's obvious to you all why that is. The world changes, and we have to change with it, just as our customers in the UK government must change their requirements for intelligence. Now if you have questions —'

Hands shoot up at once all around the table. Only the former Guards officer, Sebastian Marin, doesn't seem inclined to ask anything but sits back, crosses his arms and yawns. TD12 smiles. TD11 looks nervous.

Thomas Avery, who would prove to be a future 'C' and Bridie's boss, gets the first nod.

'You say we're a global Service, Sir Stephen. Why? The UK isn't an empire any longer, at least I hope it isn't. We no longer rule the waves and the sun set long ago. Why does SIS need a presence at all in the Asia-Pacific region or Latin America, for example?'

The question wins a fleeting smile from the boss.

'Thank you for your question — Thomas, isn't it? The Service exists to fulfil the requirements of the UK government. They might include a requirement for intelligence on oil pricing, or it could be Beijing's intentions in Hong Kong or towards Taiwan, the increased smuggling of illegal narcotics in the Caribbean, or unrest in Venezuela. Our customers wouldn't be happy if we shut up shop across swathes of the world and ignored the requirements of ministers. And I should mention that Australia and New Zealand are our staunchest allies in the Asia-Pacific region. Remember, we still have a seat on the UN Security Council, and that counts for a good deal of our global outlook. We do carry some responsibility as a result.'

Not wholly convincing, is Bridie's thought.

Next is Kenneth Roberts, the only trainee not in jacket and tie but a hoodie. He sprawls in his seat and seems to avoid looking up at 'C' when he asks his question. Instead, he frowns at the pencil he's holding.

'Why the stress on secret intelligence, yeah? Open-source intelligence is just as important, if not more so given the advances in technology, for example open-source satellite imaging. Like, the media produce tons of useful information every day, provided it's sifted and analysed. This cloak-and-dagger stuff is kinda outdated, doncha think?'

'I agree with you on the first part, Kenneth. Absolutely right. It just so happens that we specialise in secret intelligence, but that doesn't mean we would denigrate or ignore the vast resources publicly available. You make a good point.'

Bridie's turn.

'If the SIS contribution is so important, Sir Stephen, why then did SIS fail to predict the 1979 Soviet invasion of Afghanistan, the 1982 Argentine seizure of the Falklands, and the 9/11 attack on the twin towers in New York? And perhaps you could also say something about the SIS role in the flawed intelligence used to justify our invasion of Iraq?'

'C' clears his throat behind his fist. 'Well, thank you, um, Bridget. Interesting question. Who says we did fail in the instances you mention? Do you have an authoritative source for those assertions? Has it perhaps occurred to you that an intelligence service may indeed provide a succession of warnings to government of an impending or likely event, only for the advice to be ignored or simply not read by the ministers responsible for taking possible preventive action? Sometimes ministers and their advisers don't always understand the implications of the reports they receive from us. We can't *make* people listen.'

Bridie's hand is up again. She hates it when a question is answered with more questions. It isn't just evasive. It's downright dishonest. 'Supplementary question, if I may, sir. Are you saying that SIS did, in fact, provide timely warning of those events I mentioned? And that SIS was aware of the flawed nature of the intel cited by government in its decision to go to war in Iraq?'

Is she imagining it, or has she drawn dirty looks from some of her fellow trainees? Both TD12 and TD11 seem embarrassed, shifting uneasily on their feet, and even Sir Stephen appears put out, looking down and adjusting his spectacles with the fingers of his right hand. He coughs yet again. He appears to frown as he exchanges words with TD12. Bridie watches as his lips move. Did he just say, 'That's quite enough'? The Q&A session is curtailed right then, after only four questions, and 'C' turns away from the lectern, giving his audience a parting wave and a lopsided smile as he totters away.

Bridie realises she will not get an answer to her supplementary question. She's gone too far. Overstepped the mark.

'We'll meet again soon,' says Sir Stephen over his shoulder, and he's gone, followed by a flustered TD12.

Bridie tells herself she's fucked up already, before the course has even begun.

Oh, hell. What have I done now?

• • • •

THE FOLLOWING DAY, Bridie and her fellow trainees set off for the mysterious Fort Monckton near Gosport on the south coast. The dark green minibus creeps through the wet streets of Portsmouth, passing through pools of sodium light as TD12 hunches forward in the driving seat, clearing the vapour off the windscreen from time to time with a bare hand while TD11 beside him bends forward over a map on his knees, a spare hand clutching a list of twelve names and twelve Portsmouth pubs. The mood in the bus is cheerful, the trainees happy to be out and about with a fun exercise ahead of them, code named IDEAL STRANGER.

Bridie isn't quite so euphoric. She worries they have had little time to prepare. She needs a plan, and fast. She doesn't know Portsmouth; none of them do. They've barely thrown their kit into their rooms at the Fort and had a look at the place before they are summoned outside into the drizzle sweeping the central courtyard where the minibus waits, coughing diesel fumes. The details of the task are only explained once they've left, rattling over the filled-in moat by means of the wooden drawbridge — the original bridge, they are told, as if they are tourists off for a sight-seeing tour — and heading along the coast to Portsmouth's sprawl of city lights.

Cash, in the form of tenners, is dished out by TD11.

'If you want to spend your own dosh, so be it,' says TD11. 'But I wouldn't advise it. Your job is to get what you need as quickly as you can and clear out. Twenty quid should be plenty.'

They pull up outside a city pub. Nothing special, Bridie thinks. Plain, small windows covered in wire mesh, a mansard roof, dirty, whitewashed wall. Probably 1970s vintage, with interior decor to match. And the name? Mizzen and Main, though there's nothing in the least nautical about its appearance.

'Kenneth, this is your stop.' Roberts slides the door open and jumps out without a word, pulling his hoodie up over his head and jogging to the entrance, dodging the puddles as he goes. There are half a dozen cars parked outside. Not much of a crowd, then.

TD12 drives on.

'Bill, you're next.' His destination looks to Bridie like a rather fancy mock Tudor gastropub. The Gown and Mitre, black and gilt lettering illuminated with downlights, no doubt with inflated prices to match, complete with flower baskets hanging outside, only without flowers at this time of year. A Jaguar SUV and a Range Rover stand opposite, parked up on the kerb. Bridie watches Bill pull his raincoat over his head. The former RAF pilot is going to need more than a measly twenty quid before he's done winning hearts and minds.

So it goes, one after another, they vanish into the rain.

Bridie is second last out. She checks her watch: 20:18, which means she has just under two hours to complete her task before the minibus rolls up again to collect her. She still has no plan.

The place is fake in every way, a pastiche of a high-end lounge bar in a casino. Fake hunting and maritime prints on fake wood panelling under fake ceiling fans, loads of fake brassware everywhere, a horrible, swirly carpet of many colours, enough to make anyone dizzy, and fake leather chairs at varnished tables. Must have cost a pretty penny. There aren't many customers, but Bridie focuses her attention on the only group, half a dozen young people chattering and laughing at the bar, men and women in their late teens and early twenties is her guess, probably undergraduate students.

One bespectacled youngster, maybe two or three years younger than Bridie, is drinking beer out of a pint glass, and he is too engrossed in what his friends are saying to watch himself. An easy mark. Bridie steps in closer as if on her way to get herself a drink, and accidentally on purpose uses her elbow to knock the hand holding the beer, spilling it down the drinker's jeans.

'Oh, I am terribly sorry. That was *so* clumsy of me. Christ. Entirely my fault.' She asks the publican for tissues or a towel and tries with both to mop the lad's pants, but the fellow only laughs, embarrassed, pushing Bridie away and saying not to worry. But Bridie isn't having it, oh no. She keeps apologising and orders another round of whatever it is he's been drinking to make amends.

'And what about your friends?' Bridie notes the two women are sipping soft drinks, Coca-Cola or Pepsi by the look of it, and two males are drinking halves of lager. She can just cover that and a half pint for herself, with some change left in reserve, but anything more, and she'll have to pay for it herself.

It does the trick. Bridie joins the group without being invited, smiles and introduces herself as Joanna. They don't seem to mind at all. The questions she expects are not long in coming, though.

One of the students — if what's what she is — says she is Clio, and, indicating her friend, introduces Rachel. What does Joanna do? She works for an independent film company, First Trident Pictures. In Portsmouth? No, London, she replies, but scoping Portsmouth for a documentary. No, she's not a producer, nor is she the director, sadly; nothing so grand as that — she researches places, looks for suitable shoots according to the script, draws up plans for any external sets and matches them with the actors and extras they'll need. No, there isn't much money in it; it isn't a big-budget thing, but Netflix UK is already keen.

And yes, extras have a fixed daily rate agreed with their union. Are they interested, perhaps? She can't promise anything at this stage, but she's going to need a couple of dozen when the time comes. They are. All of them. 'Hell,' says Ben, 'we're students, for fuck's sake! What do you expect with the huge fucking loans we have? We'll do anything for a few quid. Well, almost anything.' Ben is reading architecture at Exeter, Rachel art and design at Portsmouth, Clio psychology also in the city, and Stan, who had lost most of his beer all over his jeans, is studying civil engineering.

'Well, in that case,' Bridie says, frowning, 'If you really mean it, I'd better have your names, mobile numbers, WhatsApp if you have it, and residential addresses so Trident can send you the bumf in the post. It might be a few weeks yet. How does that sound? You do realise they'll probably only want you for two or three days at most. You can tell your friends, too, of course. Oh, almost forgot — for payment purposes, it would help if you have your passport or national insurance numbers handy. But it's not compulsory!'

Rachel points to Stan. 'C'mon, Stan, you're the only one of us who's organised. Give the lady a pen.' Stan produces a biro. Clio tears a page out of a notebook she's carrying in a coat pocket. They put their drinks down on a table and take turns with pen and paper, writing down their details, looking over one another's shoulders, the women with their arms around each other, making fun of their entries and giving one another a great deal of unsought advice amid gales of laughter. Two have their passport details, and the rest write down their national insurance numbers. None protests at this invasion of privacy, to Bridie's surprise.

Stan also insists on buying Bridie a round this time, with just twenty minutes to go.

Clio moves around the group and stands next to Bridie. She asks how Bridie got into the film business. Video business, actually, and by accident. She'd messed up at university, getting a poor second in English Literature at Glasgow, one of those courses the government considers useless and wants to scrap (lots of heads shake along with mutterings about the fucking Tory fascists), and then, Bridie continues, one eye on the fake antique grandfather clock in the corner, quite by accident she drifted into a job stacking shelves at M&S, which, she hastens to add, she hated, and then someone had asked her at a drinks party if she'd like to help out with researching a video project in Bradford of all places, and here she is on the next project, as assistant to the director, in sunny Portsmouth...

Two minutes.

With Stan's pen and on another scrap of Clio's notepaper, Bridie writes her fake name, Joanna Masters, a fake email address and an old mobile number that no longer functions, or at least she hopes it doesn't. She's fulfilled her task and more by the time she hears the fort's green minibus turn up. Two sets of names and addresses would have sufficed, but four is a positive bonanza.

The best of the lot, as it turns out.

Bridie tells herself she's sorry about the deceit and even more sorry that she's had to say goodbye, gullible though they are. She's enjoyed their company even while whoring for the British Empire.

How wonderful to be so innocent, so trusting in the honesty of a stranger.

Chapter 20

Woking, Surrey, England, 11:37, November 14

'Would you like a mask?'

'I'm fine, thanks,' said Septimus.

The pathologist turned to Bernie. 'And you, sir?'

Bernie shook his head, but Septimus could tell his companion wasn't that sure.

O'Neill was a tall, spindly man with huge ears who chatted away as the general's remains were decanted from the refrigerator to a gurney by two assistants, one male and one female, both in long rubber aprons. He reminded Septimus of Roald Dahl's giant in *The BFG*. O'Neill himself unzipped the white body bag all the way down to the toes, revealing a head and body not unlike his own — lean, tall, bony. Only, this one was very dead, and Septimus thought it was like something carved out of a block of candle wax and so pale it was almost translucent under the harsh white light.

Septimus and Bernie had had to wait until this morning to visit. Only at the last minute, and just before setting off the previous evening, had they discovered that the Woking morgue closed at 5 p.m. on weekdays.

O'Neill explained. 'The son identified his father's remains early this morning. I'll be starting the autopsy just as soon as you're both done, and I hope to get it finished by teatime. It's pretty straightforward, or appears to be, and I should have the paperwork completed by close of play today.'

Septimus had seen many bodies in his time. He should have got used to it by now, but it didn't get any easier; rather the opposite. He'd brought along a small plastic tub of mentholated Vick's Vaporub, and he'd spread some of it on the tip of a forefinger, and he used it to smear the gap between his upper lip and his nostrils. He'd offered the tub to Bernie, who'd shaken his head. Bernie was probably regretting it by now if the ashen pallor of his face was any indication.

The white tiles, the harsh strip lighting, the drains in the floor and the gleaming metal instruments were nauseating enough even without the corpse and the smell of decomposition that seemed to attach itself to everything.

'I can't tell you gentlemen anything officially as yet,' O'Neill said, 'but unofficially, I think you can see for yourself. It seems he was stabbed with great force in the chest. You see the wounds?' O'Neill glanced at his visitors. 'You can come closer. He won't bite, not now. You see?' He pointed at each one.

Bernie did not take up the invitation, but Septimus did so and leaned over the gurney to see better. There were four wounds — puncture marks — evenly spaced out across the chest. They looked a little like insect bites. The flesh around each was crusted with dried blood and discoloured like grey bruises.

Refrigeration slowed the process of decay but did not stop it. The same went for the smell.

Bernie frowned. 'What caused the wounds?'

'A garden fork recovered at the scene was consistent with the injuries. The steel prongs were around ten inches long and 3.5 inches apart. If so, then whoever wielded the fork as a weapon did so with great force, perhaps holding the shaft with both hands and taking a run at his victim,' O'Neill demonstrated what he meant with an imaginary garden implement, then continued, 'and maybe gripping it under his elbow at the same time, a bit like a bayonet on the end of a rifle. If either of you has ever experienced the thrill of bayonet practice, you'll know what I mean. Considerable strength is needed to break through the ribs. You see? The assailant must surely have charged at the victim, who was found on his back with the fork implanted deep in his chest.'

'So that was the cause of death?'

'I'll only know when we open him up, but I'm pretty sure we'll find that the prong furthest to the right — on his left — punctured the heart. Others may have done so, and one at least probably penetrated a lung, but he died so quickly, I would suggest, that it must have been his heart. If you wait around, I'll be able to tell you. You can watch if you wish.'

O'Neill picked up a circular saw. Bernie groaned.

• • • •

'WHAT DO YOU THINK?'

Bernie drove. Septimus enjoyed watching the Surrey countryside sweep past and let his thoughts flow without trying to control them, seeing them come and go, as it were, without getting caught up in them.

'Not a lot as yet,' Septimus said. He didn't want to talk.

Bernie glanced at him. 'Still think it's our man? Not the same MO, though. This was brutal. It's one thing to shoot someone at five hundred yards, another to stab him face-to-face, don't you think? We can't be sure there's only one perpetrator. There may be a group. That CCTV image showed a man with a baseball cap, shades and a beard — hell, it could have been anyone.'

Septimus didn't respond, and he didn't pay attention to Bernie's endless prattling. Any fool could have opinions, and unfortunately, most did. Opinions didn't matter. Facts mattered. He was thinking about Bernie's little Toyota Aygo and wondering why he'd chosen such a small vehicle. Perhaps it wasn't his. He could have borrowed it. It might belong to his wife, assuming he had one. Bernie had pushed the seat back as far as it could go to give his long legs as much room as possible, but he still looked cramped. His head almost touched the roof.

A few minutes later, Septimus said, 'We might learn more at the crime scene.'

'I hope so,' Bernie said, and they lapsed once more into silence.

After a little while, Bernie glanced at Septimus. 'You married?'

Septimus didn't respond.

'Kids?'

No response.

Bernie wouldn't give it up. 'No family, then?'

'I don't do personal,' Septimus growled after a pause.

Bernie finally shut up.

The place looked deserted as they drove up, Bernie halting the car on the gravel outside the front door, but before they could get out, a young, uniformed police officer appeared from around the side of the cottage where there was an enormous clump of rhododendrons.

PC Leonard was an immense man, useful in a riot, Septimus thought. But it soon became clear he was not the most intelligent of coppers. He'd been left on his own to guard the murder scene. As Bernie and Septimus followed Leonard back the way he'd come, they noticed an old child's swing attached to the branch of an ancient oak moving back and forth. It seemed that Leonard had amused himself by sitting on it — it was a wonder that the constable hadn't snapped the ropes or the wooden seat, or both.

Leonard waved a hand at the police tape and the conservatory. 'All yours,' he said.

'Forensics are finished with the crime scene?'

Leonard looked flustered and seemed unsure how to reply to Bernie's question. At last, he said, 'Sure. Think so, yeah. Yeah, I'm sure.' Leonard nodded his head and contrived to shake it at the same time, as if trying to convince himself, while backing away and almost tripping over a flower bed.

They went inside, Septimus leading, Bernie ducking his head. At the far end they saw the glass panels of the conservatory had been cracked, and one had been shattered, the fragments of glass thrown out onto the grass. Septimus walked to the end and bent forward, hands on his knees. If he wasn't mistaken, there were drops of blood — a spray of dark matter — on one of the broken seed boxes.

Bernie went back out again, but Septimus stayed behind for a minute or two. He tried to absorb what he was seeing, to reconstruct what had occurred. He pictured the old soldier turning to face the intruder, the sudden charge, the general skewered and forced back, falling against the glass as he died. There were the footprints, those of the general's wellies mixed up with what looked like the pattern of the soles from the attacker's footwear, probably trainers. The latter must have taken a run at the general — he could make out the stride of the killer coming from the open door, then they'd been close together, a confusion of feet as the fork was driven home, and the old man had tumbled back.

Dead in moments.

Why?

Did the general know his assailant? Did he recognise his murderer?

As he went out again, Septimus saw the back door to the house was open. It was a stable door painted white with black ironwork.

He turned to Leonard. 'Anyone at home?'

Leonard shrugged. 'Nah. No one.'

'Who's been inside?'

'Not me.'

'But your colleagues have, right? And forensics?'

'Think so, yeah.'

'You think so.'

It took a while to sort out. Septimus spoke by cellphone to a DS Arbuthnot at Woking, number two in the murder investigation, but only once Arbuthnot had assured himself that Septimus was who he said he was. Arbuthnot confirmed that yes, the police had indeed searched the house. Forensics had taken DNA samples and prints. They'd found the downstairs in a mess, especially the general's study — the perpetrator had beaten them to it and trashed the place. Drawers pulled out of desks and antique tables, clothes and books tossed about — whoever it was had been in a tearing hurry. Yes, the murderer seemed to have been looking for something. A laptop was missing. According to Arbuthnot, this had been confirmed by the general's twenty-eight-year-old son. But nothing else of value had been stolen. The general had a few expensive items: pictures, some solid silver cutlery and candlesticks, antiques, rugs, regimental bits and pieces. His late wife's jewellery. Credit cards were still in the victim's wallet.

Arbuthnot said there was as yet no evidence to suggest the murderer had *not* been alone.

As they got back to Bernie's car, they decided by mutual agreement to reward themselves with a detour to a traditional pub for a liquid lunch to wash the taste of the morgue out of their mouths. None of that upmarket gastro-pub nonsense, thank you very much. They headed to Farnham and the *Lamb*, which Bernie said he'd known in the past.

After some discussion, they sat outside, notwithstanding the November chill. There was some sun, and they agreed it would be easier to talk shop without being overheard.

With two pints in front of them — Spitfire for Bernie, Whitstable pale ale for Septimus — they reviewed the morning. No great conclusions were reached. But Bernie said he'd dug something up from open-source material on Ivor Brodzinski — the name linked to the Strategy Institute at Tufton Street, and to the general's new career as its marketing consultant as well as Brodzinski's donations to the election campaigns of the assassinated prime minister and opposition leader.

Septimus wanted to eat something, but the pub didn't serve food. Hadn't they sought a traditional place? He had to make do with a couple of packets of crisps.

'So tell me, Bernie.'

'He's dead,' said Bernie, reading notes on his phone. 'Ivor Brodzinski, that is. Fatal heart attack in February, 2012 at his home in Menton, France.'

'I know where Menton is. Not far from Nice and close to the Italian border.'

'Good for you,' said Bernie, who continued to read his notes. 'Both the family business and the Brodzinski Foundation are now run by his son, Leo. The old man had an interesting life. Polish, as the name suggests, fought the Nazis as a teenager, survived Warsaw, drafted into Poland's post-war communist armed forces, escaped on board a Soviet troop train with forged papers and made it to West Germany via East Berlin's Friederichstrasse by simply hopping across from one station platform to another, then Switzerland and from there to sunny South Africa.'

Bernie took a long swig of beer and continued.

'Worked on the South African Railways as the driver of steam locomotives. An occupation reserved for whites. Preached anti-communism. Staunch supporter of the South African Nationalist Party and its apartheid policy. A big man in more ways than one, becoming heavyweight boxing champion of southern Africa for three years in succession. Built up a successful chain of hardware stores and petrol stations and invested the profits in mining shares — especially gold, platinum and iron ore. First million by twenty-eight. A fan of Margaret Thatcher and invited to tea at Number Ten in the 1980s, by which time he was a billionaire. They no doubt agreed with each other that Nelson Mandela was a dangerous communist terrorist. In fact, the Iron Lady advised her apartheid pals in Pretoria that Mandela was far too dangerous to be allowed to live and should be killed.'

'Good for Brodzinski,' said Septimus, putting his head back and draining his pint glass. 'Why didn't I think of that? Work on the footplate and make a fortune by becoming a professional racist on the winning side.'

'Here's where it gets interesting. Brodzinski became the key intermediary between the white Nationalist government and Israel in the 1960s. It was never confirmed, but he was said to have had a clandestine role in the development, with Israeli help, of white-ruled South Africa's nuclear weapons program. According to media reports, South Africa built six nuclear devices by the time the project was cancelled in 1989. A seventh bomb was under construction when they ended it. For which service Brodzinski received The Grand Cross of the Order of South Africa.'

Septimus gave a low whistle. 'Wow. A top Boer gong.'

'He left South Africa after the whites-only referendum on reforming apartheid in 1992 produced a strong "yes" vote, signalling the end of white rule. He continued his business activities abroad and maintained a strong segregationist, conservative and pro-Zionist stance right up to his death. His son Leo — a member of the new global elite — seems to maintain that tradition, with properties in London, the south of France and Tel Aviv. He invests in oil exploration, mining, arms manufacturers and in new technologies, such as AI. He donates to right-wing politicians' election campaigns, mostly in Europe.'

'Good work, Bernie, thanks.'

Septimus felt his own phone twitch and rumble in his pocket. He pulled it out.

'Yes?'

He listened.

'Okay, thanks. We're on our way,' Septimus said, then slipped the phone back in his pocket, got to his feet and turned to Bernie.

'Let's go.'

'What's up?'

Septimus explained as they hurried over to the Toyota.

'That was the boss. She says it seems they've found the killer.'

'Who's they?'

'The cops. An arrest is imminent. She thought we might like to be in on it.'

'Seems? Either they have, or they haven't.'

'Whatever, Bernie. Let's get a move on.'

Chapter 21

South London, 10:10, November 13-14
Merrick wasn't a breakfast person. He accepted Andy's offer of coffee — strong, hot and black — and peeled a banana and ate it just to keep Andy company, while Andy scoffed two slices of toast and jam. They didn't speak until it was time for Merrick to leave.

'Take this, pal. I've no further use for it.'

Andy held up an old jacket — grey, lots of pockets, modelled on the American M65 combat smock.

'You sure?'

'And this.' It was a dark green beanie.

'Why?'

'Chilly morning. And I don't have any use for them.'

Merrick knew it wasn't true. Andy had apparently decided that his guest was on the run, and he wasn't wrong, which of course meant Andy knew he needed to change his appearance often, if only to confuse CCTV and police facial recognition devices. London was stuffed with thousands of both types of surveillance.

'You don't have to do this,' Merrick said.

'I'll feel better if you take 'em.'

'Then, I will, thanks.' He put on the jacket first, then tugged on the beanie.

'Keep your head down, son.'

'Will do, don't worry.' They shook hands, a firm clasp, eye-to-eye, but Andy had pushed something hard into Merrick's right hand. He could identify it by the feel: a roll of banknotes. Andy forestalled any protest on Merrick's part. 'No, don't fuckin' argue, pal. Not a word. You can pay me back when this — whatever this is — is over, okay? It's no big deal.'

'Sure.'

Over? There's only one way it'll ever be over.

Merrick slipped out the front door and heard Andy double lock it again and put on the chain. He slunk away, hands in the jacket pockets, head down. Once around the corner, he picked up the pace.

He was going home.

He caught a double-decker heading only God-knows-where across Vauxhall Bridge and two stops later jumped off, crossed the street and continued to walk.

It wasn't that cold because it was a grey, overcast day. No rain so far. His back was clear. All he could smell were petrol and diesel fumes. The air was bitter with pollution. Merrick watched the traffic on his left with the Thames, brown and sinuous at high tide, on his right. He kept a weather eye open for any repeats — vans or motorcycles that passed him more than once.

Two uniformed police officers — they seemed absurdly young to Merrick — were pulling on white gloves as they stood next to a bench by the river. A ragged figure lay there, apparently dead — from hypothermia overnight, no doubt. A gin bottle next to him.

More likely than not, a veteran like himself.

Merrick didn't slow down, but he gave them a wide berth.

No probs so far.

In a newsagent's, he bought mints and the *Daily Mirror*. He didn't look at the old guy in a vest serving him. Fifteen minutes later, Merrick doubled back one block, ducked into a greasy spoon, and without making eye contact with anyone, ordered tea, eggs, beans and sausage from the laminated menu and found a table to himself at the back so he could sit facing the entrance. He took his time eating and drinking his tea while watching the windows.

All clear.

He counted Andy's cash in his lap. A thousand in twenties. He divided the money up among his several pockets. If he was mugged at knifepoint, the bastards wouldn't get it all.

He had on him the money, keys, one burner. That was it.

Merrick continued to move east, through the City of London to the East End. He left behind glossy merchant banks, foreign exchange trading companies, equity funds, limited partnerships and wealth management firms, streets in perpetual shadow like narrow chasms between brass-plated marmoreal towers, built on tax-free black money and offshore trusts. Since the Suez debacle in '56, Britain had built a financial empire to replace the territories it lost. As long as the money kept flowing through the world's money laundering capital, whether Chinese or Russian, no one really cared where it came from or how it was made. He passed the gilded windows of posh pubs and shiny champagne bars where City traders spent their bonuses. Wankers, the lot of them. The sounds of the city: police and ambulance sirens, the scream of gulls.

Almost there.

He talked to her.

The risk is slight, love. They don't yet have a name, an address, not even a face, just a blurry figure — a white male between twenty and fifty, bearded, shades, baseball cap. One among millions. I'll be well away by the time they come knocking. Trust me, sweetheart. I'll complete the job, and then I'm out of it and headed your way.

Three more to go, that's all, and they won't have made the connection even when I'm done with the last. How could they? They've no clue. This is all I have to offer you. For your pain. For our love. For what we had, for what they took from us. For the life and future that they stole from you.

I know it's not your way. I understand that, and I respect it. But it's mine, you see, and I have to do this if I'm ever going to rest easy again. They have to pay the debt, all of them.

Merrick paused at the front door, turned to look back at the street, glanced right and left, then slid the key into the lock, pushed the door and stepped inside. He went fast, light-footed, up the wooden stairs without pause, all the way to the second floor and his cupboard, as he called it.

He stood still, mouth open, listening. The wedges he'd pushed between the door and its frame were still in place. Two Banham locks, and he was in.

Scattered junk mail, a stale smell of dust.

Once a rather beautiful Georgian townhouse, it was badly converted in the 1970s. One day, perhaps, Merrick imagined some wealthy sod restoring it by tearing up the shoddy linoleum, ripping out the partitions and wallpaper, stripping the doors and applying lime plaster to the walls.

But he wouldn't live to see it.

Merrick stood still again, tasting the air, feeling the silence as much as hearing it.

• • • •

MERRICK STRIPPED, CLIMBED into his narrow bed, wrapped himself in his duvet. It was like being surrounded by his grief, even comforted by it because it made him feel close to her. He wore his grief like a coat. Sometimes it was the low, grey cloud pressing down on London, or the shadows that seemed to follow him, or the rattle of dry leaves rolling towards him, driven by an east wind. Sometimes it was the rain, soft, drenching, almost silent.

Merrick slept for three hours, then woke with a start and lay still on his back, staring into the dark.

He accepted the grim reasoning that told him death was the end, that the universe was a cold emptiness without limit, and in death that we become part of that void.

Merrick was convinced there was no afterlife, no return, no resurrection; logically, he had to accept it, to come to terms with this bleak truth. The past was dead. He told himself not to be stupid; we were, all of us, becoming dead. It was a becoming, just as life itself was a becoming. Yet no matter how he tried to accept the obvious, he couldn't align his feelings, his instinct, with what his head told him. It was delusion, yes. It was nonsense; of course it was. It was wishful thinking, self-pity, a need, an endless thirst. It was all manner of crap, but she was still there, so close he felt her warmth, her skin on his, her fingers in his hand, the incomparable smell of her. He heard her voice, her laugh. He saw her too, sometimes, watching him, smiling, and when that happened, his gut gave a lurch, and his vision reeled with light-headedness — as if he was about to jump off a cliff.

Merrick knew she wouldn't want what he was doing, wouldn't agree with it. She'd tell him to stop, that none of it would help either of them.

It helps me, love, it really does. It's my pathetic contribution to a better world, to fucking justice. It helps me sleep.

He got up at five, still pitch-black outside, but made sure the curtains were closed and showed as little light as possible to anyone outside looking up at his window before he switched on the table lamp. He put on the heating and gave himself a careful, close shave with a new blade. He inspected the results and approved; it took years off him, he decided. He showered, pulled on clean boxers, t-shirt and socks, brushed his teeth, applied scentless deodorant.

A new man, yes?

He smiled, turned sideways and inspected his profile.

You'll do, you handsome bastard.

Merrick gathered his equipment. Screwdriver, pliers, two tops from beer bottles, wire, standard wall plug, small folding knife, electric detonator. He set them out on his folding table.

The last item was no bigger than his little finger. It had the appearance and consistency of plasticine, like something squeezed out of a bottle.

Wearing gloves, Merrick cleaned all but the detonator and the wormlike plastic material. The last two items he kept separate from each other.

His final act, after cleaning the flat and wiping down every surface and sorting out his bed, was to dress. He put on his best shirt, white and almost new, and added a navy silk tie. His only decent jacket and a pair of dark grey trousers and socks. Last were the shoes.

All his best civilian gear.

A final check in the mirror.

Good to go.

Chapter 22

Taskforce HQ, south London, 15:26, November 14

The first person Septimus saw on entering the operations room was Bridie. She stood centre stage in her dark suit, staring up at the big screen on the wall, in characteristic pose, with her right hand across her body and grasping the upper part of her left arm, which hung straight down. An oddly protective gesture, he thought. She turned her head and glanced at Septimus and Bernie with no change in her expression. She didn't so much as nod but turned back to look again at the screen.

The room, stark white and utilitarian with its grey metal desks, was crowded. Caro was there at her desk, and she raised her eyebrows and smiled at Septimus as if she was asking what they'd been up to. There were some faces Septimus didn't recognise, perhaps additions to the investigation he knew nothing about. No one spoke. The atmosphere was tense with anticipation. Bernie nodded to one stranger, who nodded back.

That same newcomer leaned over to speak quietly to Bernie without taking his eyes off the screen, but Septimus heard every word. 'Not our operation,' the man said. 'It's the Met. They had a tip-off. We're not invited to the party.'

Bernie whispered an introduction. 'Calum Shields. He's one of ours. Counter-Terrorism.'

The screen showed a north London street of mostly Edwardian terraced properties stretching up an incline with a cluster of shops near the top, including a restaurant and a florist. The target address was at the foot of the screen: 83C Attica Street, Muswell Hill, N10. Septimus saw the live video was provided by a police drone.

The feed seemed to pull back into a wide angle, taking in not just the one home and street but the entire block. It now became clear to Septimus why. Police vans approached in convoys from two directions, without flashing lights or sirens.

Septimus counted a dozen of the navy blue vehicles with unit identifier markings on their roofs.

'Is the sound on?' Bridie asked.

'It's on,' a male voice replied. 'Volume's up as far as it will go.'

Still no sound except for the whine of the drone.

Septimus watched the vans park across the approach roads, blocking them. Police officers in yellow vests disembarked and stretched tape across from one corner to another. They set up diversion signs and started turning away cars, bicycles and pedestrians.

Squads of armed, helmeted police approached the front and rear of the property, moving fast, in single file with that odd half-run, half-hobble typical of an assault team, each officer holding a weapon in the firing position and with a free hand stretched out in front, resting on the shoulder or back of the officer immediately in front.

Two muffled bangs could be heard as they took down the doors front and back.

They were in.

Septimus counted down the seconds.

He gave up at thirty-two, just as a telephone rang on one of the desks.

'It's for you.'

Bridie took it. She listened, said 'Thank you,' and handed it back to whoever it was who'd given it to her.

'Empty house,' she announced and, without further explanation, turned around and marched out, her expression still deadpan. 'Turns out the suspect is a post office worker on the night shift.'

The tension was broken by a series of expletives from those present.

'Fuckin' hell,' was Bernie's contribution.

'We'd better write up our trip,' Septimus said. 'Suggest you do the initial part about the morgue and the pathologist's comments, and I'll do the crime scene.'

Bernie scratched his head. 'Fair enough. Or could we do it the other way around?'

'Fine.'

Septimus decided the issue they must address — they could hardly avoid doing so — was whether the general had been murdered by the lone assassin, bringing the total number of kills to five. It would be hard to prove without physical evidence. The Tufton Street connection and the link to Brodzinski might be circumstantial in a court of law, but Septimus had no doubt at all, even though the MO was different.

He and Bernie had to persuade Bridie.

· · · ·

NO SOONER HAD THEY filed their report than they were summoned to Bridie's Taskforce office.

She stood behind her desk, tapping one foot with impatience when they went in, Bernie in the lead.

'Coffee, anyone?'

'Please,' said Septimus.

'Me too, boss,' said Bernie.

'Espresso okay?'

Bridie didn't wait for a response but turned away and started pushing buttons on the complicated-looking machine behind her desk.

Steam hissed; something dripped and dribbled.

The delicious smell made Septimus salivate.

He asked, 'What happened out there today?'

'Seems the Met was under pressure from our new home secretary to do something, anything. A member of the public had called in to report that he'd seen the man in the Photofit enter a neighbouring property, adding that he'd noted the same suspect coming and going over the last couple of days, mostly outside normal working hours. I'm told Special Branch was convinced the witness was authentic. They questioned him, apparently. Over the phone.'

'Brilliant,' said Septimus, taking the tiny cup. 'I hate to think what that little lark cost the London ratepayer.'

Bridie handed another cup to Bernie as she changed the subject and prepared her own coffee. 'I didn't ask you two in here to gloat over the Met's latest cock-up. I read your report, and I have to ask you both: are you absolutely sure about this retired general being his fifth victim?'

'Yes,' said Bernie with unusual firmness.

'No doubt about it,' said Septimus.

'But all you've got is a tenuous link with some rich white supremacist lunatic named Brodzinski, a dubious far-right Tufton Street outfit and FMEDF. Oh, and a certain media empire that employs former Mossad and Shin Beth operatives to spy on its rivals. And, I should add, a former head of SIS who's on the board of FMEDF, still very much alive and kicking and highly litigious — someone who'd take it amiss if his name was dragged into this in any way.'

Septimus added, 'And the aforesaid are in turn linked to our recently deceased prime minister and opposition leader.'

'Quite so. But we need more than conspiracy theories.'

Bridie did not invite her visitors to sit, so they remained standing.

'At the risk of boring both of you,' Septimus said, 'I want to draw your attention to something odd about the Armistice Day shooting. I included it in my report at the time, but I don't think I really paid enough attention to it myself. However, I think it's relevant.'

'You never bore me, Septimus,' said Bridie, throwing him her sardonic half-smile.

'Why, thank you. You probably don't remember, but the sniper rifle the assassin used on Saturday takes a magazine with five rounds. Our shooter was trained, I think to "double-tap" his targets — two rounds for each. A form of insurance, yes? He fired off four bullets at two politicians. Then he changed magazines, leaving one round in the magazine he'd been using, and replaced it with a second magazine, containing five rounds.'

'So?' Bernie frowned. 'What are you driving at?'

Septimus put his cup down on Bridie's desk. 'He intended to continue firing. It's obvious now that I think about it.'

'But he didn't,' said Bernie.

'Exactly. I suggest he had two more targets at the Cenotaph, and he'd planned to "double-tap" them in the same manner, just like the first two. The magazine attached to the rifle when I found it still contained five rounds.

'I asked myself why this was. My opinion, for what it's worth, is that he saw through his scope the defence secretary go down, and he saw the home secretary killed. He didn't need to fire again, you see, especially as every second he stayed in the roof space only increased the risk of him being killed or captured.'

'Okay,' said Bridie, 'I understand what you're saying. But, like Bernie, I have to ask you: so what?'

'My conclusion is that our mystery man had four targets that day. All in all, he's notched up five high-value kills in what, three days?'

Bridie sipped her coffee. 'And?'

'We have to make the connections between his victims quickly and draw the appropriate conclusions, or stand by and watch the bodies pile up. He's not going to take a breather until he's done. It could be six or twenty targets for all we know.

'He's got a kill list, I'm sure of it. We have to find out who they are *before* he gets to them.'

Chapter 23

Gosport, England, 2005

G Bridie works hard as an apprentice at Fort Monckton for a trade that she's no particular desire to join, let alone master, at least not at first and even then, for all the wrong reasons.

Spying has never occurred to her as a way of making a living, respectable or otherwise, yet here she is. It has never been an ambition, unlike some of her colleagues, who seem to have had a romantic attachment to the notion of becoming a 'secret agent' since childhood, perhaps as a result of reading John Buchan, Joseph Conrad, Geoffrey Household or maybe Oreste Pinto's *Spycatcher* series at school.

Bridie imagines that they, too, must have been talent-spotted. She wonders why. They seem to her such unpromising material. Some have tried other things — such as the armed forces and commerce — and have somehow fallen into this arcane world, as Bridie has herself for lack of any better ideas. Many universities have 'spotters,' as does Sandhurst and the Royal Naval College at Dartmouth, so it isn't a surprise.

That said, she decides to make the best of the opportunity thrown her way by the history professor. Nothing else seems a worthy alternative. She throws herself into it without any of the public schoolboy's pretence of macho diffidence.

If it works out, wonderful. If it doesn't, she'll have lost nothing but the time and effort she devotes to it.

Being the only female makes a difference. She stands out in a not particularly agreeable way. She knows from her secondary school and university what most males are like. Immature. Sexist. Misogynistic. Domineering. Lechers in several cases. Control freaks. In a word, arseholes.

This is no different. They stare at her tits, at her ass, her legs and everything else. They make remarks behind her back. They not only expect her to fail; they want her to fall. Demoralising her by innuendo, mockery and gossip is part of the insecure male's deliberate effort to wear her down, to secure domination over her.

Fuck them. She won't give the disgusting creeps the pleasure of witnessing her give up or get sacked.

I'll beat you at your own game, you pathetic wankers.

Running the course must take considerable planning, for Bridie notes that she and her colleagues never seem to bump into anyone else while on their way from one activity to the next. While they belong to the only IONEC course running at the time, this takes up the accommodation, dining, kitchen and teaching space of just one of three self-contained 'wings' or sections at the Fort.

Who is being trained in the other two?

Bridie doesn't know the city of Portsmouth at all when she first arrives at the Fort, but she's quick to learn the city's layout. When it comes to tradecraft, instinct tells her that if she is to be tracked in a strange town, the best thing to do for starters is to make for a department store or shopping mall until she figures out the alleys, short-cuts, backstreets, tunnels, dead-ends, no through roads, bridges, bus routes, rat-runs, railway stations and docks that punctuate every European coastal city.

Once she's on the move inside a store, the watchers' cars and motorcycles are of no use to them, and that helps create a more even playing field. Bridie is on the lookout for back exits and side entrances, which she memorises for future use. Riding escalators is an effective way to spot pursuers and stationary watchers. It's a simple matter to lure a follower to the far end of the shoe section or the back wall of an M&S food store and trap him there, forcing him, in effect, to reveal his role.

Among Bridie's favourite 'traps' for over-eager and zealous surveillance teams — composed of her fellow male trainees — are the female undergarments sections on the upper floors of Next, Peter Jones, H&M and M&S. Nothing like racks of brassieres, knickers and thongs to make her fellow male trainees feel awkward and expose them to the hostile and suspicious stares of sales staff and genuine shoppers.

She notes that the people trailing after her — sometimes they come from the front in pairs, move in parallel or occupy static posts (and they sometimes manage all three) — might change jackets and headgear but seldom bother to change their shoes and boots. They haven't the time or opportunity. So she pays attention to feet.

She discovers early on that she isn't much of a team player for role-playing as a member of a surveillance or anti-surveillance squad, following others on foot and on wheels. Bridie much prefers operating alone, and she decides she is much more inclined to be poacher than gamekeeper (ironic, given her later function). She gets a thrill from managing a car-toss in the few seconds she's invisible in a quick turn around one corner before the next. Cars aren't much of a problem; motorcycles are far harder to evade.

About half the course time is spent outside, in all weathers, by day and by night, ensuring she's not followed by countersurveillance. Bridie enjoys these outdoor sessions even if she and her aching feet are soaked by driving rain and numb with cold. Some of her colleagues, especially the ex-military, are too obvious; they stop too often to stare in shop windows — it's called 'mirroring.' They might bend down and tie their shoelaces too often, or they might take to glancing frequently over their shoulders. All obvious giveaways.

Bridie much prefers the practical work of wearing out shoe leather to shuffling paper and the theoretical, classroom lectures. She relishes surveillance, anti-surveillance and countersurveillance, making drops at dead-letter boxes and clearing them, as well as perfecting brush passes, using secret writing ink and simple concealment devices.

The Security Service sends down an experienced officer to lecture on surveillance, while an elderly and by now famous Soviet KGB defector gives a memorable talk on his breathtaking exfiltration from the Soviet Union.

Bridie enjoys the therapeutic interludes, too: the indoor and outdoor small arms ranges, using pistols and automatic weapons, the SIG Sauer 226 having replaced the Browning High-power; she's surprised to find that her weapons-handling and marksmanship are better than that of her fellow trainees. She has better reflexes, is more instinctive (and combat shooting is all instinct), faster, and never hesitates to squeeze the trigger.

She relishes the use of a replica of the SAS Regiment's 'killing house,' a new addition to the IONEC schedule, where trainee officers wear the standard black overalls for practising tactical, urban shoot-outs, their 'enemies' mingling with 'civilians' while the student officers try to take down the former and avoid maiming or killing the latter.

In the Fort's gym, they learn the basics of unarmed combat, from defence against gun and knife attacks to temporarily disabling an opponent with a simple thumb-lock or blow to the throat. Here, the 'boys' think they can teach Bridie a lesson, but discover she's quick, fit, has better reactions and has no hesitation in going in hard for throat, eyes and balls of her adversaries. Size really doesn't count when it comes to killing.

For relaxation, there are squash courts and a well-stocked bar where the trainee IOs spend most of their time at the end of the working day, joined by the ever-watchful TD11 and TD12.

• • • •

THE INITIAL COHORT of twelve IONEC trainees has been whittled down to ten. James, the former RAF pilot complete with resplendent ginger moustache, telephones TD12 one weekend to say the early starts interfere with his social life, and now that he's become engaged, he's terribly sorry but he no longer wants to work abroad. Spying isn't for him.

Ian, the modern languages graduate from Durham, has never recovered his morale after being arrested and banged up in police cells after that first exercise involving a visit to a pub to get names and contact details of customers. He was caught up in a scuffle outside while waiting to be picked up, though it wasn't his fault and no charges were pressed. He also tells the DS he detests the endless footslog around Portsmouth and thinks the surveillance and countersurveillance exercises 'silly games.'

When faced with a full day in the 'classroom,' Bridie hauls herself out of bed before anyone else and goes for a solo run, jogging over the drawbridge and passing under the commandant's flat above, and over to the local Gosport and Stokes golf course and beyond. The chill salt air wakes her up. Seeing the Fort at a distance gives her some idea of what it must have looked like since its initial construction on the orders of Henry VIII in 1545 as a simple blockhouse with artillery to protect Portsmouth and the Solent. Abandoned eleven years later, it was rebuilt as a temporary and shoddy fortification during the American War of Independence, and by fits and starts a permanent fort was completed just before the French Revolution of

1789. Despite subsequent modifications, Bridie thinks she recognises some of the original features, including the bastions and sea-facing casemates.

With six weeks still to go, they study the Whitehall 'bazaar' of intelligence products and services, and how the Service is a buyer's market in that SIS is 'demand driven.' It isn't easy to take this on board after a late and bibulous night in the Fort's pub, and Bridie almost nods off more than once during these talks.

She finds issues of structure and organisation tedious, and by the bored looks on their faces, so does everyone else. They learn about the SIS bible, the Red Book of requirements, as well as the all-important arbiter between producers and consumers of intelligence, the Joint Intelligence Committee (JIC) in the Cabinet Office. They are lectured on the importance of the JIC's Annual National Intelligence Requirements. They discuss the role of SIS requirements and production officers with the help of a senior and somewhat severe officer from London who gives her name simply as 'Moira.' The SIS doesn't develop its own requirements, of course, but it does have an element of 'push' i.e. SIS officers can advise Whitehall 'consumers' of opportunities and 'product' the latter wouldn't otherwise be aware of. Taking the initiative is possible, even desirable — subject, of course, to the necessary approvals.

SIS is described as both formally bureaucratic and informally collegial. What would Max Weber have made of it? No doubt he would have thought its organic aspect nothing but a hopeless bloody mess. Maybe he would have been right to think so.

But had KGB double-agent Kim Philby still been top dog in the counterintelligence section for Russia, he could not betray as many secrets and fellow officers and their agents as he'd done before his defection, or so the IONEC students are given to understand in a lecture from a retired Middle East Controller. The traitor would have come up against geographical 'compartmentalisation' — bulkheads or firewalls set in place largely to prevent that from happening again. Hopefully.

In counterintelligence, joint sections with MI5 — the Security Service — are nowadays more the rule than the exception. Bridie learns that the Directorate of Counterintelligence and Security, or D/CIS, responsible for both counterintelligence and counter-espionage, runs several joint SIS/MI5 sections, for example, on China (C13), Russia (C14) and Eastern Europe (C17).

Of greater practical interest to Bridie is an intriguing phenomenon known as a 'shoebox' Station. A single Intelligence officer with an encrypted laptop messaging system equipped with a satellite link can operate as a one-person Station anywhere, even on the move, and is able to respond to fast-moving developments. Bridie pays close attention to the workings of Targeting and Counterintelligence Sections (TCIs) that recruit and run agents from hard countries using VCOs — visiting case officers — especially when handling such agents outside their home turf for their own safety and for operational security. It's especially important with China and Russia, both of them hostile environments for SIS intelligence gathering.

At last, as the long, hot summer tightens its humid grip on southern England and the almost fully qualified cohort of IOs became increasingly somnolent during postprandial lectures, it's time to prepare for the grand finale: a test of their skills and knowledge.

Codename:

OPERATION SANDCASTLE

Chapter 24

Tufton Street, London, SW1, 10:28, November 15.
Sir Thomas Brownlow, a portly figure in a dark grey, three-piece suit, exited a black cab, paid off the driver and, briefcase in hand, patted down wayward wisps of grey hair. After pressing an entry buzzer, he entered an elegant, four-storey Georgian townhouse, one of several on this narrow and relatively quiet street in central London.

He bellowed a cheery 'good morning' at the lone receptionist and, without waiting for a response, made a beeline for the stairs, taking the steps two at a time. He paused at an office door on the first floor that bore his name, along with the title — in smaller, Gothic-style letters below — of the organisation for which he worked part-time, the State Strategy Institute.

He keyed in his entry code, and when the lock disengaged with a click, opened the door and walked in, shrugged off his jacket, which he hung on a hanger on the back of the door, dropped his leather briefcase on the polished desk alongside a computer terminal and strode over to the window.

With one hand, he parted the blast curtains so he could look down at the pavement. He watched another cab pull up and smiled at the sight of his visitor hurrying to the front door.

Sir Thomas remained standing, looking out at leaves bowled along the street by gusts of winter wind.

When there was a knock a couple of minutes later, he went over to the door and opened it.

'I've only just got here myself,' he told his visitor.

'So I'm not late,' said an American voice.

'No, not at all, my dear chap. Come in, take a pew.' Sir Thomas turned away and indicated with a wave of his hand where his visitor should sit. Then he walked around his desk, shot his cuffs, and smiled at his visitor.

A framed, colour photograph of the king hung on the wall behind the desk. On the opposite wall was a signed photograph of Donald Trump.

Sir Thomas sat down.

There was a blinding flash, a deafening bang, followed by a fusillade of smoke and flying debris.

Witnesses would later liken the sound to both barrels of a double-barrelled shotgun fired simultaneously.

The explosion blew out the office window. The diaphanous anti-blast curtains worked in reverse; instead of protecting the office interior and its occupants from flying glass from an external detonation, they caught a hurricane of glass slivers as they flew outwards, preventing them from raining down on the heads of any pedestrians who might happen to linger on the pavement below.

Sir Thomas bled out in seconds.

His visitor survived unscathed, aside from a few superficial lacerations, though he was in a state of shock and quite deaf. He was also drenched in the blood, abdominal tissue and faeces of his British host.

· · · ·

'I WOULDN'T GO IN THERE if I were you, sir.'

'You wouldn't, Detective Inspector? But you're not me, are you?'

'It's like an abattoir in there.'

The faecal stink was unmistakable.

'Thanks for the concern, but as you see, I've got my noddy suit on, my gloves, booties and my mask. And I've been in many abattoirs of one sort or another.'

'Don't say I didn't warn you, is all.'

'Appreciated. Now be so kind as to move the fuck out of my way.'

Septimus pushed past from the corridor into the office. It looked as if someone had spray-painted gallons of red paint around. Even the air seemed perfused with red.

Out, damned spot! Out, I say! Who would have thought the old man to have had so much blood in him.

It wasn't just the blood, oh, no. Septimus couldn't ignore gobbets of flesh — unidentifiable gobbets — stuck to the walls, to the ceiling above the desk, the desk itself and in a rough semi-circle of bloody sludge and gore on the Burmese teak floorboards.

The stench was far worse than any abattoir.

Blood and yes, say it, fresh shit.

Sir Thomas — what was left of him — was in two parts. His upper half, from the ribs up, sprawled face-down on the desk. The lower half, from the thighs on down to his feet, was a bloody pile on the floor with charred clothing that still smouldered amid the wreckage of the chair. The middle part — comprising the guts, kidneys, liver and genitals — was gone.

Blown to bits. Vaporised.

The senior technician, Proudfoot, walked over and told Septimus in a muffled voice it'd all be in the forensics report.

'Sure it will,' said Septimus, holding up his NCA identity card. 'But I'm going to need a quick brief from you now. Now, not later.'

The technician agreed to talk unofficially out in the corridor on the clear understanding that anything and everything he said was subject to change and to final confirmation. He could give Septimus two unauthorised minutes and no more.

They pulled off their masks.

'Some of this is conjecture right now.'

'Understood.'

'Okay. Well, imagine someone sticking a shotgun up the victim's arse and pulling the trigger. Instead of shotgun cartridges, what we seem to have is a tiny quantity of C4 —'

'How tiny?'

'Less than thumb size. Or maybe the size of one of those marbles kids like to play with. Powerful stuff. Seems it was wrapped around something metallic, in this case what I believe were a couple of beer bottle tops. The fragments of the metal act like the shotgun pellets, yeah? We found a couple of these tiny pieces had penetrated as far as the victim's lungs and even his neck. No doubt we'll find more in the autopsy.'

'Go on.'

'The chair disintegrated. The explosion sent razor-sharp wood splinters vertically and horizontally into the victim, severing the femoral artery, which I think was probably the direct cause of death. I can show you some of these splinters in the wall behind the desk—'

'How long?'

'To bleed to death, you mean? Couple of minutes, but possibly less, given the extent of the other injuries. The victim was — well, you can see for yourself — ripped in half.'

Proudfoot kept his voice down, not wanting to be overheard by police officers who might well be taking cash for passing snippets to the media — a well-established Metropolitan Police tradition.

'We think a detonator had been inserted into this ball of C4, and fixed to the bottom of the chair — the underside of the seat, I mean — with a wire attached to the back of the chair. Whoever did this seems to have attached a metal spring to the bottom of one of the chair legs, so —'

Septimus completed the sentence for him. 'So when he sat down, he completed the circuit.'

'Exactly so.'

'Nasty.'

'Very, but it had the virtue of striking at the one target alone. No collateral damage...even whoever it was with the victim at the time escaped serious injury, though he was close — only on the other side of the desk, three or four feet away.'

'Who was this other person?'

'Right now, he's sitting in the ambulance, and the police are interviewing him or trying to. An American, I'm told, from something called Vision 2035.'

'I must let you get back,' Septimus said. 'You've been very helpful. Thank you.'

'It's off the record, right?'

'Of course it is. Of course.'

• • • •

THE FOUR OF THEM SAT on plastic chairs around the metal table in Bridie's Taskforce office. Bridie herself, Caro, Bernie and Septimus were the select few.

On a whiteboard were a few new police statistics. A scorecard, in effect.

Lines of inquiry: 5,400

Witness statements: 1,300

Public contacts: 4,200

Bridie turned to Bernie. 'By the way, what did LUCY find out in Nice?'

'I've sent you the report.'

'Ok. I'll get to it. Summarise.'

'Dead end,' Bernie said. 'The ex-soldier, Martin, was found dead with another unidentified male in a flat. Both shot. LUCY says the local cops will come up with the identity of the second man eventually. They seem to think it was a gangland killing.'

'What does LUCY think?'

'She thinks she recognised the man named Martin.'

'Thinks?'

'Killed with a shotgun. Messy.'

'And?'

'She believes he was among the passengers at Rome airport departures while she was watching Carstairs.'

'Was he with Carstairs, or following him?'

'She doesn't think so, though possible. Nothing to suggest either.'

• • • •

THE MEETING WAS UNDERWAY.

Caro briefed colleagues on what Tufton Street was all about — especially at No. 55 and No. 57, along with No. 2 Lord North Street, and Nos. 23 and 40 Great Smith Street. These addresses — all a stone's throw from Westminster — housed small but influential lobby firms and so-called think tanks — far-right libertarian, pro-Brexit, neoliberal economics aka austerity, promoting climate science denial and pushing the interests of such lovelies as the global fossil fuel and tobacco industries. Limited Partnerships were much in favour for avoiding tax and hiding both the owners' identities and the sources of revenue.

Loads of dosh flowed into their offshore accounts from the Gulf, United States and Israel, as well as a number of shady oligarchs the world over.

Caro explained that the big beast at 2C Lord North Street was the Centre for Economic Affairs or CEA, which described itself as an educational charity and think tank committed to the free market, and funded by the likes of BP and ExxonMobil.

'The CEA propelled Trish Loss into office, if you remember,' said Caro.

'How the fuck could we ever forget her trashing the economy?' replied Bernie.

'I think we get the picture,' said Bridie.

'Our new prime minister, Richard Carstairs, is a CEA alumnus,' Caro added as an afterthought.

Bridie turned to Septimus. 'Did you talk to Sir Thomas's visitor?'

'Not possible, I'm afraid. I did try. He was shaking and unable to speak. Shock, it seems. Also, burst eardrums. The paramedics were still trying to scrape the shit and gore off him when I left.'

'What is Vision 2035?' Caro asked.

Bernie answered. 'It's paving the way for a presidential dictatorship. Its members believe democracy gets in the way of the Holy Grail of pure capitalism, and that what the United States needs is an authoritarian leader with the power to override the checks and balances of traditional American governance. Stuff the Constitution. Screw human rights. Fuck the allies. Torch the environment. Embrace Putin and Xi. Democracy's just too messy and inefficient, and Trump's their man for the job.'

'In a word, fascism,' muttered Caro.

'Yup. Heading our way, too,' said Bernie. 'The UK isn't a democracy, only the semblance of one.'

'A plutocracy,' suggested Septimus.

'A kleptocracy,' Bernie offered.

An uncomfortable silence followed these comments. Bridie steered the discussion away from politics back to the more pressing matters of the latest murder.

'You were there at the crime scene,' she told Septimus. 'How do you know this is our killer?'

'I don't know it for a fact because we have little in the way of hard fact. But I'm sure of it. This wasn't an ideological attack on the far right. It was precise and designed to take out Sir Thomas and no one but Sir Thomas. It took a lot of thought and no little skill. If he'd wanted to, I'm sure he could have blown the entire building sky-high and left a crater fifteen feet deep.'

Bernie was sceptical. 'But why do you insist it's him?'

Septimus threw out his arms. 'Why are any of them his? We need to find out, and fast. But in answer to your question, I'd say his thorough reconnaissance, detailed prep and the skills required to carry them out. If you want to know what I think, I'd say he's planned all his kills well in advance over several months, and now he's ticking them off as fast as he can because he knows he's going to be stopped one way or another. For him, it's a race against time — meaning us.'

Bridie opened her laptop. 'Oh, this is interesting. Seems a recent visitor to Tufton Street bears an uncanny resemblance to our killer in age, height, build, and so on. Only this time he's wearing a jacket and tie and is clean shaven. We've got another image of him, this time from the building's security cameras. He made two visits —'

The three others jumped up from their chairs to stand behind Bridie and peer over her shoulder at her screen.

'And on each occasion,' Bridie said, 'he gained entry to the building by producing what appeared to be a National Crime Agency ID in the name of — Christ, I don't believe this.'

They all turned to look at Septimus, including Bridie. He read accusation, puzzlement, disbelief in their expressions.

'In the name of a Septimus Brass,' Bridie added.

Chapter 25

B *attersea, London, November 15*
Septimus Brass lived small. He lived quiet. He lived in a small flat with small rooms in a small street near Bayswater. His savings were small. He had no car. He rode an ancient, second-hand bicycle he handled with loving care and attention. He had a small number of friends — they were more acquaintances than friends, aside from colleagues.

He said little, drank little, slept little.

Septimus was satisfied with his small life, with not wanting what others seemed to crave. Not wanting in itself he found oddly satisfying. Retail therapy was not something he would understand. Over the years, it was true that he'd bought a handful of fine Kazak and Persian rugs at auction with his spare cash, and occasionally splashed out on the odd picture he took a liking to. Nothing fancy by no one famous. Abstract expressionism was his thing. Local artists, mostly, the young up-and-coming ones whose work he discovered in small galleries and studios well away from the West End. Dalston and Haggerston in east London, mostly. No one saw what he put on his walls and floors because he had no visitors.

If he won the Euro lottery, Rothko and Kline would be in his sights. Most of all, Jacques Villon, whose real name was Duchamp, older brother of the Cubist Marcel Duchamp.

We can all dream, can't we?

The lottery companies would like every fool to think so. A tax on the poor to pay for the pleasures of the rich, such as opera.

Septimus bought his books second hand, and when he'd finished them, he piled them up by the door and took them, a dozen at a time, to Oxfam in a Lidl carrier bag. It was a form of recycling for a good cause. He retained only those he considered worth reading again, and the survivors crowded windowsills, cupboards and shelves and the floor.

He had neither wife nor children living with him. Septimus was comfortable in his own skin, with being alone, with not speaking to another human, sometimes for days. He didn't watch television and didn't own one.

He took pleasure in telling the television license authorities where they could get off.

He found silence a comfort on a small planet of eight billion people.

When he was younger and less sure of himself, Septimus bore the hallmarks of the true introvert. He had the urge to go out and have fun like everyone else but couldn't bring himself to leave home. He wanted to have people around for drinks or a meal, to welcome them to his small life and small living room, to show generosity, but when he did so, he regretted it, for within a few minutes of baleful conversation, he suffered from an almost overwhelming desire to rid himself of his guest or guests as soon as possible, barely able to resist the urge to push them out. He wasn't a good host.

Not entirely alone, though, and not totally silent, either. His companion was Trooper, a four-year-old border collie with one blue eye, acquired at five months from a North Yorkshire farmer, the runt of a litter of six deemed unsuitable for sheep herding. Not steady enough, the farmer declared, and lacking in the ability to concentrate, apparently. A wayward adolescent. A canine version of failing one's GCSEs, Septimus thought, but not the end of the canine world.

Like most of his breed, wall-eyed Trooper had an inexhaustible appetite for exercise and stimulation, which was fine because Septimus enjoyed walking and cycling through London's several parks. He talked to Trooper a good deal, though it wasn't clear to Septimus whether he was talking to Trooper or to himself, and no doubt Trooper felt the same way.

A bit of both, most likely.

Trooper did talk back in his own way.

He wasn't sure what to make of his human's latest preoccupation. The work space set aside for it was against one wall in the living/dining area, the dining table itself (which had never been used for eating or entertaining). It was reserved as a work surface and was piled high with paper, files and reference books, along with the obligatory computer, refurbished and third-hand. And a straight-backed dining chair rescued from a tip. The wall itself had a newly installed diorama of detection; it was decorated with six enlarged passport mugshots, and below them four rather fuzzy copies of Photofit images from police and private security cameras of the alleged killer. There were snapshots of locations, too. Streets, buildings, parks, rail and bus stations. Brief details of the individual in each mugshot were provided on yellow post-it notes below each image.

Once Septimus completed his latest puzzle and stood back to admire it, thoughtfully scratching his belly, Trooper came up and stood before the display, took a long look, barked once and turned tail, then headed for his basket, his expression miserable.

He didn't approve, especially when his human's latest activity took up any of his outdoor walking time. Septimus knew his companion well enough to interpret Trooper's body language and solitary bark as 'Fuck it, you crazy old bastard, it's so unfair!'

Septimus provided a commentary in a low voice. 'So, there we are, Trooper. All six names and their six faces. Six victims. Edwin Lufkin, our late prime minister. Tasmin Quaife, late opposition leader. Kevin Tomlinson, recently departed defence secretary. Melanie Members, until Saturday, our home secretary. Humphrey Ocean, much-decorated former army chief of staff. And the latest murder victim, one Thomas Brownlow, ex-permanent secretary at the Ministry of Defence.

'What do you think, Trooper? An unattractive bunch? Corrupt members of our political establishment? Right-wing carpet-baggers after a quick profit at the expense of the public? Agents of foreign influence? Recipients of dodgy donations from far-right billionaires? They're all that and more. You agree, don't you?'

Self-exiled in his basket, Trooper was in a sulk, muzzle between his paws.

'I've read about these people, Trooper. I know what they are. I know what they've done, pretty much. Seems to me, though, none of this is sufficient a reason to kill them. You don't murder people and put your own life and freedom in jeopardy because they're warped, because they're sociopaths or narcissists — there are just too many evil bastards. You stay away from them; that's what you do. You ignore them. You vote against them. You emigrate to New Zealand or Ireland if you can. No, it's not that. It's something else. Something I'm not seeing. Something staring me right in the face, but I'm still not seeing it. It's not their values or lack of them. It's not their ideology, their stupidity or their nasty prejudices.

'It's something they've all done. Or something they've all *not* done.'

Rain tapped insistently on the window. *I know*, it seemed to say.

Septimus put on the lights to ward off the crepuscular November afternoon he found so depressing, especially London's winter world of greys upon grey — grey sky, grey river, grey buildings, grey streets, grey people. There were times, though, when Septimus liked to sit at the window without putting on the lights, watching the city lights come on and wink back at him, making up stories about the mysterious shadows of people behind curtains in homes across the street. At these times, he felt the tentacles of his dreams, the dreams he would have that night, reach out to him. For dreams mattered to Septimus. Often, they stayed with him on waking from the previous night's sleep, lingering all day. Their atmosphere, their colours, their smells and even their taste, they stayed on, and before night fell, they came out of hiding to take him in again. To Septimus, they were a part of his life, as real as the supposed reality of his investigative work. Old friends.

He was able to be both awake and dreaming, conscious of the fact that he was in a dream. He could cut the dream short if it was too unpleasant to continue or alter its direction. Sometimes a dream was episodic — he was able to come out of a dream and go back into the narrative again all in the same night, or sometimes night after night he was able to plunge back into the same current, though it often changed and brought in new characters and situations. He dreamed in colour, and the colours appeared to reflect his mood. Lucid dreams, they were called, and Septimus had been able to manipulate his own dreams from childhood, and likely as not this had developed as a way to deal with what his parents had called his 'night terrors.'

Septimus has dreamed of what he thinks may well turn out to be the killer's next target. He's seen the victim's face, heard his voice, seen him going about his business. The imagined target has even spoken directly to him. A pompous, fruity, Old Etonian voice of a conman. Was he awake, or was he dreaming? At times, Septimus couldn't tell which. Mostly, he was aware of what he was dreaming.

Which begged the question whether wakefulness was itself a dream, and whether Septimus was living a dream inside a dream. What was reality, after all?

The killer was getting far too cocky. Somehow, he'd learned that Septimus was the lead investigator, in just four days. How come? Then he faked an NCA identity, and in his name! Bloody nerve. Septimus hadn't appeared by name in the media as far as he knew. The killer must have excellent sources — was that what the assassin was telling him? It was a threat, obviously, and was probably meant to be seen as such. If he knew his name, he'd also know where Septimus lived, and how he got to and from work. And *where* he worked.

The bastard knew far too much and wanted Septimus to know it.

'Thing is, Trooper, I'm pretty sure who's next on the list. I'm not going to mention him by name, not yet. I can tell you he's a household name. Can you guess, Trooper? Here's a tip. He's in the middle of a messy divorce, or so the tabloids would have us believe. They say his girlfriend is pregnant, and an ex-girlfriend who bore him a daughter out of wedlock is suing him for paternity payments. I'm sure you know who I mean. Everyone would know if I said this much, but I'll not say anything yet. Let's you and I make a wee sporting bet on who it is, and in the meantime, I need to check a few dates.'

No response. Trooper was asleep.

Septimus didn't notice. 'You can see for yourself I've left a blank space for murder victim number seven, see? For his picture, and for my notes. If I'm right, he'll be our killer's toughest assignment yet. Maybe the last. He's well protected 24/7. Close protection team wherever he goes, inside and out, and never alone. Armoured vehicles, motorcycle escort, helicopter overhead, the works. It'll be no pushover, this one, especially now everyone's alert. He'll be taking on a small army this time. A real challenge.

What do you think, Trooper? Will he pull it off?'

Chapter 26

P *aris, March 19, 2005.*
It looks simple because it's meant to. Bridie knows enough of what SIS represents and the tricks it employs to know it will be anything but easy. For the purposes of SANDCASTLE, she is Amy Vernon, with a passport in that name. She will meet a local agent, British businessman 'John Scobell.' It won't be his real name any more than hers is Amy Vernon, and she guesses he'll be an IO out of Paris Station playing the role of the agent who will introduce her to a Russian with something juicy to sell for hard currency. Half a million U.S. dollars. Code name TASKMASTER.

Namely, the detailed plans and technical specifications of the latest Russian subsonic anti-ship cruise missile, KAYAK, a much cheaper, smaller weapon than its predecessors, and with what is believed to be a much greater range. Of vital interest to NATO navies, therefore.

But is the seller a 'dangle'? Are the goods fake? Is the handover a trap set by the SVR, successor to the KGB? Once in possession of the material, Bridie aka Amy is to deposit it in a dead letter drop and await word of their receipt from Scobell at another meet. He will then drive her to the airport.

Why? The last step seems suspect. Why not allow 'Amy Vernon' to take the Metro alone or hail a cab? Why the car journey? It seems unnecessarily risky. SANDCASTLE is only an IONEC exercise, of course, and it's the last of its kind on Bridie's course, but somehow the flaw in the entire scheme seems so obvious that Bridie is tempted to break the rules for once and improvise her own exit. She doesn't, of course. She's far too competitive to fail. She wants to score well and emerge triumphant in the race against her male rivals. There has to be a reason for the planned car journey.

'Amy Vernon' flies to Amsterdam then on to Paris. She knows she isn't doing the environment any good by flying, but in her new role, she has no choice. She keeps an eye open for possible surveillance — her own team's or the opposition's. Nothing strikes her as unusual. Not the young couple with a toddler, nor the elderly man in a flat cap who uses a walking stick to navigate the queues. From a window seat in economy, she is gratified to see that, as the plane takes off, the cloud has parted, revealing a sky of delicate blue worthy of Poussin. Looking down when the aircraft reaches its ceiling of 30,000 feet, she sees that the sullen grey Channel has given way to a wrinkled parchment of cheery cerulean winking back up at her in the reflected sunshine.

'Beautiful, isn't it?' The voice comes from a male two seats away. Bridie has been aware of someone moving into the aisle seat, leaving the middle seat free, but she's resisted the temptation to inspect her fellow passenger. Now, she does so. 'You're lucky you got a window seat,' he adds when he sees her turn.

He's in his thirties, she guesses, lean, quite good looking, in a navy blazer, open-necked blue shirt with a button-down collar, tan corduroys. She can't see his footwear — well, she could if she leant over a little and stared down toward his nether regions, but she won't go that far. She marks him down as a competition tennis player.

He's speaking English with a slight French accent.

'Isn't it just?' She gives one of those fleeting, automatic smiles — a brief stretching of the lips without smiling with her eyes, indicating that she doesn't wish to be rude by ignoring him and by failing to respond, but on the other hand, making it clear even to a moron that she wants to be left alone, thank you very much. She returns to the book in her lap.

'You're an architect?'

Bridie counts to three before she looks up from the page and turns towards him.

'No.' She shakes her head and goes back to the book.

'I saw what you're reading and thought —'

Bridie doesn't care to know what he thinks. Not at all bad looking, though. Good eyes and in great shape. Is he SIS? Or one of 'theirs'? Whoever 'they' are supposed to be — the Russians or their local help. Bridie isn't going to go along with it, whatever it is, this play-acting. The fellow is surely a plant, someone positioned to befriend her, to discover what personal information she can be persuaded to give up, such as where she's staying, what she's doing in France, and whether she'll accept an invitation to a drink and who knows...a romantic, candlelit supper in an expensive restaurant?

Fuck that. I'm not stupid.

He tries again when the cabin crew come around with drinks.

'You're a historian, right?'

'No.' This time, Bride doesn't look at him or even raise her head from the page she's pretending to read.

The stranger switches to French. No doubt to see if she understands and can respond in kind. 'But you're reading *Paris: An Architectural History* by Anthony Sutcliffe. It's quite famous, not so?'

You can read. Bravo!

Bridie gives no sign she's heard. God, does SIS think she's dumb and pliant enough to go weak at the knees when someone presentable tries to chat her up? How sexist can they be?

It's fucking disgusting.

Her neighbour tries again, in English. 'So what do you do?'

'What's it to you?'

'Nothing. I was trying to make light conversation.'

Bridie has injured his *amour propre.*

Good.

'Do I seem to want to talk to someone like you?'

'No, I...'

'Do you think I like being asked personal questions by a strange male?'

He throws up his well-manicured hands. 'I'm sorry, okay?'

No l'esprit de l'escalier moment for Bridie.

'You should be. Do us both a favour, will you please, and fuck off.'

That's offensive. It's unkind. It's aggressive. Bridie knows this. On the other hand, it has the desired effect. The prick doesn't speak to her again, nor she to him, for the rest of the journey. When Bridie visits the lavatory, careful to take her purse, laptop and phone with her, she speaks to one of the female cabin staff on the way back to her seat, saying that her fellow passenger is a pest, and asks for his name on the passenger list. Rather an irregular request, it has to be said, but it works.

Claude Lantier, whoever he is.

Bridie is offered and accepts an immediate and free upgrade to business class.

The modest three-star Hotel du Quai Voltaire is perfect for her purposes, but there is more to it than that. She'd stayed there as an undergraduate with her first 'real' boyfriend on a two-night break. Back then, it seemed to her to be what she imagined a run-down, *fin de siècle* bordel might have been like. Red velvet curtains, blood-red carpets, a lumpy mattress, noisy pipes and a lingering smell she couldn't identify. Americans would hate it, naturally, which had only added to its shabby allure. It was romantic; back then, everything in France had been romantic to Bridie, from the tapwater that could not be drunk to the rats and even the tarts who lined a street near the Gare du Nord and literally stank of sex.

The rats and whores might have moved out of the centre of town, but the place is still, well, atmospheric, the rooms small, no air-con, a room fan that clanks like a steamship's boilers, street noise of course (but much better on the second floor, where Bridie has booked a room), along with those sinister stains she remembered on the filthy carpet and bedcovers, but it brings back fond memories. It's also central, with a fine view of the Seine and the Louvre. Better still, for Bridie's purposes, it's only a few minutes' walk to the Tuileries, the Invalides, the Musée d'Orsay and the metro on Rue du Bac.

It's like being in love all over again.

She takes a taxi from the airport to the Pompidou Centre, walks a few blocks with her small wheelie suitcase, and flags down another cab to take her to the hotel in the 7th Arrondissement. The taxi driver is miffed at having such a short journey and swears under his breath. Too bad.

Paris is still Europe's most attractive capital, though Prague and Lubljiana come close, especially after France surrendered her capital city to the predations of the motorist in the 1970s by carving highways through its heart. On a good day, with winter sunshine, it's stunning. Yet its very beauty seems to Bridie to be fragile, edged with suspicion and shadowed with danger. Paris couldn't lay claim to being the spy capital of Europe — who would want that title, after all? Surely that falls to the likes of Belgrade, Berlin, Brussels and Vienna. Still, for a sceptic like Bridie, central Paris seems too good to be true. Too agreeable, too pretty, too charming, too fashionable, too well-dressed and too well-endowed with the arts.

Bridie is to meet John Scobell at Brasserie Le Florès on the corner of Rue de Grenelle and Rue du Bac the next morning at 10:30. Following the unwritten rules of tradecraft, which dictate that one should never arrive or leave a contact on time, and never together, she arrives at 10:42 — twelve minutes late. Scobell is already there, sitting at the bar, having had a coffee and a cognac. He has a copy of *L'Express* in front of him, while Bridie removes a Liberty's scarf from her head and reties it around her neck once she reaches the counter. She's already prowled around the neighbourhood for more than an hour as part of her route surveillance detection.

Having thus provided their respective recognition signals, they move at Bridie's suggestion to a quiet table for two at the back. The brasserie — which opens at 10 a.m. — wasn't crowded at that hour. What Bridie thinks are likely regulars come and go, half a dozen office workers by the look of them, all but one male, each throwing back a *petit café* and sometimes a brandy as well at the bar, then hurrying away. The barbaric, Anglo-Saxon habit of starting work by 9 a.m. sharp has not yet taken hold. How civilised! A young couple with a small child in a pushchair occupy a table near the windows, but that is about it. Bridie thinks she hears them speaking Spanish.

Scobell is a pink-faced Englishman with a soft mouth, sleepy eyes of pale blue and receding blond hair. He doesn't look Bridie in the eye but lets his gaze drift over her head or shoulder. Is he nervous? Afraid of women? She's met several Englishmen like that. His clothes seem too tight; he resembles a rather slippery, plump seal basking in the sun. She judges him at once, perhaps unfairly, as someone both lazy and evasive, who puts his own comfort and safety before everything else and not someone who would go at once to the assistance of anyone in trouble. Businessman? She didn't think so; more like a Foreign Office time server and stooge, enjoying his tax-free status and all the allowances, expenses and perks he can grab. There's no wedding ring, Bridie notes, only a crested signet on the fifth digit of his left hand.

She's already made up her mind about 'agent' Scobell in the first couple of minutes; she doesn't like him or trust him — but then she isn't supposed to.

They get down to business.

TASKMASTER will be at the Tuileries at 14:35 local. He will have an umbrella and hold a bag of oranges. As far as recognition signals go, it seems to be very Russian. Very much Moscow rules. He will want to talk money, and Bridie — or 'Amy' — will negotiate him down to a reasonable cash sum of 100,000 dollars from half a million, but only to be paid once the provenance of his material has been established. She'll demand a sample of the goods he's selling in return for an advance of 10,000 U.S. dollars for which he must sign on a blank slip of paper, meaningless in itself but part of the process of psychological entrapment. She's to sound him out about his work and his suitability for long-term recruitment. Defection is out of the question. Russians come cheap nowadays. They all seem to want to escape Putin's empire, even if it means joining the American one. TASKMASTER will have to be close to the top of the Russian food chain to be even considered for exfiltration and resettlement.

There was a time a few decades ago when a Red Army sergeant in the Strategic Rocket Forces would have been regarded as a great catch. When the Soviet Union collapsed, colonels were a dime a dozen, and even generals were old hat. The Western allies could pick and choose. Now, only very senior and specialised individuals are worthy of being resettled abroad with a new identity, a house, a lump sum, and a job. Who is TASKMASTER anyway?

First on the agenda, though, is their administration — where and when 'Amy' and 'Scobell' would next meet, what emergency signals they will use if it all goes pear-shaped. 'Scobell' will meet her with his car outside the Musée d'Orsay rail station. Scobell announces a change to the game: Bridie will hand over whatever TASKMASTER gives her directly, so no need for a dead letter box after all. He won't park or leave the vehicle — a grey-green Renault Mégane — but will keep moving as slowly as possible until she spots him and gets into the car. She'll hand over the Russian's sample and the receipt for the cash. Then he'll drive her to Belgium.

Bridie senses something isn't right.

'But why? That's three hours by road. And why Belgium? Makes no sense, not to me.'

'Orders. A change of plan.'

'Makes no sense,' Bridie repeats.

The porcine Scobell looks irritated. 'My car is registered in France, so we won't be logged. There are no permanent border controls, Belgium and France both being in the Schengen area. Whatever TASKMASTER gives you, we don't want it scrutinised by police or anyone else. Understood?'

'And then?'

'I'll drop you at Luxembourg airport, and you can fly home.'

Bridie has to remind herself not to take things too seriously. Especially Scobell. This is a field exercise, after all. Although it's supposed to be realistic, the plan has its flaws, obviously, but she has to make peace with it and not appear too critical or obstructive, or this Scobell will give full vent to his misogynist bigotry.

Just before they split up and go their separate ways, Bridie asks the man who calls himself Scobell if he knows the name of someone she met on the way over.

'Who?'

'Claude Lantier.'

'Can't say I do. Why?'

'He tried to chat me up on the flight. Pretty clumsy attempt, too. Maybe you could look him up, if he exists. He's probably one of your people, Mr Scobell. A colleague, perhaps.'

· · · ·

TASKMASTER, HIS UMBRELLA and bag of oranges are where they are supposed to be. He's a small, rumpled figure in a black beret and beige coat, his face partially hidden in a red woollen scarf. He speaks with a Russian accent. Fake or real, Bridie can't tell. Good enough to fool most people, anyhow, including Bridie with her First in Modern Languages.

She sits down on the bench he occupies — there's plenty of room. He doesn't look at her but absently offers her one of his oranges, holding it out. She leans over and takes it, thanks him, peels and eats it segment by segment in front of him, sucking the juice off her fingers. What else is she supposed to do?

'You know what I have?'

'I do. I want a sample. A sample of the originals, not copies.'

She leans forward to avoid orange juice dripping onto her clothing.

'And you know what I want.'

'Of course, but it's unrealistic. I'm authorised to offer you 100k, with an advance now of 10,000, the balance when you provide the rest of the material. If it's genuine.'

TASKMASTER snorts through his scarf. 'I'll go to the Americans instead.'

'By all means. Please do. I'm sure they can afford it. It'll save me a lot of trouble anyway. You can always try the Germans.'

Bridie wipes her sticky fingers with a tissue and gets to her feet.

'Wait.'

She hesitates, her back to him, looking around. A group of children are racing their bicycles down the paths.

TASKMASTER relents. 'Okay.'

Bridie sits down again. That was easy. She takes a brown envelope from her coat pocket and puts it down between them. She doesn't look to see if anyone is watching because if they are, they'll ensure they aren't visible anyway. They'll use optics of some kind, possibly a camera to record the transaction at long range.

TASKMASTER takes the envelope, pushes it into his coat pocket and puts in its place a larger, A4-sized white envelope.

'Photographs of the originals, but odd pages. A thumb drive, too.'

Bridie scoops it up and secretes it under her coat.

'Do you want to work for us?'

He shakes his head. 'No. I love my country.'

'Is this going to be a one-off, or do you envisage something more long term?'

'I can get you a lot of secret material. If you pay. Technical, most of it. You wouldn't understand it, but there are people in your country who will want this. They'll appreciate it. If they don't, or they can't afford it, the Americans will pay well for it.'

'You're a scientist?'

'No.'

'So what are you?'

'I am official in government. Military procurement.'

'Why are you doing this?'

'Stupid question. Money, of course — what else? We're all capitalists these days, my dear. Or maybe you hadn't noticed.'

'Our next meeting —'

TASKMASTER doesn't let her finish. 'We will meet again in one week. Same time, same place. You will wear the same scarf. Yes? You'll have the rest of my money for me, and I will give you all the original material on KAYAK. Good?'

'Good. But how do I contact you if there's a problem?'

'You don't. No meeting, no deal.'

And that's that. Bridie aka Amy stays where she is and watches the grizzled and patronising TASKMASTER get to his feet. He has a slight limp and shuffles off, taking his time and clutching his umbrella in one hand and the remaining oranges in the other.

• • • •

BRIDIE ESTIMATES THEY are about an hour from the unmarked Belgian border when it starts to rain, fat drops smacking the windshield. It's also the moment when both Scobell and Bridie see the roadblock ahead.

'Oh, shit. I thought you said —'

'I know what I said,' Scobell says. 'The police set up temporary checkpoints sometimes near the border to catch smugglers.'

'Do we count as smugglers?'

Scobell slows the Renault, and he's waved to a siding. A uniform appears at the driver's window and another on the passenger side, where Bridie sits.

She notices these are not the national police but the Gendarmerie, with black jackets and blue trousers under their rain slicks. Armed, of course. Scobell hands over his driving licence, car registration and ID without a word. Bridie hands over hers too, in the name of Amy Vernon. One officer walks off with their papers and speaks into his radio while three of his colleagues stand around the Renault and watch its two occupants. A minute later, he's back. Scobell and Vernon are ordered out of the car. 'You and you — out!'

They're pushed up against the Renault, their hands placed on the wet roof, patted down and then roughly handcuffed, hands behind their backs.

One officer addresses Scobell. 'Monsieur. Allow me to inform you that you are under arrest.'

'And I thought this was a date.'

The same officer isn't amused. He grabs Scobell's hair and slams his head none too gently against the edge of the door. Twice for good measure.

'*Enfoiré*!'

Which Bridie translates as: 'Motherfucker!'

Bridie and her 'agent' — blood trickling down the side of his head — are separated, each placed in the back of different Gendarmerie vehicles. She sees one officer get behind the wheel of Scobell's Renault. The convoy sets off, one Gendarmerie car in front, one behind, the Renault in the centre. It seems the checkpoint had been set up just for them.

Bridie listens to the crackle of voices on the police radio. From what she can make out, the Americans and British have launched an invasion of Iraq only hours previously.

One uniformed officer turns in his seat and glares at her.

'Shit,' he said. 'You English and Americans are so stupid!'

Bridie can't argue with that, but she has other matters on her mind. She realises that her final SIS 'test' has only just begun.

Chapter 27

South London, 08:50, Thursday, November 16

Was it Sun Tzu who was credited with the phrase 'Keep your friends close; keep your enemies closer'? Whoever it was, Merrick took the advice to heart.

When he trudged up the ramp out of Vauxhall Underground station in the company of an immense column of office workers, he could see the Ziggurat right across the street, and once he'd turned sharp left and walked south underneath the railway bridge, he was faced by the stand-alone SIS annexe with its blank windows and CCTV cameras where the task force pursuing him had set up shop. All he had to do to find out who was on his tail was spend a little time watching who came and went. He turned right this time before he reached the building, pausing at the traffic lights outside the Vauxhall Tavern and crossing over the busy street. He headed westwards along the South Lambeth Road, with Vauxhall Park on his immediate left.

He'd chosen the rush hour; Merrick reasoned he'd be hard to spot in the legions of mortgage-paying zombies who staggered in by train from the suburbs and affluent southern towns. He didn't look at their exhausted, pinched faces and sullen expressions, and he avoided eye contact. He kept his face down. He looked at feet and hands. He was one of them this morning, moving in a synchronised, automated production line like mineworkers emerging exhausted from the pithead at the end of their shifts. Many, if not most stared at their phones — TikTok or texts — or listened on bulbous headphones to audiobooks or to playlists of their favourite artists. Here, but not here. Not watchful, not looking. On autopilot. Using maybe three percent of their brains. Which was how Merrick liked it.

The Underground was foul. The air stank with the musty odour of wet clothing and sweaty feet. It was overcrowded most of the time. Everyone knew it was infested with bedbugs and a unique variety of large, spotted mosquitoes that survived down in the tunnels on the cocaine-infused blood of City of London traders.

None of that mattered. What was important was that Merrick's adversaries wouldn't think of looking for him on the local CCTV right under their noses, not five days after his first attack. At least, he hoped not. They'd assume he was hundreds of miles away by now. In any case, he was wearing glasses perched on the end of his nose and a beanie on his head so that he resembled one of the seven dwarves. Not a killer.

Merrick didn't think he looked anything like his usual self. He looked, well, nerdy, bookish, even. Dare he say it, scholarly.

At the junction with Fentiman Road, Merrick moved to the right and waited for the lights to change before crossing and heading down a small alley opposite, Miles Street. He was alone, or seemed to be. He passed an innocuous red brick Anglican church like a crouching armadillo on his left, grandly named St Anne and All Saints. He faced the railway embankment ahead and a series of arches converted for various activities, from nightclubs to fitness centres and firms such as Garage Services and Stone Theatre, whatever that might be. En route, he strolled between two new high-rise blocks of flats. Right at the end of Miles Street, a rust-stained sign on the brick rail embankment declared storage for hire. One of the nearest arches to the right had a blue metal shutter. There was no sign or name. Merrick approached, looked around to make sure he wasn't followed, bent down, and unlocked the padlock. He used both hands to haul up the shutter with a metallic rattle and squeal. Behind it was a conventional door, which he also unlocked. He felt for the light switch, entered, and closed the inner door behind him.

The long, cavernous, semi-circular interior was almost empty. It felt damp. It reminded him of a Nissen hut. The walls were whitewashed but streaked with mould. There were a couple of big plywood tea chests at the end that contained bits and pieces of his that wouldn't fit into his tiny flat. An army camp bed and a folding chair were placed next to the boxes with a couple of blankets for emergencies. Along one wall was an old carpentry bench with a few tools hanging above it. But there was something else in there that was far more important to Merrick.

He pulled the covers off two bikes.

The first was a new BMW F750GS — an 853cc mid-range all-rounder and, to quote the brochure, a water-cooled 4-stroke, in-line two-cylinder engine, four valves per cylinder, and two overhead camshafts, offering 77 hp and a top speed of 190/kph or 118 mph.

More than fast enough for Merrick's purposes and sufficiently agile for manoeuvring in urban traffic.

The other was a second-hand, well-used 2011 Honda CBR1000RR Fireblade, larger and much faster than the BMW and dressed in the fiery livery of red and black, with a black helmet and black leathers on the seat.

Merrick's latest acquisition was all white, and it was no coincidence that it was almost identical to the new BMW machines of the Met's Special Escort Group (SEG). All it lacked was the word 'police' in small black letters painted low down on each side panel, but who was going to notice when he was mobile? The white helmet and black gloves were there on the bench, and hanging from a bracket in the wall was a yellow, waterproof, high-vis jacket with the Velcro strip on the back that read 'police' in black capital letters. A police whistle on a lanyard hung on the hook too, for the SEG didn't use sirens, only whistles.

Feeling under the bench with one hand, Merrick withdrew a handgun, a SIG Sauer P226, designated in the UK as L105A1. He checked the 15-round magazine and one spare. He wasn't planning on a firefight if he could avoid it, so he reckoned thirty rounds of 9mm calibre would more than suffice. It was just there if needed. As for comms, Merrick was aware of the Tetra Airwave digital radio used by SEG, and the standard operating procedure or SOP the group employed. It didn't differ much from the military equivalent.

SEG officers were routinely armed.

Merrick started the BMW and listened to the engine. Its gravelly whine sounded perfect to his ears. After a minute or two, he shut it down.

He would take the Fireblade out for a spin through west London. It was chilly and damp outside, so he pulled on the leathers. The traffic would doubtless be heavy, but that's what he needed for this outing.

Merrick had studied the SEG. He'd followed them on the Fireblade, hanging back to watch them, or else cutting across their path and stopping to let them pass by as he counted and timed them. Merrick admired their operational methods. He summarised their style in three words: calm, courtesy, discretion — not terms commonly associated with police anywhere. They might well be unique. As armed police motorcyclists who protected VIPs, domestic and foreign, they seemed to work in small numbers, matching the number of vehicles in any cavalcade, normally two bikes per vehicle.

The centre of gravity was the lead biker, who controlled the speed of the escorted vehicles by staying just ahead of the first and occupying the centre of the lane. That's where he or she stayed for the duration, issuing brief commands and listening to the acknowledgements and brief sitreps from the team over the encrypted radio link.

The other bikers streamed ahead one by one, positioning themselves at junctions or where there was a likely traffic holdup. They used hand signals and whistles to keep a lane open. They'd say 'thank you' to cooperative motorists, bus drivers and taxis. If an SEG cop had no option but to close off an intersection or side street, it was for seconds, or perhaps half a minute. Roads and highways were never shut down in the U.S., French or Russian sense of the term. Whether the VIP was royalty or a minister of the Crown, the VIP and the protection teams were expected to blend into the stream of traffic like anyone else without causing the public undue inconvenience.

From Merrick's point of view, it meant that the SEG leader couldn't have eyes on all his team at any one time, with the exception of the start and end of a journey. Two, if not more, would always be well ahead and most of the time out of sight, checking the route and reporting back, and if there was an SEG officer bringing up the rear, he or she wouldn't be in the leader's rearview mirrors continuously. This was an important element in Merrick's calculations.

No system, no matter how professional, was perfect.

It was also a concern that Merrick's next target would be close to civilians. It would be a challenge to strike the target without causing collateral damage.

He was through west London and on the A40 headed for Greenford, then Beaconsfield, and beyond that Amersham and Great Missenden in south Buckinghamshire. He didn't push hard, for he didn't want to attract attention. Merrick's Honda slowed right down close to the objective, growling through the village of Ellesborough at the foot of the Chilterns. Merrick checked his watch: the entire journey had taken one hour and seven minutes.

The traffic turned out to be moderate, but it might not be moderate tomorrow when it mattered.

Merrick had timed each stage as he always did.

He believed his target was a creature of habit, a lazy slug, what's more, one who believed himself to be entitled to the privileges of his office without having to do any work, especially the privilege of his weekly escape to the Grade 1 medieval country manor where he could show off to his guests — at taxpayers' expense, naturally. Tomorrow should be no different. The security 'packet' shouldn't vary much, either. The VIP's armoured Range Rover SUV would lead, armed driver and co-driver in the front seats, the VIP and possibly his partner in the back. Firearms officers usually occupied a second vehicle, most likely also a Range Rover, and Special Branch plainclothes officers brought up the rear in another.

Three vehicles would suggest an escort of only six SEG officers, including the escort leader.

He could be wrong. Ever since Merrick carried out his first assassinations on Saturday, he'd been aware that the authorities had increased security, especially the protection for all senior government and opposition leaders and, given his most recent kill, for senior civil servants as well.

Not that he was surprised.

Central London already resembled an armed camp, with temporary checkpoints taking on a permanent appearance on major roads and intersections with the introduction of coiled razor wire, oil drums, sandbags, searchlights, and gabions in the form of Hesco barricades. Ugly but effective.

Armed police patrols in navy blue, wheeled armoured personnel carriers (APCs), had replaced the military and had become the norm in the current state of emergency. He had seen some of these APCs himself, no doubt deployed as a deterrent and intended to boost public confidence, parked at both ends of bridges over the Thames, including Waterloo, Charing Cross, Vauxhall, Battersea and Chelsea.

Merrick had taken this into account, which is why he decided to launch his next op outside London. He reckoned it was also time to organise a diversion to throw his pursuers off the scent and keep them looking the wrong way.

Or so he hoped.

Chapter 28

Pimlico, London, November 16, 12:10

For his meeting with LUCY aka Calista, Bernie picked *The Constitution*, a family-run pub on Churton Street in Pimlico. He reasoned it was close enough to both the Ziggurat and Southwark across the Thames where LUCY lived, but not so close to the SIS HQ that it would be crowded with SIS suits on their lunch break. It was also Bernie's idea of a traditional pub with plenty of beers on draft to choose from, along with good pub food — especially the fish-and-chips — and none of the gastropub pretension (or inflated prices) that plagued much of London.

Calista selected a pint of Proper Job from St Austell Brewery for herself, while Bernie plumped for Cold Harbour lager from Brixton Brewery.

'So what is this?' Calista demanded once they'd settled down with their pints. Weak sunlight found its way in from the window to bathe part of their table in a poor facsimile of warmth, but it was better than nothing.

'It's a meeting between a case officer and his agent. Do you remember those?'

'No shit.'

'Cheers,' Bernie said and drank. Calista did too, but without a response.

'You got my CX report,' Calista said as if it was a statement of fact and not a question.

'I did. For which, thanks. Now, I want to hear from you everything you didn't mention.'

'I wrote the facts as I knew them to be. Everything else is speculation. Guessing. That's not intel.'

'I'll be the judge of that.'

Calista picked up her glass again and drank some more, watching Bernie all the while.

'Okay,' she said at last. 'Seeing as the Office is picking up the tab. The French national known as Jean Martin flew into Luton airport on November eight and vanished. Three days later, on November eleven — Armistice Day — I saw him in the departure lounge in Rome, along with a dishevelled Carstairs, awaiting a flight to London. They didn't sit together or speak to each other. I saw Carstairs board the flight, but there was no sign of this Martin person doing so.'

'Why do you think that is?'

'I truly have no idea.'

'Could he have spotted you watching Carstairs and taking pictures of our future prime minister, and maybe that scared him off?'

'I suppose it's possible,' Calista said. She picked up her fork and prodded her prawn salad.

'Tell me about your visit to the flat in Nice.' Bernie hadn't touched his fish and chips as yet.

Calista told him about meeting SPENDTHRIFT aka Godfrey at the cafe by the port and walking with him to the flat in the old town. How he couldn't bring himself to enter the place because of the stink, and she described him fleeing down the stairs only to throw up on the cobblestones. She mentioned the writhing swarms of bluebottles inside.

Bernie said, 'According to you, this Jean Martin aka Erich Karscher died between the time you saw him on the morning of November eleven in Rome and the afternoon of November thirteen in Nice. Yes?'

'Correct. Aren't you going to eat?'

Bernie wasn't sure he wanted to now. 'How could putrefaction have been so advanced after such a brief period — just two or three days — given that he'd spent several hours travelling between cities?'

'I suggest Europe suffered an unnaturally hot summer this year, and it's continued well into November, remember? The flat was on the top floor under the roof. People weren't wearing coats or jackets. It was like mid-summer. That would account for it. In any case, internal organs start to decompose around seventy-two hours after death. That means gases, which means stink, which brings the flies. Even a dead mouse will attract them.'

Bernie turned to his food despite the turn their conversation had taken.

'You were questioned by the French police?'

'I was. By a cop named Couture. An inspector. He was polite. It didn't take long, maybe thirty minutes, no more.'

'Did he tell you the name of the other man you found dead?'

'He didn't know at that stage who it was. Oh, he told me Godfrey's real name was Mahoney. SPENDTHRIFT, I should say.'

Bernie was tackling his fish and didn't answer, so Calista decided to relax. She emptied her pint glass and watched Bernie try to get ketchup out of the bottle on the table without splattering them both with the contents.

Fork in mid-air, Bernie asked between mouthfuls, 'Any word on someone named Costa?'

'Nope. Couture said the dead men were probably the victims of some gang-related dispute.'

'Now, I've got something to show you.'

Bernie produced a photograph from an inside pocket and pushed it across the table. 'Take a look at this, if you would, please, and tell me if you can identify any of them.'

Calista put her plate and glass aside and peered down at the print. 'It's a party picture, taken with a flash. Christmas lights already up in the background.'

'Uh-huh. And?'

'That's Carstairs in the centre, smirking, holding a glass —'

'Dry martini,' said Bernie. 'He likes them very dry.'

'I wouldn't know or care. He's got his arm around the shoulders of some fat guy I don't know.'

'That's Leo Brodzinski, wealthy extremist.'

'Okay, if you say so. Whoever that might be. On the other side of Carstairs, if I'm not mistaken — the guy with the big toothy grin and also holding a glass — is a Russian named Vishinsky. I only know him from social media.'

'Excellent. Top marks. This is from the party in Rome you reported on. Igor Vishinsky was the host. And who is that in the background? Can you make him out?'

Calista bent her head and looked. Several seconds passed before she looked up again at Bernie.

Her forefinger tapped the image. 'I'd swear that was the dead man in Nice — the ex-legionnaire Jean Martin I saw at the airport.'

Bernie nodded. 'Thank you,' he said, taking the photograph back and putting it back in his jacket pocket. 'You've been very helpful. I've got one more print to show you.' He placed it on the table, face up, and pushed it across. Calista leaned forward and stared down at it.

'Yeah. Same guy, right? Our new unelected leader. Carstairs. And that's the owner of the party venue, if I'm not mistaken, the one and only Luca Pacioli, big-cheese financier and backer of the Italian far right. Likes young girls, so they say. Owner of the villa where the event was held. As well as a donor to our very own Tory Party. Where did you get these?'

'Italian social media,' said Bernie.

'The prawn salad was delicious,' Calista said. 'I should thank you — or maybe I should thank the UK taxpayer. Do we have time for coffee? I'll have a latte, thanks very much. Sweetener, no sugar. Ta.'

Chapter 29

Helmand Province, Afghanistan, January, 2018

At first, Lieutenant Merrick isn't sure if the figure standing in front of him is male or female. Could be either.

Merrick is halfway through his third tour in Afghanistan. He squats on his heels in a strip of shade provided by an immense mud wall four feet thick at its base that marks the perimeter of what the British call a compound. It's a family home, albeit deserted, and serves as Merrick's temporary halt. He rests his back against the wall, his rifle across his knees. Merrick has discovered there are only two ways of being in Afghanistan in the winter months: either extremely cold or extremely hot. There seems to be no middle ground.

Merrick is warmer than he would like to be, but he's cooling down fast now his latest ten km patrol has ended. He knows if he keeps still in the shade much longer, he'll start to shiver. Right now, icy sweat runs down his neck and back.

At night, the temperature will plummet to below zero.

He squints up at the Afghan's outline. Merrick can't make out facial features against the white sky. The only obvious sign that this might be a female is the slight stature — around five-one. Maybe another couple of inches to account for the combat boots. He puts up a gloved hand to shield his eyes so he can identify whoever it is. The Afghan from Commando Force 333 wears a helmet, has a scarf wound around the lower half of said commando's face, shades hide the eyes, and the soldier carries what might seem to a civilian to be an immense amount of gear: body armour, backpack, webbing, ammunition pouches, grenades, water bottle, combat knife, semi-automatic pistol on the right-hand thigh, an AK-74 on a sling.

'I found him, Lieutenant.'

A woman's voice, speaking heavily accented English. A woman named Zala.

Merrick squints up at her. 'Where?'

'Thirty, maybe forty minutes on foot south of here. He's got a local kid in there. Taken from his home yesterday.'

Fuck this. I've got to stop this shit.

Merrick rises from his squatting position, using one hand against the wall to help himself up. He feels like an old man. What he really wants to do is lie down and sleep, right there, right now. An hour would be enough, but he knows it's not going to happen. He can't remember when he last had a straight three hours' kip.

He bellows at the top of his voice. 'Jake!'

'Sir?'

Sergeant Jake Stringham clatters down a ladder from an observation post on the top of the wall.

'Get a squad together. We're heading out.'

'You only just got back.' Stringham looks and sounds concerned.

'Thanks for reminding me, Sergeant. Now, get on with it. We leave in five minutes.'

Merrick turns back to Zala. 'If you need to eat or drink, I suggest you do so now. If he's there as you say, we need to go right away. I don't want to miss the chance of taking a crack at the bastard. Oh, and bloody well done by the way. Good work.'

Zala has unwound the scarf and taken off the shades, revealing her face. She gives Merrick a broad smile. It's so cheerful, so utterly unexpected, that he's taken aback and, just for a moment or two, can't think of anything at all, let alone speak. He recovers, telling himself that he's knackered, and he knows only too well that when he's tired or hungry — and both apply — his temper gets the better of him. So too, apparently, does a green-eyed young woman's spontaneous grin.

Merrick checks his M-16 and ammunition. He checks his other gear, too. He fills his water bottle. He tells Zala she should consider leaving her backpack. They're going to be in and out, no hanging around. Light and fast. They'll come straight back once the job is done. He's not taking his pack.

He knows Zala wants to go even more than he does, which is why he doesn't ask if she's up for it.

Merrick heads over to the water truck. He puts down his gear and washes hands, face, head and neck — without soap — just to get rid of the worst of the thick yellow-pink dust and dried sweat that cakes eyes, ears, nostrils, hair. The water feels marvellous on his skin. Sheer luxury. It's better than all the vintage champagne in the world! He goes into the mess tent and emerges

with coffee in a tin mug and two green plastic packets known as MREs —
the standard American ration packs or Meal Ready to Eat.

He throws one to Zala.

Merrick would appreciate a hot shower, if only to 'wash his weapon' as
the Army has it, meaning to stop crotch rot from developing, but it will have
to wait.

After a swig of coffee, he tears open the pack and consumes whatever
he finds in it and in no particular order. He eats standing up, and although
Merrick thinks MREs pretty disgusting compared to UK rations, and
certainly inferior to enviable French military cuisine, it provides the calories
he needs for his next saunter in what passes for the Afghan countryside.

He scoffs the lot: cheese, cold beef casserole with vegetables, chocolate
brownie, dried fruit. Yuk! It's baby food. But he feels almost human again,
especially now he has a firm target in his sights.

Jake has assembled a section of eight, equally divided between UK and
Afghan special forces members, but Merrick only wants four. He picks them
himself, choosing the soldiers he knows to be reliable and who have had at
least some rest. He dismisses the others back to their posts. As he's Merrick's
2/ic, Jake will stay behind, too. With Merrick himself and Zala, there'll be six
all told in the hunting party.

. . . .

THEY TRUDGE ALONG A tree line, boots moving in a farmer's narrow
irrigation channel, now dry. The country all around is mostly flat. To their
immediate right is a field of opium poppies, already harvested, the stalks dry
and cracked. The sun beats down on their heads from a white sky. They work
in pairs, well-spaced. Two up front, two bring up the rear and two in the
centre, the pair in the centre being a radio operator and a soldier burdened
with the squad LMG, or light machine gun.

Taliban are around, though they tend to lie low in daylight. Merrick
knows they've brought in some of their best fighters from Pakistan, and
they're good at what they do. Very good. Those who weren't any good, or
had taken too long to learn, are dead, wounded or captured. The ones they're
fielding now are veterans, experts at laying IEDs — improvised explosive

devices. They conceal them well and cover them with fire teams who know how to set an ambush, how to move and how to cover dead ground.

They're formidable.

Merrick wants to move fast, but he also knows that unless he exercises caution, all he'll achieve is his patrol's destruction, and his own. So they watch for wires, for a footprint that shouldn't be there, for a clod of earth that somehow isn't right, for scuff marks in the sand, for fallen leaves and broken twigs out of place, for newly disturbed soil that doesn't match the immediate surroundings.

Tourists on safari in Africa or South Asia are likely to complain to their guide that they can see nothing when they first venture out. The guide will explain that for the first few days in the bush, it's natural if his clients see little if any of the wild game they want to photograph. Everyone's different, of course, but within three days or thereabouts, the tourists' eyes start to adapt to not only the colours of the bushveld but to the finer shades of brown and green, to shadows and above all, to shapes. It's a matter of survival for prey and predator alike.

Merrick's target isn't Taliban, but an Afghan police officer with the equivalent rank of captain. He's feared and hated by local people. At best, the Afghan police deployed to Helmand by the Karzai government are lazy and useless. Some are thieves. Many take drugs. Many also like to fuck one another. But this man is a monster, and he's by no means alone. He and his kind are the reason that the Taliban have been so effective in returning in strength. Villagers are afraid for their women and children, and with good reason. The good Captain Lodi has his men abduct women and boys for him so he can rape them at his leisure in police stations, which he does often and with impunity.

The sad truth is that when the Taliban were in power, most ordinary people — workers, farmers — felt secure despite the harsh, discriminatory treatment of women. Like people everywhere, the Afghan civilian population wanted to work, earn a wage, eat, raise a family, and live in peace in what passes for a normal life. Opium production was outlawed and fell abruptly. But Merrick is well aware that when the Taliban were toppled, the drug lords came back, sometimes with official government titles and Kabul's backing, bringing with them their own private militias thousands strong, many of them former Taliban fighters. And with them came a corrupt national police force that now terrorises towns and villages.

It hasn't taken long for Taliban spies to detect a shift in public opinion, a desperate desire for stability and an end to the exploitation. The village elders have bowed to the inevitable and secretly welcomed them back — not with any enthusiasm, mind — and Merrick is of the opinion that the maliks had no real alternative, given the failure of international forces, including the British in Helmand, to provide adequate protection.

It's usually the Taliban who attack police stations. Today, it's likely to be a patrol of the joint Afghan-British special forces.

• • • •

THE COP SHOP IS A NEW build. It was opened with great fanfare a year ago. It has — or rather, had — sleeping accommodation, a sports centre, lecture rooms, decent bathrooms. All mod cons, as well as the usual police cells and charge office. Paid for by U.S. and European taxpayers. Six months later, it was attacked by the Taliban and partially destroyed.

It commands Route 61, a strategic road linking the Helmand provincial capital of Lashkar Gah with the only other Helmand towns of any significance, Gereshk and Sangin, and running all the way to Afghanistan's second city, the former royal capital of Kandahar.

Zala approaches the front entrance while the rest of the patrol spread out. Two CF333 members dodge out of sight around the back. She bangs on the door and shouts out in Pashto to open up. She says she wants to speak to a Captain Lodi. There's no response, but a face appears at a barred window and vanishes.

There's the sound of a door banging shut, angry voices, shouts. Captain Lodi and two of his confederates — wearing light blue police uniforms, Lodi armed with a 9mm Smith & Wesson pistol in a shoulder holster and his subordinates carrying two Romanian AKM rifles — have tried to escape out the back, clambering over a wall and kicking open a door to an alley. When Merrick and Zala investigate, they find the policemen have been disarmed, lie spread-eagled face down in the dirt, and are covered by the rifles of two grinning Afghan special forces soldiers.

Inside, a young male is discovered naked and cowering in the corner of one cell, chained to a bed frame. He's filthy, streaked with dried blood — his own — bruised, hungry and thirsty. It's not difficult to work out what's happened to him. He tells the Triples he's twelve. He's been held there for two days. He's freed, offered a bucket of water to wash, as well as food and water to drink, and someone finds him clean clothes. On Merrick's orders, his place in the cell is taken by two of the three police officers.

Merrick decides to question Captain Lodi himself in the charge office. Zala will translate.

They exchange glances. In that look, much is meant but is left unsaid. Does Merrick know she knows what he's about to do, and that he'd decided even before the patrol had set out?

He uses a trenching tool. It's like a short spade. But with the blade folded out and clipped in place, it's more like a hatchet.

He looks at Zala and gestures with his head. She goes out and waits, making sure no one interrupts what's about to happen. Merrick doesn't want witnesses. When the job's done, he mutters two words.

'Filthy bastard!'

In the routine report Merrick submits the following week to his commanding officer, he states that during a visit to a police station, a notorious rapist, Captain Sibghatullah Lodi of the Afghan National Police, while under arrest, went for a handgun, a 9mm Makarov, hidden behind the counter of the charge office. Merrick had no option but to defend himself, cutting him down with his army-issue trenching tool, killing him instantly. Zala is the only witness. She backs up Merrick's account with a brief, hand-written note in Pashto and English to the effect that Merrick acted in self-defence. She signs it, and Merrick attaches it to his report.

Nothing more is said, by Merrick's CO, the UK's Special Forces Command, the British Army hierarchy or anyone else. As far as Merrick and Zala are concerned, a brutish but essential justice has been served.

Chapter 30

The Ziggurat, south London, 16:22, November 16

An encrypted one liner from 'Mother' summoned Bridie to a meeting presided over by 'C' somewhat late — what little daylight there was had faded into twilight gloom.

'C' sought Bridie's presence in the conference room next to his office. Asap. No word of explanation and no apology for the inconvenience were offered. It wasn't far from the Taskforce offices, a mere ten-minute stroll, but it was pelting down. It had rained all night and all day, and it was forecast to continue without respite for the next few days and nights. Hundreds of flood warnings were in place across soggy England. The Midlands were already transformed into an inland sea. Only Scotland, hardbound in an iron mantle of ice and shrouded in fog, would escape the wet. Such was the nature of global warming and the failure of government to repair flood defences. At least, Bridie consoled herself, there was little or no wind.

She pounced on someone's golfing umbrella in reception — Bridie had no idea whose, but hopefully, she'd be back by the time the owner noticed its absence. She set out at once, frowning at the thought that she'd end up with soaked feet and wet legs no matter the size of the red and white contraption decorated with an ad for Santander Bank that she held up with both hands over her head. At least the Vauxhall railway bridge would provide some cover for part of the way.

On Bridie's arrival, Madge took the still-dripping umbrella from her without a word and opened the conference room's double doors. Bridie walked in. She saw that 'C' faced the window, his back to her. He didn't turn when she entered. Sir Liam Venables, his opposite number at Five, was slumped in his chair and impassive as usual. It was impossible to know what the man thought. He paid Bridie no attention.

The atmosphere, Bridie thought, was a little strange.

At the end of the table, nursing what looked like a large measure of scotch, was someone Bridie recognised but had never met.

Lord Neville Sacristan, life peer for his services to national security, long retired from the civil service, at least officially, was a living legend in the intelligence and security establishment for half a century and perhaps longer.

Bridie's glance took him in at once: long, unkempt white hair, white beard and beetling eyebrows, heavy spectacles, cavernous cheeks, watery, pale eyes, and round shoulders. An old man who seemed to have shrunk inside his thee-piece black suit, which now seemed far too large a chrysalis for its living fossil. A character from one of Tolkien's books. An ogre. If it wasn't for the suit and the whisky, he could have been Robinson Crusoe stuck on a desert island. A former 'C' and subsequently head of Five, with a reputation as a moderniser in the bad, shabby old days of the impecunious 70s. A hawkish Cold War warrior. Adviser to Thatcher. Ruthless hunter of traitors. Also, a maker and breaker of politicians. A tough man with the old-world manners of what used to be considered a gentleman. It was rumoured that he carried a garotte in his pocket as someone might carry a handkerchief; in his case, the garrotte was said to be not cheese wire but silk.

And now?

Bridie did not wait to be invited to sit. She helped herself to a chair halfway along the coffin-shaped conference table and sat down, kicking off her wet shoes and enjoying the feel of the thick carpet on her damp stockinged feet and toes.

Now she could see that Venables was hiding a phone on his lap and watching something. Netflix, perhaps?

She would have liked a whisky, but she wasn't offered one. A coffee would do, but she wasn't offered that either.

The silence continued. No one so much as moved a muscle. Rain streamed down the windows like the Victoria Falls, and Bridie wondered if 'C' could see anything at all out there.

Probably not.

Her eye fell on a few items on the table and, without asking or waiting to be invited, Bridie sat forward, reached over and pulled them towards herself one by one. No one seemed to take any notice, nor did anyone object.

She recognised them all. A CX report from agent LUCY about a Rome party for far-right politicians that Bridie had graded as two stars in the hope it would languish unnoticed at the bottom of the pile. Obviously, she had failed. Ditto, a CX transcript of a discussion between TCO Bernard Cuttle and LUCY describing the state of newly appointed Prime Minister Richard Carstairs spotted by chance at Rome airport on the morning of Armistice Day. Ditto, a more recent report by the same TCO on LUCY's confirmation that very morning of the identities of people photographed at that same Rome gathering on November 10, the eve of Armistice Day.

Those persons being Luca Pacioli, billionaire supporter of Italy's far-right Fdl and donor to several European far-right parties, including Britain's Tories; Igor Taras Vishinsky, expat Russian oligarch with oil exploration and gold interests in Mali; Jean Martin, French ex-legionnaire, pimp and far-right muscle for hire; Richard Carstairs, old Etonian, inveterate liar, deputy prime minister and now Prime Minister of the United Kingdom. Oh, one more — Bridie almost forgot the grinning billionaire Leo Brodzinski, resident of Monaco.

Bridie felt the hair rise on the nape of her neck.

This is a lynching party, but who's the victim?

'C' seemed to speak to the window as if he'd watched her reflection in the streaming glass. 'May I ask, Bridie, why those CX reports were graded two stars?'

'They fell into the category "interesting if true," at least without further elaboration or context, which wasn't then available.'

'You've seen the photographs?'

'I have.'

'Do you feel, now that you've seen them and the subjects have been identified, that those same CX reports might merit a higher grade than two stars?'

'Possibly.'

'Possibly?'

Bridie did not respond. She would not walk into a trap by her own volition.

Silence.

'C' turned from the window. He pulled out a chair and sat down. He made no attempt to introduce her to Lord Sacristan but put his hands together as if in prayer, the tips of his pianist's fingers touching his lips.

'I understand Brodzinski funds something called the State Strategy Institute, based in Tufton Street. A think tank.'

'Junk tank,' growled Sacristan.

'C' gave no sign of having heard. 'And furthermore that both the late Sir Thomas Brownlow and General Ocean were on the Institute's payroll as consultants.'

'Consultants, my arse,' rasped the combative Sacristan. 'They were employed to flog arms and spyware to anyone who'd pay. Myanmar. Saudi. Kazakhstan. Iran. Israel. Syria. The world's deepest shitholes, palm trees an optional extra.'

Bridie thought it better to say nothing at this point and stay out of what seemed to be shaping up to be an interesting argument. Five's director general had so far said nothing. He was still staring down at his screen hidden below the surface of the conference table.

Personal phones were supposed to be left with security at the entrance. Bridie had surrendered hers on arrival as a dutiful servant of the state.

'C' pushed his chair back and got to his feet again. He looked agitated. He turned back to the window as if trying to hide his expression.

Sacristan turned to Bridie. 'I should perhaps explain, Ms Connor, that I'm not here in any *official* capacity and not as chair of the Parliamentary Intelligence and Security Committee. I've been invited to offer advice in a purely *personal* capacity.'

'I see,' Bridie said, not seeing at all. Sacristan's accent was public school, as one might expect, but somewhat dated by half a century or so. He would pronounce 'golf' without the letter l, and 'often' as 'orfen.'

Sir Liam Venables cleared his throat and spoke up at last, his voice pitched so low that Bridie had to listen hard.

'The State Strategy Institute is part of the Globe Network, which is linked to the Legacy Foundation, our very own Centre for Economic Affairs, and several others promoting extreme neoliberal politics, from Buenos Aires to Seoul. Your colleagues in Six know this better than we do. We keep an eye on the worst of them, as do our friends on this side of the river,' he glanced at 'C,' 'but I see no conspiracy here. Simply greedy people, a parcel of rogues more than willing to take dark money from anyone wealthy and willing to line their pockets. After all, the government does all it can to encourage Russian and Chinese oligarchs to park their ill-gotten gains in our banks. Climate change deniers. The fossil fuel lobby. Tobacco companies. Arms manufacturers. Look at the City of London, if you will. Look at the Commons and the so-called Lords. If you do want to stop them, reform electoral law and tighten financial regulation. It's not really a national security issue but one of poor governance and corruption. More than half a century of it.'

A neat argument in favour of inaction, Bridie thought.

'Sir Thomas,' said Sacristan in his deepest voice, turning to 'C' who still had his back to the table. 'It's time we stopped beating about the bush and came to the point. Is Prime Minister Richard Carstairs part of this cabal, or is he not? Is he working on behalf of a hostile foreign power? Is he an agent of influence, and if so, whose? More to the point, what are we to do about it?'

'Nothing,' said Venables in his subdued voice. 'How does any civil servant inform his or her prime minister he or she is an evil idiot and a traitor who deserves to be hanged, drawn and quartered? I for one am not going to volunteer to bell *this* particular cat.'

Sacristan wasn't done. 'As a matter of fact, it wouldn't be the first time an incumbent prime minister is suspected of working for hostile foreign interests. You know it. I know it.'

Bridie realised his lordship was referring to the late Labour Prime Minister, Harold Wilson, and suspicions on the part of some senior Security Service officers in the 1970s that he was a Soviet penetration agent. Nonsense, of course, but paranoia was a necessary ingredient in all counterintelligence operations — until it got out of hand as indeed it had.

'Socialising with unsavoury characters isn't evidence of anything except execrable taste,' Venables added in his quiet voice. 'Carstairs might well be a cunt, but that in itself isn't a crime. Westminster's full of 'em. One solution would be to compel all public figures, especially would-be MPs, to submit to a brain scan every election year for signs of psychopathy. If they fail, then they should be barred from public office for a minimum of ten years.'

Bridie wasn't sure if Venables was being serious.

'C' turned around. He was known to dislike 'foul language.'

'Thank you all for coming in today and letting me have your views. It's much appreciated. Lord Sacristan, my driver will be happy to take you wherever you want to go, as long as it's in London.'

'The Cotswolds, actually,' said Sacristan and showed his tobacco and coffee stained teeth in a mischievous grin as 'C' blanched in dismay. 'Only joking, old boy.'

Bridie recalled someone — she couldn't for the moment recall who — as having said that the old goat was a bibliophile who owned a first edition *Hypnerotomachia Poliphili*, known in English as *The Dream of Poliphilus*, said to have been written by Frances Colonna and published in 1499 by the remarkable Venetian Aldus Manutius. It was a fine example of incunable, or early printing, apparently, in which Sacristan specialised as the owner of a tiny but world-renowned bookshop devoted to such rare works and located somewhere in the depths of South Kensington.

Excellent cover for an old spy, no doubt. An old spy who managed to be both cynical and patriotic, whatever that meant these days.

The meeting was over, and like most meetings involving senior civil servants, Bridie thought, it had expended much hot air and decided nothing.

It was still pissing down outside.

'C' approached. 'Bridie, a word, if you have a moment? My office? I'd appreciate an update on our assassin.'

Maybe she'd get her dram of single malt after all.

• • • •

IN THE EVENT, SHE DIDN'T. Madge brought them both coffee in Sir Thomas's precious 'Italian' blue Spode chinaware instead and, glancing pointedly at her watch, announced her own imminent departure.

'C' didn't seem to mind. He played mother, and when he'd served them both, he sat back in his leather club chair, straightened his legs out, crossed his ankles, admired his expensive footwear and asked, 'What did you think?'

'About what?'

'The meeting,' 'C' said.

'It didn't seem especially urgent.'

'It wasn't, but I wanted you there so I could get a second opinion on the discussion.'

'I'm afraid I don't have one. Nothing was resolved, after all. It seemed to be no more than an airing of views.'

'And Sacristan's line on Carstairs?'

'Lord Sacristan didn't express an opinion, exactly, but asked the question. As for my opinion of Sir Liam Venables and his remarks, I thought he took a sensibly cautious approach.'

'Quite. I'm glad you think so. Liam is a calm voice and a steady hand in a crisis.'

They drank their coffee, watching each other warily.

'What I want to know, Bridie, is whether our mysterious assassin is targeting members of these Tufton Street, er...'

'Junk tanks,' suggested Bridie.

'Oh, right. Yes. Junk tanks. I must remember that. Do you think this is some sort of crusade on his part — assuming the killer is a he — against the Right?'

'Definitely a he. The only evidence so far is circumstantial. My chief investigator believes the motive to be personal rather than ideological.'

'That would be Septimus Brass of the National Crime Agency, right?'

'Indeed.'

'And how does he come to that conclusion?'

'Not entirely sure as yet, but Septimus claims to be very close to identifying the assassin.'

Not true. He never suggested such a thing, but Bridie feels she must throw the boss a bone in the form of hopeful news, even if it is a lie. It's five days since those first assassinations, and they seemed no closer to catching the murderer than they were at the start.

'You'll let me know as soon as Brass does, won't you?'

'Of course, sir.'

He's feeling the pressure. Bridie wouldn't be at all surprised if ministers were demanding the shutting down or at least 'downsizing' of the Taskforce because of the spiralling cost, while the Met would want all its officers back on normal police duties.

It wasn't a good time to lower their guard.

• • • •

IT WAS ONLY WHEN SHE reached home that Bridie realised she'd forgotten the umbrella she'd 'borrowed' and had left it behind at the Ziggurat.

Never mind. Madge aka 'Mother' would take care of it.

Alec had made a salad, and now Bridie was home, he proceeded to make them both mushroom omelettes. She loved his omelettes, not least because he always added a *soupçon* of oyster sauce to boost the flavour.

He'd also found a reasonably priced bottle of Frascati at Lidl, at least of good enough quality to remind them both of their romantic breaks many years ago on the Amalfi Coast.

That felt like a world away. Another life of sunshine and leisure.

They were both ravenously hungry, so they ate first, talked later.

'Have you caught the brute yet?'

Bridie shook her head. She was nibbling cheese. They'd polished off the wine, and Bridie was wondering if they had any red. She was in the mood for drinking and reaching the stage of feeling pleasantly squiffy.

'Do you know who he is?'

'If I did and told you, I'd have to kill you.'

'Very bloody funny.'

'You know I shouldn't talk shop outside the shop.'

'But you want to, I can tell.'

'Am I that obvious? You know I do, yes.'

'Maybe a postprandial drop of single malt will help break down the ramparts of professional rectitude.'

'I love it when you talk dirty. We could always try, couldn't we?'

So they did.

Sprawled together on the sofa, wrapped in each other's arms, Bridie confided in Alec — up to a point, a point beyond what she knew was safe, sensible, permissible, lawful.

But who would ever know?

'Here goes. There's a feeling among senior members of the security and intelligence community that our mystery assassin is on a one-man crusade to kill off members of a network of the far right — wealthy financiers, business people, politicians — and that at the centre of this target group is our very own esteemed and unelected prime minister, Richard Carstairs.'

'Do you share this so-called feeling?'

'No.'

'Why not?'

'It's premature. The evidence is circumstantial. Everyone he's killed so far has indeed been on the right, it's true. Yet my people believe this isn't ideological at all but more personal.'

'Personal — how?'

'I don't know as yet.'

'But if you're wrong, and their conspiracy theory is correct, and this dickhead Carstairs is next on the killer's hit list, or on the list at all, what then?'

'I can say goodbye to my illustrious career and end up serving out the rest of my days as assistant station chief in Malawi until statutory retirement at fifty-five. Or Vanuatu. If they have assistant station chiefs in those places, which I doubt. I'd better check it out tomorrow. Or maybe as senior analyst in Registry here, in the depths of the Ziggurat. My male peers would dearly love to see me brought down a peg — several pegs.'

'I like the sound of either place, especially Vanuatu at this time of year, at least while it's still above water. But not Registry. It would drive you bonkers.'

'I know. Thanks.'

'I'd come with you,' Alec said, hugging her.

'That's sweet. But it may not come to that.'

'Pity. Let's go to bed and dream of Pacific islands. We'll do the dishes tomorrow.'

They read a little in bed.

'Any good?'

Bridie had begun Benjamin Labatut's latest novel.

'Very good,' she answered, also smiling. 'So far.'

'I haven't read — what's his name?'

She held up the front cover so Alec could read the author's name for himself.

'It's a novel?'

'I suppose it is,' Bridie said, 'but it's partly non-fiction and partly fiction. Sometimes, it's hard to know where the non-fiction ends and the fiction begins. Like spying. It's very clever. Disconcertingly so.'

'It's about what?'

'Oh, just about everything. Life. Death. The universe.'

She didn't manage more than three pages before they were both asleep.

• • • •

THE EXPLOSION — A GIANT *whoomph* — shook the building and seemed to Bridie to lift their home up and drop it down to earth again. It was followed by the sound of glass windows shattering outside.

The bedside clock read 03:31.

She thought at first that whatever it was had happened inside their home, which must logically mean a gas explosion. An accident.

Heart thumping, Bridie pulled on a bathrobe and pushed her feet into slippers. Alec dragged on jeans and shoes but left the laces undone. They rushed downstairs, holding onto each other, not knowing what to expect, trembling in a confusion of fear, excitement, shock.

The front door was missing. The night outside gaped blackly in at them, with street lights flickering in the rain. Splinters of wood and shards of glass were scattered throughout the hall, a plume of destruction stretching all along the floor. The doorframe, what was left of it, was blackened by fire, so too the wallpaper in the hallway.

Flames licked hungrily at fragments of the coir doormat and the bottom right of the charred door frame. Alec leapt forward and beat at them in fury with his pyjama top, suppressing them but failing to put them out. The pyjama top also caught fire, and he flung the smouldering striped cotton outside into a puddle on the stone path.

'Jesus Christ,' he said. He repeated it over and over. 'Jesus Christ.'

When the firemen and police turned up, sirens blaring, they found the couple standing outside their home, clinging to each other, soaked, both of them shaking with cold or shock, or both.

'We're on the bastard's hit list,' Alec said out loud to no one in particular, clutching around his shoulders a foil thermal blanket a fire officer had given him.

Bridie, also cloaked in silver foil and resembling a wet Tin Man in *The Wonderful World of Oz*, turned her face to Alec and whispered in his ear. 'No, Alec. No. Shush now, darling. It was just a warning, that's all. Don't speak.'

She blamed herself; she shouldn't have said anything at all to him about the mystery assassin.

Chapter 31

K *andahar Province, Afghanistan, June, 2019*
Merrick's latest tour is nearly over, with only a fortnight to go. He should be happy. He's survived. He's going home. That should be enough for anyone who's emerged alive and whole from what most people would think of as an ordeal.

The brief interval of two weeks is taken up with final reports, debriefings, handing over to a new team and surrendering equipment. British Army tours are far too short, only six months. That means the first two months are spent learning how to carry out the given task, two months doing the job — if that — and two months winding down, handing over to the newcomers and counting off the days. It takes most people six months before they're getting into their stride, in Merrick's opinion, so they never really do. It also means that deploying a single brigade of 3,000 troops involves five other brigades of similar size — one just arrived and taking over from one about to leave, one already left, yet another about to deploy and a fifth being lined up to deploy in turn. A military production line. As rotations go, it's grossly inefficient. Even worse, in Merrick's view, is the unfortunate fact that the brigade headquarters itself only serves in theatre for six months before being replaced in its entirety. The result is that on arrival and for some considerable time thereafter, no one knows anything, not the country, the politics, or what they're supposed to be doing until of course, it's time to leave again. The reality falls far short of the stated objective; far from bringing peace and stability to the Afghan people, it degenerates into claims of kinetic battles as victories (as opposed to gaining the trust of the locals) and the acquisition by egoistical officers of a gong or two on the way home.

Captain Merrick has mixed feelings. He knows he needs a rest, and a fortnight of alcohol-fuelled self-indulgence somewhere agreeable would see him right. But his departure from Kandahar comes with a reluctance caused by the most unsoldierly of reasons: a strange and, for him, uncharacteristic tug of the heart over someone he barely knows.

For one thing, there's no sneaking off behind rock or hill for a quick snog with Zala, even if she wanted it, nor is there any hope of an hour in a lone, olive green Army tent used for the purpose of sexual congress between consenting and usually married partners serving in the military. Such a tent does exist unofficially (officially, no one is aware of its existence), with a generator to power a single light bulb over the entrance; when the light's on, it's a signal that the tent is occupied, and whoever is next in line must stay back and await their turn. There's a secret booking system, and husband and wife (or boyfriend and girlfriend, for the Army has yet to adapt to the notion of same-sex partnerships) can spend the best part of an entire night together, especially if one partner has had to travel a great distance on a twenty-four-hour pass, hitching rides on helicopters and fixed-wing transport aircraft, followed by a lift on a Snatch Land Rover to reach their destination.

That's all very well for members of British forces; it would be another matter entirely for a UK serving officer to have sexual relations with a single female Afghan noncom and subordinate, even with her enthusiastic consent. Zala would be disgraced and shamed; Merrick would be court-martialled, in all likelihood, for a breach of discipline and gross violation of regulations.

Only once during his tour has he seen Zala without her full equipment on her back, shoulders, waist and thighs. Quite by accident, he stumbles upon three female Afghans, all members of CF333. On returning from a patrol, they've dumped their gear in neat piles — weapons, backpack, helmets, elbow and knee pads and so on — and are helping to wash one another's hair, faces, feet, hands with the aid of buckets and with much throwing of mud and water and immense merriment. As noisy and carefree as kids, he thinks. They are fully dressed, of course, in green t-shirts, camouflage combat pants, web belts and sandals.

Unfucked lovelies, all.

Like some prudish nineteenth-century Presbyterian, Merrick turns his back at once and retreats in haste, almost tripping over guy ropes and his own boots, embarrassed and mumbling apologies in his poor Pashto, their musical laughter ringing in his ears.

What strikes him most is how slim Zala is, how womanly and firm her youthful flesh, the grace in the sweet curve of her neck like a swan's, the sheen of her hair as glossy as blue-black crow's feathers, those white, even teeth, the wide smile, the melodious birdsong of her voice.

Those extraordinary eyes.

It's an image that pursues him day and night.

He's hooked. None of this delicious but painful feeling that arises in the stoical and diffident Merrick is made any easier by the distance between them while they must yet serve together. A distance that is imposed by gender, culture, rank, and her faith. (Merrick has no faith; he considers the words 'faith' and 'belief' to be the most dangerous in the English language). He leads her and her comrades out on patrols himself into hostile territory. At other times, he watches as she and her unit leave the base for the unknown: for raids, patrols and intelligence missions from which he knows she may never return.

Today, she has an intelligence assignment of the kind she excels at but which poses the greatest danger. With two other females from the Triples, she will reconnoitre a village that's thought to have welcomed the resurgent Taliban. It will take great courage, which Merrick knows she possesses in spades. She wears a midnight blue burka. She's unarmed. There's nothing on her person that might identify her as an operative working as a Triple with the British under the auspices of the Karzai government in Kabul. In terms of protection, she and her comrades are stark naked in their vulnerability.

Merrick stands on the top of the compound wall and watches them leave in a cloud of beige dust, sitting in the back of a battered white Datsun pickup driven by a male Triple in threadbare Afghan civilian shalwar kameez and turban, none of it new or costly. A peasant, then, with a valid civilian identity as a farmer, who will drop them off at a crossroads so they can complete their approach to the village on foot.

All the women have in the way of protection is their wit, the sodality of their gender, their shared experiences of forming almost from birth an underclass under the domination of an austere and cruel patriarchy, of family and friends and of their own lives as villagers themselves. As women, then, they will talk to the village women to whom they have access simply by being women. They won't be perceived as a threat, even if their physical access is limited to their hosts' tiny yard and kitchen space. They'll accept what hospitality they're offered, sit on the packed earth, drink the green tea, laugh and chat, maybe help with preparing the family meal, careful not to ask too many leading questions, but listen closely to what is said and by whom.

So far, that has proved enough to come out of it unscathed, but will it be this time? So much of survival comes down to luck.

Zala is of the Barakzai, once the paramount Pashtun tribe of Afghanistan, descended from soldiers who served Nadir Shah, founder of the short-lived Afsharid dynasty in Iran, and who were settled on land seized from the Ghilzai. Influential in Pashtun circles even now, the Barakzai occupy large tracts of land between Kandahar and Herat in the west.

Merrick watches through binoculars until the Datsun has vanished in the wilderness, and even the dust cloud has dispersed. He resolves not to seem unusually glum while she's away — not so glum that anyone would notice — and he'll make every effort not to appear unduly cheerful if and when Zala returns.

At times like this, he senses a flutter of fear in his gut, bordering on an unfamiliar feeling of panic. For the first time he can remember, he cares about someone else.

He needn't bother. His secret is already out.

They can't help it, for they've failed to conceal entirely the enjoyment they derive from each other's company. They can't help it as much as they try. They laugh a lot when together off duty, although it's not always clear, even to them, what they find so amusing. Merrick tries to be especially stern when leading his little force into the field and gives Zala no special favours. Rather the opposite. He tries to find things to criticise and comes across as harsh. That, too, is noticed by others.

Partly, it's language. Zala speaks English, more or less, and he tries and usually fails in his efforts to speak Pashto with a terrible accent, in itself an entertaining horror show to Afghan ears. They both have to translate mentally their respective tongues — Pashto to English, English to Pashto — before they can speak, leading to much hesitation, many blunders, much repetition and a great deal of confusion for both. All of which they find hilarious. It has to be said, though, that Zala shows every sign of progressing in her mastery of English, while Merrick offers little hope of learning anything much at all.

Officers and other ranks of the joint special forces teams live in close proximity. Only the males and females are segregated in their tented accommodation. They all eat together. They share the same food. There's no such thing as an officers' mess. It means that Zala and Merrick see each other rather more often than they otherwise would, whether or not they intend to do so and despite the wide gap in their respective ranks.

His last official act of his tour is to promote Zala to corporal.

. . . .

THE LANKY, ALMOST CHINLESS Lieutenant Colonel Godwin Cootes-Maycock, OBE, offers Merrick a clammy hand in farewell.

They're standing outside the squadron headquarters, a green tent tethered to the ground that puffs up like a balloon and then shrinks like a beating heart of canvas, pushed and pulled by a stiff wind that whips their legs with horsetails of sand. There are seven tents in all, set out in a triangle, protected by Hesco barriers, razor wire, sandbag strongpoints and slit trenches. A miniature fortress.

'Is it true what I hear, Peter, that you're spending your well-earned leave in-country?'

'It is. Only two weeks. I thought I'd try to see something of the country and people.'

'Sightseeing in the middle of a war? Good God, man! I hope you know what you're doing.'

'I hope so, too.'

'You'll be unarmed, on your own, without a uniform and no means of asking for help — not that we could offer it even if we were inclined to do so. You'll be off the books as far as we're concerned. You do know, I suppose, what'll happen if the Talibs get their claws into you, don't you?'

'I do.'

'Well, each to his own, chum. I'd have preferred the fleshpots of Singapore, Hong Kong, Manila or Bangkok myself. Let off steam, I would. At least I'd be able to enjoy some serious drinking, if not whoring.' Merrick thinks the colonel sounds almost wistful. 'I have to remind myself that I'm a married man, so it's out of the question. But you, Peter, on the other hand...' he doesn't finish the sentence.

Both officers are clad in clean, starched and ironed desert camo, though Merrick's combats are somewhat faded by now, plus desert boots, stable belts in their respective regimental colours, berets, their sleeves rolled up. Cootes-Maycock is clean-shaven, while Merrick has allowed his facial hair to grow into a piratical beard of unruly curls of reddish hue. Merrick knows what his soldiers say about Cootes-Maycock. One old wag, a staff sergeant, said of the colonel: 'This officer will undoubtedly go far. He should start straight away.'

Merrick is going to visit Zala's family, but he tells no one. It's the respectful way to do these things here. Zala has left for home the day before, escorted by an uncle and a cousin. They'll travel by taxi, bus and motorcycle, and the journey will take them two or three days, depending on the state of the roads — and the war. She has given Merrick precise details of the location. They can't be seen travelling together, for obvious reasons.

Cootes-Maycock: 'By the way, Peter, I felt I should tell you — if you don't know this already — you're in line for a crown on your shoulders. You'll be a major sooner rather than later. If you're unwise enough to put yourself forward for yet another tour, you'll probably find yourself in command of a squadron.'

'I've already put my name down, Colonel.'

'You're a bloody fool. Or mad.'

'Thank you. I'll take that as a compliment.' Merrick takes a step back, draws himself up ramrod straight, pulls his elbows into his sides, and salutes. Instructors at the Army's Pirbright Training Centre would have approved.

'No need for that here, old chap,' mutters Cootes-Maycock, embarrassed, but he returns the courtesy with a leisurely flap of his right hand as if waving away a fly. It's out of habit, perhaps.

'I know,' Merrick replies. 'But I'll salute who I fucking well like. Sir.'

• • • •

TWENTY DAYS LATER, a few minutes after noon, Trooper Mark Tearney notices a plume of dust approach along an unmetalled road from the northwest, the only road. The plume becomes a dust cloud at the foot of which is a dot that grows in size and eventually materialises as a motorcycle. In another couple of minutes, he can make out two men.

Tearney, who's on guard duty, informs his guard commander, a lance sergeant. The lance sergeant, Travers, joins him on the wall, and they both watch through binoculars as the motorcycle — a 150cc Honda — comes to a standstill about 400 yards away. The driver and passenger dismount, the driver handing his pillion rider a bundle that he's kept up front between his knees. The passenger hands the motorcyclist something in return, possibly the fare. They exchange a few words, give each other slight bows, right hands on their respective hearts out of mutual respect, no doubt saying their formal farewells; then the passenger picks up the bundle, throws it onto one shoulder and starts walking towards the patrol base.

The motorcyclist kick starts his machine, turns it around, and it put-puts off in the direction it came, trailing blue smoke and dust.

'Doesn't appear to be armed,' says Tearney.

Travers grunts. 'You can never tell with these bastards. He's probably carrying under his shirt. Could be one of those fuckin' suicide bombers.'

Tearney cocks his SA-80 rifle. He watches the figure through the sight. Travers shifts himself over to the seat behind the .50 cal, slams a round into the breech, pushes the safety catch off and swings the barrel over to cover the target.

The man comes on directly. He's left the road, such as it is. He doesn't amble but strides along with a sense of purpose. Tearney notes he wears traditional clothing: grey shalwar kameez, brown waistcoat, grey blanket or pothu folded over his left shoulder, a grey and silver turban on his head. His brown face is lowered as he watches where he places his feet, feet encased in sandals of the traditional kind and made of leather strips and tractor tyres — cheap but hard-wearing. He's taking care not to step on a mine or a scorpion. His beard is full and auburn.

The stranger stops some eighty yards away. He drops the bundle, flings the pothu down on top of it, removes his turban and adds that to the pile. He looks up at the two soldiers, arms akimbo, and waits.

Tearney asks, 'Is that really an Afghan? He's got blue eyes.'

'Loads of them have blue eyes, mate.'

The man below raises a hand to his eyes to see them better against the rays of a low sun.

'Are you fellas going to just sit there sunbathing all bloody day or let me in?'

'Christ, he's one of ours,' says Travers in astonishment.

Two soldiers are sent out for a closer look. They're told to inspect the stranger and to search him and his belongings for weapons. Or explosives. They are wary, rightly so, and approach from two sides, rifles at the ready, as one might advance on a poisonous snake.

One steps in close, pats the stranger down quickly, then jumps well back while his mate examines the pile of belongings, poking gingerly at it with the muzzle of his rifle. Up on the wall, Tearney and Travers watch, weapons trained on the visitor.

The bundle turns out to be Merrick's Army-issue backpack, full of his military gear, save for weapons and ammunition.

A Scouse accent: 'Christ, sir, we didn't know, yeah?'

West Yorkshire: 'Sorry, Captain. No one told us you was coming in today, like.'

They look embarrassed, guilty as schoolboys who've failed a test. Merrick grins at the lads, showing his teeth through his ragged beard. They are so young, so innocent and yet to be blooded, to use a fox-hunting term. Scarcely weaned, he thinks, and Merrick imagines he can see the residue of their mothers' milk on their lips even now. Innocent. He was like that not so long ago. Untested. Comradeship and a sense of belonging to a military community — regiment, battalion, company, platoon, section — yes, this can be taught to a large degree, forcibly hammered into tractable young minds and bodies on the parade ground and assault course, along with its very opposite, the lessons in the dehumanising of opponents as 'the enemy.' Both blunt instruments are necessary to turn teenagers into warriors.

But there's a deeper, unspoken, inexpressible *geheimschaft* — an invisible bond that marks all who've killed and emerged unscathed, physically at any rate. These uniformed children have not yet seen how shockingly bright hot blood looks when freshly spilled, nor have they breathed in the fierce tang of it. But they will, given time and opportunity.

Merrick tells them he's back from his wee sightseeing trip to Herat. They don't know what to make of that. Is he kidding them? Sightseeing, really? What is Herat?

Verminous and undeniably dirty, of course, stinking, hungry, certainly — missing Zala already, it goes without saying — but in one piece, and that's something for which Merrick is grateful.

Zala is due back on duty in two days, and he can hardly wait to see her.

Chapter 32

Taskforce headquarters, south London, 18:50, November 16
Bridie sent a message to Septimus and Bernie to the effect that she'd like a brief meeting with both of them in her Taskforce office right away, please. *Now.*

Septimus managed to get in the first words as he knocked and entered, Bernie close on his heels.

'Heard what happened,' Septimus said, moving to a chair and dropping into it. 'Hope you're all okay. Your family, I mean.'

Bridie nodded. 'We are, thanks.'

Bernie's eager curiosity overrode discretion. 'Was it him — our assassin?'

'Who else could it have been?' Bridie regarded Bernie with her head slightly tilted, watching him take a seat alongside Septimus, that sardonic twitch in the corner of her mouth in play. Did he perhaps know something different?

'Then he knows who you are, where you live and what you do,' Bernie added, having sat, the palms of his hands clasped together and pressed between his knees as he rocked back and forth. He frowned, worried. 'Not good. It suggests he's getting information from the inside.'

'From here,' Septimus said. 'From inside the Taskforce. Someone's talking out of turn.'

'That's not the reason I wanted this meet,' Bridie said, brushing the memory of her scary overnight adventure aside. 'We can deal with that a little later, not right now.'

'It's a diversion,' Septimus said. 'That IED, I mean. Simple device, little more than a thunder flash and not intended to kill or maim. An attempt to throw us all off track. He knows we're close, and he's rattled. Tossing sand in our faces. A sign of desperation, I'd say.'

'You think? Wrecked my front door and could have wrecked us, too, if we'd been stood there,' Bridie said. But I assure you I'm not thrown off anything. And I hope no one else is, either. Do you know something you haven't yet told us, Septimus?'

'No, not really. No.' Septimus wore a devious expression and looked away, not wanting to meet her look. He seemed to find her out-of-date calendar fascinating all of a sudden.

Bridie continued, still watching him. 'I wanted to ask you both about Costa, the individual whose phone number was found on the body of the unidentified individual shot dead by police in Dover. You remember. It was in Costa's flat in Nice where two people were found murdered. Both killed with a shotgun. One of them being the former French Foreign Legionnaire named Jean Martin, who'd attended the Rome party and was present at the airport along with Carstairs the next morning, on Armistice Day. We still don't seem able to identify the second man also shot dead in Costa's flat that night. Maybe it was the mysterious Costa himself. French police spoke of a feud among gangsters. Do we know anything more?'

Bernie hunched his shoulders up around his long neck in a shrug and shook his head.

'No,' said Septimus.

'Do we have anything more on what went on at the Rome party Carstairs attended — aside from the party pics?'

Septimus and Bernie exchanged looks.

'No,' they said simultaneously.

'Perhaps, Bernie, you might ask LUCY to tap her contacts on what went on during the event Carstairs attended. And what goes on generally at that location. A luxurious mansion, right? Drugs, tarts, secret cameras, maybe? Gambling? Unless, of course, your agent's busy doing something more important.'

'She's not,' said Bernie. 'I'll get onto it right away.' He half rose, then fell back again into his seat when he realised Bridie wasn't finished.

'Who spent time with whom? Who was fucking who? Who was snorting coke? Who was smoking smack? Who was dealing? Who spent time together in the bedrooms? What deals were done? Facts, rumours, gossip. I want it all.'

'Sure,' Bernie said. 'No probs. LUCY's great at this kinda thing.'

'As for you, Septimus, when are you going to tell me whatever it is you're *not* telling me?'

'Soon, yeah,' Septimus said. 'I promise. Very, *very* soon.'

'You bloody well better, you sly old fox,' said Bridie, 'or I'll set the hounds on you. Don't think I won't. I wouldn't want to be in your shoes if I find you've been holding out on me. My door is always open to you both. Use it.'

Someone tapped once on Bridie's door and came straight in, not waiting for an invitation. It was Caro, looking slightly flushed and short of breath.

'This, just in. Minutes from here. Miles Street, Vauxhall. It's him, no doubt about it.'

She grabbed the remote off Bridie's desk and pointed it at the screen.

'When?' Septimus demanded. 'How long ago?'

'This morning. Look at the time group in the bottom left corner. 08:50. It's a CCTV camera he must have missed as he walked past that new block of flats. We missed it too, until a few minutes ago. A private security firm. There he is, going into a storage site under the arches. I'll speed it up. Here he comes out again, this time on a Honda Fireblade. Time: 09:20.'

The figure they saw was visible for a little over three seconds at an acute angle, and it was only partial, with half the man's body off-screen. They had a better look at his face as he emerged on the bike before he dropped his visor.

Cora repeated the take four times until all were satisfied.

'That's our man, alright,' said Bernie. 'Where'd he go?'

'Our people and the Met are on it,' Caro said. 'We're going to reconstruct his route if we can, using CCTV footage. We've got the bike registration, and we're distributing it nationally. We'll find it.'

Bridie had a suggestion. 'Perhaps the Met might consider putting out a public statement with the registration and an image of the bike itself or one of the same make and vintage. Good for the evening news if the ongoing bombing of Palestinians and Yemenis doesn't push everything else aside.'

'Sure thing.' Caro dropped the remote back on the desk and hurried out.

Septimus said, 'I'll organise a search of the premises right away and go there myself. 'We'll do a thorough sweep and try to get prints, DNA — all of it.'

'Wait.' Bridie held up a hand. She knew that a good manager had very little to do once his or her team was working smoothly, and it seemed clear to her that the Taskforce was doing so. Occasionally, though, the well-oiled machinery had to be tweaked. This was one of those moments.

'Odds are our killer will return and lock his bike away again. If so, we might follow him from there to wherever it is he sleeps and snatch him in the small hours when his guard's down. I'm assuming he has to sleep somewhere. He must have a base. So I suggest we should stay clear until we've figured out his movements — and put a tracker on the bike, too.'

Septimus said he'd sort out a stakeout.

'Professionals, Septimus. We're up against a pro. One slip and we'll lose him. He's no fool. This guy will smell a plainclothes cop within a half mile.'

'Right,' said Septimus, whose expression said this much was obvious.

'I can't use my people,' Bridie added. 'We don't operate on UK territory. We can ask the Met, maybe Special Branch. Or the Security Service.'

Septimus didn't trust the Met. Too many officers were corrupt, on the take or slapdash and lazy. He suggested his own people from the National Crime Agency.

Bridie turned to him. 'Can you rustle up a team right now — at such short notice? We'll need a static crew and a mobile one. Experienced people.'

'Sure.'

'Will you be part of it?'

'I'd rather leave it to the specialists. He's already proved that he knows my name and what I do. He might recognise me. Same goes for you, Bridie.'

Bernie looked up, cleared his throat. 'What if he's already on his way to his next target? He might not return tonight. Just asking....'

'All his targets have so far been London-based,' Bridie replied. 'It's always possible he'll make an exception and strike elsewhere, but I'm willing to risk it.'

Septimus had a question. 'Which reminds me. Where's our illustrious prime minister spending the night — the Honourable Richard Carstairs? Is he going to be out partying, or joining his fellow Bullingdon Club veterans for a riotous piss-up?'

Bridie was emphatic in her reply. 'Nope. The latest Special Branch report states he's intending to spend the night in the bosom of his family at Number Ten.'

Bernie snorted in derision. 'Scrabble night. How touching. We won't ask which of his several families.'

'Enough, Bernie, thank you,' Bridie said. 'We're very close to nailing the bastard, so let's keep this airtight. No leaks, no false steps.'

'No leaks,' Bernie repeated. 'No false steps.'

Caro walked back in again without knocking. 'Sorry. He's back again. Without the bike this time. Right now — in real time.'

They couldn't be sure in the failing light. It might be him; then again, it might not be. Opinion was divided. Miles Street was not well-lit, and the storage site was in shadow.

The phone on Bridie's desk rang. She listened then put her hand over the receiver. 'They've found the bike,' she announced. 'In west London. That was quick. Somebody reported it parked in their street after seeing it on the news.'

· · · ·

SEPTIMUS WAS WOKEN during the small hours, and it took a few seconds to locate and unscramble whatever had woken him from a dream in which he was watching himself scrambling up a mountainside. He had no idea why, and the experience was far from pleasant. He kept sliding down the dry scree of sand and rocks, scraping shins and knees. Afghanistan, by the look of it.

Trooper, for reasons best known to himself, was scratching at the front door, using both paws in a rapid digging motion, tail wagging. It was the frantic behaviour more typical of a Labrador than a Border Collie.

A furious Septimus was up at once, out of bed, on his bare feet and down the hall in an instant.

'What the hell do you think you're doing, Trooper?'

Trooper paused, looked up, whined, and went back to his digging, only more energetic than before.

'You've been fed and watered. You've had your evening walk and done your business. Stop that. Sit, damn you. *Sit!*'

Trooper sat, unwillingly, but Septimus saw he was ready to spring back into action.

'Down!'

Trooper lay down, watching Septimus with a sorrowful expression, muzzle between his front paws.

'What the hell is it with you, Trooper?' Trooper's tail thumped twice and was still. He didn't take his eyes off Septimus, gauging his master's expression. Why was his human so agitated?

Trooper had been given his Christmas present early because of the winter chill that had followed on the heels of all that rain. He'd seemed pleased with it when they'd gone out to the park that evening. Septimus had picked the warm, waterproof winter coat in Hunting Stewart plaid rather than the darker Black Watch tartan. He knew the Black Watch was a distinguished Highland regiment, of course, but it had been raised, or so he understood, to keep the Highlanders in their place as a defeated and subjugated nation. It seemed to him that most if not all colonisers recruited compliant members of the conquered people to keep the latter in check. The French had used Alawites in Syria, for example, and the British had used Sikhs in India.

Septimus cared little for colonisation or subjugation. Not that Trooper was bothered. Being warm, dry, well fed and taken for walks was all he cared about.

'Go to bed, Trooper.'

Septimus put an eye to the peephole in the front door.

Nothing.

He stretched out his right arm, fingers finding the switch for the light over the porch.

For a moment, he thought he saw movement, but decided he was imagining things. There was nothing out there. The street seemed empty except for parked cars, their windscreens and roofs already frosted, glittering in the streetlights. Septimus turned back to Trooper, who was still watching him, head lowered.

Septimus roared, '*Bed*!'

Trooper slunk off to his basket, looking back over his shoulder, and Septimus put off the lights in the hall and porch. He went back to his own bed, hoping his home was not going to be attacked with an explosive device.

Before burying himself under the duvet, Septimus satisfied himself that there were no messages, no texts on his phone on the bedside table. He told himself the NCA surveillance team should be in place by now and about to change shifts.

It was right then, at that very moment, lying on his back under the duvet, that Septimus realised what it was he'd been looking for all this week. It was if a window had opened just a crack, letting in a sliver of light. It came to him in the form of four digits and was accompanied by an image in colour of a crowd of people, male and female, entire families in some cases, at an airport.

He'd studied the assassin's victims since Saturday in every detail and had gone over the facts of what was publicly known about them again and again.

Of all people, he should have known, given his own experience.

He'd been there himself, hadn't he?

You're slower than you used to be. You're too old for this crap.

He knew the when and the where.

Just as he'd thought, it wasn't something they'd done, the murder victims, but something they'd *not* done. Something they'd failed to do when they'd been in positions of authority and could have done the right thing.

You stupid prick; why did it take you so long?

All he needed now was the name.

Septimus turned onto his right side. He heard Trooper whimper in his sleep. Then he, too, slept. Once again, it wasn't long before the next episode, and he was aware of himself once again — conscious of being in his subconscious — scrambling up that same fucking mountain, his boots full of sand and stones.

Chapter 33

Paris, March 19, 2005.

Bridie has no idea where she is. Initially, she intended to remain calm whatever happened, not saying anything at all and making no effort to resist arrest. She decided she would play at being nice, polite, respectable, even submissive up to a point, yet silent. But when a black hood is produced in the car, she changes her mind. She can't prevent the escorting officers from hooding her, but she fights back. Bridie lashes out with her feet and twists violently from one side to another in the back seat.

'No!'

She screams as loudly as she can, and that's extremely loud. She attempts to head-butt one of her captors and nearly succeeds, and when that fails, she tries to get hold of the door handle with her cuffed hands. The doors are centrally locked, naturally.

The gendarmes yell at her to be still, to shut up, to cooperate, or, as they say, things will go much worse for her. Bridie swears in English, then uses every French curse she can remember. She continues her piercing shrieks, hoping to draw the attention of other motorists. She stops yelling only briefly to demand a lawyer, then resumes. She demands the right to call her country's embassy. She wriggles and kicks some more and accuses her escorts of assault.

It gets to them, finally. She's slapped in the face and punched, none too gently, in the ribs. The officer in the front seat cocks a pistol and presses the muzzle against her cheekbone under the hood.

Yikes! It is getting serious.

As SIS exercises go, this seems to be turning out to be more realistic and entertaining than most. When they arrive at their destination, wherever it is, she is seized, dragged out of the car and forced to bend forward almost double, at least three pairs of hands gripping both her upper arms and the back of her neck, propelling her forward into a shambling run. A ramp, sliding doors, some sort of reception area, a lift, stairs, corridor, metal gates clanging open and shut, a heavy metal door squealing open, keys jangling, she's pushed in roughly and held up against a wall, then chained to something by one wrist.

The hood is pulled off, and she's alone.

Bridie finds she's been chained to an iron bed. There's no mattress. The only other object is out of reach: a bucket. And yes, the place stinks of urine and shit. The single, barred widow is small and set far too high to see anything at all beyond the walls.

Bridie doesn't know how long she's there, sitting on the brown-tiled floor, but guessing by the changes in light and temperature, she estimates it's around four hours before they come for her.

By now she's hungry, thirsty and badly needing a pee, all of which is no doubt the intention.

Two people, a man and a woman, sit in front of Bridie at a table. Mid-forties, possibly, not in uniform but office wear. Unsmiling suits, both. A plain brown folder lies on the table. As for Bridie, her cuffs have been removed, and she is sitting in an upright chair with armrests. Quite comfortable, she thinks to herself, rubbing her wrist where the cuff had cut deep into her skin, and much better than the floor of her cell.

The woman does most of the talking in English.

She opens the file. 'Will you confirm your name, please?'

'I need the bathroom.'

'Certainly. It's behind you.' The woman raises her right hand, palm up, in what is apparently intended as a conciliatory gesture, indicating that there really is a bathroom and that Bridie is free to use it.

No one watches her, and she can close the door. She looks around, but there is nothing she thinks she can use to escape or employ as a weapon, and no window she can escape through. When she returns and sits again on the chair, feeling much relieved but a failure for having failed to escape, she sees her fake passport in the file.

'Your name?'

'I want a lawyer.'

'You don't need one. You have not been accused of any offence.'

'I have a right to legal representation.'

'You have no rights,' said the man in a gruff tone.

'I demand to speak to my consulate.'

'Only after answering our questions truthfully.'

Portentous creep, Bridie thinks. He takes some papers from the file and pushes them over to her.

He switches to French. 'These were found in your car.'

'I don't understand. Please repeat in English.'

He does so.

She glances down at them just enough to make out the Russian's documents.

'Never seen them before, and it's not my car.'

'Your friend's car. Mr Scobell is your friend, not so?'

'The car was rented. Probably the papers were left by someone else before. They're not mine.'

So it goes. Little by little, Bridie feeds them her cover story and repeatedly denies knowing anything about any papers. No, she has never heard of KAYAK, and she knows no Russians. She's never met a Russian. She appears to give ground slowly, only revealing what she means to tell them, nothing more.

A battle of attrition to gain time.

She is taken back to her cell, chained to the bedframe again, thrown a thin grey blanket that's none too clean, and after an hour or so, she's given a tin cup of lukewarm black coffee, unsweetened, and a chunk of stale bread. The evil smelling bucket is kicked closer so she can use it, and the ceiling light is left on.

A restless, cold, and uncomfortable night follows. Bridie dozes on and off, woken by the pain of her stiff joints and cuffed wrist, a cycle that repeats several times. She has to use the bucket; there's no other option. Before first light, the questioning resumes.

Dragged into the same office, forced to sit on the same chair, Bridie feels bruised all over. She feels dirty, her hair is a greasy mess, and she's groggy from lack of sleep. She can smell her own body. She wants sleep more than anything else. All of which she knows is deliberate. She's meant to feel this way: demoralised, fearful, eager to be freed, homesick, exhausted, sorry for herself, willing to capitulate to anyone who has a kind word for her.

No breakfast, naturally. She develops a sharp headache and becomes thirsty as the questions are repeated over and over again.

Who did she meet in the park? Did she pay him? Was he her agent, or was she his? Who was the man who called himself Scobell? What was his job? What was their relationship? What did she know about KAYAK? Who did she work for? Was she a British spy? What was her real name?

Sooner or later, it will end.

• • • •

BRIDIE IS FROG-MARCHED back to her cell, and on the way she thinks she recognises a man's laughter on another level, upstairs perhaps, but she can't remember whose it is — she's too tired to think clearly. A little later, her grey cell door swings open, and in walks TD12, Tom Gowers, the senior of the two instructors — the messy dresser Bridie regarded as sympathetic and yes, that had been his hearty laugh.

'Well done, Bridie. You played a blinder, let me tell you! Let's get those chains off you and find you a decent cuppa and take you home, shall we?'

And that's that. Or is it just another fucking trick?

She wants something stronger than a cuppa, thanks very much.

Back at Fort Monckton that evening, Bridie enjoys a long, hot shower, a change of clothes, a casual supper — pizza, ice cream and beer — and a solid ten hours of uninterrupted sleep.

The next morning, it's time for their grades.

Like school kids, the student spies sprawl at their desks, feeling anxious and trying but failing not to look nervous, casting surreptitious glances at one another. They are supposed to write up their reports on the final exercise, but few do so. Bridie tells herself they'd all ten of them passed, or they wouldn't still be there, so what did a grade matter? *A great deal* is the true answer. The grade determines the nature of the first appointment as a fully qualified SIS Intelligence Officer.

Names are called, and people leave the room for their final interviews with the two course instructors as part of the formal staff appraisal, the culmination of six months' training. It's an agonising wait. A score of one is outstanding — and rare. A score of two is above average. A three is the norm, pretty much, and Bridie understands four is below standard, while a five reflects poor performance and spells a likely termination of a would-be spy's career. She hopes for a two, but will settle for three.

At last, it is Bridie's turn. She's so tense she finds herself sweating hard. Her hands tremble, so she tries to hide them behind her back. Her mouth is dry and tastes of metal. The instructors both stand up when she walks into their office. 'Brilliant job,' says TTD12, coming forward. 'We couldn't fault your performance. Not that we didn't try,' he adds with that laugh of his.

'Congratulations,' adds a grinning TD11, the younger Andrew Cornwall, who pumps Bridie's right hand up and down with enthusiasm. 'You're only the third candidate ever to have received a score of one in IONEC's history. And the first and only woman to do so. Bravo!'

She's beaten all nine of her colleagues to the finishing line, excluding the two early dropouts. She remembers how they'd stared at her at the start, their sniggers and their snide remarks. Beaten by a woman? Suck it up, dickheads!

And the job? That's what really matters.

'You're going to catch Russian spies trying to worm their way into the Service,' says Gowers. 'Loads of travel, five-star hotels, great places to visit. Important operations, too. Huge fun, in other words. I envy you. You're going to love it.'

They make counterintelligence sound so glamorous, but it won't be like that at all.

Chapter 34

R Trastavere: an ancient enclave huddled in a loop on the west bank of the Tiber, fighting a rearguard action against mass tourism. Fortunately for Calista, by mid-November, the invaders had retreated and tranquility had been restored. Unfortunately, rain fell in remorseless torrents on the tiled roofs, piazzas, gardens and alleys. Calista took an H bus from Termini Station to Piazza Belli bus stop — a journey of some fifteen minutes. Armed with an umbrella, she made her way on foot to the Piazza di San Cosimato, where Andrea was waiting.

Happy to see her and looking forward to enjoying a late breakfast together, he wasn't at all pleased by the real reason behind her surprise visit.

'It's unfair,' Andrea said, gesticulating with both hands. 'I don't pry into your profession as a British spy, but you want me to compromise my intelligence work — I could lose my job, even go to jail just for being seen with you.'

He was being rather melodramatic. Calista put a hand on his arm and gave it a reassuring squeeze. 'You misunderstand, my love. I only want what's in the public realm — open source stuff. Not your secret work at all.'

'Then buy a newspaper or talk to anyone on the street,' Andrea said, almost upsetting his coffee as he waved an arm at an imaginary crowd in the flooded piazza, which was actually empty of people because of the heavy downpour. 'Why ask me? This is a domestic matter for the police, I think.'

'Only because I know you, because I trust you, and because you keep yourself informed about what's going on. You hear stuff. My Italian isn't good enough.'

'You're right, it isn't.'

Ouch. That was bitchy.

He still looked sulky, though mollified by Calista's piling on praise. Andrea was about five-ten and twenty-six, Calista's age, dressed in a navy blazer, a maroon, open-collared silk shirt, white jeans, loafers, and no socks. A camel-coloured coat and paisley scarf folded over the back of one of the bar chairs, along with a compact umbrella, completed the look. A fashionable young Roman who'd taken the day off to be with his English girlfriend.

Calista thought him amazingly sexy but somewhat spoiled. She loved his olive skin, bedroom eyes, and glossy black hair. He had a good body. Great shoulders and a broad chest. He smelled good. A touch of Versace cologne, if she wasn't mistaken. Even so, she wasn't sure the relationship would last. He was too soft, too self-absorbed. Great in bed, sure, but that wasn't enough. How long before the male egoist started chasing other women? One sign was that he spent longer in the bathroom playing with his hair and skin products than she did.

'Okay, look. I'll tell you what I know. Not much. The villa where the party was held is well known for its lavish events — I mean, a lot goes on there that people talk about in hushed tones, pretending to be shocked. Coke, of course, freely available. And girls — not off-the-street hookers, of course, but the high-end kind.'

'Go on.'

'I'm told they charge around two thousand euros an hour or ten thousand a night. Courtesans, or so they like to think of themselves. They won't go with just anyone, though a present of a Rolex watch helps if the client is fat and ugly, or so I hear. Some are top models earning pocket money on the side. There's a guy who provides this service for Pacioli. French, I believe.'

'You have a name for this pimp?'

'He runs security for the villa and muscle for Pacioli personally. I can get you the name if you want.'

'I do.'

'I'll make a quick call to a friend who writes a gossip column and knows all this society stuff if you're interested. My friend might be willing to talk to you. Off the record, though.'

Rapid exchanges in Italian followed on his cell — too rapid for Calista to keep up.

'Jean Martin is the name. Pimp. Dealer. Muscle for hire. Ex-soldier. Specialised in trafficking Ukrainian and Romanian girls.'

'Past tense?'

'Shot dead in Nice about a week ago along with his associate, Costa. Police said it was gang-related, but my friend believes they tried to blackmail the wrong people with sex videos they'd had taken at the Pacioli villa.'

'At that same party?'

'Sure. And others. It's one of their several businesses.'

'Anyone in particular they've blackmailed?'

'Libel laws are strict in England, so my friend has to be careful.'

'So what?'

'My friend is worried this will cause trouble if it gets out.'

'I'm not a journalist, Andrea. This is confidential, I promise.'

'One of them was your friend. Yes? Taped during a threesome in one of the suites. Lots of coke, too.'

'My friend? What are you talking about?'

'Carstairs. The one who is now prime minister of your wonderful country. How's Brexit these days? By the way, you didn't say — have you caught the assassin yet?'

Calista shook her head.

'Listen. Calista. I think we have an early lunch, you and I, and then we go to bed. Too much rain to do anything else. You agree with me, carissima?'

'What about your friend? Can I meet him?'

'Tonight we will meet for drinks if you're agreeable. And it's a her, not a he. She will tell you how these people take videos and sell them to the highest bidder. They don't do the blackmail themselves. They see themselves as artists and don't care for the rough stuff.'

'And who was the highest bidder with Carstairs?'

'I think Isabella might know. Somebody called Brodzinski, I think. Oligarch. He was there — at the party. Let's eat, shall we? I know an excellent place I'm sure you will like. It's nearby. We can walk. I want you to tell me all about this assassin.'

Calista gathered up her jacket and umbrella. 'I'm sorry, Andrea, but I know only what I read in our media, and they know nothing.'

'I don't believe you.'

At least the rain had stopped. Off they went, arm in arm, a handsome couple of young lovers and spies. Calista was enjoying herself, but she couldn't help wondering if this mysterious Isabella really knew enough —

and would tell her enough — to justify her expenses and a couple of CX reports.

Andrea recommended the pachero all scoglio, and he was right. It was scrumptious, and bed seemed the right place to digest it after all.

. . . .

ISABELLA WAS QUITE something. Andrea called her contessa without explaining why — he might have been teasing her, but as the evening wore on, Calista came to the conclusion that Andrea looked up to her. She could see why this was. Isabella was a tall woman, aged somewhere between late fifties and early sixties, with an impressive and well-preserved figure partly hidden by her long, black woollen coat. It was stylish and probably from Fendi. Expensive, and way out of Calista's league. Black trousers, a striped blouse, enough buttons left undone to show ample cleavage. A brunette with a marvellous head of thick, curly hair down to her shoulders, which shook and danced every time Isabella laughed, which she did a lot. A wide mouth, big white teeth, aquiline nose and flashing eyes that seemed to miss nothing. Lots of rings and bracelets. Diamonds and gold were her thing.

The contessa, whether in her own right or by marriage, was someone at ease with herself, Calista decided. She was both supremely confident and happy with her lot in life.

Calista was envious.

Isabella wasn't shy. She pressed her cheek against Calista's and captured her arm with her own and marched her into the twelfth-century Basilica of Santa Maria on Trestavere's main square, Andrea tagging along behind and looking lost.

'He hates churches,' Isabella muttered with a chuckle.

Isabella suggested to Andrea that he find a seat at the back, well out of everyone's way because it was still a working church, as she explained to Calista. 'I'm taking my new friend on a little tour' she said with a toss of her mane. And she did. They strolled around, admiring the golden mosaics, which Calista found extraordinary.

It was only much later, after a couple of bottles of wine, that Isabella leant across their table and spoke in a low, confiding voice to Calista.

'You can't touch those people, believe me. They're litigious and won't hesitate to hire the best London lawyers in lengthy defamation actions that would leave you or me penniless. So I can say little. I have to be very, very careful. Being right isn't any kind of defence under British libel law. You know this, yes?'

She explained how it worked. One group of people — no names — from the porn industry made the videos, with a generous cut from the proceeds to the property owner. Pacioli, in this case. They then 'marketed' the product to those likely to be interested. Big money changed hands. Millions of dollars. Whoever bought the so-called product would no doubt attempt to blackmail certain people — business rivals, celebrities in sport and entertainment, but also politicians. Careers and marriages had been destroyed by leaks to the media of these 'artistic' performances.

'Carstairs?'

'You didn't hear this from me. A careless, overgrown schoolboy who thought he was inviolate. He wasn't. He was caught with his pants down — literally.'

'For cash?'

'No. Not the political ones. Carstairs, they wanted for his influence and to provide intelligence. He belongs to them now. He's rumoured to have been successfully recruited. They may not have had to use what they have on him. His ego is enough, his greed. A few big donations through offshore accounts might have been enough.'

'Who are we talking about?'

'The Russian and the Pole, of course, Vishinsky and Brodzinski, billionaires working together. They own Carstairs and many others. V & B set the targets for the intelligence they want and sell it on.'

'To whom?'

Isabella sighed, and her voice dropped to such a low murmur that Calista could barely hear her. 'Putin's SVR. The Chinese. Israel's Mossad. The Iranians. The Saudis. American white supremacists. Global corporations. Whoever can afford to subscribe to this exclusive and private intelligence service. The intel they offer usually contains lists of dissidents. For V & B, I understand it's not ideology or politics — just business.'

Andrea hadn't said a word throughout, but he turned to Calista and hissed at her:

'You have what you want. Just remember who risked her life to tell you. Don't you dare forget!'

Chapter 35

Kandahar Province, Afghanistan, June, 2020

The road to Zala's home is long and arduous.

By the time he leaves Peshawar in northwest Pakistan for the frontier town of Parachinar in the so-called tribal areas, Merrick realises he isn't alone. Maybe they're Barakzai, members of Zala's extended family and clan from up-country. Maybe not. They don't speak to him, nor he to them.

His training has alerted him to their presence, and at first, he thinks they're probably agents of Inter-Services Intelligence or ISI, Pakistan's ubiquitous military spy agency that has done so much to support the Taliban with arms, training and combat support. Merrick stands out as a foreigner when he arrives in jeans, t-shirt and trainers at Peshawar airport. He takes a taxi driven by an irascible old Afridi Pashtun into the town. The driver asks him if he's American. Merrick tells him no, he's not. English? Canadian, he replies.

Merrick is out buying his Afghan gear when he notices his minders for the first time. They loiter outside the tailor's, standing on the pavement, gazing at nothing, one using a toothpick, another eating something out of a brown paper packet and gazing at tattered Bollywood posters fluttering on the walls. The third wanders into the shop, listens, looks at the displays, the glass-fronted shelves, pretends to inspect the wares on sale, and saunters out again.

Merrick doesn't try to shake them off as they fall into place behind him and tail him all the way back on foot to his downmarket Greens Hotel, a budget stopover for many a foreign backpacker in pursuit of cheap hash or opium since the 1960s. He'd intended to stay at the historic Dean's Hotel, which he's read about, with its seven acres of magnificent gardens, a colonial sprawl of whitewashed rooms and balconies, complete with ballroom, where King Zahir Shah, Kipling and Churchill had once stayed, but he discovers it's been torn down and replaced with a grotesque concrete 'plaza.'

Consumerism has hit Pakistan, too.

They're with him on the rickety municipal bus out of the city. His followers, watchers, minders — whatever they are — don't give any sign that he's their responsibility, and he notices that these three — all men, all Pashtuns — sit well apart from him and one another. One sits near the front, one at the back, and one on the opposite side of the bus, two rows ahead of Merrick.

His ruse is simple.

Merrick dozes, or rather he pretends to do so, sitting forward on his bench seat, forearms on the back of the seat in front, and rests his forehead on his arms, keeping his turban on. He adopts this position each time the bus slows, and Merrick spots through the dusty window a barrier across the road with oil drums and a Pakistani flag. He counts three checkpoints. On each occasion, two Frontier Constabulary members, in a uniform of dark grey shalwar kameez, black berets and carrying Kalashnikov rifles, climb on board. After questioning the driver, one stands at the front, watching the passengers, weapon at the ready, while his companion moves down the aisle demanding papers from passengers, seemingly at random.

Merrick doesn't look up. He keeps his eyes closed. He doesn't know how or why, but each time, they leave him alone. He expects to be nudged, kicked, slapped or shouted at, maybe asked for money — maybe all at once — but he's ignored. Has money changed hands before they reached him, perhaps?

Parachinar is a squalid settlement set in a bowl of hills, a kind of Wild West one-horse adobe and wood shithole of Central Asia. It teems with people from across Afghanistan and Pakistan. Merrick recognises the facial features and clothing of Uzbeks, Hazaras, Tajiks, Turkomen and Pashtuns of almost every tribe — they swagger about, well-off and poor alike, most of them armed.

It's Merrick's turn to walk. He'll start at once, for he's unwilling to spend a single night in this dump. The countryside itself, with shimmering lakes, green farmland, deep woods and the hazy blue outline of the Hindu Kush, looks to Merrick like a lost world — a place belonging to a pristine era before so-called modern humans made such a mess of things.

• • • •

MERRICK DOESN'T MIND the hike. He keeps going without complaint, maintaining a steady pace even uphill. His sandals take some getting used to, and that means blisters, but it doesn't slow him down. When darkness falls, it's more difficult, given that it's a rough mountain path, stony and unpredictable in its direction, rising and falling, with the rocks and boulders hard to make out once the moon has set. His minders have changed — his escort on the bus has been replaced by three much younger men, the age of undergraduates or young soldiers still in training. They're physically fit and more curious than the men they replaced; they watch Merrick all the time out of sheer inquisitiveness. All three are armed.

They rest well away from the path. They don't light a fire but roll themselves up in their *potus* and try to sleep. Merrick drifts off, only to be woken after a couple of hours by rain. They all rise to their feet and, without a word being said by anyone, resume their march. It's better to keep moving in the wet and cold.

During daylight hours, his minders avoid the roads and towns. Merrick notices their skill at field craft. They stay off the skyline, keep to whatever natural cover they can find — shielded by ridges, depressions, tree lines, a copse — and freeze, motionless, wherever they happen to be at the instant a helicopter or fixed-wing aircraft takes them by surprise, sweeping low from behind the mountains. They avoid other travellers. They clean their weapons every day. Merrick shares his bars of chocolate and nuts with them, and they try everything he has to offer, again out of curiosity rather than need. In return, they share their loaves of flat unleavened bread and green tea with him.

Five days and four nights after Merrick left Peshawar, they arrive at their destination. He offers his guides money, but they're shocked if not insulted, unsure whether to be angry or amused, and they leave him standing there, turning and waving as they walk away.

· · · ·

FROM A DISTANCE, THE home resembles a typical Afghan 'compound' of tall, thick and extensive mud walls — a defensive structure with high, ancient wooden gates. The traditional structure blushes bright pink in the declining sun. Around this fortress-like structure, small fields are marked out by a crisscross of irrigation channels. On the banks of these sprout bushes and trees. Merrick recognises orchards of apple trees, pistachio, pomegranates, almonds, and also vineyards — not grapes for wine, obviously, but of the sweet dessert varieties. There's also a large grove of walnut trees behind the house, rising up the slopes of a small hill.

Inside the wooden gates, it's a different matter.

First, he encounters a well, windmill and a pump powered by a generator surrounded by a bank of prickly pear, then a courtyard through another inner wall.

Zala is nowhere to be seen, and Merrick knows better than to go looking for her. Her absence is to be expected. Even so, Merrick is anxious to see her. He's led to the first building, an annexe shaped like a longhouse in the Scottish Highlands. Like the main building, it's built of concrete with a corrugated iron roof. He realises this is the guesthouse where all male visitors are welcomed by other males from the main house.

After jettisoning his sandals, he's led into a large living room, carpeted with a huge red and black wool Bokhara rug. The walls are lined with cushions — flat and as wide as a single mattress, for sitting or reclining, and plump ones along with traditional, triangular cushions for leaning against. The reception leads to two sleeping areas and a bathroom. Merrick discovers a real, Western-style affair with two handbasins, a bath, shower and flush toilet. Running water, hot and cold. The floor and walls are covered in white tiles.

It's a guesthouse of some substance; it signals to Merrick that the owner — presumably Zala's father or one of several uncles — is someone substantial, wealthy, educated, a moderniser. It's also Merrick's new home for the next fortnight.

• • • •

THAT EVENING, THE RECEPTION area is packed with Afghans of all ages, sizes and classes. All male. They sit side by side, shoulder to shoulder. Two postures seem to be permitted, either cross-legged, or with the legs tucked together, bent, and the weight on one or other cheek of their owner's arse. Either way, Merrick finds the position excruciating, and after about twenty minutes, he feels compelled to change from one posture to the other as his legs and backside go numb.

Boys — Merrick estimates their ages to be between eight and twelve — spread plastic tablecloths in the centre of the floor, covering most of it. Spittoons, copper or brass, Merrick can't tell, are deployed at intervals around the rectangle.

There's much chatter in Pashto. Merrick snatches the odd word or phrase but nothing more. He's ignored, though he catches the younger guests — if that's what they are — looking at him curiously. No one attempts to talk to him.

Jugs of water and bowls follow, along with cotton towels over the servers' forearms; one lad holds a bowl, the guest puts both hands over it, and a second server pours the water as the guest makes a washing movement. It's a ritual cleansing. The guest is offered the cotton towel — it resembles a dishcloth — but by the time it reaches Merrick, it's neither dry nor clean, and he declines.

Vast metal platters are set out: grilled chicken, roast mutton, what appears to be vegetable curry of some kind, immense mounds of rice, both white and saffron, some of the rice containing almonds and raisins. Piles of freshly baked bread loaves or *nan* are distributed. Merrick wonders if they feast like this every day.

No one reaches for the food. The conversation, once so loud and continuous, falls away.

The host arrives, a tall, dignified figure with white hair and goatee, wearing a Kandahar-style shalwar kameez, much embroidered on the sleeves and around the neck of his collarless silk shirt. Everyone rises to their feet, but the host, whom Merrick thinks must be in his sixties or early seventies, gestures for them to be seated.

He makes straight for Merrick, bends, reaches out with his right hand, his left hand holding his right forearm.

'*As-salaam aleikum.*'

'*Waleikum salaam,*' Merrick responds, struggling to stand up straight.

They shake hands, then place their right hands over their own hearts — a gesture of respect. As they do so, they exchange greetings.

'*Sanga yaast?*'

'*Manna*.'

His green eyes smile at Merrick. How like Zala's eyes!

This has to be the father.

Bartakzai senior makes it clear that he will sit next to his honoured guest, so the others move over to give him space. Still, no one eats. They wait. Instead, the host starts piling food on Merrick's plate. Merrick always has a good appetite, and he is hungry, but this is too much. He protests, holding up his hands, and his host laughs.

At that moment, a kind of spell is broken, and people load up their own plates. Merrick tries to serve the old man with food, but his efforts are dismissed with a wave of the hand and a smile. The diners aren't doing much talking because the business of eating is far too important, especially at a feast. The men tear off bits of bread and use them to scoop up food or use four fingers of their right hands to do so. Boys bring glasses and take around pitchers of water.

At the end of it all, there's another round of handwashing.

For the next four days, a pattern is established. Merrick is woken at 7 a.m. and is offered hot, green, sweetened tea with a sprig of mint. There's always bread or fruit. There's also milk tea with cardamom. Merrick can't get enough of the latter.

After breakfast, he walks out of the compound. He watches the farmers — or farm workers, he's not sure which — and tries out his Pashto with mixed results. He visits the local mosque and is welcomed by the elderly village imam, who encourages him to attend prayers even though he's not a participant. He sits at the back, trying to be as unobtrusive as possible.

The evening meal in the guesthouse is similar — males only again, fewer of course, and a more modest but equally delicious meal. Merrick is joined by one or two male relatives of Zala. Maybe they have a duty roster and say to one another something along the lines of, 'Oh, no, do I have to? Not the boring Englishman again! I can't understand a word he says!'

A gaggle of boys follows Merrick on his walks. They try to talk to him, and he to them. The latter ends with general hilarity on both sides. They're interested in his footwear, his clothing, his wristwatch, whatever he has in his pockets, taking each item from him, turning it over, examining it and passing it on to the next boy. They offer him their favourite possessions: a football, a catapult. They especially enjoy playing football with him; Merrick versus the rest, which assures them a victory every time.

On the fifth night, everything changes.

Merrick is led to the main house in the late afternoon, removes his shoes and enters. Zala's father greets him, takes him through to what Merrick thinks must be the family living room. It's furnished with overstuffed sofas and armchairs, several side tables and footstools, and dominated by an immense glass chandelier in the centre of the ceiling. The carpet is of a blue and beige Chinese design.

'What will you have to drink, Peter?'

He speaks fluent English, after all.

'Oh, anything, sir. Whatever you're having.'

'Call me Faisal. Oh, yes, I know — I'm so much older than you, and I'm Zala's dad. But I'd like us to be friends, Peter, if that's possible, and if you agree.'

'There's nothing I'd like more. It would be an honour.'

'Here.'

Faisal hands Merrick a glass.

'Yes, it's whisky. Black Label. And you're right. Moslems shouldn't drink. I'm a Moslem, and I do drink — occasionally, on special occasions, and only in private. Correct me if I'm wrong, Peter, but this is a special occasion, is it not?'

'Your good health, sir.' Merrick raises his glass and sips the golden liquid, feels the delicious heat run down his throat. It's a triple dram, by the look of it.

They sit down opposite one another in the armchairs. 'I've watched you, Peter, while you've been here. I've also listened to what Zala says about you — and it's a great deal, I assure you. She never stops talking about you. I think we've reached the point at which a Western father asks his daughter's boyfriend — if I may call you that — what his intentions are. What are yours?'

Merrick dives right in. 'My intentions are honourable. I'd like to ask your permission to marry Zala.'

The silence that follows seems endless to Merrick.

'Do you have any idea what that involves, Peter? Of the difficulties you would both face, and the sacrifices both of you would have to make if this is going to have any chance of success?'

'I do. At least, I think I do.'

'Then you have my permission, and my blessing, subject to an understanding on both sides about what this involves. When we've finished our drinks, I'd like to introduce you to the family, and please join us for supper.'

Chapter 36

West London, 06:29, November 17
The doorbell rang long and hard until Alec ran down the stairs in his bare feet, pulling a raincoat around himself. He looked through the peephole.

The doorbell now chimed in short bursts.

Bridie called down to him. 'Who is it?'

'One of yours,' he shouted back.

He pressed the intercom button. 'Who is this?'

'Septimus for Bridie,' said a gravelly voice.

'Let him in, Alec. He's a nuisance, but he doesn't bite.'

Alec unlocked the door, drew the bolts top and bottom, took off the chain, and opened it. He saw it was cold, wet and still night out there.

'I'm sorry...' A Scots accent.

'Don't be. You're in time for breakfast. Come on in.' Alec opened the door wide and stood back. He watched the street beyond the front gate. No strange cars, no odd behaviour he could see. Everything looked normal for the time of day.

Septimus stood on the hall mat, shaking the water off umbrella and coat.

'Wow. I see it's all repaired and repainted,' he said, looking at the doorframe and wallpaper. 'That was fast.'

'Paint's not quite dry, so be careful with your clothing. Come through to the kitchen. I'll make us all coffee and then leave you both to your nefarious business.'

'That's a wee bit strong,' Septimus said with a grin. 'There's nothing nefarious about us. We're just harmless paper-pushers in the civil service.'

'Oh, right,' said Alec. 'Apologies. I stand corrected. Department of Work and Pensions, is it?'

As he trailed Alec along the corridor, Septimus saw Bridie appear at the foot of the stairs, pulling her hair back with both hands and fixing it in place with a large clip. She wore a nightgown, thick socks and a scarf — items she seemed to have grabbed in a rush. No makeup, still sleepy, but Septimus thought the laconic smile more than made up for these deficiencies.

'Sorry, Bridie,' Septimus mumbled, embarrassed by his intrusion. 'We need to talk. I've some of those answers you wanted.'

'No problem,' replied Bridie. 'Will the kitchen table be all right?' She and Alec exchanged glances. He had the coffee on the go and said he would heat three croissants in the microwave. There was also fruit. What would Septimus like? Sainsbury's 'easy peelers,' apples, bananas or grapes? The guest accepted an easy-peeler tangerine just for something to do with his hands.

While he peeled, Septimus watched the little domestic play-acting in front of him. 'The trouble with answers is that they usually give rise to yet more questions,' he said. 'I think you'll find that's the case here.'

• • • •

'WELL?'

'All the victims have one thing in common, without exception. In August, 2021, they were all involved in one way or another with the disastrous evacuation of civilians from Afghanistan.'

'I remember it. The military withdrawal, given its sudden nature, went surprisingly well, I thought at the time. But the civilian side of things was chaotic.'

'Aye. First, Lufkin, our dear departed leader, was a junior minister in 2021 with responsibility for admitting and settling the evacuees in the UK. That he was vocal in his opposition to allowing Afghans who'd served with the British military into this country is well known and is on the record. It's in Hansard. I checked. Yes?'

'You have been busy.'

'Enough of the sarcasm, okay?'

'Sorry.'

'Two. Melanie Masters, the late home secretary, was a junior minister in the same department. She was responsible to Lufkin for the inter-departmental program known as the Afghan Relocation and Assistance Program or ARAP. It was slow, and frequently it rejected perfectly valid applications on the flimsiest excuses — unless the media kicked up a fuss, which sometimes happened, fortunately. Some people were saved because of public petitions and so on. For others, it was too late.'

'Okay.' Bridie held her mug with both hands to warm them, and occasionally she took a sip, watching Septimus. He had a story to tell, and she told herself he would not be hurried. He would tell it his way and in his own time, and she'd have to put up with it.

'Three. Kevin Tomlinson, our defence secretary, fatally wounded by the shooter. He was at the Foreign Office then, on the ground in Pakistan, in fact, and liaising with both our people at the embassy in Kabul, with the Kabul government, and with the Pakistani authorities. An influential role. When many of the Afghans who'd been turned down by ARAP fled across the border into Pakistan, he did not try to help them. When Pakistan deported them back to Afghanistan, he made no intervention on their behalf. He didn't make representations or lodge a protest. His performance was characterised by inaction, and it set the stage for his entry into the Commons on an anti-foreigner ticket.'

'More coffee, Septimus? How about a croissant?'

Septimus shook his head. Glancing out through the French doors, Bridie saw it was light. Rather grey, but light, nevertheless.

'Number Four,' Septimus continued. 'Tasmin Quaife, Labour leader. She made no effort to press the government to do anything. She was especially passive, in contrast to her forthright demand that refugee status be granted to thousands of Ukrainians after the Russian invasion. She stayed silent. She was criticised for being opposed to Moslem immigrants of any origin, even if they were Afghans who'd fought with us. People quit her party because of her perceived Islamophobia.'

Bridie's mobile rang. She hauled it out of a pocket in the gown, saw it was 'C' calling, and switched it off. Some things were more important than whatever Sir Thomas Avery wanted. He could wait.

'Did you want to take that?'

'It's fine. Carry on.'

'Victim number Five. General Ocean. He was in command of the operation. The UK Special Forces commander, no less. He didn't believe the UK, and especially the military, had any responsibility for Afghans who'd served with British forces. He argued they were serving their own country and fighting their war, not ours, and that we were there to help. His position was that no obligation was attached to their military duty, whether they were interpreters putting their lives on the line or Afghan special forces — the so-called Triples — we had trained, and with whom our troops had served. Music to the ears of the government of the day, of course.'

Septimus looked up. 'Could I take you up on the offer of another coffee?'

'Of course.'

Alec put his head around the door and blew Bridie a kiss.

'I'm off to work, you guys. All the best, Septimus. Talk later, sweetheart.'

Mugs of fresh coffee on the table, Septimus resumed.

'Six. Thomas Brownlow. Blown literally to bits in Tufton Street. Former permanent secretary at the Ministry of Defence in 2021. Speaks for itself. Did all he could to follow his minister's line and more, namely, that Her Majesty's Government was doing all it could and all that it was required to do. Anything else was the woke fantasy of the lentil-munching, champagne-swilling, suburban Marxist Left.'

Silence.

'Great coffee,' said Septimus.

Bridie thought all this seemed plausible, but where was the evidence? Was there any, or was it nothing but clever speculation?

'What about the next victim?'

'You're referring to our esteemed prime minister, Richard Carstairs.'

'It was you who said he's the next likely target.'

'I did. Carstairs was this campaigning commentator and journalist, if you recall. Witty, sarcastic, a columnist in two right-wing tabloids, deputy editor of the Tories' favourite weekly magazine, wrote for online US media, too. Fan of Trump. Fought his own campaign against bringing back Afghans after they'd served with us against the Taliban and al Qaeda. Overtly racist. Called them towel-heads and worse. Made fun of the Prophet, which only seemed to make him more popular among his constituents. Actively supported the 'stop the boats' anti-immigration campaign, too.'

'Okay. I see what you're getting at.'

'Good, Bridie. God be praised.'

'Do you have a name?'

Septimus took another swig and smiled.

'I do indeed.'

He put his mug down and looked at it, turning it round with the palms of his hands. He seemed to be enjoying his moment and the build-up to it.

'There was no point in looking at every serviceman out there, right? It would take years. I didn't need to. You'll recall that UK military operations ceased — officially — in December, 2014. Then, on April fifteenth, 2021, NATO confirmed the withdrawal of allied forces. Four months later, on August thirteenth that same year, the UK pulled out fifteen thousand troops but redeployed one thousand to protect the evacuation.'

'And?'

'I'm getting there, Bridie. I excluded everyone except special forces and the paras, because whoever it was had the skills and chutzpah beyond the usual call of duty in a regiment of the line. That saved time. I found someone who fitted: a decorated army officer. He started out with the Volunteer 22 SAS, served three tours, became a regular, twice mentioned in despatches, climbed the ranks to major and commanded his own squadron, serving two more tours, and was awarded a gong for his efforts.

'He married an Afghan woman who worked with the Triples, a special forces group trained by us, and which worked alongside us. She was a sergeant. She belonged to a joint UK-Afghan unit commanded by our man, which is possibly how they met. He was then a lieutenant. She started out as an interpreter and became an intelligence operator. They lived together for a short while, though he kept this liaison quiet. She was turned down by ARAP, fled across the frontier, was deported by the Pakistanis....'

Bridie wanted to hear about the woman, of course she did, but she could stand the suspense no longer.

'His name, Septimus? What's his name, for God's sake?'

She was grinding her teeth in frustration.

Septimus polished off his second coffee and set the mug down.

'The name? Oh, yes, of course. Sorry. Right. It's Major Peter Merrick, DSO. He's our man. I'm sure of it.'

Chapter 37

Number 10, Downing Street, 11:45, November 17

The flesh-coloured earpieces crackled and sputtered into life in two dozen sensitive eardrums.

'Confirm BADGER en route. Thirty seconds.'

The drivers, the Special Branch officers, the firearms police officers, the leader of the day's Special Escort Group and even Callsign 98 — the pilot and copilot of a metropolitan police Eurocopter EC145 circling overhead — all received the message, some instinctively putting their hands to their ears. It wasn't their first heads-up that morning, but the seventh.

He's coming. No, he isn't. Yes, he is. Wait. No. Yes.

BADGER was late. Again.

The glossy front door swung open at last, a burly uniformed police officer stood aside, and Richard Carstairs bustled out of his official London residence, a plump, shambling figure under a thatch of unkempt hair. He waved to everyone and no one in particular, muttering in his ripe voice, 'Sorry, sorry,' almost tumbling over his own feet into the arms of the close protection team of brawny men in suits with military haircuts. Several hands reached out to thrust him firmly, like an unruly child, onto the back seat of the Range Rover. The door was shut, and the several escorts jogged to their own vehicles.

BADGER wore weekend gear. Yellow cords, brown ankle boots, padded jerkin over a heavy brown pullover that helped conceal the paunch. The would-be country squire with a double chin was irritable; he'd come off the phone after tearing the Met commissioner off a strip for trying to bully him — him, the prime minister of this great country, no less — into accepting a doubling of his escort detail. More vehicles, more armed police, another chopper. Susman demanded that he wear body armour, too. Susman could insist all he liked, but Carstairs wasn't about to indulge in something so ridiculous and embarrassing as a U.S. presidential cavalcade.

Not good at all for his popular image as a man of (some of) the people.

This was his weekend, dammit. He had every intention of enjoying himself after his first week in office. No advisers, civil servants — only a discreet domestic staff who could be relied upon to fulfil his every wish. He'd promised his partner, Angela, he wouldn't touch a red box all weekend. No paperwork. No late-night conferences or transatlantic calls with his Republican friends. None. He wouldn't even glance at the headlines of his favourite papers: *The Times*, the *Mail* and the *Daily Express*. An informal supper with close friends on Saturday evening was the only social engagement he'd planned.

The weather forecast wasn't bad. Dry, some watery sunshine, little wind. Perfect for an invigorating stroll in fresh country air. Didn't he deserve a break? Wasn't he entitled to a rest? A little time off? Of course he bloody was. Leo Brodzinski and his wife — he couldn't remember her name, but it would come to him — would be impressed by Churchill's country retreat; they'd never been to Chequers before.

Leo was a generous man, a major donor to both Party and Carstairs' own election campaigns. The prime minister pondered the possibility of presenting his dear friend Leo with a special present. How about a peerage? It would be the very first of his premiership.

Why not, indeed? It was within his gift, after all. 'Lord Brodzinski' had a certain ring to it. Foreigners loved all that sort of thing, parading in ermine and scarlet.

They were on the move, pushing into traffic. London slipped by. Scudding clouds, dog walkers, red double-decker buses, homeless sleepers in doorways, the majestic plane trees dipping their branches as if in salute from London parks. Uniformed police officers on corners watched the three vehicles pass, headlights on. One or two saluted, but through the hardened and darkened glass, they wouldn't be able to make out the important passenger slumped in the back.

Carstairs was behind the driver, and between the man's shaved head and that of the senior police protection officer in civvies in the front passenger seat, The prime minister could make out the leader of the SEG team in white helmet and yellow jacket right in front of the Range Rover.

As they picked up speed, passing the tall black railings of Wellington Barracks, another SEG rider surged past on the inside left, hurrying ahead on his white BMW — closely followed by a third on the right, while the SEG leader stayed where he was in the centre of the lane, setting a steady pace.

Call-sign BADGER was aware of the throb of the helicopter's rotor blades overhead as he turned on his phone and went to his WhatsApp account, which he liked for its end-to-end encryption.

Six messages from Angela already. Oh, crumbs.

where the fck r you?????

11.46

have you left??????

11.34

your late!!!!!!

11.25

do u know what time it is???

11.15

r u leaving?

11.00

honey hi look forward seeing u in about 90 mins confirm pse xxx

10.50

Carstairs told himself he'd better say something before she went ballistic, but it wasn't easy on the phone while on the move, especially with his sausage fingers. He and King Charles had had a good laugh at the Palace earlier in the week about their respective plump digits, and he smiled fondly at the memory.

After several attempts and much deleting, he finally composed something he thought appropriate.

darling so sorry held up by security well on the way dont worry love honey bunch ccan't wwait to spend weekend togetherr ETA 1330 xxxxxxxxxxxxx

12:14

That should mollify her for a while, or so he hoped. He put the phone down on the seat next to him, sat back, folded his hands across his stomach, and closed his eyes.

· · · ·

WHEN HE OPENED THEM again, Carstairs saw that the convoy of three Range Rovers and six motorcycles had stopped on the circular gravel driveway of what appeared to be a mock Tudor pub and hotel, *The Artichoke*, complete with fake wood beams and mullioned windows.

He sat up.

'Where are we?'

No one answered. That was because the glass partition between the passenger seats and the front was up, though Carstairs didn't remember having done that himself or having requested it. It occurred to him he might have snored loudly during his brief nap — not unknown by any means — and that one of his trusty companions had done something about it.

He found the right button, and the partition slid back down.

'Where are we?'

'Beaconsfield,' said the driver.

Wherever and whatever that might be. Oh, yes, he remembered now: the fourth wealthiest town in the UK. Lots of Tory millionaires.

'And Tom? Where's he got to?'

'Having a wee chat, Prime Minister.'

'About what?'

'There's talk of a diversion for security reasons, sir. Would add maybe thirty minutes to our journey, depending on the route they decide to take.'

Bloody hell. Angela will go berserk.

'No diversion.'

By sitting up straight, he could see a conference under way through the windscreen: a tight cluster of people, arguing. A Special Branch sergeant, an armed police officer, the leader of his own close protection team, Tom, and the SEG team leader in his bright yellow jacket, also a sergeant. They were looking at a map on someone's iPad.

'Go tell them. Now. Go!'

The driver was startled. 'What?'

'No diversion. Didn't you hear me? No fucking diversion! Get out and tell them. We stick to the original plan. No diversion. Got that, have you?'

'Sir —'

'Do it, man. Unless you'd like an immediate change of career. Go!'

So he did.

They stopped their discussion and looked back at the Range Rover. They exchanged a few more words. One or two shook their heads; another shrugged. The SEG leader jogged back to his bike and started it up. His team followed suit, two of them going ahead and vanishing around a bend in the road. The others walked back to their respective vehicles. They avoided looking at Carstairs, but of course they couldn't have seen him in the back and behind the rear window.

Carstairs saw faces at the windows of *The Artichoke* peering out at them. Two held glasses of beer. He almost envied them; he wouldn't have minded a pint himself with the locals. They were sure to be solid Tories, given this was Beaconsfield.

He didn't sleep. He sat back, watching the scenery, utterly relaxed now, enjoying the comfortable ride. The interior smelled of good leather; whether it was the new leather seats themselves or the scented spray used to keep the SUV smelling fresh, he couldn't tell.

The radios crackled again. *BADGER en route.*

Something startled him and made him turn, peering out of his window. His face showed surprise, not shock or fear. He was merely curious.

It had sounded like a muffled thump, as if someone had kicked the outside of his door, or hit it with a knee by accident. A bloody Stop Oil demonstrator? Or Palestine Action? He was just in time to see a yellow-jacketed rider and his white BMW flash past.

Maybe the SEG officer had passed too close to the Range Rover.

Carstairs did not move away from the door. The vehicle was armoured, after all. He was aware in the next instant of the physical sensation of being lifted up, and as he put his hands out to brace himself on the back of the front seats, he was thrown sideways. *Whoops*! An immense white flash as bright as a sun, only very close, blinded him. He was pushed violently, thrust feet first outside the vehicle, suspended in space, rolling, flying in a cascade of glass, before tumbling to the ground, knocking the breath out of him and snapping a collar bone.

No words or thoughts.

Not even the sensation of pain, nor eyes swimming in blood.

Carstairs heard nothing but a whistling inside his head. It started as a low moan and rose to a high-pitched shriek.

Darkness. Someone or something had turned off the lights.

Chapter 38

K*andahar Province, Afghanistan, August, 2020*
Merrick must convert. It's no big deal.

He's never been religious in any sense of the word, though raised as a Protestant and schooled in the doctrine and rituals of the Church of England. His attitude is straightforward. Merrick doesn't give a jot for any religion, but he knows he loves Zala. He wants to marry her, and she wants to marry him. That much is clear. It can't be done unless he does convert. It's a matter of family, of Zala's relationships with her parents and her extended family, and second, of her public reputation.

They've talked it through. After that first family meal in Zala's family home — no more male-only exile in the guesthouse — they spend more time together. At first, they're chaperoned in public by an aunt or cousin trailing them at a respectful distance so they can talk without being overheard. Later, they can be alone together during the day, provided it's within the compound walls.

One morning, they walk through the family's apple orchard, hands touching.

'We could just leave,' Merrick suggests. 'You could join me in Islamabad, and we could fly together to the UK, have a simple civil marriage on our arrival so that everything's legal and above board, and that would be that. Done.'

'I could never come back, though. I could never see my family again. Look, Pete, I know you find it old-fashioned and unfair, but I would be an outcast. It would break my mother's heart. My dad would be ashamed and dishonoured. I can't do that to them. I can't hurt them like that. It's bad enough that you're British and a soldier — but if you're not a Moslem, it's just not possible.'

And that's it in a nutshell. Merrick says he understands.

So, while still serving as the CO of his squadron, he finds pretexts to sneak off to Kandahar city, where an imam at the central mosque has been recruited by Faisal to teach him the rudiments of his new faith. The imam, a national treasure of sorts, speaks some English, hates the British and the

Russians, at least historically, and is a fiery orator, drawing large crowds to hear his Friday sermons against foreign invaders, occupiers and the many evils of colonialism. But he has a wicked sense of humour, and they get on well, perhaps mindful of the fact that a conversion of an unbeliever such as Merrick represents a spiritual credit for himself, too. He teaches Merrick about the Koran, the life of the Prophet, and the moral precepts of Islam.

The old man instructs him in the Five Pillars: *shahadah*, or statement of faith; *salah*, prayer; *zakat*, almsgiving; *sawm*, fasting; *hajj*, pilgrimage to Makkah.

Stripped down to the most essential tenet of belief, all Merrick needs to do to gain entry to the world community of Islam is recite the shahadah in front of three witnesses:

Ashhadu Alla Ilaha Illallah wa Ashhadu Anna Muhammadarrasulullah

Which he does.

And again in English, just for good measure:

There is no god but God; Muhammad is the Prophet of God.

Merrick has adopted a new name to match his new religious affiliation: Mirwais Hakim Barakzai.

He can now marry Zala, in theory, at least.

• • • •

IT'S ANOTHER SEVEN months before they can get around to it.

Zala has been promoted again and commands her own contingent of Triples in an intelligence role that takes her to Paktia Province; Merrick, as a squadron commander, ventures much less often into the field but must manage and lead from his fly-blown headquarters in the far corners of Zabul Province. They don't see each other for weeks at a stretch.

They both sense that, with the passage of time, things aren't getting any better. Security is deteriorating.

The Taliban are resurgent. Their attacks increase in number and ferocity; they've both read the official figures. Those Afghans who work for the International Security Assistance Force, or have worked for it in the past, are prime targets throughout late 2020. Splits appear within ISAF itself — perhaps not that strange as it's the biggest and longest-running coalition that

NATO has ever deployed. The Pentagon tries to paper over the cracks in its own strategy by stepping up airstrikes and changing its top commanders. Merrick knows airstrikes don't win wars; for the past two years, the number of Afghan civilians killed by allied air attacks has exceeded those killed by the Taliban.

It's increasingly obvious to anyone on the ground — that is, anyone who works outside the air-conditioned hotels, embassies and military headquarters of Kabul — that the newly trained and constituted Afghan National Army and Afghan National Police cannot hold the ring; they're disintegrating, even with U.S. air support.

The Taliban are gaining. They are everywhere, even in Zala's home district. She tells Merrick they may include some distant members of her own family. Popular opinion in rural areas has swung their way, especially among the majority Pashtuns. Merrick knows it, and Zala even more so.

On March 17, 2021, two huge marquees are set up within the outer walls of Zala's home. Armed men stand guard at the entrances to the property. Merrick notices one carrying an old Czech Skorpion machine pistol shiny with age under his *potu*.

The initial ceremony is brief and attended by family and a handful of the closest of Zala's friends. Merrick has no one there he can call family, which is odd by Afghan standards, but which is excused — so Faisal, Merrick's father-in-law says to everyone — because Afghanistan is in the middle of an internecine war.

Merrick's hot and uncomfortable in his absurd finery, compelled to sit still on a dais under a canopy of red and gold, stared at and his appearance commented on by everyone, or so it seems. He's an object of curiosity. He's relieved when the ritual is over. Zala, who looks wonderful, nevertheless appears to feel much the same way, though less self-conscious.

On that first afternoon, celebrations in the marquees begin with formal greetings. Those guests arriving by car or people carrier have decorated their vehicles with ribbons, flowers and greenery. At dusk, they feast, men in one tent, women in the other. Some 400 people have been invited, from extended family to followers, workers, neighbours, local farmers and their families.

A government minister has accepted an invitation, and so have the provincial governor and the provincial chief of police, all three rascally rogues, according to Zala.

The older, more important males sit at tables with white tablecloths and place names along with members of the host family as food is served. Merrick realises he's marrying into a prominent family, the equivalent perhaps of landowning English gentry.

Merrick must greet the guests in person on the first day, paying special deference to the older men. The second day is more of the same, except he and Zala sit together on the dais in their finery.

The younger men dance, long black hair flying, stamping the ground in time to a fast drumbeat; clouds of dust soon fill the tent, reducing people to blurred outlines. The dancers brandish sticks, apparently mimicking fighting, and they emit bloodthirsty yells like Highlanders on the attack.

The dance changes, and men form circles — to Merrick it seems not unlike the Arab *dabke*, holding one another's hands, prancing forwards and back, bending and straightening. It's called the *Altan*. Someone grabs Merrick. and two men drag him into their circle. He has no choice but to join the dance, pulled back and pushed forward, and his appearance raises a cheer despite his being clumsy and out of step with his fellows.

At around 8 p.m. as Pashtun folk singer Zarsanga croons in the background, he's advised by a brother-in-law that he can withdraw and return to the house. The formalities are over; the guests can relax and enjoy themselves without the restraining influence of Faisal — the bride's family and the groom.

It's their first official night together under one roof. No more stolen, hurried moments under canvas or a hidden embrace in a ravine. A special bedroom has been prepared for them with the family's best linen. Rose petals have been scattered over the bedspread, and the room scented with musk.

The young women Merrick encounters in the house draw their scarves over their smiles, suppress their giggles and run off when they see the foreigner approach.

Zala is waiting for him.

. . . .

THEY SIT TOGETHER AMONG the walnut trees on the rise behind the homestead. Between them, balanced on the rock they're sitting on, is a basket of walnuts they've collected, and they take turns fracturing the hard shells with a nutcracker and eating the contents. Zala feeds Merrick, and he feeds her.

A week has passed. This is the last day of their honeymoon before they go their separate ways. Such is the nature of married life in the military. Merrick has enjoyed it, though he wishes it was much longer and that he could have spent it with Zala alone and without her family. If only they could have left together, flown off somewhere to have a real honeymoon, just the two of them.

He's struck by her strong family bonds, the huge warmth of affection she has for her parents, and their love for their daughter; it's obvious to him that their only concern is for her happiness and well-being. It's shown every day in their laughter and smiles, their hugs and kind words for one another. He realises that they've achieved a level of what the Greeks called *eudaemonia* — well-being and happiness — that he can only dream of. Merrick is strongly affected by the experience, and he asks himself if he has what it takes to be a partner worthy of her trust and love.

They've talked everything through; Zala is returning to duty but only for another three months, while Merrick attends his advanced leadership course at the Defence Academy at Shrivenham, some eighty miles west of London. They've also discussed Afghanistan's future, and the Taliban, and what will happen when Kabul falls, which seems both certain and imminent. They've talked about Zala's family; she assures Merrick they'll be safe inside the compound walls, for her father has certain 'connections' and will be left alone.

Merrick has helped her fill in the appropriate form for relocation to the UK. He's checked the details and made sure she follows procedure to the letter. He's made copies. As her former commanding officer, he's added a formal commendation of his own, and he's persuaded his CO — Colonel Cootes-Maycock — to write a brief note on Army headed notepaper in support of her application.

An hour later, Merrick is back in his old Afghan clothes, along with sandals and turban. Old, inexpensive clobber, necessarily so to avoid attention, but at least clean. Mirwais Hakim walks to the outer gate and is let out by the two guards. Zala watches from the front door of her home until the gates close and a motorcycle carries her husband away.

Chapter 39

Rome, 12:55, November 17

Calista knew she had her work cut out. Isabella supplied the bones of what she needed on the private intelligence network run by V & B Enterprises, and she was grateful, but she also knew she must have corroboration and put flesh on those same bones if it was to qualify as a CX report of consequence. Without that, it was rumour. Mere second-hand, sensational chitchat from an Italian gossip columnist.

Nothing wrong with that, but the SIS expected verification.

She had Andrea's help in getting the name of one of the catering firms employed at the parties where guests were said to be trapped on camera in *flagrante dilecto*.

From Isabella, she had the name of a mainly gay nightclub where some of the expensive and sought-after 'courtesans' pimped by the late Jean Martin were said to hang out when off-duty.

Calista could start there.

The three of them were on their feet, gathering up coats and bags. Andrea kindly paid the bill, refusing offers from Calista and Isabella to split it three ways.

They were still arguing about it when Calista glanced up at the big television screen over the bar. She noticed it was Sky News, and there was an eye-catching red banner at the bottom that read 'Breaking News.'

Calista paused.

It was the image of a disaster of some kind.

No, it wasn't Gaza. It wasn't the occupied West Bank. It wasn't Ukraine. It wasn't the British bombing of starving Yemenis. It wasn't the Sudan or Eritrea. It wasn't even Trump's claim of victory in the presidential elections.

Those weren't Italian but UK police cars, ambulances, and a close-up of a police helicopter.

The dateline was Beaconsfield.

TERROR ATTACK ON UK PREMIER CARSTAIRS

Shit.

Isabella was talking to her, but she didn't hear. Andrea took her arm, but Calista pulled back.

Calista had one question.

Is BADGER alive or dead?

Chapter 40

Basingstoke Road, Buckinghamshire, England, 13:33, November 17

B Septimus pulled on his flat cap and buttoned his coat up to his neck. He hunched his shoulders, put up the collar, and shivered. The wind was bitter. It pummelled and punched him the moment he stepped down from the police helicopter, ducking the rotor blades.

The Eurocopter rose, rotating slowly until its nose pointed down the length of the road, and there it stayed. It amazed Septimus it could fly at all in the gale.

The metallic voice rasped in his ear.

- Headed straight for you, Charlie India.

Septimus — aka Charlie India — adjusted his mike and spoke.

- If you have a clear shot, Tango Victor, take it.

- Roger that.

Septimus would never forget authorising a killing. He would not forgive himself, either.

He saw that this stretch of the road where they'd set up the roadblock — one of three to trap Merrick — was straight for about 300 metres at least, lined on both sides by substantial detached and semi-detached homes, set well back from the street and screened by walls and trees.

Septimus saw the target — a dot, growing fast, heading straight for him at speed.

It wouldn't be an easy shot, Septimus thought. He could see the rider clearly now, moving like the clappers.

Behind Septimus, police officers were getting out of their cars, four of which formed the barricade. They positioned themselves behind their vehicles. The armed officers had their weapons drawn and trained on the motorcyclist speeding towards them.

The voice crackled in Septimus's ear.

- Target has ditched his helmet.

Septimus raised his binoculars.

It was true.

What the fuck?

There could be only one reason for doing so.

- He's ten seconds from you, boss.

- Tango Victor, do you have a clear shot?

- Negative, Charlie India. Collateral damage risk.

He doesn't want to live. He wants us to take the shot.

Or —

- Six.

He's going to kill himself if we don't.

- Five.

- Four.

Merrick was clearly visible, bare-headed and leaning as far forward and as flat as possible over the handlebars. Septimus dropped his binoculars onto his chest.

- Three.

Septimus took three rapid steps backwards to the edge of road as the high-pitched scream of the BMW's engine reached him. He shouted out one last command to the police before the impact.

- Two.

- Take cover!

Chapter 41

M Lord Sacristan's Sunday lunches were legendary in the upper reaches of London's intelligence community, if only because they went back decades. Invitations went out to those whom Sacristan found useful or interesting, or both. Position, rank, age, gender, class, sexual orientation, education, length of service counted for nothing.

Sacristan was interested in people with something to say; just because an individual qualified as a Whitehall mandarin didn't count. Tedious, self-important pillars of what passed for the British political class did not appear on the guest list. Politicians were seldom if ever invited because Sacristan considered them lower on the evolutionary scale than pond life.

In the light of recent events, who could disagree?

The meals varied little. It was one thing or the other, depending on the week. One week it would be roast beef and Yorkshire pudding, followed by sherry trifle; the next time it would be a leg of lamb with mint sauce, succeeded by apple pie and custard. Traditional British food — albeit cooked slowly with garlic — for an eclectic gathering of international spies, adventurers and ruffians.

Bridie explained to Septimus by way of warning that no one talked shop during the event, starting with preprandial drinks served on the ground floor of Sacristan's Georgian townhouse at 12.30 — scotch, gin-and-tonic, sherry, brandy. No vodka — something to do with the Cold War, perhaps.

Like any self-respecting officers' mess, sex and politics were forbidden subjects, on pain of immediate expulsion by Mr Masters, the ex-Royal Marine household steward, rumoured to be a black belt in both karate and jiu-jitsu. No one had had the temerity to challenge Mr Masters or raise the taboo topics to discover if any of this was true.

The wines, which were judged as excellent by those who claimed to know such things, came from Sacristan's own cellar.

'He'll want to fill in the gaps,' Bridie said on the way there.

'Gaps? What gaps?' Alec wanted to know.

'Gaps in his knowledge of what happened this past week. Since the first killings on Armistice Day.'

'He's not cleared for it,' said Septimus.

'He doesn't care,' said Bridie. 'I don't think anyone does.'

A frowning Septimus grunted in disbelief. 'How will he do so if we're banned from talking shop?'

'Like you, he's a good watcher and listener — let's just say that he listens to everything between the lines, and he reads people the way you and I might read a novel.'

Septimus was wondering how someone who'd retired so many years ago could still be plugged into a supposedly secure system two generations later — a system very different from the one Sacristan had himself shaped and controlled in his day.

Alec was also invited. All three travelled together, Alec behind the wheel of their family car, an elderly Saab, Septimus on the back seat. The latter wore a brown corduroy jacket frayed at the sleeves and elbow and a soup-stained tie he'd dug out of the bottom of a cupboard — out of respect for the old man, he said, not that he needed to dress for the occasion.

Sir Thomas Avery aka 'C' had arrived ahead of them, looking sleek in blue jeans and black polo neck, and for once not trying to out-tweed the tweedy Lord Sacristan. He was holding a G&T while inspecting the titles on Sacristan's shelves. In a corner, almost hidden by the curtains, Cora and Calista, strangers an hour ago and now best buddies, were whispering to each other and sniggering at private jokes.

Bernie arrived late and flustered, and forgot he was still wearing bicycle clips.

Sacristan made a point of staying away during this phase of the proceedings; it wasn't until Masters announced that lunch was being served and he'd shepherded the guests to their places at the dining room table that Sacristan put in an appearance, dressed in a sailor's heavy jumper of oiled wool, matched with grey flannels and slippers.

His lordship carved and served the beef and Yorkshire pudding; the gravy boat and vegetables were passed around, and everyone helped themselves, watched over by Masters and his wife, Mrs Masters, who was the cook. Sacristan liked his beef rare, so rare it was.

Sacristan wanted to know Caro's opinion on contemporary novels, and he then asked Calista about her favourite films; they were happy to oblige and were soon arguing with each other, to Sacristan's amusement. He challenged Alec on the issue of nuclear energy, and encouraged him to hold forth on the subject, which he did, thankful for the captive audience.

Sacristan's strategy was to draw people out and encourage them to share whatever they cared about.

Dessert was followed by coffee and cheese.

Alec hated trifle but pretended to eat it by moving it around his plate.

Then port for those who wanted it. Everyone did.

Bridie had a special favour to ask of their host. Could she possibly see his copy of *The Dream of Poliphilus?*

He was pleased, and he took her to see it in its special glass display case.

On one wall of the library was a painting that caught Bridie's attention. 'Is that what I think it is? A Titian? A self-portrait?'

'You know your painters, then, Ms Connor. It's a fake. Not really so much as a fake, but wrongly attributed. That's a polite way of putting it. You and I, in our professional lives, deal with fake people and fake tales all the time, do we not?'

At Sacristan's insistence, everyone had to go for a walk while Mr and Mrs Masters cleared the table. The weather was dry; the wind had dropped, and it was not that cold. So he said. There were several pairs of Wellington boots in different sizes to choose from. They took several turns around Cavendish Square Gardens.

Bridie and Septimus led, followed by 'C', then Caro and Calista, finally Sacristan and Alec. Sacristan was asking Alec about quantum mechanics.

There was no mention of Carstairs aka BADGER, who was reported by the media to have been placed in an induced coma in the intensive care unit of a private London hospital.

'Septimus, what I don't understand is why he killed himself. Merrick, I mean.'

'It's in my report, which I sent you two days ago, Bridie.'

'I haven't had a chance to read it, but if you could explain in your own words...'

Septimus sighed. 'Fucking hell. Do I really have to?'

'If you would be so kind.'

'I'll keep it brief.'

They passed the same holly tree for the third time.

'Of course. Thank you.'

'Merrick's mother was a Bosnian Moslem. She was murdered by Serb nationalists at Srebrenica during the Bosnian war. His father, who was British and worked for the United Nations High Commissioner for Refugees, was based at Sarajevo airport, running aid convoys to the besieged enclaves and towns. There was nothing he could have done. Merrick himself was a schoolboy back then.'

'It must have left a mark.'

'It must have, yes indeed.'

'Go on.'

'Merrick converted to Islam while serving in Afghanistan so he could marry an Afghan woman who'd served with him in an Afghan special forces unit. Merrick was a major by this time and had been awarded a DSO. He was well thought of. He had a promising career ahead of him in the military had he wanted it.'

Septimus looked back. No one was in earshot. The people who'd started out behind them were now ahead as they circled the park. The beech, oak and lime trees were bare, their naked branches pointing at the sky in supplication. Leaves scurried about the path.

'And?'

'His wife applied for resettlement in the UK. It was denied, though she qualified under the terms of the Afghan Relocation and Assistance Program. She had all the right papers as well as Army recommendations. She had her ID and her payslips. No reason was given for the refusal.'

'Shit.'

'It was shit, aye. She and other members of her family had to flee to Pakistan, where she tried again. Merrick — who was at the Shrivenham defence college at this point — intervened in the UK on her behalf. He pulled every string he could. To no avail. He started a petition which garnered seventy thousand signatures. It was too late. Pakistan deported Zala, along with several thousand other Afghans, back to Afghanistan. She headed home but was caught by the Taliban. Someone had informed on her.

You can imagine. She'd fought in an Afghan special forces unit, the famous Triples, alongside the British, and what's more, she'd married a British officer.'

'So what happened?'

'It could hardly have been worse.'

'Tell me.'

'If I must. They took her to her home district. She was beaten, whipped. They buried her up to her neck and forced villagers at gunpoint to stone her to death. It took a while. *Pour encourager les autres.*'

'So that's why —'

'That's why Merrick wanted revenge. Not on the Taliban, who were only doing what the Taliban do, but on the British authorities who'd betrayed her trust — and his — out of indifference, indolence, incompetence, and no doubt institutional racism.'

'Why did he kill himself, though?'

'If he hadn't, we would have done so. I'd already authorised taking the shot. What did he have left to live for, Bridie? Can you imagine the humiliation of being arrested, charged with multiple murders, held on remand, tried, pilloried as some kind of monster in the media and then banged up for life in the maximum-security prison at Belmarsh? Can you? And the images in his mind's eye of his wife being stoned to death...'

Septimus had the image once again of the BMW ploughing into a police Volvo with a crunch of metal and glass, shifting the big car to one side, folding itself around the BMW, the bike rearing up and standing on its nose, catapulting the rider into the air so that he somersaulted over the roof, only to crash down in the street on his back and break his neck.

Bridie was saying something, her voice reaching him as though it came from a great distance. 'He would have had people give evidence in his defence, and surely his military record, his courage...'

Clearly upset, Septimus interrupted. 'Oh, c'mon! He didn't stand a chance any more than his wife did. I think the final straw was his discovery that the woman he adored was pregnant with his child when she was stoned to death. Do you see now?'

'Oh, God. I'm so sorry, Septimus —'

He turned away so she wouldn't see his face, dismayed to discover that he was weeping despite himself. Merrick hadn't seen his wife die, but the imagining of it — over and over again, a thousand deaths endlessly repeated — would have been infinitely worse.

Pull yourself together and stop being so bloody pathetic.

He halted on the path, overcome with anger and shame.

'Just read the fucking report, will you, Bridie? Please?'

Postscript

London, November 26

His employers at the National Crime Agency owed Septimus six weeks' paid leave, so he applied for a fortnight off right away and got it authorised by a manager in human resources. He had to visit her office for a signature.

She was businesslike and sympathetic. She asked if he thought he needed counselling. He said he didn't. The two-week rest would do very nicely, thanks, and that was that.

The same day, he heard on the news that Richard Carstairs had died of his injuries sustained in the attack on his car. A shaped charge had been used, not unlike the improvised IEDs used by insurgents in Iraq and Afghanistan.

No doubt Merrick had built the device in his Miles Street lockup.

There was to be a general election.

Septimus didn't go anywhere. He couldn't run away from himself.

For one thing, he had Trooper to think of, and Septimus had no intention of leaving him at some kennel where they'd charge a hundred quid a day — or whatever ridiculous sum it was — for failing to look after him properly. Trooper himself would be distraught at being deserted. He might only be a dog, but even dogs knew what betrayal was.

Septimus disliked mass air travel. That was another reason. It was uncomfortable and expensive. He'd tried it in pre-Trooper days. He'd been to Tenerife, Turkey, Cyprus and so on. The usual. All horrible. Package tours to popular places, and that had been his fault. He should in retrospect have travelled alone, picking a few less popular locations. Kiev or Novosibirsk, perhaps. At least he'd have had a window seat there and back. He'd disliked having to rub shoulders with so many talkative strangers in such close proximity — especially as they were embarrassingly semi-naked, their ample flesh spilling out all over the place, lathered in sun cream and roasted a weird shade of deep orange.

As for the UK, it was winter. No sun cream required.

So Septimus and Trooper settled for long walks every day, tramping through and around the parks and town. Septimus spoke of his recent adventures when they were alone, while Trooper remained silent, which was probably wise of him.

Septimus sometimes visited dog-friendly cafes for coffee and a cinnamon bun. Trooper would snooze at his feet, content in the warmth.

They enjoyed themselves in their quiet way.

In the evenings, Septimus read, and when he slept, he entertained himself with his lucid dreams, observing his own narratives and his role in them. Trooper also dreamed, if his whimpers and twitches were any indication.

Flashbacks featuring Merrick's death were fewer and less intense as time passed.

After ten days of tranquility, the same manager from human resources called him at home, which was unusual.

How was he? How did he feel? Had he rested?

Septimus grunted something that sounded vaguely positive to the effect that he was fine, thanks, and yes, he had indeed rested.

There was a new investigation being set up, the manager said, but she didn't have the details. Which presumably meant she didn't have the required clearance. Someone had asked for him. Would he mind awfully if she were to call him at home to discuss it?

Who was the mysterious she?

He would complete his leave, of course, the manager hastened to add, just in case Septimus ended the call before she'd finished, but they needed to get things straightened out ahead of his return to the office on the Monday. Would that be okay? It would only take a few minutes. Perhaps they might fix a time now.

Septimus closed his eyes like someone trying to ward off a bad headache. 'Who wants to call? Do you have a name?'

Like Merrick, I too am the servant of the monstrosity we call the British state.

Trooper wanted a walk. He wagged his tail and looked up at Septimus with a beseeching expression.

'Yes, of course, Mr Brass. It's someone who says she's worked with you before and asked if you were available. Bridget Connor — does that name ring a bell?'

Acknowledgements

I'd like to doff my cap to Philip H.J. Davies for his scholarly book, *MI6 and the Machinery of Spying* (Frank Cass, London, 2005), which provides details of the structure of the Secret Intelligence Service. Richard Tomlinson's autobiography, *The Big Breach: From Top Secret to Maximum Security (Cutting Edge Press,* Edinburgh, 2001), which Margaret Thatcher tried to suppress, contains useful material on his selection as a volunteer in 22 SAS Regiment, along with his experiences on the SIS Intelligence Officers' New Entry Course at Fort Monckton. (Perhaps I should mention my own training at Fort Monckton as a 'contract labourer' for SIS, but my preparation for the role of 'head agent' was much shorter and a lot less demanding).

Friend and former colleague Roger Crabb has lost none of his sharp-eyed skills as a senior World Desk editor at Reuters; he gave up several hours of his time to check every word and comma in the first draft, while another pal, Sinclair Molloy, volunteered as a Beta reader and offered useful insights. Margo Trogadis quickly identified the main weakness in the plot. My thanks to Nick Venables, who designed the great cover, and also to John Hopton, copy editor and proofreader. Stu Grant, who knows everything there is to know about authors' websites, has rebuilt my online presence and I'm grateful to him for his skills and cheerful enthusiasm.

That said, any errors are my responsibility, and mine alone.

Finally, *The Independent* newspaper reported the following on January 29, 2024: 'At least six Triples' members have been murdered by the Taliban since the West's withdrawal from Afghanistan in August 2021.'

GET YOUR FREE BEST-SELLER, NEWSLETTERS, BLOGS AS WELL AS EXCLUSIVE SEPTIMUS BRASS MATERIAL.

Building a relationship with my readers is the most rewarding aspect of writing. I send out occasional blogs and newsletters about my books, my characters and the peculiar business of writing. If you sign up, you'll also receive a copy of my standalone political thriller, *Emperor*.

Sign up here:

https://johnfullerton.org

Did you enjoy this book? If so, you can help.

I'd really appreciate a review. Reviews help more readers find my work, so a positive review can make a huge difference. It doesn't have to be more than a few words and shouldn't take more than a couple of minutes of your time. Amazon, Goodreads, and booksellers such as Waterstones and Blackwells all accept reviews.

BY THE SAME AUTHOR:

Emperor

Spy Game

Spy Dragon

Spy Trap

The Reticent Executioner

This Green Land

A Hostile Place

Clap (JW Diaz)

White Boys Don't Cry

The Monkey House

The Soviet Occupation of Afghanistan (non-fiction)

You can find out more at: https://johnfullerton.org

Facebook link: https://www.facebook.com/johnfullertonauthor.scot/

About the author

John Fullerton is the author of 11 novels. He worked during the Cold War as a 'contract labourer' in the role of head agent for Britain's Secret Intelligence Service, also known as MI6, an episode that triggered an interest in spy thrillers. As a newspaperman, freelance journalist and Reuters correspondent, he's lived or worked in 40 countries and covered a dozen wars. The latter have provided settings for his novels, including Beirut, Kandahar and Sarajevo. He has an MA in Buddhist Studies, and in 2006 was appointed a Fellow of the Royal Literary Fund.

https://johnfullerton.org.

Excerpt from a work in progress:
How To Kill a Spy
A Septimus Brass Novel
By John Fullerton

Chapter One

The following is the recording of a call from a cellphone to the emergency number 999 at 11.23 on Tuesday, August 20, in London:

- What service?

- I want to report a missing person.

- Your name?

- Bow, Jessica Bow.

- How long has this person been missing, Jessica?

- He didn't turn up for work last Monday.

- That would be...eight days ago, correct?

- That's correct.

- What's your relationship with the person you're calling about?

- We work in the same office.

- I'm putting you through to the police, Jessica. Stay on the line, please.

- How can I help you?'

- I want to report a missing person.

- What's the individual's name?

- David Jones.

- How do you know he's missing?

- He didn't turn up for work last Monday.

- Monday, as on August 12? Eight days ago?'

- Correct.

- Did you check his home?

- I called a few times, but there's no answer.

- What's his home address?

- 24A Tuncliffe Road, London, SW1V 1JU.

- May I have his work address if you have it?'

- It's 58, Albert Embankment, Vauxhall.

- One moment. Please stay on the line.

- Sure.

- Sorry to keep you waiting. Number 58 is the location where you work?

- It is, yes.

- Is that your current location - where you are now?

- It is.

- It's a government department, yes?

- It is, yes.

(Pause. The sound of breathing.)

- I have that listed as the headquarters of the Secret Intelligence Service.

- Yeah, that's right.

- Are you Mr Jones's employer?

- No. We work in the same office.

- So you and Mr Jones are colleagues?

- We are.

- Are you sure he's not on holiday, or off sick?

- Yeah, I'm sure. I'm afraid something bad might have happened.

- Have you spoken to his family?

- He lives alone as I understand it.

- Can you contact his next of kin?

- I'll be doing so after this call.

- Can we reach you on this number, Jessica?

- Yes, during normal working hours..

- We'll send someone around to the address as soon as we can. We'll let you let you know if we find out anything.

- Thank you.

- Take down this reference number, please, as a record of your call...

LE

MARCHÉ MONÉTAIRE

ET SES CRISES

DEPUIS CINQUANTE ANS